Praise for *The B*

"An elegantly told story of friendship, full of meaty issues and wonderful characters, this is a book that will make you sob and cheer. A book that will stay with the reader long after the last page. Absolutely brilliant."
—Kristan Higgins, *New York Times* bestselling author

"*The Bookshop Sisterhood* is everything—dramatic, heartwarming, heart-wrenching, funny, relatable, and most of all, a truly enjoyable read!"
—Kimberla Lawson Roby, *New York Times* bestselling author

"This is an enjoyable read, filled with drama, conflict and friendship. You'll laugh, you'll cry and you'll ultimately rejoice in the bond of sisterhood."
—Brenda Novak, *New York Times* bestselling author
of *The Seaside Library*

"An inspiring read about the power of friendship and resilience.... This drama-packed page turner will warm your heart, and fill your TBR pile!"
—Eliza Knight, *USA TODAY* and internationally bestselling author
of *The Mayfair Bookshop*

"The ups and downs, joys and pains, and unyielding power of friendship are on full display in this funny, heartwarming tale of sisterhood. The perfect book club read!"
—Farrah Rochon, *New York Times* bestselling author of *The Hookup Plan*

"A novel rich in sisterhood and emotion, friendship and forgiveness, readers will savor the poignant journey to a satisfying conclusion proving that books really do bring us together."
—Rochelle B. Weinstein, bestselling author of *This Is Not How It Ends*

"The unwavering friendship was the true magic that shined through and captured my heart. Michelle Lindo-Rice skillfully brought to life the dreams and aspirations of the women. These characters became my friends, and I didn't want their story to end!"
—Rhonda McKnight, award-winning author of *The Thing About Home*

"*The Bookshop Sisterhood* is brimming with warmth and humor as four friends open a bookstore and a new chapter in their lives—along the way learning to embrace new beginnings and daring to dream of happy endings."
—Annie Rains, *USA TODAY* bestselling author
of *Through the Snow Globe* and *The Charmed Friends of Trove Isle*

The
BOOKSHOP
Sisterhood

MICHELLE LINDO-RICE

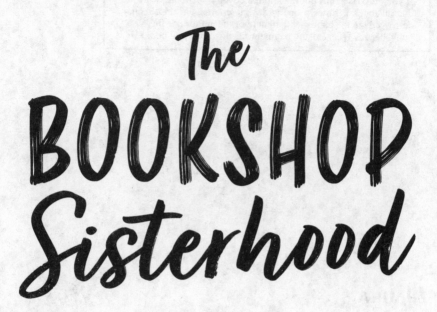

MIRA

//II MIRA™

Recycling programs
for this product may
not exist in your area.

ISBN-13: 978-0-7783-3438-5

The Bookshop Sisterhood

Copyright © 2024 by Michelle Lindo-Rice

For questions and comments about the quality of this book, please contact us at
CustomerService@Harlequin.com.

TM is a trademark of Harlequin Enterprises ULC.

Mira
22 Adelaide St. West, 41st Floor
Toronto, Ontario M5H 4E3, Canada

Printed in U.S.A.

For my husband, John.

1

Celeste

JANUARY 2

"This is going to be the best year of our lives," Celeste Coleman said with forced cheeriness, tucking her long legs under her dining table. She lifted her coffee cup toward the other three women seated in her spacious eat-in kitchen.

Leslie and Toni propped their elbows on the table and held up their iced lattes.

Yasmeen was the last to raise her cup of peppermint tea. "I sure hope so." Her foot rapped on the natural hardwood floors. She was convinced coffee wasn't good for her skin, though Celeste had repeatedly told her it was rich in antioxidants. But Yasmeen's dark skin was smooth, flawless, so Celeste stopped arguing and let her drink her tea.

It was Tuesday, a few minutes after 9:00 a.m. on the second day of the new year, and her friends had gathered in her home in Dover, Delaware, with two purposes in mind: to talk about their first read of the year, *Just the Nicest Couple,* and then plan the grand opening of their bookstore. The closest major bookstores were an hour away, and the friends believed they had a solid chance at launching a successful business selling what had bound their sisterhood for years: books. No matter what was going on in their lives, books were their therapy, their escapism, their companions—and pretty soon, they would share that love with other young girls. Celeste could hardly wait.

They had to decide on a name, their brand and a location.

The women tapped their cups gently.

Seeing Yasmeen's slumped shoulders, Celeste's heart squeezed. Yasmeen had been working two jobs at two nursing homes and had lost one of them just before the end of December. Now she was sleeping on her parents' couch in their one-bedroom apartment. She eyed Yasmeen's jeans, sweater and black kitten pumps from two seasons ago and kept her face devoid of any pity.

"It will be amazing. How can it not be? Four friends with off-the-chart skills starting a bookstore together can only be amazing," Leslie chimed in, her green eyes sparkling. She patted her sleek blond bob out of habit, because not a single strand of hair was out of place. She wore a blue-and-red sweater set with black slacks—no-nonsense clothes for a no-nonsense, plus-size woman. Celeste was taken back to the first time she had met Leslie—a white woman attending an HBCU, who showed up to pledge in her sorority. The other sorority sisters had balked, tried to freeze her out, but Leslie had spunk, so Celeste had welcomed her to the sisterhood.

The fourth woman at the table rolled her eyes. "Yes, as long as we each play our parts—no slacking—everything will be alright," Toni said, flashing her five-carat engagement ring and giving Yasmeen a pointed glance. Mirroring her icon, Tracee

Ellis Ross, Toni had donned a Galvan sunshine-yellow dress with matching Louboutin heels. After leaving her advertising executive job to become a social media and book influencer, Toni had garnered hundreds of thousands of followers, who tracked her every move. Her bank account made her more than happy to share her life and her love of books with the world.

Celeste couldn't understand the phenomenon that was vlogging, but Toni had doubled her six-figure salary by just sharing moments of her personal life and her book recommendations with her fans. Her success was why Toni would be their publicity manager to take their store nationwide. She was eager to hear Toni's ideas.

Of course, Yasmeen wasn't about to let that jab slide. "What's that supposed to mean?" She popped gum in her mouth and pinned Toni with a glare. "I'm bringing my knowledge of books. I have been an avid reader for years and I have actually worked in a library, been around books. Granted, it was in high school and only lasted a few months but still..." She cleared her throat and sipped her tea. "It takes skill to keep on top of what's trending in the book world. I know what's hot right now and I know how to organize our bookstore. I might not have a degree, but I do bring something to the table."

Celeste smiled. It was for that reason that Yasmeen would decide what books they needed to purchase for their main target audience: minorities and other underrepresented communities.

"Why did you make the assumption that I was talking to you?" Toni asked, drinking her coffee and peering over the mug.

Celeste could see the mischief in Toni's eyes. She raised her brows, giving Toni a silent warning, but Toni batted her mink eyelash extensions, toyed with a section of her midlength chocolate locks, and ignored her.

"Because I know you." Yasmeen's head snapped back and forth, her thick, natural curls swaying with each movement.

"You've been shading me every chance you get since you showed up." They engaged in what felt like the thousandth staredown since the three women graduated high school together. First it had been just Celeste and Yasmeen, then when Toni came to town the last semester of high school, they had become inseparable, but Toni and Yasmeen had always butted heads.

Yasmeen was way too sensitive when it came to her lack of education—which admittedly tried Celeste's patience—and Toni knew that.

"Ladies—notice I said *ladies*, not *girls*—let's refocus," Leslie said in a singsong voice, her Philadelphia accent strong.

Celeste smoothed her off-white pants suit, tugged on her pumpkin-colored tank and tapped her matching Blahniks. Often the peacekeeper—unless she was the one bickering with Yasmeen over their differing opinions on each other's relationships—she knew from experience their meeting could go sideways if she didn't jump in. Something she had never hesitated to do, until...

No. It was best not to think about that.

Keeping a calm voice, Celeste ignored her hammering heart and addressed the group. "Listen, it's a new year. A chance for new beginnings for all of us. We need to be in solidarity if this venture is going to work. Wade has already predicted we're going to fail because, and I'm quoting him, 'we're too catty to work together,' so I for one need to prove him wrong."

She pressed her thighs together to keep from squirming. Her hand was shaking and threatening to spill the contents of her mug, so Celeste placed the cup on the mat. Glancing around, she was relieved to see her friends hadn't noticed. Bringing up her husband of fourteen years made her think about their marriage and the nonexistent intimacy between them over the past few months. That hadn't been the case when she had gotten married at twenty years old, her third year of college. They had been…insatiable. Inseparable. Now it was like he couldn't stand the sight of her. He didn't say it, but his eyes didn't lie. Oh, he wanted her. Very much. He just couldn't stand her weakness.

She shook her head, blinking back tears as she scanned each woman at the table before looking out the sliding door that led to her backyard. If it weren't for her friends, she wouldn't have made it to another new year.

"What does he know?" Yasmeen said, giving Toni a light shove. "We bicker but the love is real. You mess with one of my girls, you mess with me." She and Toni high-fived.

Pointing to the folders on each of their woven table mats, Leslie said, "Can we get back to the plans? We need to agree on the name and set the launch date."

When Leslie had approached the four friends with the idea of going into business together the year before, Yasmeen had been enthusiastic but Celeste and Toni had declined. Celeste held a lucrative position as chief financial officer at a healthcare administration center, where she oversaw the financial management and expansion of several facilities. But then the carjacking happened. And her life changed. Her marriage changed. Her love for the job changed.

Then Leslie brought up the bookstore again. They'd flourished during the pandemic, and with streaming services making movies out of books, Celeste had reconsidered and so had Toni. It felt like it could be fun, something new and a risk worth taking. Celeste was not one for risks after almost losing her life, but she needed a fresh start. She planned to devote as much time as she could to getting the bookstore on solid footing. Shaking off the memory of the attack with a toss of her shoulder-length auburn bob, she reminded herself to take long, deep breaths. Remain calm. She was safe. Among friends.

Toni opened her folder. "Being the overachiever that I am, I prepared a slideshow to present my ideas on how to get us to another level, start some buzz, and I'm stoked for you all to see it."

The women gestured for Toni to go ahead. Celeste wanted to say they should talk about the name or the finances first, but she didn't want to dash her friend's exuberance. Toni dipped into her large tote and retrieved her iPad mini.

"You sound like a woodpecker," Yasmeen said, referring to Toni's pointed nails clicking on the screen. It was a mystery how she could operate her smart devices with them, but Toni was a pro.

Celeste bit back a chuckle. She knew Yasmeen was in payback mode. She was probably still low-key upset with Toni's barb from a few minutes ago. Thankfully, Toni didn't retaliate. With a swoop of her arm, she turned the screen and they huddled to take a look.

"That's you in your wedding dress," Leslie said, scrunching her nose. "Didn't I choose this one?" The friends had ventured with Toni to several bridal stores across several states. Toni had yet to ring the bell for the right one.

"Oh, my bad." She squinted. "I think this was your choice but I haven't decided." She tapped her screen again and pulled up a PowerPoint, her light brown eyes sparkling. "I've been researching some bookstore websites and I'm excited about forming a larger in-person book club." Before anyone could respond, she tilted her head. "By the way, Yasmeen, I would be honored if you'd design a one-of-a-kind bouquet ensemble for my big day."

Outsiders might have found the shift odd, but toggling between conversational topics had always been part of their flow. At Toni's sincere tone, the four women joined hands in the center of the table. It wasn't often Toni got emotional.

"Aw, I would love to." Yasmeen's voice caught and she lowered her head. In one of her many gigs, Yasmeen had worked at a florist shop and had been really good at it, even though it wasn't her passion. But she viewed them as great gifts, so each of the women had hand-crafted arrangements in their homes. "Do you have a date yet?"

"Actually, since Kent and I have a small circle of friends and family, we planned on doing something small. But then I thought about my fans, and the bookstore, and…" She paused and gave them each a look.

"You are not live on social media," Celeste said. "Spit it out."

"I thought we could get married at the bookstore. It would be a launch and a wedding," she squealed, shaking her shoulders.

"Oh wow. What a great idea," Yasmeen said. "That's thousands of people tuning in to watch you get married, while putting our bookstore on the map."

Toni bobbed her head. "Yes, plus instead of sending us gifts, I would ask them to buy books instead. You know any of the ones I recommend on my streams end up hitting the bestseller lists, which gives me even more followers. So this would be a win-win for all of us." She cheered. "It was Kent's idea, actually."

"Kent?" Celeste gasped. "Sheer genius."

"Yes, that man has been good for me in so many ways."

"That is beyond dope," Yasmeen said. "Cha-ching."

Celeste chuckled and rolled her eyes.

"I'm so happy for you," Leslie breathed out. "That man is so sprung I think if you asked him to jump off Niagara Falls, he would. He'd do anything for you."

That was no exaggeration. From the moment Kent Hughes met Toni, he had been smitten. Celeste had witnessed the astute, sharp corporate attorney reduced to a gushing schoolboy because her friend batted her lashes.

"You're his arm candy," Celeste teased and Toni's smile wavered for a fleeting second. Celeste's brows furrowed. Was Toni offended by her choice of words? But Toni tossed her hair and struck a pose. Maybe she had imagined it…

"I'm envious of your well-shaped arms, Toni," Leslie said, touching her own "mommy's paunch," as she dubbed her rounded belly—a remnant of her pregnancy and C-section twelve years prior. And sweets. Mostly sweets.

"Thank you. If you're going to be fluff, you might as well be fit fluff," Toni said, lifting both arms to show off her muscles.

Though she laughed, a sadness showed in Toni's eyes, like she wanted to be…more. But then, one couldn't take Toni seriously because she was such a hoot.

"I love the idea of a book club at the bookstore as well," Celeste said, returning the conversation to business. "It's brilliant, so thank you." She looked at Leslie. "Since we're each investing fifteen thousand dollars, we can put some funds into advertising and creating a buzz for our big day. I'll also look into investing a portion into some stocks that will give us a quick turnaround." Celeste was an expert at all things money.

Too bad she couldn't say the same of her marriage.

Ugh. Think of something else, Celeste.

Yasmeen's chin tucked into her chest. Celeste knew it was because her friend was self-conscious about not being able to contribute. Instead, Toni, Leslie and Celeste each had donated equal amounts toward her portion. Of course, Yasmeen had vowed to pay them back.

Leslie filled the silence. "I've already begun scouting for a location. I'll let you guys know when I have a few suitable places for us to check out, and I'll get us incorporated."

Yasmeen lifted a hand. "I wanted to bring up the idea of us making this a bookstore-café combination."

"I think we should focus on one thing before another," Leslie countered, her tone firm.

"I like the idea of a café, but I'd have to do some research on that." Toni made some quick notes. "My mind went to possible bug-and-rodent infestation."

Yasmeen rolled her eyes. "I love being able to enjoy tea or cookies while I read."

They all pinned their eyes on Celeste, waiting for her input.

She tensed, resisting the urge to cringe into her seat. She counted to three before siding with Yasmeen. "It could be a great investment. I actually ran the numbers on bookstores with cafés and they've showed profit."

"And don't forget I was a barista."

"Yeah, I think that was job number ten?" Toni chuckled. Then she gasped and snapped her fingers. "Maybe you could come up with a special blend. Something that makes our store stand apart. I could get behind that."

"Ooh." Yasmeen nodded. "I like that idea, but since I don't drink coffee, I might do a tea blend or a refresher."

"I'm feeling that," Toni said, giving Yasmeen's arm a squeeze.

Celeste nodded. "Alright. I guess we're doing a bookstore-slash-café. We just need a name…"

"I think I might have a solution for that." Toni clicked on her PowerPoint. "How about… Four Besties Books?" She bit her lower lip and gave them an expectant look.

Yasmeen held up a finger. "And beverages."

Leslie's mouth popped open and her eyes went bright. She mouthed the words several times before she squealed. "That's it. That's it. Besties, Books and Bevs."

"It's perfect." Celeste breathed out and thumbed away a tear. This was really happening. "I think we have a name, guys."

"You know what's cool? The fact that we will have a Black-owned bookstore in our city," Toni said.

Leslie pointed to her chest. "Um, white woman here."

"Well, seventy-five percent of us are Black, so that makes it Black-owned," Celeste said. "I did my research. And besides, you invited to the cookout, so make sure you bring your mac and cheese, because it's off the charts."

"You know it's good too." Leslie cackled.

They clinked their cups again, toasting to Besties, Books and Bevs.

"Good. Now that all that's settled, can we choose our book for February?" Yasmeen asked.

"You just picked the book, Yas," Celeste warned. "And you did in October and November. Someone else needs a chance. Let's hear everyone's book pitches."

She pouted. "I have a really good one. Just hear me out. *American Queen* is—"

"Nope." Toni raised a hand. "Save it. Don't want to hear it. It's my turn and I say we finally read *Walking in My Joy: In These Streets.*"

"Whatever. You only want to read it because it's written by a celebrity," Yasmeen griped.

"And?" Toni rolled her eyes. "Jenifer Lewis is a legend. Plus, she has style."

"Actually, it's my turn," Leslie said. "Don't you remember you chose the book in December? I think we should read *I Will Never Leave You*, by a new author, Kara A. Kennedy."

Celeste rolled her eyes. "We just read a thriller though. How about Rochelle Weinstein? We didn't read *When We Let Go* last year. Or, we could choose another Marie Benedict book? She's all about empowering and uplifting extraordinary women."

"I agree," Leslie said. "Marie's books make great company at night when Aaron is off working and Nadya is in bed."

"I guess if that floats your boat," Toni joked.

Celeste gave her a playful shove. "You enjoyed her. Admit it. Plus, you guys couldn't stop raving about *The First Ladies* last year. Remember that? The one she wrote with Victoria Christopher Murray?"

"Oh yeah, didn't they coauthor another book together?"

"Yes, *The Personal Librarian*," Yasmeen chimed in. "The audiobook is amazing."

This was how it was when they talked about books. The discussion could go on for hours. Toni continued, "My other book choices are Michelle Obama's *Becoming*, or Cicely Tyson's *Just as I Am*, since it's Black History Month."

"I've read those already," Yasmeen said.

"Read it again," Celeste countered with a sigh. "You read almost everything we mention."

"No. No. I got it. I got it." Yasmeen's eyes flashed. "I say we read Rhonda McKnight's *Bitter and Sweet*. Or…since Valentine's Day is coming up, we can pick a romance. By a Black author. Like Toni Shiloh's *The Love Script*."

"Ooh, I could get with that." Toni rubbed her hands. "But FYI, Rhonda's book won't be out until June or so."

"Wait, how about *When No One Is Watching*, by Alyssa Cole? It's a thriller and she's a Black author," Leslie suggested.

"It sounds like we have quite a list for the next few months," Celeste said. "Why don't we write them all down and pick one for each month?" The women recorded their choices on slim strips of paper and then plucked the name for February.

"*When No One Is Watching*, it is," Leslie yelled, doing a dance. They then chose the other books for the rest of the year.

"That took way longer than it needed to, but now that it's done, I'll put some plans together for our launch and my wedding," Toni said, rubbing her hands together. "I think summer is the best time, like mid-July."

Leslie nodded. "Summer works, but let's push for late June, before people go off on holidays."

Yasmeen nodded. "I agree."

Celeste raised a brow at Toni. "Keep the launch party classy."

Jangling the pearl bracelet that had been an heirloom from her mom, Leslie looked at her watch. "If there's nothing else on the agenda, I need to tackle my to-do list if I'm going to get Nadya to her gymnastics class on time later this afternoon."

"Take it easy on my goddaughter," Celeste chided with a smile.

Leslie had completed her master's degree in business management, and she ran her home like she did the multimillion-dollar industries she had dreamt of leading. Under her leadership, Celeste was confident their customer satisfaction would be un-equalled. That was one of their goals.

"You mean *our* goddaughter," Yasmeen corrected. "I'm pretty sure I was there when she screamed her way into the world."

"Yes, but I was the only one who stayed in the delivery room," Celeste said, her lips twitching.

The women began gathering their personal belongings and slipping into their coats.

"Whatever. We're not going down that rabbit hole with you. I've got a doctor's appointment," Toni said, stretching.

"Doctor?" Celeste raised a brow.

"Just a routine visit." Toni shrugged, not quite meeting her eyes.

"Well, I've got to fill out some job applications. Hopefully, somebody will call me," Yasmeen said, touching her beautiful natural mane. At her depressed tone, Celeste gave Yasmeen's hand a squeeze.

"So that's it for now." Celeste stood. "I have a facial and hair appointment here at the house so I can be ready for this work event Wade insists I attend." Her stomach knotted at the thought of going out at night.

"Will you be okay?" Leslie asked, rubbing Celeste's arm.

All Celeste could do was nod and swallow her fear. Or to use Wade's words, her *irrational* fear.

The women hugged each other. Yasmeen wiggled her hips. "I'm real excited about this bookshop."

"I am too," Celeste answered, her heart light. "In a few months, we're going to have a classy event to remember."

"You best believe it." Toni snapped her fingers. "People will be talking about our bookstore launch for months to come. No, make that years."

"As long as our launch is smooth and well-organized, I'll be happy," Leslie added.

Toni pointed to Celeste, "You'll bring the class." Then to Yasmeen, "You'll add the creativity." And to Leslie, "You the co-ordination." She pointed to herself. "And I'll bring the crowd."

Yasmeen gave her a look. "How long did it take you to come up with that?"

They all cracked up.

"I just did. I'm that good," Toni said, which led to even more laughter among the friends.

Celeste looked at each of her sister friends, her heart overflowing with love. She broke out into a spontaneous jig and her girls joined her, shaking their booties and egging each other on.

"You know," Celeste said, "there's a warning that friends shouldn't go into business together. But I am quite sure we'll be the exception."

Toni

JANUARY 2

Antoinette "Toni" Marshall would be the first to declare she had never been in love. Until now. For thirty-four years, she had avoided the *L* word. Now it blossomed within her like a flower bursting open in the sun. She was so in love that this man had the power to contort her heart like a pretzel. Not that she had voiced that aloud often. In fact, when Kent Hughes had declared his love for her, she had responded with a breathless "Ditto," like Demi and Patrick from one of her favorite movie classics, *Ghost*.

Recalling it now as she navigated the U-turn to the gynecologist's office, she chuckled. Kent had cracked up, too, before giving her a scorching kiss. Two reasons of possibly a hundred, no, make that 1,228, as to why she loved him. His sense of humor and positive attitude.

His optimism was the equalizer of her internalized trust issues.

She pulled into the closest space to the entrance of the building—yes, she was an unapologetic space hog—and opened the door to her Mustang, an engagement gift from Kent. He had insisted on the car even when she told him the five-carat pink diamond—her favorite color—had been enough and she had her own money to spend on grown-up toys.

Slapping on a pair of oversize shades, she exited the car and pulled down her dress, which had ridden up during the twelve-minute ride from Celeste's house. Usually, she would pull out her selfie stick and post a quick story to Instagram, highlighting her whereabouts, but today's visit was personal. Humming the timeless tune of "Endless Love," her intended wedding processional song, she signed in at the reception desk for her ten-thirty appointment and then sat in one of the comfortable chairs, avoiding making eye contact with the other two women in the room. Maybe it hadn't been such a good idea to wear yellow. Nothing unobtrusive about it.

But back to her thoughts… Thinking about her fiancé was one of her favorite pastimes, right up there with reading. She had also been known to doodle his name like she was a teenager enthralled with her first crush. Once, she had even written Kent's name inside the front cover of Yasmeen's book. In her defense, she hadn't realized what she was doing until she was done. Yasmeen had been hot for days, and Toni had had to buy her a brand-new copy.

Yep. She hummed now. Doodled and hummed. Love made her steps light and gave her strut extra confidence—emphasis on the *extra*, because you best believe that she had plenty before. It made her hips move with the kind of swagger that comes from the security of knowing she was loved by a trustworthy man. A man who didn't play games. A man who gave of himself boldly.

And without condition. For that man, she had willingly agreed to wait for marriage to consummate their relationship. Kent had been inspired after reading *The Wait* by DeVon Franklin and Meagan Good. Without the pressure of premarital sex, they devoted their time to getting to know each other and being satisfied with long, sensual kisses and an abundance of hugs.

She could pinch herself, but she wasn't about to damage her unblemished skin. She had to maintain picture-perfect status as always.

She sent Kent a text with kissing emojis. Within seconds he returned the same. Her honey was quick with it. And dedicated to her. No matter what he was doing or where he was, if he was awake, he responded. Like she was important. Like she mattered. Was it any wonder her heart had tripped with the inelegance of a model wearing ten-inch heels on a slippery runway?

And to think if Yasmeen hadn't dragged her to speed dating (Toni had gotten ten thousand followers from just posting about it), she would have never met Kent. A moment she'd dubbed "random perfection."

The physician's assistant came to the waiting room door, clipboard in hand, and called a name Toni forgot within seconds. One of the women held the sides of her chair and stood belly first in an awkward but adorable way. Toni's eyes went wide. She hadn't realized the woman was pregnant. She took in the rounded abdomen from under her lashes and quashed the immediate pang. The flashback. The envy. The what-if…

No. She wouldn't, couldn't, go down that path.

Shoving that memory aside, Toni picked up an old edition of *Essence* magazine with a rapper-turned-actor gracing the cover. She admired how the performer had maintained his physique and youthful looks, before flipping through the pages. Then she tossed the magazine on top of the others, losing interest. She wasn't one to dwell on an unattainable fantasy. Not when she had a man who made her want to be something she had once vowed never to become.

A mother.

The door creaked open, and she heard her name. Her purse tucked under her arm, she tossed her hair and followed the physician's assistant to a room that had an ultrasound machine. "Okay, Ms. Marshall, I'm sure you know the drill," the woman said in a cheery tone, as she pulled the protection paper to cover the exam table. "You can get undressed, just the bottom half, and have a seat on the chair. I grabbed two gowns so you can put one on facing toward your front and the other toward your back—it's chilly in here. Is your bladder full?"

"Oh yeah. I drank so much water and coffee, I feel like a camel. Although, I suppose if I was a camel, I would be able to hold it, but I am ready to go." Her voice sounded breathy, a sure sign of her nervousness. *Breathe, Toni, breathe.*

The other woman chuckled. "You'll be glad to know that you're next, so you'll be able to use the restroom soon. I'll be back in a few minutes to give you some privacy. The doctor won't be long." Placing the hospital gowns on the chair, she vacated the room.

Toni changed into the drab blue-grey gowns, her body shivering, more from nerves than the cool room, before sitting on the table, hating the feel of the crinkly paper. She had come in for her yearly pap smear the week before, but the doctor had ordered a transvaginal ultrasound when Toni stated she'd had irregular periods over the past six months. She stared at the posters of the female anatomy before she retrieved her cell phone to scroll through her social media accounts. She was curious to learn her fans' reactions to her post that morning.

One in particular made her frown. Someone with the moniker @BLSTFRDAPST posted a comment in all caps.

I KNOW WHAT YOU DID. DON'T LET ME TELL.

Because of her social media presence, Toni was used to all sorts of hecklers. But something about this one caused dread to fall like boulders in her stomach. She'd first seen this username about a month ago when she shared her wedding plans and talked about how she wanted to have a baby right away. Her fans had posted all sorts of encouraging words, except for this @BLSTFRDAPST.

And here they were again. Her palms became sweaty and her heart moved faster than a gamer on a PlayStation release day. She fretted on her lower lip. This could be anyone. Or a certain someone… Her heart thundered. If this was who she thought it was, things could get ugly. He could damage the life she had built, slash her good-girl facade and expose her for the hypocrite she was. The only reason she had become a social influencer and plastered her face on social media was because she didn't think this person could ever get to her again.

She took a screen shot. Hopefully, her sudden anxiety would be a simple overreaction. Before she could dwell on that eerie comment, the doctor entered the room with his assistant close behind.

They closed the door. Dr. Hadden greeted her, tapped her shoulder and then directed her to lie down. His assistant placed a blanket across her abdomen and the procedure begun. Staring up at the ceiling, Toni gritted her teeth and willed herself to relax. His assistant took picture after picture, which made Toni look at the grayed image on the screen.

Suddenly, the physician's assistant paused and gave the doctor a look. The doctor leaned forward, brows furrowed. He peered at the screen before taking over. Alarm punched her gut. That wasn't a good sign.

Her heart thumped. "Do you see anything?" she squeaked out.

The doctor gave her a bland smile. "I need to study the pictures a little more. That's all."

No. That wasn't all. She knew it. "What is it?" she asked, her tone insistent and shaky.

"Let me go study the labs and then we'll talk." His words were followed with a patronizing pat on her shoulder. Toni wanted to scream that she wasn't a child and she needed the doctor to tell her what was going on *now.* But that would make her sound like a child throwing a tantrum. He addressed his assistant. "Once Ms. Marshall's ready, you can bring her to my office."

Oh no. Now she knew it wasn't good. Her body trembled. She crossed her arms, blinking back the tears of fright. She wasn't a crier, so her over-the-top reaction was surprising. While she used the restroom and dressed, her mind churned over scenarios on what the look on the doctor's face could mean. Her legs felt wobbly and unbalanced in her heels, and she had to concentrate on putting one foot in front of the other as she followed the assistant to Dr. Hadden's office.

She took in the deep chocolate armchairs, the solid desk, the bookshelf stuffed with medical books, the soothing water sounds playing in the background, and slipped into the chair across from him.

The doctor didn't hesitate. "The ultrasound shows that your ovaries have shrunk. That's a classic indicator of POI. Primary ovarian insufficiency. What this means is that your ovaries aren't working the way they should to produce enough estrogen or release the eggs every month." He pointed toward her. "This is why your periods have been irregular."

Toni drew several deep breaths. "What are you saying?" Her mind hadn't been able to process past the words *ovaries have shrunk.* She cupped her abdomen with the palm of her hand. "Spell it out for me, Doc, because I can be quite dramatic and I don't want to be drawing conclusions and making assumptions, like the big *C* word."

Leaning forward and clasping his hands, Dr. Hadden rushed

to explain. "No, you don't have cancer. I didn't see any evidence of it in your lab work—"

She cut him off, released a small laugh and dabbed at her eyes. "Whew. Let me tell you, you had me worried there for a second. So, am I going to have to take estrogen pills? Because I don't mind telling you since you're bound by patient-doctor confidentiality I am ready to do whatever's necessary to have a child. Not right away, though I know I'm probably considered ancient in gestational years. I want to enjoy married life for a bit. But after a year…" Dr. Hadden rubbed his eyes and gave her a grave look. She trailed off. "What is it? What aren't you telling me?"

"I'm sorry, Ms. Marshall, but…" He paused before uttering four words that crushed her to the core. "You can't have children."

Her mouth dropped open. "That can't be true." She jumped to her feet and paced the small space. "I'm healthy. I eat right. This is so random."

As if his assistant had timed it, she opened the door and ducked her head inside. She avoided Toni's gaze but spoke in a calm, deferential tone. "Dr. Hadden, your next patient is here." She backed out of the room, closing the door with a final click.

"I'm afraid the images confirmed it. You're infertile." His eyes held sympathy, and she spun away from him, hot, furious, disappointed tears rolling down her face. She sniffled and grabbed a tissue from the box strategically placed at the corner of his desk. How many women had received similar devastating news in this very room? How many tears did the walls hold secret? There was no way she was going to accept this. Toni would demand a second opinion.

Because if this were true, it would mean she wouldn't be able to bless Kent with a child. Kent—the most perfect man, who wanted one thing from her.

It took every ounce of willpower she possessed to walk out

of the doctor's office with composure. She wanted to howl and scream and cry and rage, but she had to pretend. Pretend her heart wasn't breaking. Pretend those four words hadn't smashed her dreams of becoming a mother.

Slapping on her shades, Toni strutted outside with a tight grip on her purse and an even tighter smile. She wanted to go home and curl under the covers and hibernate with this pain for days. But she couldn't.

Going home meant seeing Kent, since they were supposed to meet up at her place. But she needed alone time to get her mind right before she saw him. Before she revealed that if he married her, he would never be a father. From the time they became engaged, he'd often talked about having a son like him or a daughter like her. That's why he had purchased a house with five bedrooms. To fill it with children. To make a family. Kent had even ended a previous relationship because that woman hadn't wanted kids.

Her case was different. She wanted children. Desperately. She just couldn't have any. But would that matter, if the result was the same? She still couldn't make Kent a father.

She sniffled. How she hated the thought of Kent putting on a front and pretending his heart wasn't breaking, that choosing her hadn't been yet another big disappointment in his life. Because that was the kind of man he was.

She was a failure. A disappointment. And her parents had already shown her what happened to those who disappoint. They got abandoned.

She couldn't tell him.

She couldn't even tell her friends. She wasn't ready to voice her new truth. Not to herself or anyone else. Besides, why get everyone all riled up and emotional? Why bring them on this emotional roller coaster when it could all be for naught? Maybe this would be a fluke and she would get a better outcome at her second–opinion appointment. It was better she rode this one solo until she knew for sure.

As if on cue, she got a text from Kent.

How did everything go?

On instinct, she started to compose an honest response. They were best friends. They shared everything. Her heart pounded. Her mind pressed her to confess. But fear of losing him stopped her fingers from typing out the truth. Instead, she wrote four different words from the ones she had just heard. Four words that would change the paradigm of their relationship.

Everything is just fine.

Yasmeen

JANUARY 2

"I'll meet you by the gas station," Leslie whispered once they had stepped outside Celeste's home. Then she scuttled toward her vehicle.

Yasmeen nodded before her eyes went wide. *Drip. Drop.* She could see the nasty gunk falling from her car onto Celeste's immaculate pavement as she dashed down the driveway.

She knew she should have parked on the curb. But no, she just had to pull into Celeste's driveway with her old clunker. Yasmeen Adams needed to listen to Yasmeen Adams. Now the newly paved driveway was ruined. She hopped in her car, hunched over her steering wheel and backed up onto the street. Leslie was already in her vehicle and Yasmeen had to follow her. She would call Celeste later and apologize.

That's all she could do, because her account had a whopping $66.42 to feed herself and her parents over the next two weeks, which was why she had called Leslie for a ride so she could get to the meeting today.

But thank God for caring, intuitive friends. Leslie had told her to drive and offered to fill her tank. Though her friend would do more for her, that's all Yasmeen would allow. Even now, she was mortified to accept this help but she had to get to work. She couldn't lose another job. Tears rolled down her cheeks. She wiped her face. Her life was like a dark, slippery pit, and try as she might, she couldn't get a good leg up to make her way out.

Her muffler made an obscene amount of noise in the otherwise quiet neighborhood, but she had to keep up with Leslie.

Peering through her rearview mirror, Yasmeen saw the people in the car behind her pointing and holding their noses. Her muffler released dark, blotchy puffs of air. The car next to her honked and gestured for her to roll down her passenger window. If she did, she would have to manually pull it back up, so at first she ignored them. But when they pressed her at the stoplight, she complied.

"You need to get that two-bit crap off the road!" the man yelled.

"Yeah, your car is only good for scraps. If that," his partner bellowed before falling over in laughter.

Biting on her lower lip, Yasmeen resisted the urge to counter with the fact that they both could be related to Squidward from *SpongeBob SquarePants*, but her training as a certified nursing assistant refused to let her. Service without sass.

Some of her patients disrespected her while she fed or cleaned them, and she had to cater to them with a smile. They saw her as lower, inferior. And it wasn't just them. Even some of the nurses behaved that way toward her. But Yasmeen didn't mind. She needed the paycheck and she loved helping people. Besides, as her father would say, "love isn't love if you only love the lovable." The real test was loving the unlovable. Personally, she thought Michelle Obama said it best: "When they go low, we go high."

Keeping her eyes on Leslie, who had stopped at the light ahead of her, she gave them a small wave and proceeded. She shivered from the cold, due to her now-open window, and turned up the heat, which she had repaired just before losing her second job. Leslie turned into the local gas station and hopped out. She strutted over to Yasmeen and asked, "How do I open the tank?"

Yasmeen moved to open the door. "I'll get it."

Leslie waved her off. "Stay put." She pressed on the latch, then slid her card in the card reader. Yasmeen watched her friend move with confidence, never once doubting or praying her card wouldn't get declined. She was sure Leslie must be inhaling the fumes from her exhaust but her friend didn't say a word. Her heart squeezed. Leslie placed the gas nozzle into the tank. Once it was going, she returned to the window.

Yasmeen put a hand over Leslie's. "Thank you, again, friend."

"It's nothing."

Not to Yasmeen, it wasn't. This car was the means for her to remain employed for the next couple weeks.

Leslie switched topics. "I am so excited about this bookstore." A sharp wind blew some of her hair into her mouth. She sputtered and used her finger to scoop it out before gagging. "Ugh. I tasted gas. I wasn't thinking or I would've used my other hand. Do you have hand sanitizer?"

"Of course." Yasmeen had bottles in every door. She held one out to Leslie, who poured a generous amount into her palm.

Rubbing her hands together, Leslie continued, "When you get a chance, email me your first book suggestions for the shop's inventory." She tilted her head. "I still can't believe you read ten books over the past three days. I wish you had gotten a degree in library science or something. You could be a librarian now."

Yasmeen froze and gripped the wheel. The praise flattened her spirit like a boulder on cotton. The familiar ache made her chest tighten.

Leslie gasped and placed a hand over her mouth. "Oh goodness, my love. You've got to forgive me. Sometimes I just blabber on and…"

"It's okay," she said in a small voice, patting her hair, her throat gripped with regret. She could do so much more if she didn't struggle with heavy reading and test-taking. A fighter, Yasmeen overcame her reading difficulties through the use of audiobooks. She defiantly used that medium to read, read and read, especially since she had a Libby account from the library. (Did somebody say free books?) But the test-taking was another story. No matter how she tried or what she did, Yasmeen couldn't pass the NCLEX-PN exam to become a licensed practicing nurse. She had taken the test three times and failed. That had ended her heart's desire to become a nurse and had been the beginning of her deep-rooted self-disappointment.

Never mind that her father had become disabled, causing him to leave his job as a carpenter before entering into ministry full-time. A fulfilling but low-paying position, as most of the congregants were retired. Yasmeen generally tried to help her parents pay the utilities because his disability payments were just enough to pay the rent, but losing that second job hurt her contributions. Her Jamaican parents never complained because they were grateful for the opportunity to make a better life in America, but she knew she was a big disappointment to them, since she hadn't become a nurse or a doctor. Instead, she was a community college and tech school dropout on their couch. They never criticized, but she felt their unexpressed pressure to succeed.

The gas pump clicked, sparing Leslie and Yasmeen any further awkward conversation. Leslie went to return the hose to its holster and get her receipt. She tried to apologize again but Yasmeen assured her that she was okay.

Even though she wasn't.

Leslie dashed off to run more errands. Yasmeen sat by the pump, caught up in the memories of her past pain. It took years for Yasmeen to admit she might have a learning disability. But even though she researched strategies to help herself, she didn't have the guts to get evaluated. To learn the truth. To see her shortcomings displayed in black-and-white.

Her stomach rumbled, reminding her that she had promised her parents to bring them something to eat from the dollar menu at the drive-through. All they had in the refrigerator was eggs, and that had been their dinner the night before. She started the car and dug in her purse for a fresh piece of gum, only to discover she was all out.

With a huge sigh, she turned off the car and headed into the store. The wind blew her curls in all kinds of directions but she wasn't worried about it. She hoped the gas station had her Big Red cinnamon gum. As she shuffled inside and ambled toward the candy aisle, her phone rang.

Pookie came up on her screen—the nickname for her on-again, off-again boyfriend, Darryl—and she allowed the call to go to voicemail. She grabbed two packs of gum and made her way to the checkout queue. There were three people ahead of her and each one of them bought a lottery ticket. Apparently, the local lottery was a little over ten million dollars—10.5 million dollars to be exact. Her father's words echoed in her head: "God disapproves of gambling." She inched closer and chewed on her bottom lip while she considered. Spending a couple dollars on a lottery ticket would be a major sacrifice. It would mean foregoing her burger and drink at the drive-through.

Her body swayed back and forth, matching the indecisiveness of her mind. For some reason, before he left the store, the man in front of her addressed her. "Take a chance. Buy a ticket.

You never know." He held up his own ticket. "Today might be my lucky day."

Her lips twisted. She bit the inside of her cheek to keep from asking "But how much money do you have to spend to make the jackpot?" Yasmeen slid her gum across the counter and tapped her feet. Then, right before the cashier added up her total, she found herself saying, "Let me get a ticket."

"What's your number?"

Yasmeen didn't know what to choose. She had made enough bad decisions to last both her and her parents' lifetimes. Her father wouldn't like this move. He would see it as taking the easy way out. Daddy was all about hard work. She swallowed; her forehead beaded with sweat. "I'll let the machine decide."

"Alright, bet."

Yasmeen swiped her card, already regretting her spontaneous purchase. She tucked her ticket into her purse and skulked out of the store. The drive-through food made her mouth water, and she had to pop her gum in her mouth to ease her hunger.

When she arrived home, her parents greeted her with drawn faces. They were sitting side by side on the living room couch, which doubled as her bed.

"What happened?" Yasmeen dropped the bag of food on their small eat-in kitchen table, which boasted a plastic tablecloth from the dollar store.

"They turned off the electricity." Her father's shoulders slumped. Willie Adams was a proud man and to see him so despondent pierced her very core.

"They did that even though Mom's asthmatic?" Yasmeen raged. "That's inhumane. In a few hours, it's going to be twenty-nine degrees outside."

"They said they couldn't give us another extension." He released a sigh.

"We have candles," her mother, Dixie, said. "I can read the Vanessa Miller book you got me from the library by the candlelight. I'm falling behind and I heard a lot about *The Light on Halsey Street*." Dixie had instilled a love of reading into Yasmeen. Her mother tore through books with the speed of a snag in pantyhose. Now, though, the image of her mother striving to read in the dark made her heart hurt.

"I can renew it at the library, Mommy. It's no problem. How much do we owe for the electric bill?" Helplessness wrapped around her psyche.

"Seven hundred dollars plus a connection fee of seventy-five dollars."

Yasmeen knew she could call any of her girls and they would help her out, but she was so tired of being that friend. The one who was always begging for a bailout. The one who always had money problems. Yasmeen closed her eyes to keep in the tears threatening to spill. She was thirty-three years old and should be in a position to be an asset to her parents after all they had done for her. Instead, she was on their couch, mooching off their generosity. Adding to their burden.

Good thing she hadn't bought herself anything, because her appetite deserted her. She prodded her parents to eat. "We can head to the library until closing."

"Our God doesn't sleep nor slumber. Day or night is the same to Him." Her father's quiet words did little to comfort her. Not when she knew the sun would leave in a few hours and darkness would descend.

Her cell phone shrilled again. Pookie was persistent and consistently broke. She strolled into the bathroom, the only place she could have a private conversation, and answered his call. Her ear welcomed the deep timbre of his voice, and her brain flashed an image, reminding her of his unnatural fineness. The man should be on a runway instead of running the streets.

"Hey, baby. I've been trying to reach you all day… I got a situation."

"I got one too," she shot back with major attitude. He didn't even ask how she was doing.

"What's going on with you?" he asked.

"Our lights are out."

Darryl whistled. "What are you going to do?"

"I don't know." Of course, he wasn't looking at it as a "we" problem. It was all up to her and—as he liked to call Leslie, Toni and Celeste—the Upper Crust Crew. She shook her head imagining what Celeste would have to say if she heard this. Yasmeen and Celeste had gotten into spats because Yasmeen refused to end things with Darryl. Well, Celeste was a fine one to talk when she couldn't see she had a goldmine in Wade.

Sure enough, Darryl returned with, "You need to signal the Upper Crust Crew."

"What's the matter with you? You think this is an episode of *Batman* or *Spiderman* where I just need to put out a distress signal for them to throw money at me?"

"Ease up. You know they would help you but you're too proud."

That jab hit her heart. He was right. She did have a lot of pride. Just like her daddy. "Unlike you, who has none."

"If I don't ask for help, how will I get it?"

She couldn't argue with that point. "I've got to go figure out what to do with my parents."

"Listen, if you don't hear from me, it's because I might be incarcerated."

Yasmeen almost dropped her phone. "What?" A light tap on the bathroom door made her jump. "Hang on a minute." She pressed the mute button. "I'm coming out."

"Okay. I have to go."

She could hear her mother's feet shuffling in front of the door and told Darryl she would call him back. Washing her hands out of habit, though she hadn't used the restroom, Yasmeen wiped them on the towel and let her mother inside. Seeing the worry on her mother's face made Yasmeen cave.

Darryl was right about her pride. She squared her shoulders and texted Celeste, hoping her friend wasn't too busy with her nails to read the message. There was no way she was going to ask Toni after their unpleasant exchange earlier. Not that Toni wouldn't give it, but Yasmeen didn't want to deal with any snippy remarks. Celeste didn't make Yasmeen grovel or ask why. Within seconds, twelve hundred dollars appeared in her cash-transfer app.

She fired off a thank-you text and promised to pay her back. Celeste sent her a thumbs-up emoji.

Don't worry about it.

Yasmeen called the electric company and paid their outstanding balance. Fortunately, since their service had just been disconnected, the electric company was able to send someone to turn on the power. Then she used some of the extra cash to order pizza and pay their water and gas bills. She wasn't about to take any chances.

Her parents rejoiced, thanking her profusely. Praising her, when she was a leech. They pulled out their board games and Uno cards while Yasmeen swallowed back tears. She hadn't done anything meaningful to deserve their gratitude. Celeste was the real hero and she told them so. Cupping her head with her hands, Yasmeen welcomed the relief of a problem averted. At least for today.

4

Leslie

JANUARY 2

Five minutes to spare for Leslie Bronwyn meant she was late, and she couldn't abide being late. She pulled her luxury vehicle into the spot reserved for parent of the month, which she often was. Leslie was among the top volunteers and sponsors for Nadya's gymnastics team. Through the mirror, she eyed her daughter in the back seat and smiled.

Nadya had grown an extra foot over the past six months and was almost Leslie's height. She often wore her long blond hair parted down the middle, and unlike Leslie, she had blue eyes. Her slender brows, pert nose sprinkled with freckles, full lips and slender build had been the reason Nadya's face had graced many of the gymnastics team's brochures.

"You'll be alright, honey." Leslie turned to tap her twelve-year-old on the leg.

Nadya shook her head and looked out the window, massaging her temples, her bun tight against her scalp. Celeste had suggested Leslie use this edge control, that was 'the truth.' No matter how much Nadya moved, her hair remained in place.

"I don't get why we couldn't skip one day. I told you I wasn't feeling well," her daughter whined.

Leslie thought about Siobhan, Nadya's chief competition for first place. "We can't fall behind. Missing one day could mean losing your chance at getting the lead floor routine at comps."

"Yeah, 'cause that's what's most important."

Ignoring her daughter's crabby remark, Leslie opened her door and got out. She shivered under her down coat. The weather had dropped about ten degrees. She opened the passenger door, picked up her laptop bag and gestured to Nadya to hurry up.

With a dramatic sigh, Nadya scooted outside the vehicle. Leslie's eyes narrowed. Nadya's cheeks looked flushed. Maybe she should have stayed in… But Nadya had the potential to be the next Simone Biles, if her coach could be believed. And her daughter could be laid-back, which irritated Leslie to the highest degree. She hated to see wasted potential. Naw, she would give Nadya the push she needed. Nadya would thank her in about two decades or so. She was sure of it. For now, Leslie would be the villain. Shooing Nadya toward the entrance, Leslie hurried behind her, texting Aaron to find out if he was on his way.

His response came in just as she took her seat upstairs, slipping her coat on the back of the chair.

I might not make it. Can you record it?

Leslie clamped her jaw to keep from bellowing in frustration.

This is the third session you have missed. Nadya needs you here.

I need you. She released a plume of air and looked around to see Siobhan's mom, Ruida, studying her.

Straightening in her chair, Leslie gave a wave and plastered a smile on her face. Then she zoomed in on her daughter stretching on the mat with the other girls. She squinted. Nadya seemed sluggish, but maybe her energy would pick up once they moved from floor exercises to the pommel horse.

The girls moved single file behind the instructor until they were by the balance beam. Leslie pulled up the camera app on her phone. She would wait until it was Nadya's turn before she hit the video option. Leslie liked to record her daughter's session so she could review Nadya's performance and then provide her pointers on how she could improve. Having taken gymnastics herself as a child, until her late teens, Leslie knew all the jargon and what was needed to perform a well-executed move.

Nadya was last in line. Leslie studied each gymnast as they performed, noting that none were as good as her daughter. Under the surface, she was squealing, but on the outside, she strove to appear unbothered. She eased back into the chair and relaxed. Nadya was going to kill it. Picking up her cell phone, she tapped record.

Her daughter mounted the balance beam before swinging into a handstand. Leslie's lips widened into a smile. Then her breath caught. Nadya's entire body was shaking, her chest heaving, like she was exerting herself beyond control. Leslie's heart rate accelerated and she stood. "C'mon, baby," she whispered.

Nadya then slowly bent backward and placed her hands on the beam. Her hands shook and each move appeared to be labored, like Nadya was struggling to breathe, but she finished the flip. Leslie ended the recording and lowered the cell phone, her eyes planted on her offspring. Something was wrong. She was sure of it. All of a sudden, fear sprung like a well threatening to overflow and she scampered down the stairs to run across the gym, heedless of her spiky heels damaging the mat.

"Stop," she yelled, waving her arms. "She's got to stop."

The coach gave her a stern reprimand but Leslie only cared about getting to Nadya's side. Nadya lifted her head, cheeks red, frozen in position. For a beat. Then, with a determined grunt, she dismounted before swooping her arms in the air.

Leslie placed a hand over her mouth and looked around to see all eyes pinned on her, looking at her like she was bananas. All except Nadya, who refused to meet her gaze, her hands still in position.

"You're going to pay for the holes in the mat," the coach bit out, pointing toward the exit. "You need to return to the waiting area."

Her shaky hands ran through her short strands. "I—I'm sorry. I—I thought that…"

"Thought what?" Coach put a hand on her hips. "Keep it up and I'll have you banned from coming to any more practices."

"Nadya… She looked like…" Leslie shook her head. "I overreacted. I'm sorry." She backed up. "I'll return to the observation area. I won't be any trouble. I promise."

But then Nadya's eyes rolled to the back of her head. Her legs bent. And she crumbled.

All the air rushed to Leslie's lungs. "Nadyaaaaaaaaaa…" She twisted her ankle in her haste to get to her daughter's side but ignored the pain. All the other gymnasts and the coach surrounded her prostrate child. Leslie wasn't having it. "Move the children away. Please. And call 9-1-1." The coach, now appearing apologetic, did her bidding. Her heart thundered and her body felt weak, but Leslie couldn't fall apart.

She heard a low groan and heaved a sigh of relief. That meant her daughter was alive. Alive meant hope. She dropped to her knees and called out, "Nadya? Nadya? Can you hear me?"

The owner of the gym came bounding across the floor,

holding an emergency kit. She opened the rectangular box and held up an EpiPen. "Could she be having an allergic reaction?"

Leslie twisted the hem of her cardigan. Breathless, she replied, "No. No. Not that I know of..." All she could see was her daughter falling to the floor as she remembered ignoring how Nadya felt, because of her competitive nature.

"Did she eat anything new?"

Leslie's lips trembled. "No. We had pasta in a creamy tomato sauce—her favorite—for lunch."

The EMTs arrived and took over. Within minutes, Leslie was running behind them as they toted her daughter on a gurney. Nadya appeared lifeless. Leslie's composure cracked. She called Aaron, but he didn't answer, so she left a frantic message for him to call her back, before jumping into the ambulance. Leslie held her head in her hands, sobbing for most of the ride. She vacillated between calling for Nadya to wake up and praying for God to not take her baby from her. Then she texted her girls in the group chat to tell them what had happened and ask if one of them could pick up her vehicle.

Yasmeen was quick to volunteer. I'll go. Keep us posted on Nadya.

Thx.

Her hands shook, but she texted Yasmeen separately to provide the code to enter her vehicle. Leslie kept a spare key under the mat of her driver's seat in case she ever got locked out. Never had she imagined it would be needed for a reason such as this. As the ambulance swerved into the emergency entrance, Leslie couldn't help but think how she had a backup plan for every aspect of her life. Except Nadya. She gulped. Her only child. Her miracle baby. The one thing in her life that was irreplaceable. Although her daughter didn't seem to think Leslie felt that way.

Nadya was a daddy's girl, and Leslie was alright with it because she was one too. Everything Leslie needed, everything she wanted, had been given to her by her father. Leslie hadn't *needed* a husband, and because of her dad, she hadn't accepted anything less than 100 percent from any other man. Thinking of her dad, Leslie called him to let him know about Nadya's passing out.

"I'll be right there," Edwin Samuels said and hung up the phone.

Knowing nothing would stop her father from rushing to her side was the kind of comfort she needed. He'd enfold her in his arms and assure her that everything would be alright. Because if her daddy said it, she sure would believe it.

5

Celeste

JANUARY 2

With her one-of-a-kind evening gown and designer shoes, Celeste knew she would be a standout at tonight's charity event. And that worried her, had her grinding her teeth as she stood in front of the floor-length mirror in her walk-in closet. She plumped her lips to still their quivering.

The stylists had done an amazing job. Once she had registered their bookstore as a company and applied for the LLC licensing, Celeste had devoted the rest of her day to getting primped and prodded. She was fab-u-lous. Flawless.

On the inside though, she was a mess. A hot mess of churning, bumbling fright that intensified with each passing hour.

After Leslie sent the SOS text, her hands turned shaky and

she was on the brink of a panic attack at the thought of driving Leslie's car home. She hadn't driven at night in months. All because of the carjacking on her anniversary night fifteen months prior. Wade had been behind the wheel and narrowly missed an accident at a stoplight. One minute she had been laughing at Wade cracking a joke about his driving skills and the next, a rap on her window revealed a gun pointed her way. Every moment of that interaction had her heart throbbing with fear, visualizing her terrible end.

When Yasmeen texted she was available to retrieve the SUV, Celeste almost crumbled with relief. To be clear, it wasn't the driving that terrified her, it was the necessary stops at the red lights. Red lights that were like dragons making her sweat and hyperventilate under their glare, making the minutes feel like an eternity, while she clutched the steering wheel and prayed. It was too much for her equilibrium. That and the four tickets she had received for gunning past red lights at night. It was a good thing the Coleman name had clout in the city or she would be out of a driver's license.

Celeste glanced at the clock, drawing deep breaths and willing her heart to slow down its heavy beating. Seven o'clock was showtime. And it was one hundred and twenty-eight minutes away. Wade would be walking into the house any minute to get dressed. Celeste could already see his upturned lip if she displayed any anxiety. She could hear the low hum of his voice, stating she couldn't back out of the party now.

Maybe this time would be different.

Maybe Wade would show some compassion, show a thread of understanding. But that thread had shriveled at his company's New Year's party. The one where she spent most of the time hidden in the women's restroom, trembling and crying.

No. This time would be different.

So…she needed to get herself together. Celeste inhaled and exhaled. Inhaled and exhaled. Looking down at her hands, she gasped. She had forgotten her diamond solitaire. Since the carjacking, she wore only a simple wedding band. But Wade would insist she wear the showpiece to his work event. Hurrying to her jewelry collection, Celeste donned the gem, marveling at how weighty it felt on her finger. Pinching the ring with the thumb and index finger of her right hand, Celeste turned it so the diamond was hidden under her palm. Just in case. Choosing a pair of tassel earrings and a matching choker, Celeste slipped them into her clutch. Once they were safe inside the venue, she would put those on. Then she would be showcase-ready. Ready to compete with the other sparkling, tittering wives from Wade's firm.

Ugh. To think she'd once craved to be in their circle. Had been in their circle, actually, welcomed, revered, until she dared to show fear, weakness. That was a contagion to be avoided. Now she was subjected to the whispers behind hands and the eyes filled with pity—and for some, spiteful satisfaction over how the Dame of Dover, as the newspapers dubbed her, had fallen. Celeste despised all the attention. She groaned. She wished she could just…be. Eat, drink, blend in. But Wade wanted her to be the standout he had married, the swan spreading her wings on command before hundreds.

Not this cowering mass of incompetence.

His words.

Words she hadn't allowed to take ownership of her soul, though they had pierced her core. Celeste knew she was capable. She still excelled on the job. She was just…stuck. Stuck in time. In a moment. And if Wade couldn't understand that, then that was his problem.

Antsy, Celeste walked into their master suite and sat on the edge of her bed, her clutch under her arm. The sun had set and she could see the beautiful array of stars beaming through the night. This would be a good time to curl into bed and read one of the books Yasmeen had recommended.

Just then, Wade sent a text saying he had gotten dressed at the office and was about a minute away. Some of his colleagues wanted to go out for cocktails before the gala. Never mind that neither Celeste nor Wade drank alcohol. He was very much a schmoozer.

She sent him a thumbs-up. Texting was their primary mode of communication unless words were absolutely necessary. She hadn't spoken to him much after he had tossed those harsh words her way, his lips curled with contempt.

Tonight though, they would be the loving, laughing couple, putting on a show designed to impress the city's elite.

From her position on the bed, she saw the black Range Rover turn the corner and shot to her feet. Giving herself a final once-over, she rushed down the stairs and out the door. Then she stopped short. The tarantula was in the front seat.

Celeste marched forward and opened the passenger door, scoffing at the nickname Toni had bestowed on Tula James, the only woman in a leadership position at Wade's firm and one who did nothing to disguise her fascination with Celeste's husband.

Tula stopped midsentence and gawked at her like she expected Celeste to jump into the back seat. *As if.*

Celeste arched a brow, daring the other woman to say something. Wade dipped his head, taking in the scene, but kept his mouth shut, hiding a smile. Tula was dressed in a red form-fitting dress more suitable for a video vixen than for a classy event. The woman had paired it with some clunky, brassy gold heels. The kind you knew were expensive but were just plain ugly. And her makeup transformed her into a completely different person every time Celeste saw her. Celeste almost clucked her tongue but she was determined to behave as unbothered as she was. Money couldn't buy taste. According to Wade, Tula outearned most of the men in the firm—including him. With a mental shrug, Celeste greeted the other woman, her tone polite and cool.

Tula gave Celeste a onceover before raising her chin and giving a smile as fake as the makeup on her face. "Hey, girl. I was going to move. Just busy talking shop."

Yeah, right. Envy poured from Tula's very pores.

The other woman got out and moved into the back seat while she continued her yakking.

Tula wanted Wade, with evident desperation. Wade would come home and regale Celeste with stories of Tula attempting to weave her way into his life and they would laugh at her not-so-subtle tactics while they ate the donuts that Tula ordered special delivery from across the nation. Celeste's heart squeezed. She couldn't remember the last time she and Wade laughed or even chuckled at something just because.

Now they had these practiced smiles and flat jokes that fooled everyone but them. Celeste struck a pose, loving the hunger in Wade's eyes as he checked her out. She resisted the urge to see if Tula noticed. That would give the feline an importance she didn't have in Celeste's world. That's why Celeste hadn't even asked why Tula was there. Insignificant.

"Hey, baby," he said, "you looking exquisite as usual."

"Thank you." Slipping into the vehicle, Celeste leaned over to kiss her husband on the cheek, taking in his fineness. His skin was smooth like milk chocolate and he tasted just as good. No, better. He sported a low fade and his mustache covered a set of generous lips. Lips that had trailed a path on every crevice of her body.

Celeste crossed her legs and welcomed the unexpected desire snaking through her veins. She gave her husband a glance from under her lashes, wondering if he had noticed her reaction to his presence. His eyes met hers, holding promise. Familiar, silent communication. Maybe they could get back to how they once were.

It's on later, she mouthed.

He smiled, flashing white, straight teeth and put the car in gear.

She gripped the door as a stronger emotion took center stage in her mind, stomping down the passion and replacing it with fear. *Irrational fear.* They weren't even driving far, but Celeste clutched her stomach, now relieved that Tula had engaged Wade in conversation, for once appreciating the chatter, hoping it would distract her husband from seeing the terror building, threatening to overtake her.

But that was like asking a well-tuned guitar to play out of tune.

Of course he saw. He reached over to grip her hand, giving it a squeeze. A silent plea for her to keep it together. Like she could help it. Celeste could already hear the argument, the four words he voiced on repeat: *go back to therapy.* Something she insisted she hadn't needed after four sessions of her rambling and the therapist not offering any advice. All she really needed was time and his patience.

Tula seized that moment to utter something witty that made Wade laugh. A genuine one. Watching his shoulders shake with mirth, Celeste swallowed.

"That's a good one, Tula," he said, wiping his face.

The tarantula was slowly crafting her web, and Celeste's husband was the unsuspecting prey. She should say something. Instead, she turned her head, tuning out the conversation, and watched the people in other cars driving without a care in the world. How she longed for that…

She tucked her chin into her chest and took long, deep breaths before realizing that they had yet to stop at any red lights. Her brows furrowed. She leaned forward and paid attention to his route. Wade was making extra turns and taking the back roads to the highway to avoid the traffic signals. Despite their cold war, he cared. Her heart melted at this thoughtfulness and she turned to look at him.

Again, their eyes met. She knew hers held appreciation, and his held understanding. Celeste covered her mouth and struggled not to fall apart at his sweet actions. Since he was steering with his left hand, she lifted his right and pressed her lips against the back of it. Wade tightened his hold briefly. Then she released him, feeling hopeful. Maybe tonight wouldn't be all an act.

"I wish I had what you two have," Tula said, not even hiding her envy.

"She's one-of-a-kind," Wade said, repeating the words he had stated when Celeste asked why he'd chosen her from the swarms of women hankering after him back in the day. They still did. Everywhere he went, the man found a new addition to his fan club. When she pointed it out, he would give a dismissive wave and kiss her until her toes curled. It didn't matter where they were, either. Wade was all for the PDA. He was proud of his woman. Again, his words.

But that was then.

It could be once again. All she had to do was try.

Celeste settled into her seat and forced herself to relax. Her heart rate calmed. They were now on the highway and almost at their destination. She could do this. Tonight, she would allow herself to have a good time. Tonight, she would make her husband proud. Wade dropped the women off out front and went to secure a parking spot.

And for a moment, she did do it. She smiled and schmoozed and ate appetizers while a couple of Wade's pals and their wives enjoyed cocktails. Then they caravanned to the venue and all that positivity disappeared the moment she entered the building and saw the theme was Ain't No Stopping Us Now. That's right, they were giving away a car.

There were hues of red, green and yellow in the darkened room. Celeste immediately battled images of the carjacking. She scanned the room taking in the smiling, clueless faces while her throat closed on her. Curling her fingers, she clenched her jaw to keep from screaming, her nails cutting deep into her palm. Celeste darted to the bathroom and dabbed at the beads of sweat on her forehead, careful not to ruin her makeup.

Tula must have seen her panic because she entered the bathroom. "Are you okay?" She licked her lips. "Wade told me all about what happened and I just came to check on you."

Wade had told her? Celeste wagged a finger in Tula's face. "Don't pretend to care about me and don't think I don't know your true motives." She shoved the door open and exited the restroom. Back into the dark. Back to the flashing lights. Her panic rose.

Tula rushed to her side and took her arm. "Celeste, calm down. Take deep breaths."

In her peripheral view, she could see people checking her out, but Celeste flailed her hands to shrug off the other woman. "You think I don't see right through you? You think I don't see you sidling up to my husband as if he would ever give you the time of day?"

A loud gasp filled the space and she knew all eyes were on her. Her reaction was over-the-top and undeserved, but it was like a dam had busted open and she had to spew. She had to release all the fear building up inside her.

Tula placed a hand up and took a few steps backward. "Look, I don't want any trouble."

"You don't want any trouble?" She faltered for a moment, the terror overwhelming her. She cupped her eyes but all she saw were the lights. Wade had to have known but he'd brought her here. Brick by brick, fear had built a wall that kept her from her life, that kept her huddled inside the four walls of her home. Yet here she was, venturing out. Yes, she had been coerced, but still. Her emotions were running wild, and she couldn't cap them and remain civilized. Celeste could cry about it or she could attack. Fight, like she was doing now.

It wasn't appropriate and the timing was off, but it felt right. Nancy, Wade's boss's wife, and a couple of other women circled close. This time Celeste was the one who backed up, feeling surrounded by a pack of hyenas. Wade entered, and from the corner of her eye, she could see him storming toward her.

"You're making a scene, dear," Nancy said, her tone condescending. The older woman put a hand on her chest.

"Celeste. What are you doing?" he asked, gripping her arm. "I could hear you yelling from all the way down the hall."

She jabbed an index finger toward Wade. "Quit coming at me like I have a problem. You're the one who brought me here when you know my...situation."

His brows furrowed. "What are you talking about? Why are you making this charity event about you?" His voice held fury and surprise. She watched him gather his composure. "You know what? Let's leave."

Wade cupped her arm to lead her outside, but Celeste shrugged him off. "I'm not leaving until I say my piece." Her chest heaved. "It took everything within me to agree to come to this pretentious farce of a gathering because you insisted I slap a smile on my face and show up," she screeched. By this time, all eyes were on her. She was definitely the center of attention.

Wade's boss, Craig, stormed over. He cut her a scathing look before addressing Wade. "I suggest you get your wife out of here. She's out of control."

"She is right here and she can speak for herself," Celeste raged, her neck rolling from side to side.

"We're leaving."

Through her haze of anger, Celeste registered Wade's disapproving glare. She could see the embarrassment on his face and suddenly realized she had made a mockery of herself. This wasn't who she was. Celeste didn't even understand why she had erupted. Lost control.

She placed a hand to her mouth. Her anger dissipated, leaving her body in slow, long waves like a sandcastle on the beach. Sudden tears pricked. "I'm sorry." Shame engulfed her in waves. "I wasn't thinking. I..."

Wade spoke through gritted teeth. "Let's get out of here."

Seeing the pity in their eyes, Celeste lowered her head and sniffled. What was wrong with her? She trailed behind him, a meek minion, her husband remaining silent until they were back inside their vehicle. Wade was too furious to say a word. In fact, when she tried to speak, he cut her off, telling her that they would talk once they were home.

So as soon as they walked through their front door, Celeste turned and confronted him. "Wade, I'm so sorry I fell apart like that."

He spun on her, unleashing his fury. "Fell apart? That's how you see your behavior back there?" He rubbed his head. "That was an avalanche, a category five hurricane. That wasn't merely falling apart."

She wrung her hands. Celeste couldn't recall ever seeing Wade this upset and she was still in shock from her outburst. "I'm as confused about my behavior as you are. But I will apologize to your boss and Nancy tomorrow."

"And Tula?" He raised a brow.

Celeste put a hand on her hip and engaged in a staredown. "She had it coming. That woman has been after you for two years and I've looked the other way."

Wade tapped a foot, the sound a nervous rattle on the floor. "That's your defense? Please don't pretend to be jealous because we both know you aren't. You have no reason to be and you know it. You're just trying to rationalize your atrocious actions." He curled his lips. "Look at you. You're wallowing in embarrassment right now, and you want me to cuddle you and tell you I understand." He gave her a look of contempt. "Well, you're not getting that because I don't."

Tears streaked down her face. "You're ashamed of me," she choked out.

"Yes. I am. In abundance." He drew several deep breaths and shook his head.

The fact he didn't try to deny it slashed her gut. She wrung her hands. "What can I do to fix this?"

"There's nothing you can do or, rather, that you want to do, and I'm tired of trying to force you to get help." Wade squared his shoulders. "But you know what? I'm done. I'm done debating." He had a finality in his tone that would scare her if it weren't for the fact that this was Wade. Her rock.

"I'll do anything," she said, and then squared her shoulders, expecting "Go back to therapy." This time, she would even attend a session or two to appease him. Instead, her husband uttered four words that shattered her soul. Four words she never thought Wade would ever think, much less say.

He used his index finger to lift her chin and whispered in a pained voice, "I want a divorce."

6

Toni

JANUARY 2

A bright light pierced the dark of the night. Toni clenched her jaw. In her peripheral, she could see someone holding their cell phone, recording her. Internally, she sighed and groaned. But outwardly, she whipped around and struck a pose, before blowing a kiss at her eager fan outside the nail salon. Then she sauntered to her car with a calculated, carefree head toss, when all she really wanted to do was run.

After she had told Kent the bald-faced lie that everything was fine, Toni had put her phone on silent, tossed it in her bag and then engaged in a few hours of meaningless retail therapy, killing time, so she wouldn't have to tell Kent any more lies.

When she was done shopping, Toni had decided to get her

nails done. It was either that or call Kent because she missed him and wanted to hear his voice. It had only been a few days between nail appointments, but it was something to do. A distraction. The technician did her thing and Toni tipped her accordingly.

Opening her car door and slipping into the driver's side, Toni slung her purchases onto the passenger seat. Settling into the soft leather, she studied her zebra-striped nails, staring at the painted pink flower on her ring finger.

Then the interior lights went out, leaving her with nothing but quiet. Her public persona began shedding like a snake out of its skin, until she was left with her true self.

She inhaled. The questions she'd kept at bay rushed to the forefront of her mind. Doubt and fear gnawed at her. From low in her gut a tightening began, climbing its way up her chest, twisting her insides and constricting her heart. Unable to contain the swelling of emotions, she coughed, the sound a sputter expanding into a guttural groan. Her body shook and she curled her fists. If she let this out, she feared she might never regain control. Sucking in her cheeks, she swallowed. And exhaled.

She couldn't stop the tears leaking from the corners of her eyes. Sniffling, she wiped her face with the back of her hand. That's all she would allow herself to feel.

Since her purse was propped on her leg, she felt her phone vibrate inside, shaking her out of her introspection. Another notification. For a second, Toni considered ignoring the calls like she had over the past hours, but then it vibrated again. And yet again.

Her curiosity piqued. Her mind begged for something else to occupy her thoughts.

Toni reached into her purse and dug around for her phone. Curling her hands around the smooth, rectangular frame, she unlocked her phone. There was a ridiculous amount of social media alerts. She dismissed those and tapped on the text messages icon. As expected, there were several messages from Kent asking for her whereabouts and if she was okay. She skipped over those, swallowing her guilt. When she read Leslie's text messages, she took in a deep breath and her eyes went wide. Nadya had collapsed and was in the ER? Heart pounding, she hurriedly texted the group chat.

Just seeing these. You need me to come up there?

While she waited for a response, Toni pressed the brake and turned on the car, intending to head over to the hospital. It was the only one around, the next hospital close to an hour away.

Not yet. My dad is here and we're just waiting.

Ok... Let me know if you need anything.

I will. Hoping she'll get discharged soon.

Catching up on the rest of the messages in the chat, Toni breathed a sigh of relief knowing Yasmeen had volunteered to retrieve Leslie's car from the gym. Then her thoughts returned to Kent.

Gathering her courage, Toni pulled up her voicemails and listened to that deep bass voice that made her breath catch. He had left three messages. First, he sounded unbothered, then there was a hint of worry, and finally, deep concern.

"Baby, I need to know you're alright. Please call me."

His worry fanned her guilt, wetting her face with fresh tears. She flung the phone on the passenger seat next to her. She couldn't call because she was scared. Scared. Scared. Scared to hit him with her failure. Her inability. Then he'd find her lacking like the last girlfriend who refused to be "saddled with a child." Would her fate be the same? She thought of her parents, who had been quick to chastise, almost never telling her she was loved. Would he love her, but just a little...less?

No. This was a man who spoke words of affirmation to her daily. He loved her, treasured her. Love bore all things... Love grounded. She moistened her lips. Maybe if she told him her diagnosis, it would bring them together. She had to have faith their love was strong enough to withstand *this* truth.

Maybe it could. But she wasn't sure it could withstand the *whole* truth. Her infertility was only the skin of the onion. There were scales and layers to her past that could taint the way Kent saw her, dim the glint in his eyes. Like the fact that she had committed a crime...

A call came through, cutting her thoughts.

"Hey, Celeste," Toni said, her tone forcefully light and calm.

"Girl, where you at?"

Toni's ear pricked. Celeste sounded frantic, off-kilter. "I'm not too far from you. What's going on?" She pressed the video icon, and a second later, Celeste's face appeared. Her eyes were filled with worry. She was steadily pacing her living room area.

"I—I need you. Can you stop by?"

Clutching the phone, Toni backed out of the parking space. "I'm on my way."

Celeste released a deep breath. "I'll see you when you get here."

Toni made it to Celeste's home in half her usual time. She noted Wade's car was missing and parked her Mustang behind Celeste's vehicle to leave space for him. Before going inside, she sent Kent a quick text apologizing, saying she was okay and that Celeste had an emergency. She knew he would assume she had been too caught up in that situation to respond to him earlier. He answered with a kiss emoji. She told him she loved him, once again swallowing her mountain-sized guilt.

Her heels click-clacked up the driveway and she pressed the doorbell. Celeste called out that the door was unlocked, and Toni went inside. There wasn't a single light on in the house. Celeste lay prostrate on the couch, a hand over her eyes.

"Hey, friend. What's going on?" Toni asked, turning on the lights, ditching her shoes and rushing over to join Celeste on the couch.

Celeste sat up and grabbed Toni's hand. She was still dressed in her gown, but her updo had come undone, and her eyes were red and swollen from crying. Yet her first words were not about herself. "Is Nadya alright? I haven't checked my phone."

"I think so. Leslie wrote in our chat that she was waiting on results and her father is there, so she told us not to come. Most likely the poor baby's worn out. You know how Leslie is about gymnastics." She patted Celeste's hand. "Now, what's going on with you?"

"Wade asked me for a divorce."

Toni's head reeled. "Wait. What? Wade? Come on. You can't believe he meant that. You two are my couple goal."

Though her voice sounded hoarse, Celeste explained all that transpired earlier that night at Wade's firm's supposedly swanky affair. It sounded downright tacky to have a stoplight in the middle of the dance floor. Toni couldn't imagine her friend falling apart to the point where she would cause a scene and become the "spectacle of the night," but Celeste assured her that was the case.

Rubbing the top of Celeste's hand, Toni said, "I don't think he's serious though. Not for one minute. He'll be back once he's calmed down."

Those words were not just to reassure Celeste, they were very much for Toni as well. If Celeste and Wade couldn't work out, then what hope was there for her and Kent? She wasn't nearly as put together as Celeste, and if Wade, one of the most patient men she had ever met, was ready to let his relationship end over this speed bump, what's to say Kent wouldn't do the same if she told him about her infertility and her past?

Celeste's mouth curved into a wishful smile. "I hope you're right..." She cocked her head. "You think this is a stunt to get me into therapy?"

Toni doubted it. Divorce wasn't something you should threaten your spouse with to make them conform. She tapped her chin. And the Wade she knew wasn't one to bluff. So she tried another tactic. "I don't think it's a stunt but I do think it's a wake-up call. I think your meltdown tonight is a sure sign that you do need counseling."

"I don't want to keep talking about that night. I don't want to relive the horror over and over. I just want to move on."

"But you haven't. That night is ruling your life and now your marriage." Her words dropped like a hammer between them.

"He'll come to his senses," Celeste insisted. Toni could tell Celeste wasn't ready to hear what she had to say, so she stopped talking and hugged her. Celeste yawned. "Will you stay awhile?"

"I'm not going anywhere."

With a nod, Celeste closed her eyes, her breathing slowly becoming even.

While she was glad to see Celeste get some rest, Toni grappled with the fact that, just that morning, their world had been turning as it should. Yet, mere hours later, their axis had been tilted off-kilter.

From where she sat, she could peer through the slats of the blinds. Squinting, she tried to see if it there was a full moon tonight. Because that was the only explanation she could think of for the bizarre turn of events. Her diagnosis, Leslie's daughter, and now Celeste's marriage. Yasmeen was the only one who seemed to have been spared. Thank goodness, because Toni didn't think she could take any more drama today.

A loud ping made her jump. Toni checked her phone. Seeing a message in her DMs, she tapped to read, thinking it was probably just one of the pizza chains offering her a sponsorship.

@BLSTFRDAPST: TIME TO PAY FOR YOUR PAST SINS.

"Skins," she whispered. A nickname he had earned because of his love of sharp knives and his propensity of leaving three light gashes across the wrists of his victims. Goose bumps rose on her flesh and she rubbed her arms. But it couldn't be him. Skins was behind bars for life. She tapped on the search bar and typed in the words, *Lamont Fisher, gang member, murder.* Articles surrounding the young man who had killed three people in a home invasion gone bad popped up. She scanned a few of them, but there was nothing indicating he had been released. Her shoulders slumped with relief. Lamont was where he should be. Locked away for good.

Now that she knew that, Toni hit the block button. Although she knew for hecklers it didn't make sense since they would just create a new username. Still, she wouldn't have to worry about him again, for a little bit at least.

Careful not to awaken Celeste, Toni headed upstairs toward the spare bedroom where she knew Celeste kept toiletries and nightclothes, prepared for their numerous, on-the-fly sleepovers. Her feet welcomed the feel of the plush carpeting. Once she had changed into a pair of long-sleeved pajamas featuring tiny Christmas decorations, she went down to the kitchen to make a cup of coffee.

The heating system groaned to life, which was good, because it was getting colder and colder. Sitting at the small dinette in the kitchen, she allowed her memories to take her back to a different time. A time when she wasn't Toni Marshall, publicist extraordinaire, and she was simply Antoinette Masters from Hollis, Queens.

A foolish young girl craving her parents' affection who had sought refuge in the arms of the bad boy on the block. The one in the house across from hers that her parents told her to stay away from. A wannabe-gangster. Correction, an actual gangster and self-proclaimed king of the 'hood. Lamont had been twenty, five years older than she was. She had skipped classes to hang with him, get high with him, and he had been her first foray into sexual discovery. He had been a considerate lover and partner until she had come up pregnant.

Then he'd turned. Called her a ho and accused her of sleeping with his friends. Bad talked her to the whole neighborhood. All of which she'd denied. Just as fast, he had comforted her and apologized. She'd been too naive to end things. Instead, she'd let him take her to someone he knew to get an abortion. A quack who had no clue what she was doing. Bleeding heavily the next day, Toni had passed out at school and had been rushed to the emergency room. It was then her parents had learned of the botched abortion. They had been mortified, disappointed and had demanded she stop seeing Lamont.

Of course she hadn't listened. How she wished she had!

It took a scary incident before she broke things off for good and told him to stay away from her. Well, Lamont wasn't one to be told what he could and couldn't do. He tormented her and threatened her parents. Scared of Lamont's affiliation, her parents legally changed their names and relocated to Delaware. Once she turned eighteen and graduated high school, they had cut ties with her, saying their obligation to her was done and she had been an embarrassment. They blamed her for making them have to give up their life in New York to live in the "Podunk, no-class city" of Dover, Delaware.

Toni hadn't spoken to them since. The last she heard, her parents had returned to New York and were living it up in SoHo. But Toni was fine with that. She sipped her coffee, which had cooled considerably.

She had reinvented herself and made the best friends a woman could ask for, though she had never told them her sordid past. Because after all these years, Toni had a good life, great friends and an even better man. Not for one minute was she going to lose all she had worked for, all she deserved.

That meant she needed to find this person, figure out what they knew and quash this nonsense before it became something. And she had to do it fast.

Yasmeen

JANUARY 3

"I can't believe this is my life right now," Yasmeen yelled in the parking lot of her parents' apartment building, before firing off a text to Toni, who she knew was an early riser.

Can you give me a ride? I've got to take my parents to the doctor by 8 plus get to a job interview and my car won't start.

Huddled under an olive green puffer jacket she had purchased at a garage sale, Yasmeen shivered while resisting the urge to kick the car's tires. The issue was probably the battery because overnight, the temps had dropped until it was brick cold. She had come outside while her parents were getting dressed to make sure her temperamental vehicle was ready to go, and here it was, sitting duck-still.

Her ears burned from the brutal morning chill. It had to be in the low thirties this morning. The zipper to the fur hoodie of her jacket had gotten damaged, so she couldn't even cover her head. Not that it would fit over the two large Afro puffs that she had woken up early that morning to style. She hadn't gotten around to starting her braids, because she didn't think she had enough synthetic hair and needed to get some more. Something she couldn't do now because her car refused to co-operate.

Ugh. She could scream. Well, she already had.

Toni's answer was almost immediate. Girl, you have a vehicle you can use. Use it.

She shivered. But I don't feel right asking Leslie.

Her cell rang and Toni came on, her voice a whisper. "Leslie's all caught up with Nadya at the moment and you know she don't care. We all got your back. Now, go do what you have to do."

"Why are you whispering?" she asked, her lips quivering. Then her eyes went wide. "Don't tell me you and Kent finally did the deed? 'Cause I don't know why you two are holding out." She dug into her purse for Leslie's keys, stomped over to the SUV and unlocked the door. Pressing the ignition, she welcomed the blast of much-needed heat and turned on the seat warmer.

"Girl, please. You know Kent isn't budging on that and I'm good with it. I spent the night at Celeste's house." Something about Toni's tone told Yasmeen that it hadn't been a social call, otherwise she would fuss about not being invited.

"What's going on?" she asked, putting the phone on speaker so she could warm her chilled hands. When Toni filled her in about Wade mentioning the dreadful *D* word, Yasmeen felt her eyes go wide. Celeste was one stubborn woman. If Yasmeen had a man like Wade, she would do everything she could to keep him. Especially if all she needed to do was go to therapy to help herself. Chile, please. She would *welcome* the luxury of talking about her problems to someone twice a week. Peering under the visor, she looked to see if her parents were coming out of the building. "Listen, I've got to go, but as soon as I get done, I'll be over there."

"Alright. Talk to you soon," Toni said, then added, "I'm going to make Celeste some grits and eggs."

Yasmeen rolled her eyes. "That's your answer to everything and you aren't even from the South." Her stomach growled. "You know what? Save me some."

"I got you," Toni chuckled.

Once they disconnected, Yasmeen called Leslie. She didn't feel right pulling out of the lot without getting her friend's permission first. When Leslie responded, she sounded frantic, saying she hadn't slept the night before and was still waiting to hear from the doctor. Through that conversation, Yasmeen managed to slip in that she needed to use Leslie's SUV. As Toni had predicted, Leslie didn't mind, telling her to use it as long as she needed. She did say something about Aaron not being there, so Yasmeen promised to stop by as soon as she could. Seeing Darryl approaching, Yasmeen cut the call short and rolled down the window.

"Pookie, what are you doing here?" she asked, though she had a suspicion. There was only one reason why this man was out of his house before 10:00 a.m. He needed money. Sure enough, he fixed his mouth to ask for some cash. She cut her eyes at him, hating herself for admiring those long lashes and full lips. "Where do you expect me to get it from, when just last night you heard me say the lights were shut off?"

At the same time, she kept glancing toward the entrance to look out for her parents. Hopefully, she would get rid of Darryl before they came down. Yasmeen didn't want to spend the car ride to her father's colonoscopy exam hearing about her "no-good boyfriend." Never mind that Darryl did have serious cooking skills—of which they could testify—and wanted to go to culinary school. But he kept getting into his own way because of his so-called friends for life.

Darryl stuffed his hands in the pockets of his beaten leather jacket. "I figured one of your friends might have come through and slipped an extra something something your way." His breaths came out in choppy puffs in the cold.

"I don't have anything."

"Look, I really need it." Something about his tone made her pause. He sounded...desperate. She remembered his words about possibly being incarcerated.

"Are you in some kind of trouble? What did you do?"

"Why does it have to be that I did something?" He cocked his head. "I know things tight with you right now but I wouldn't ask if I didn't need it."

He thought he was slick. "I see you didn't answer my question."

Furious flashing lights followed by a couple of dark sedans raced into the parking lot and stopped in front of the SUV. Her heart thundered. "Darryl, oh my goodness, what's going on?" She moved to crack open the door.

Darryl didn't even try to run. He placed a finger over his lips and shook his head before telling her to remain inside the vehicle. Then he backed up, and slowly, painstakingly, lifted his hands high. "I'm unarmed and my pockets are clear." His voice rang out in the space while Yasmeen fought to tamp down her fear.

The cops rushed toward him and tackled him to the ground.

She grabbed her cell phone and hit record even as her body shook, her teeth chattered and the tears fell. Just in case. Yasmeen had seen too many cases of cops getting trigger-happy for no good reason. At that precise moment, she saw her parents dashing across the lot, arm in arm. Great. This is just what she needed. She could see her father's frowning face and her mother's eyes were wide.

Her father got in the front beside her and her mother climbed into the back seat. Yasmeen wrinkled her nose, inhaling the distinct smell of an egg sandwich. That's what had taken them so long.

"Daddy, please tell me you didn't eat."

"Your mother made it for later. When I'm done," Willie said.

"I hope so. Because the doctor emphasized several times that you need to be empty."

"He didn't take even a small bite," Dixie said, making Yasmeen slump with relief.

"Great, because I can't take too much time off from work."

"Let's get out of here," her father said, his voice shaky, while the police read Darryl his rights. "We don't want the police coming over here to question us."

She gritted her teeth. "Daddy, I can't leave now." She held her shaking hand with her free one to keep the phone steady while she recorded. "Driving off would raise suspicion."

"What is he doing here?" her father asked, his hands trembling while he buckled into the seat.

Yasmeen for sure wasn't going to answer that.

"You can do so much better than him," Dixie chimed in.

Hoisting Darryl to his feet, the cops shoved him into the back of their vehicle, and within seconds, they were gone. It was only because of her parents' watchful eyes that Yasmeen didn't completely lose it. She stopped the recording and dropped her phone into the console. Then she wiped her face with the back of her hand and willed herself to breathe. She repeated, *He will be okay, He will be okay*, on the inside, all the while hoping and praying it was true.

From the corner of her eye, she saw her mother waving an old McDonald's napkin she must have gotten from inside of her purse.

"Thanks, Mom," she whispered and dabbed at her eyes.

"Never mind, my daughter. He'll be alright."

"It's not just that," she said, breaking down at her mother's tender tone. "It's everything. I can't get it together."

Her daddy spoke up in a voice filled with compassion. "It's alright. It's alright. God has a plan."

Yasmeen wanted to tell him that God's plan sucked and that she needed to find her own way out. But she bit her lower lip. Not for one moment would she light that match and start that fire. Sniffling, she said, "I don't want you to be late."

After a few minutes of silence while she navigated through traffic, her mother said, "You're a good daughter to us, Yasmeen. And I know your faith in God might be shaky at times, and you don't want to hear about Him, but He's going to reward you for your faithfulness."

"Yes, Mommy." Yasmeen didn't have the stamina to argue. She and God had a special relationship. She stayed out of His way and she asked Him to do the same for her. It wasn't that she didn't believe or have love for Him, but look at her life. It was hard to remain positive and keep praying, when the only answer she seemed to get was no. No to school. No to a good job. No to nursing. No to a good man. No. No. No.

But, again, she didn't utter a word. The ten-minute drive was ample time for her father to deliver a fire-and-brimstone sermon and she had enough to think about.

Like her car.

Darryl.

Her job. Her boss hadn't been too happy to hear she needed to take the morning off to help her parents. Her dad was a man of strong faith, but he was very much a man who was scared of being put under. Her mother had confided to Yasmeen that her daddy was scared he wouldn't wake up from the anesthesia. A fact proven by the intensity of his prayers the night before, and just now, before entering the building.

"I'll be back in a couple hours. I just have to run some errands first." With a wave, her parents went inside. Yasmeen hated lying to them but they wouldn't approve of where she was going if she told them. Never mind that it was honest work. Her potential job prospect was at the local casino in Dover. She had grown up hearing enough messages against gambling, but the hours and pay were too good to pass up. If she got this job, she could quit her other one.

She pressed on the gas and headed down US 13. Just as she was about to make a right turn, Yasmeen thought she saw one of the church sisters at the intersection. She gripped the wheel. Since the casino was a part of a hotel, she wasn't worried about the news going back to her parents.

Not that she didn't plan on telling them if she got the job. It was all about the *how*. She found a parking spot and a car similar to Aaron's caught her eye. She leaned close to the windshield. Was that his vehicle? Naw, it couldn't be. She debated texting Leslie but decided she had better be sure before she created a potential rift in Leslie's marriage.

Grabbing her purse, she exited the vehicle and rushed toward the casino entrance.

She stepped inside and gasped at the number of people sitting by the slot machines. She spied a grandmotherly-looking lady at one of the games, with her cane propped against her knee, unrolling coins in a plastic bag. Yasmeen stuck her tongue between her teeth to keep from telling her to go home. That wouldn't do if she was going to get a job here.

She dipped around the table games to see if she spotted Aaron by the player portals, her heart pounding. But she didn't see him. She exhaled a long, deep breath.

Thank goodness she had been mistaken. She wouldn't have to do any snitching today. Because with all she had going on, Aaron gambling again was the last thing Leslie would need. Aaron was a good man and all that nonsense was in his past.

Shame filled her for doubting him, judging him based on a past incident when he was now out there grinding, taking care of his family.

She would give her arm for a man like that, who was able to provide, be a strong financial support. And she knew what it was like to be counting pennies and she didn't want that for her friend. Especially now.

Speaking of counting pennies… She needed to get to this interview so she could make these coins.

Leslie

JANUARY 3

If she continued to stare at the opaque walls, she was going to lose it. Leslie had been waiting in this room for sixteen hours, enduring frigid temperatures, and her daughter still didn't have a diagnosis.

Her bottom burned and her back ached from sitting in this rickety chair for most of the night, and she had a tension headache climbing across her forehead. She ran her fingers through her strands and placed a hand over her eyes. Eyes that were puffy from the nonstop crying and lack of sleep.

The wait was maddening. Interminable. The constant beeping and the bright lights made resting impossible. Not that she could sleep knowing something was wrong with her child. She had already been to the nurse's station about five times for an update. Each time she was told the same thing. To wait.

She heard a creak and straightened to face the door. Her father walked in holding two coffee cups, ducking his head to avoid colliding with the doorjamb. Edwin Samuels was six foot five and in above-average physical shape. He kept his head shaved, his beard trimmed and had an active dating life. But he always made time for her. Edwin had been there with her for most of the night and Leslie had insisted he use the padded armchair.

"Any word yet, baby girl?" Edwin asked, handing her the steaming foam cup.

She gave a quick shake of the head.

The doctors had taken Nadya for a fourth scan of some kind but so far she had learned nothing.

"At least you know they're being thorough."

"Yes. But I'm going out of my mind not knowing. And I haven't been able to get in touch with Aaron." She placed her cup on the floor next to her. She was too unsettled to put anything to her mouth.

He took a sip of his coffee. "Is that the norm?"

She raised a brow before resting her head against the wall. Shaking her head, she closed her eyes. "Not now, Dad. Please." On the inside though, she seethed. The more worried she was for Nadya, the more her anger toward her absentee husband grew. It was the silent simmer under her gnawing concern.

"He's probably stuck in traffic," her father said. "I heard the Bay Bridge was closed because of crosswinds."

She bristled. "Even if that is the case, he can still call." Aaron was an executive in pharmaceutical sales for hospitals and several physicians in the state of Delaware, so he was in high demand. The It Man for Drugs was his nickname. He had also ventured out to Philadelphia and Maryland, which meant many overnight visits and road trips. Leslie applauded Aaron's ambition, but that meant he wasn't able to devote time to his family, his home.

The more he stayed busy, the more she relied on her dad. Her hero. Her rock. A role befitting the former navy SEAL. There had never been a time when she needed him that Edwin Samuels hadn't been there. Aaron knew it. It was a vicious cycle. But she wasn't one to whine and complain about her husband not being there. She simply called her father, who had been her steady force, and her only parent, since she was seven.

Aaron knew her father would be there. But that was no reason for her husband to shirk his responsibility when Nadya needed him. When their daughter returned from her scan, Aaron was going to be the first person she asked for, and Leslie would have to lie and cover for him. *Ooh.* Just thinking about that made her fume some more. Neglecting her was one thing. Not being there for Nadya was another matter.

Her father hadn't approved of her marrying Aaron, especially not after what happened the day before their wedding. Aaron hadn't been able to pay his portion of the balance of the reception costs and she found out he had gambled it away. A one-time fluke, he'd said, and the result of his getting carried away at his bachelor party. Her friends had been livid. Edwin had been the one to settle Aaron's tab—she hadn't told her friends that part—but even knowing that, her father never interfered in her relationship. Instead, he tried to be supportive. Not that she divulged what was going on in her marriage, but it was hard to cover for someone who wasn't there.

The door opened and a man entered wearing a white lab coat embroidered with blue script. She jumped to her feet to greet the doctor. Dr. Khalid was about five-five with thinning hair. After preliminary introductions, Leslie asked about Nadya's release.

"I'm afraid she isn't going anywhere. We're admitting her to monitor her. Mrs. Bronwyn, it's highly likely your daughter will need a blood transfusion."

Blood transfusion. She almost buckled at those two words, but her father scooped her close, tucking her under his arm. She inhaled his Old Spice, the familiar scent grounding her. "What's wrong with her?" she squeaked out.

"Based on my experience, I suspect this might be severe aplastic anemia," the doctor explained in a sympathetic tone.

Her father rubbed his beard. "Isn't anemia caused by a lack of iron? We're meat eaters and Leslie has her on a balanced diet. Can't you prescribe iron pills?"

"I'm afraid not. The only possible cure is a stem-cell transplant. This isn't about her body lacking iron. With severe aplastic anemia, your immune system is attacking the stem cells in your bone marrow."

All Leslie could do was shake her head. She couldn't process anything past the word *transfusion.* "Then, why didn't we know this before now?"

"Sometimes the symptoms aren't present early on."

The doctor further explained that Nadya's red, white and platelet cell levels were low and that he might need to do a biopsy. Leslie would have fallen if her father hadn't maintained his tight grip. She struggled to concentrate on Dr. Khalid's words. All she now heard was *biopsy.* Biopsy. Biopsy.

Clutching her stomach, she held herself and drew shaky breaths, her body trembling. Her father squeezed her shoulders and she burrowed into him. Her baby was sick. Sick, and she hadn't known. Snapshots of her daughter falling flashed across her mind, making her insides knot and her heart palpitate with a new kind of fear. She could lose her child.

"Whatever it is, it'll be okay," her father said, patting her back, his tone filled with disbelief.

Air left her body in a whoosh, her shoulders sinking in. She slumped onto the chair she had vacated, holding on to her father's hand.

The doctor cleared his throat. "The nurse will be in to review the necessary paperwork. I've started her on antibiotics and we will give her a blood transfusion to see if that helps. But with your permission, I'd like to perform the biopsy really soon. I'll have a scheduling call to get you an appointment as soon as possible."

"A biopsy." Whew. She ran a hand through her bob. "I need time to process. To think. Her father isn't here…"

The doctor pushed his glasses up the bridge of his nose. "Mrs. Bronwyn—"

She waved a hand. "Leslie, please."

"Leslie, I can't emphasize enough how important it is for us to act quickly. Does Nadya have any siblings?"

"No… No. It's just her." She swallowed, thinking of the miscarriages she'd had: one at four months, and the other at six. Two major losses before Nadya, and now… She gulped. She might lose Nadya too. Her baby girl. The thought was unimaginable. This couldn't be real. She grabbed her forehead and looked around the room at the twin-size adjustable bed and the medical equipment. Terror seized her heart. Nadya shouldn't be here. She should be in school with her friends. But this room could become her daughter's home.

A sob broke free, releasing her tenuous dam of fear. Her composure crumpled like a wooden house in a tornado.

Transfusion.

Biopsy.

Bone marrow transplant.

Those words that hammered away at her heart, plunging her into a whirlwind of emotions. The most terrible words she had ever heard. While she sobbed, she vaguely heard Dr. Khalid ask that all family members get checked as possible donors.

"There's just my dad and my husband. But what about my friends?" she stammered out.

"Sure. They can as well. But nothing beats family. Of course, everyone willing to donate must have a medical history screening first and also be tested for any transmissible viruses."

Next to her, her dad stiffened. She gave him a side glance, wondering why he would be nervous. Maybe it was the thought of the needles. She massaged her temples.

The doctor cleared his throat. "But let's wait for the results before you do anything."

She nodded, and as soon as he departed, Leslie was on it. Acting on what she could control. Reaching for her cell phone, she texted SOS in the group chat. That's all she could get out. Her girls would understand and come. Leslie would fill them in as soon as she caught her breath.

Then the door swooshed open and two cheerful-by-design nurses entered the room with fixed, determined smiles. And Leslie stopped crying in an instant. Thumbing away her tears, she donned the same act, ready to join their charade.

"Here we go, Nadya. You were so brave," one of the nurses said. After they settled Nadya into bed, she retreated, leaving the other nurse to hook her baby up to the monitors.

Her father excused himself and she assumed it was to call her husband, or to keep from falling apart.

"Hey, baby," Leslie said.

"I'm hungry," her daughter croaked out, after the remaining nurse fed her ice chips. "How much longer do I have to be here? I want to go home."

"We'll get you some broth and then ice cream," the nurse said, seeming to ignore the other question on purpose. "I'll be right back. Okay, sweetie?"

Nadya gave a beatific smile. "Okay, thank you."

Leslie's heart broke and her chin wobbled. She knew that smile. That was Nadya's manner of being sweet to get her way—

in this case, to get out. Only Nadya wasn't going anywhere. To Leslie, she looked pale and…fragile.

"I'll be back in a jiffy," the nurse said, giving Leslie a sympathetic glance before she slipped through the door.

Sure enough, as soon as they were alone, Nadya lifted her face, so trusting and hopeful, to Leslie. "When can I go home?"

Smoothing Nadya's hair out of her face, Leslie found herself using the same kindergarten-teacher tone as the nurses. "You might be here a few days, honey."

Her daughter's eyes widened. "But I have a quiz at school tomorrow. And practice." She threw off the sheets. "I can't be absent without a good reason, Mom. Do you think they will give me a doctor's note?"

Eyes glassy, Leslie sniffled. "I'll explain to your teachers. Don't worry about that now," she whispered, all the while wondering how she was going to tell Nadya about the blood transfusion and biopsy.

As if sensing Leslie's internal distress, Nadya's eyes filled, "Where's Daddy? I want my daddy."

"He must have had an emergency at work." She pressed her lips together and rushed to get her phone and place another call to Aaron. Again it went to voicemail. She bunched her fists to keep from throwing the device at the wall.

"Did you get him?" her daughter asked.

"No, honey. I'm going to text him." Leslie held the phone in her hand, looking at the keyboard, trying to gather her scattered thoughts to compose a civil message when all she really wanted to do was hurl insults and curse Aaron's selfishness. Even if he was working, the man could at least check on his family. If he had been thinking of them, he would call or text.

Leslie's father trounced back inside the room and dropped into the armchair. His lashes looked spiked, like he had been crying. The idea of her father, her support, shedding tears almost made Leslie collapse, but Nadya was keenly looking on.

"How's my princess?" her father asked, scooting close to Nadya's bed. The two started talking about some warrior movie and were soon laughing over something. Leslie envied her father's ability to behave as if everything was normal. When it wasn't. Being in a hospital at 10:00 a.m. on a school day was far from normal.

Her phone vibrated. Seeing it was Aaron, her heart surged with relief. She was glad that he was okay. But she was also furious.

She peppered him with questions, barely taking a breath. "Where are you? Didn't you see I was trying to call? Why haven't you checked your cell phone?"

"What's going on with Nadya?" Aaron asked, breathing hard, like he was running. She could hear the echo of his pounding footsteps. "I'm on my way."

After telling him her location, she bit out, "Don't think I didn't notice that you're ignoring my questions."

"Look. Right now, my daughter is sick and I've got to get over there to see her. You can curse me out later."

"Oh, I will. That's a promise. Just get here."

9

Celeste

Celeste stretched in her king-size bed. Despite the drama in her life, she'd slept well, which was surprising. She'd woken up before eight in the morning, much later than her usual five-thirty time.

After she'd moved from her couch to her bed the night before, she had worked on the paperwork for the bookstore and submitted it. That simple act had made her feel as if she'd accomplished a lot. They didn't have a location, so Celeste had used her home address since she had space in her garage to store supplies. Once they had a building, she would switch it out.

She dug in the sheets for her cell phone, texted the group chat with that update and checked her other messages. Wade had indicated he was on his way over. Just before her eyes closed last night, her husband had texted to say he would be by this morning to get his things.

She plugged her phone in to charge and placed her laptop on top of Tia Mowry's *The Quick Fix Kitchen*. If only it had a recipe to fix her marriage. She ran a hand down the cool sheets on Wade's side of the bed. It was odd not having him there beside her. If Toni hadn't been in the house, she doubted she would have slept.

Inhaling, she sniffed the air. The house smelled like cornbread. No, Toni was here, so it had to be grits with eggs and sausage. And she was pretty sure Toni was recording the whole thing for her viewers to watch her every move. Celeste would take her time going down there.

Her stomach growled, and she swung her legs off the bed and went into the bathroom to engage in her morning rituals. Examining herself in the mirror, taking in her swollen eyes and her pale skin, she frowned.

This wouldn't do. Wade would be here in a few minutes and she needed to look her best. Show him what he was missing.

If he wasn't already missing her.

She pursed her lips, holding back a chuckle. Celeste knew his texts about picking up his things were just an excuse to see her, make things right, while keeping his pride. And she would apologize, reprimand him for staying out all night—a first and last time—then give him the best lovemaking of his life. She stepped into the walk-in shower and washed up quickly.

Then she chose a long satin gown and matching robe before putting on lip gloss and fluffing her hair. Checking herself out in the floor-to-ceiling mirror, she did a little two-step before bounding down the stairs, her steps light, her confidence high.

Her heart raced in anticipation of Wade's return. Now to get Toni out of her house before her man got home. After she had eaten, of course.

Celeste arrived in the kitchen while Toni was still streaming live on Instagram. She had changed out of her pj's and was wearing what she'd had on the night before. She didn't know how her friend kept up with such a demanding social presence. If Toni were Celeste, she would be exhausted and irritated. And she could see having to pump herself up to be that upbeat every day. Not today though. Today, she would have nailed it.

She stood in the shadows while Toni yakked on, holding up a bowl. "So, I decided to make grits today and you know Toni's gotta talk about her books. Grits is one of the seven things Jocelyn Delk Adams mentions in her cookbook, *Everyday Grand: Soulful Recipes for Celebrating Life's Big and Small Moments*, that you should have in your pantry." She switched the bowl for the book.

"Grits have always been a part of Black culture, and when I'm all up in my feelings and need to do some thinking—" back to holding the bowl, her flow smooth, effortless "—I put on a pot and get to stirring up some of this medium-ground goodness." Toni placed a spoonful in her mouth. "Mmm. I tell you. Nothing like it in the world." She leaned over. "Now, I'm going to go finish grubbing on this, but I'll post some pics in the comments. Talk to you soon." She blew a kiss and ended the stream.

"You are phenomenal," Celeste said, sauntering into the kitchen.

"Thanks. Gotta do my thing." Toni snapped the photos. "I'll post these in a few. Did you see the one I posted about Kimberla Lawson Roby's nonfiction book?"

Celeste shook her head. "I don't think so. I've got to check it out."

Just then, Toni's cell phone beeped. Her brows furrowed before she started typing, chewing on her bottom lip.

Toni normally did that when she was troubled or nervous, which made Celeste give her a pointed look. "Everything good?"

"Yes, it was just Kent checking up on me." She waved a hand but didn't look Celeste's way. Avoidance. Her friend-*dar* went up. Something was definitely wrong.

"Oh? You didn't look too pleased…"

"It's all good," Toni insisted, sounding frazzled. She patted her headscarf. "Let's just change the subject for now, okay?"

Knowing her prickly friend wouldn't be pushed into talking about something before she was good and ready, Celeste moved the conversation to a safer area. "Guess who completed the paperwork for our bookstore?" She rubbed her hands, her mind on the delicious food before her. The steam and smells made her mouth water.

Toni had been in the process of adding salt to the eggs when she paused. "We're still going ahead with it?"

"Of course, why wouldn't we be?" she asked in a singsong voice. Goodness, she was so cheerful this morning she even annoyed herself. But the joy she felt at her husband's imminent entrance bubbled within, and now it was pouring out.

Toni's eyes narrowed. "I figured all this unexpected drama would be a deterrent. You spent most of the night crying and drooling in my arms, so…" She cleared her throat before resting on the balls of her heels, while Celeste got a kick out of seeing her verbose friend's struggle with words. Toni tried again. "With things the way they are with you and Wade, I thought…" She shrugged. "You know. I don't want to be insensitive and spell it out."

Celeste cracked up. "You can say the *D* word all you want, Toni. Because that doesn't apply to me, and it never will. Last night was a fluke and one never to be repeated."

Handing her the plate with a generous helping, Toni lifted a well-arched brow. "Someone is real chipper and confident, and that someone is you. Am I missing something?"

"Wade texted to say he is coming back this morning." She

dipped her fork to scoop up some of the grits and took a taste, waiting for her words to sink in.

Toni's mouth popped open. "Why didn't you say something earlier? I could have been long gone." She started stacking up the pots in the sink and wiping down the counters with a cloth. "Let me hurry up and get out of here. The last thing I want to do is be in your house during that reunion." Her voice filled with tenderness. "'Cause if I'm not mistaken, it's been a minute since the two of you...connected."

All Celeste could do was nod. Toni was being tactful about her almost nonexistent intimate relationship with Wade. The women were silent for a minute, each caught up in their thoughts—Celeste dwelling on the carjacking, and how it was still causing ripple effects in her marriage, her job and her executive functioning.

"It wasn't your fault, you know," Toni said, retrieving a couple of to-go containers from the pantry to pack up some food. Toni always cooked large portions. Sometimes, she would take food to the nearby shelter, if Celeste or Yasmeen or Leslie didn't take it all.

"Logically, I know that. And I know enough time has passed that I should be over it, but I'm not. Every time I see a red light, I freeze. Last week, I had a presentation, and I was tripping over my words for no good reason. My heart was pounding in my chest." She shook her head. "This isn't me." Looking Toni in the eyes, she said, "I'm never going to be the same."

"Oh, honey. I know it feels that way. One minute your marriage could be over—" Toni snapped her fingers "—and the next... Let's just say, it looks like Stella is getting her groove back," she joked.

"I know that's right." Celeste chuckled, gyrating her hips, relieved that the tense moment had passed. "I plan on laying it on him. But I don't think he'll be here—" The front door handle jiggled. Toni placed a hand on her hip and gave her a look. Celeste giggled and then shrugged.

Hearing Wade's shoes clicking on the tile, she braced herself and straightened up, trying to appear unaffected. Toni on the other hand was scuttling out of the kitchen. From behind her, Celeste could hear Wade's low rumble greeting her friend before Toni grabbed her coat and headed out the door, singing "Let's Get It On" by Marvin Gaye.

A not-so-subtle hint.

Slipping out of her chair, with her butt popping just so, Celeste executed what she hoped was a sexy turn to face her husband, her food forgotten. He was dressed in a dark blue suit and the scent of cedar and sage was strong, stirring her senses.

Her eyes dropped to his pants, admiring the snug fit. "Good morning." She tilted her chin and puckered her lips, waiting for him to draw close. Running her hands down her hips, Celeste enjoyed watching his darkened eyes following their trail.

Then he snapped his head up, as if to clear his mind. "I'm here to get a few of my things. I'll be back sometime this evening to pack."

Her mouth dropped at his gruff tone. "P-Pack?" She spoke the word, registering the disbelief in her voice and the large canvas bag in his hand. Her heart dropped to her stomach.

If "duh" had a look, it would be her husband's face. "That's what I said last night." He stalked past her to head up the stairs. Celeste trailed behind. He sped up, moving like he was being chased by an angry dog.

Holding on to the rail, she marched right along with him. "You're really serious about this whole leaving-me thing?"

"Listen, I don't want to get into this with you right now. I just want to get my things and get to work in time to meet with my client."

"Stop. You're overreacting." She grabbed his arm. He swung

around to face her, his eyes stone cold. She released him and narrowed her eyes. "Is there another woman? Is that it?" Her breath hitched while she waited for his answer. Even as her heart rebelled.

"You really going there?" He huffed. "I'm not dignifying that question with a response because you know me better than that. I'm a straight shooter. I told you exactly why I am leaving. You refuse to help yourself, and I can't stay and watch you crash and burn—like you did last night." Shaking his head at her as if she was a speck of dirt, barely discernible, insignificant in his life, he stormed into their bedroom, gaze straight ahead, ignoring the enlarged photos on the wall of their wedding day, their anniversary and their just-because moments.

She trudged behind him, her lips quivering. "Wade, don't do this. I love you as much as you love me. That means something."

He opened his chest of drawers and took out a handful of underwear with calm precision. Then he proceeded to pack, ensuring everything was neat and organized. Just like he liked his life. She was a loose thread to be snipped and tossed with heedless carelessness. She clutched her stomach. He was serious. He was really leaving her. Her stunned hurt flipped into sudden rage.

"I can't believe you," she yelled, flailing her hands. "I can't believe you're giving up on me when I'm down on my face, at my lowest."

His lips curled, his demeanor unshaken, and he continued filling the bag with his clothes. "Save the theatrics for your mama, or your girlfriends. We both know you're not on your face. Self-pity doesn't look good on you." He moved on to place a handful of toiletries into the bag.

She bunched her fists and pressed her feet deep into the plush carpet to keep from exploding. Her eyes misted. Forcing herself to keep her tone calm, she whispered, "I was a victim."

He whirled around to stare at her, his face contorted, breath choppy. "So was I." He jabbed his index finger to his chest. "You weren't the only one there. I was in the driver's seat. I was right there when that punk placed a gun to your beautiful face, and all I could do was sit there and beg them, beg them to let you go." He drew in a deep breath before releasing a whoosh of air. "Don't you think I wish it was me? I wish I had followed my instincts and driven off. Or jumped out the car and tackled them to the ground. I wish I had done something. But they had a gun so—so close to your face. I didn't want to take a chance."

His voice cracked and corresponding tears trekked down her cheeks. She had never heard Wade talk about that night like this. She moved to grab his hand, but to her surprise, he shrugged her off and put distance between them.

He lowered his head and avoided her eyes. In a low rumble, he poured out, "I should have. I should have protected you and I failed." The words seemed to tear out of his soul.

She wanted to interject that he was wrong. That she thought he was brave and she applauded his strength in holding back. That she had been just as afraid to lose him, fearing he would do something like kill or be killed. But she swallowed her words. After he rejected her attempt to make physical contact, she remained still. And listened. And waited.

Like a flash storm, his mood changed.

Wade jutted his jaw. "But you know what I did? I went to therapy." She placed a hand over her mouth. He hadn't told her that. For some reason, the knowledge that he had gone to seek professional help without her pierced her core.

"How did I not know this?" she asked, shaking her head.

"I went during my lunch hour." He didn't answer but asked a question instead. "You think I would tell you to do something without my doing it first? I didn't tell you because I was embarrassed. Men in my family are supposed to be tough. We don't do therapy. I didn't want you to see me as weak as I felt I was, but I knew I needed help." Then he continued, while she remained riveted at his outpouring. "The guilt was like a noose around my neck, keeping me up at night. I could hardly breathe. I had to hack that cesspool out of my mind or I would wallow in it for life. And Therese helped me."

He gave a small chuckle. "I hated every minute of the process but I hated it less than I hated myself. It wasn't easy, but eventually, all the doubt about my manhood and my ineffectiveness as a spouse oozed out of my being. Eventually, I knew I would be able to look you in the eyes and tell you I loved you and feel within me that I do." He took a tentative step toward her and spread his hands wide.

Celeste had no inhibition. She rushed into his embrace, engulfed by his love. "I love you, Wade." She felt his nod and then he mumbled something.

Lifting her head, she asked, "What did you say?"

Instead of answering, he crushed his lips to hers and kissed her long and hard. Long enough for her to realize he was telling her goodbye. Wade ended the kiss, licking his lips and closing his eyes, as if he were committing her taste to memory.

Her shoulders shook and she cupped his face, her panic rising. "Don't do this to us, baby."

Wade stepped back. "I love you too, but you have to love yourself. And until you do, things won't be what they need to be between us."

A part of her knew he was right, but she still had to fight. "Okay, but divorce isn't the answer. I'll get the therapy for you."

His eyes saddened. "All this talking I've been doing and you're still not listening." He touched her cheek. "You need therapy for you, sweetheart. Not for me."

"I tried it. It didn't work."

They stood at an impasse. Celeste's heart raged at her to tell

Wade what he wanted to hear, but she was afraid he would see it as a stunt to avoid divorce. And she wasn't about to beg a man to stay. There weren't shackles on either of their feet. She had pleaded and shared what was in her heart. That was as far as she would go.

Her cell phone pinged with a notification. She fretted with her robe, bunching the soft material in her fist. "I'm sorry but I've got to get that." The sound seemed to jar Wade into motion. He lifted his bag. Celeste darted over to her nightstand, unhappy at the intrusion, but she was worried about Leslie.

Just as he was steps from the bedroom door, Celeste shouted, "Wade, you can't leave. Not yet."

He paused, then turned to face her. "Give me one good reason why I shouldn't?"

"I got a text from Edwin. Nadya might need a donor."

10

Toni

JANUARY 3

There weren't a lot of women who had the view she had when she walked through her front door. And Toni wasn't talking about the pristine white floors, plush carpeting or the graceful high ceilings. It wasn't the arched doorway and accents of art that added a splash of color to her photo-ready abode. Rather, it was the smooth chocolate specimen of a man who was half-leaning, half-lounging against her kitchen countertop. He must have let himself in with the spare key she had added to his key ring when they became engaged. She hung up her coat and dropped her bag on the counter.

The scent of wood and sea teased her nostrils. Shuttering her lashes, Toni took a moment to drink in the sight of him. His bald head, his glistening beard and those full lips. He had on a tailored navy suit and a yellow shirt with a coordinated tie that enhanced his great physique. Her baby spent hours in the gym to be able to showcase such fineness.

Then he opened that beautiful mouth, his lips spreading wide. "Morning, beautiful." He held up a bag, his long-tapered fingers curling around the edges. "I brought you breakfast." Boy, she would love to feel those hands trailing her body.

Desire fanned through her insides like a wildfire. She squeezed her eyes shut for a second and exhaled. *Stop it. Think about something else.* Then she addressed him in what she hoped was a casual tone.

"Thank you. I thought you had a new client meeting this morning." She strutted over and pecked him on the cheek. She didn't trust herself to do anything else.

"I pushed it back. I had to come see you," Kent said, embracing her. "Make sure you weren't avoiding me." He chuckled.

She stiffened before forcing herself to relax in his arms. Then she gave his bulging biceps a playful slap. "Quit talking nonsense."

"I was worried you had gotten some unexpected news."

His voice held humor but Toni registered the serious undertone. Kent's mother had died from cervical cancer. She pulled away and rushed to reassure him. "I don't have cancer. Nothing is wrong." Immediate guilt swirled in her stomach. He had provided the best segue for her to tell him the truth and she had lied.

He studied her with narrowed eyes. "You would tell me if something was, wouldn't you?"

"Of course." Heart thumping, Toni dropped her eyes to his broad chest. She slid into his arms, her hands smoothing his back. He tensed under her touch. He was acting like he didn't believe her. So she did the only thing she knew would distract him.

Flicking her tongue against his ear, she moved to kiss his neck, exulting in the accompanying groan. He tightened his embrace before placing his lips to hers. Taking the lead, Toni ground her hips into him as their tongues engaged in a tango. Body ignited, she tugged off his jacket and undid his dress shirt with speed, ignoring his warning plea. His muscles jumped when she placed her lips on his chest, before using her tongue.

"Whoa." Holding her hands, Kent took a step back. "We can't go further. Remember our vow."

Chest heaving, she said, "I want you. I need you. Please."

With a moan, he reached over to grip her head before giving her a deep, searing kiss. Yes. Yes. He was caving. A couple seconds later, he tore his lips off hers.

"This is the toughest thing for me to do, but I'm backing away." He sounded out of breath and unsure. If she pressed, they would end up in bed. She knew it.

She lifted her chin and shucked off her clothes. Standing before him in her undies, she watched his eyes devour her trim, fit body. Licking her lips, she dared him, "Tell me you don't want me." Oh, how she needed him to want her. Because she was broken and this was all she had to offer. All she could give. Toni prayed she would be enough.

If she gave him the best loving of his life, maybe he would find it hard to let her go once she told him the truth. And she planned to. *After.*

"I do want you." He dropped to his knees, laying his head against her abdomen and wrapping his arms around her waist. "But I treasure what you have to offer too much to take you now."

Her breath caught. "You wouldn't be the first." She spoke her truth, soft and timid, challenging him.

"I know. But I most definitely will be your last. And you, mine." He stood and held up her hand to touch her engagement ring. It sparkled clear and bright, a direct contrast to her lies and omissions. "When you're Mrs. Hughes, I will give you a night to remember." He waggled his brows. "You'll probably leave our honeymoon with a little bundle inside."

His certainty, his hopefulness made her knees almost buckle. She couldn't do this. She couldn't keep lying to the man she loved. "Kent, I have to tell you something—" Her phone buzzed. Then buzzed again.

"You'd better get that."

"It can wait. I—I really need to talk to you."

But then there was another buzz.

Waving a hand, he said, "Go ahead and see. It might be something urgent."

Thinking of Leslie, she said, "You're right." She pulled her phone out of her purse and then gasped. "I have to get to the hospital. Leslie texted SOS in our group chat." She dropped her phone into her purse and jammed a foot into a pair of slacks, hopping around on one leg in her haste to get dressed.

"Hospital?" Kent was already rebuttoning his shirt.

"Yes. Nadya passed out yesterday and the doctors were running all kinds of tests. Leslie said she would text if she needed us…" Then, when she reached for her bag, it tilted over, tossing the contents onto the floor.

He helped her gather her stuff and then grabbed his keys. "I'll take you. You're too distressed to drive."

Toni didn't argue. Voice shaky, she filled Kent in on everything she knew while they made their way to the hospital. Leslie then texted the words **severe aplastic anemia** in their group chat when Yasmeen asked her to elaborate. When Toni googled it, her heart raced with fear for her goddaughter. Nadya could die. As in actually lose her life. She was too young. Far too young.

"Was this what you were about to tell me?" Kent asked just as he found parking near the emergency entrance.

"Y-yes." She avoided his gaze and opened the door. Even as they rushed inside the building, she berated herself for once again lying to her fiancé. Though this time, she justified her actions due to Nadya's dire situation. Skittering down the hall toward Nadya's room, Toni told herself she would set everything right later.

Kent followed close behind her, his hand on her back a grounding source. "I can't imagine how Leslie is feeling. A sick child must be a parent's worst nightmare. All we can do is pray for a healthy child when we become parents."

She would never know, and if he was with her, neither would he. That thought made her lose her footing, twisting her ankle.

Gripping her waist to keep her from falling, he asked, "Are you okay?"

"I'm fine." She bit down on her lower lip and dabbed at her eyes before entering the room, ignoring the light throbbing. Celeste and Wade entered seconds later. Aaron, Edwin and Leslie were huddled together. Nadya wasn't in the room and Yasmeen hadn't arrived yet. She had put in the group chat that she would be there after she had taken her parents home.

Toni asked, "Where's Nadya?"

"Doing more tests. I can't keep up." Leslie spoke with bitterness. Her eyes were reddened and her face was etched with worry. "I'm glad you are here." Her voice broke. "I'm going to need all of you," she said, then proceeded to let them know she'd like them to get tested in case Nadya needed a stem cell transplant.

"I'm more than willing to," Toni said.

"You can count us in as well," Celeste said, sidling close to Wade.

Toni noticed that Wade shrank away from Celeste ever so slightly and wondered about that before telling herself that she was imagining things. Wade and Celeste had reunited that very morning.

"Awesome. Since I didn't have any more children, not for lack of trying, you guys are my best hope—along with Daddy and Aaron, of course," Leslie said.

Her offhand comment about her miscarriages hit Toni deep. Leslie had indeed wanted more children, and watching her suffer through those losses had been torture. After Toni's botched abortion, she had wondered about whether or not she would be able to have children, but she had shrugged it off, telling herself that she would eat right and work out, which would fix things.

She stole a glance at Aaron's devastated face and then at Kent's. He appeared empathetic. That wouldn't be the look he gave her if she told him her truth.

And she wasn't just talking about her recent diagnosis. Telling him about the infertility would lead to questions, and those answers would possibly bring even more questions, and they would venture to a place she didn't visit much: the real her. And he might not like who he saw.

She might lose him just as she had her parents.

You know what? She wasn't telling him anything. It was better that way.

"What happens if none of us are a match?" Aaron voiced the question Toni was afraid to ask.

Leslie gave him a fierce look before snapping at him. "There will be a match, so keep that negativity to yourself. If you're going to spout off at the mouth, you might as well go back where you came from because you look a hot mess."

Aaron's shirt hung out of his dress pants and his eyes had dark circles like he had been up all night. The fact that Leslie hadn't held her tongue around her friends and father was a true indication of her stress level. Because Leslie would never bad-talk Aaron with her father present.

The couple engaged in a staredown, chests heaving, making the tension in the room tighten. Both looked exhausted. Toni would have expected Edwin to scold them, but he was uncharacteristically quiet.

Ever the peacemaker, Celeste stepped between them. "Guys. Right now, it's all about Nadya. We all love her and that's what's going to get her through."

"Easy now," Toni interjected, glancing back and forth between them. "Our emotions are high but Celeste is right. I don't know what's up with you two, but your daughter takes priority over whatever this is."

"You're right," Leslie said, blowing out a breath. "I'm just... frustrated and scared and worried." Aaron opened his arms, and after a brief hesitation, she flung herself into him, releasing her tears.

Just then, a nurse entered and directed them to the waiting area down the hall, stating there were too many of them in Nadya's room. Everyone except for Leslie and Aaron departed. As soon as they entered the room, Celeste dropped into a chair and pulled out a copy of *Help Is on the Way*. Wade turned on the television, putting on the news. He sat a few seats away from Celeste, like he didn't want to be close to her. Toni frowned. She'd taken a step to approach Celeste to find out what was going on when her cell pinged with a message.

She scooted to the farthest corner of the room. Her heckler was back with an update to his username.

@BLSTFRDAPST2: THERE'S NO 4GETTING WHAT YOU DID.

Her heart thumped.

Who is this? Breathless, she waited for a response, but all she got was a laughing emoji. This joker was messing with her. Well, she was about to give him a piece of her mind. Call his bluff.

"What's going on?" a voice said in her ear.

She jumped, almost dropping her cell phone. "Eek!" Then she gave Kent a light shove. "You scared me half to death just now." She slipped the phone into the pocket of her slacks. Toni had been so focused that she hadn't seen him come her way.

"You looked so intense, I had to come investigate and make sure my babe's good." Kent gave her a searching glance.

"I'm good. I was just…" No way was she going to tell him about the person harassing her or what they might know about her past. Or her inability to have a child. Her don't-tell list was growing as long as Pinocchio's nose. "I was looking at wedding dresses."

"Oh, you'll know when you find the right one. I did." Kent tapped her nose. "I can't wait to see you gliding down the aisle."

"We won't have much of an aisle at the bookstore. And, gliding?" she snickered, trying to ignore the somersaults going on in her heart. "What am I? A ghost?"

"You'll be a vision." He ran his fingers through her hair. "Our wedding day is going to be something."

If they even had a wedding. His eyes held promise, love and trust and made her hope for things she didn't deserve. It was all too much. Toni rubbed her eyes to break eye contact and deflected. "When do you think they will need to check to see if any of us are a match?"

"I'm guessing right away." He lifted her chin to peer into her eyes. "Are you sure that's all that's bothering you? Not that this isn't monumental, but I can't shake the feeling there's something more."

She wished she knew what it was in her body language that triggered his concern, so she could stop. She searched her mind for the right words that would dispel his doubts.

At that moment, Yasmeen rushed into the room, sparing Toni from having to answer.

"Has there been any word on Nadya? I had to drop my parents back at the apartment before coming. Everything went well with my dad." She tugged off that hideous jacket and dropped it on a nearby chair.

Kent held up his phone to indicate he had a call and left the room.

"Yeah, we're waiting to get tested to see if we're potential donors," Toni said, going over to give Yasmeen a hug.

Celeste came to huddle with them. "We haven't seen Nadya yet, but Leslie is a wreck."

Yasmeen nodded. "Understandable. Is her dad testing first?"

"Funny enough. He's been really quiet," Toni said.

"He's probably in shock," Celeste defended, jutting her chin toward Edwin, who was sitting away from everyone with his arms folded. He looked troubled. Like he was holding everything inside.

Feeling two sets of eyes on her, Toni raised her brows. "What?"

Yasmeen chimed in, "You need to go talk to him. You're the people expert."

"Maybe he wants to be alone. To process."

"Have you ever known Leslie's dad to stand back when something is going on with his baby girl?" Celeste asked in a whisper.

Toni spared him another glance. Now he had his hands over his face. She turned to her friends. "I think you're reading way too much into this and the last thing I want is to get snapped at for not minding my business." But when the nurse came in to ask for the first volunteer to complete the pre-donation physical and Edwin remained seated, Toni reconsidered. Yasmeen was the first to go, saying she had to head to work once she was finished.

Shoving her hands in her jacket pockets, Toni sauntered over to stand in front of Edwin. "Do you need me to get you a cup of coffee or breakfast from the café?"

He looked at her with tortured eyes. "No. Coffee won't help my situation, I'm afraid." Then he mumbled, "Nothing will."

Slipping into the seat next him, she reached over to take Edwin's hand. "I know you're worried about Nadya and Leslie, and this must be hitting you on another level. But I believe in positive thinking. You could be the match Nadya needs. All it takes is faith."

Sadly, instead of perking up, Edwin slumped into his seat.

"Faith don't trump facts." The dejection and certainty in his tone made her stomach turn.

"Edwin, what's going on?"

His jaw clenched. Tears welled in his eyes. He squeezed her hand. "I'm about to hurt my baby girl in a way I hoped I never would."

Her heart raced. "What do you mean?"

Instead of answering, he wiped his face and shook his head before mumbling, "The truth always comes out. Years could go by. Years. And it rears its ugly head, hurting everyone in its path." His shoulders shook and he bent forward, clutching his chest. "I should have told her when I had the chance."

His words were a warning, which scared her. An eerie foreboding of regret over withholding the truth from Kent. But she had to stay focused on Edwin's obvious pain. "Edwin, what are you talking about?"

He suddenly jumped to his feet. Then he pierced her with a sad expression. "I have to talk to Leslie first. Promise when this all comes out, you'll be there for her. She's going to need you."

Edwin's cryptic words made fear run through her body. It sounded like his truth was going to be a wrecking ball to Leslie's existence. Toni hoped he was exaggerating. Seeing Edwin waiting for a response, she nodded. "I—I will."

He dragged his hand over his beard. "I've got to talk to my daughter." Then he stormed out the door with the gait of a determined man.

Thinking about her friend made Toni scurry out of the room and call after him. When Edwin paused outside Nadya's door, she rushed forward. "Are you sure now is the time to unload? Whatever it is, it can wait." She placed a hand on his arm. "Wait until all this is settled with Nadya. Leslie has a lot on her plate right now."

"If only I could. But it has to be now. Before she finds out."

"Before who finds out what?"

Toni gasped and swung around to see Leslie standing behind them, holding a cup of ice. Panicked, Toni spouted out the first thing that came to mind. "We're talking about the bookstore. Celeste submitted the paperwork this morning and I was saying that with all of this going on, we might have to wait with the store."

Though she knew it wouldn't grow, Toni touched her nose as a reflexive action.

"Oh…" Leslie tugged on her blond strands. "I forgot about that. Celeste placed a portion of our funds in a short-term investment opportunity, so I don't think we should stop. Our health insurance is only going to pay so much and we'll need to pay the hospital bills. Unless you guys feel I need to step back."

"Nope. We're all in it together. To be blunt, you put your money in and we can't give it back. We're going to need every dime to keep the business afloat."

She tapped her feet before shrugging. "I don't know… I guess you're right. We'll sort it out somehow." She marched up to her dad and rested her head on his chest. "I was about to give Nadya some ice and then come look for you. You didn't have to leave."

He gave her an awkward pat. "I have to talk to you."

Gesturing to the cup, Toni realized there was no stopping Edwin from pouring out the truth today. She decided to give them some privacy. A part of her envied Edwin's strength. He was ready to face the consequences of whatever lie he had told. Toni knew she couldn't say the same for herself. If she could, she intended to take all the lies of her past to her grave.

11

Leslie

JANUARY 3

Edwin led her into an empty room. Closing the door behind her, Leslie asked, "What do you want to talk about? And bear in mind that I am balancing on a tightrope right now. It won't take much to tip me over."

Her father rested his hands on her shoulders to steady her, or himself, she wasn't sure. "Believe me when I tell you the last thing I want to do is add to your plate, but I…" He removed his hands and closed his eyes. Tottering backward, Edwin leaned against the bed for support. "I'm sorry, baby girl. I'm sorry."

Leslie had never seen her father so distraught. She patted his back, her heart pounding, its rhythm a bass drum in her chest. "Dad, why are you apologizing? You're really scaring me right now, so I need you to tell me what's going on."

"Your mother made me promise," he said, now caught up in his grief. "But—after a while, I didn't want to tell you. I didn't and now…"

"Daddy!" she yelled, trembling as fear conquered her resolve. "Spill it out. Please."

Raising his head, his nose runny, face wet, he grabbed on to her hands and swallowed. "I'm not your father." He cleared his throat. "Well, I'm your father in every way that counts, but I'm not your biological father."

Her world as she knew it stilled.

Then a slow quiet hum built from deep within. She blinked.

"Wh-what?" Snatching her hands out of his grip, she thumped him on the back, wondering if he needed to get a CAT scan. "Daddy, what kind of sick joke is this? Are you trying to distract me from Nadya with this nonsense?"

He shook his head. "N-no. I should have told you sooner, but I was scared and…" He shrugged his large shoulders. "No, I'm not being honest. I wouldn't have ever told you, but Nadya's sick and you need…family. And, I am but I'm not."

His words settled into her brain. Her stomach soured. Her left eye twitched. "What do you mean you're not my father?" she bellowed.

"I… You were adopted." He made a move toward her.

Lifting a hand, she stepped back. "Adopted?" She spoke the word like it was profanity. "How can I be adopted?" Leslie was yelling now but she didn't care. "Both your and Mom's names are on my birth certificate."

"We got an amended birth certificate after the adoption."

"You're the only father I've ever known."

"Because I am your father in every way that counts."

"Yeah, well, tell that to Nadya." She spat the words and watched his face twist in shock and hurt and pain. All the things she was currently feeling, right along with confusion. And disbelief. This couldn't be happening. This couldn't be real. But her indomitable father appeared shattered and broken, so it must be true.

Rage whirled within. A tornado brewing, gathering up all the uncertainty of the past hours with her daughter, along with this new uncertainty of her origins.

The door opened and Toni and Celeste came inside. She must have been louder than she thought. Her friends flanked her sides, each taking a hand.

"Is everything okay?" Celeste asked.

"We heard yelling and came to see…"

"No, everything is not alright. This man…" She drew up her shoulders. "This man claims he is not my father and that I'm adopted, and I don't quite know what to do with myself right now."

Two gasps.

Then silence.

Stunned silence. Followed by the heavy breathing of all the women in the room, their eyes trained on the man who was bent forward, clutching his stomach, his body racked with silent tears.

"He is very much your father," Celeste finally spoke, voice firm.

"Give her a minute to process," Toni muttered. "This is some heavy stuff."

Celeste waved a hand. "Nadya is sick and is going to need her mother, father and grandfather. We can sort this out later."

Leslie clung to Celeste's words like they were a lifeline. All she could do was nod and give Toni's arm a squeeze to keep her friend from continuing that debate. She couldn't look her "father" in the face at the moment. Not after the way he had betrayed her. She knew it was physically impossible for her heart to be sliced because of words, but it hurt like it had been shredded with a boning knife.

"I'll still see if I'm a donor," Edwin said, voice hoarse. Then he added, "She might have other family too…"

She felt his gaze upon her but refused to make eye contact, gripping her chest. The pain was too new, too raw. She massaged her neck, feeling stifled, her emotions topsy-turvy. Seesawing within, Leslie knew she couldn't deal with this bombshell plus handle her daughter.

"I've got to go see Nadya. I don't know if Aaron is back yet. He was sorting things out with the insurance company." She commanded her feet to move, but her father stopped her.

"This doesn't change anything."

If only he hadn't spoken. If only he had let her leave while she had a tenuous grip on her emotions. "It doesn't change anything?" she spat out. "Are you serious right now? You were a major part of Nadya's hope of getting a donor." Her eyes raked his body from head to toe. "As far as I'm concerned, it changes everything. Why don't you just go home? You're no use to me right now." She marched toward the door using all her reserved energy, determined to erase her father's crumbling face from her mind.

"You don't mean that," Celeste said, following her closely.

"Leave her be," Toni cut in. "Give her a minute to breathe."

"I'm going to be here for my granddaughter." Edwin's low voice from behind sounded like he wasn't going to argue.

"She's not your granddaughter," Leslie raged, spinning back toward him. Edwin drew in a harsh breath. Both Toni and Celeste's eyes went wide at her cruel words. Leslie wilted. "I don't have the energy to fight with you," she whispered and left.

When the door slammed shut, she collapsed to the floor and folded her knees under her. Her daddy wasn't her daddy. Her daughter could be on her deathbed. Her heart raged, torn and battered from the sudden onslaught. And all she could do was lie here and sob. She coughed, struggling to capture her breath.

A pair of hands cupped her armpits and forced her to stand.

Through her tears, she made out Aaron's face and touched his day-old beard.

"They just took Nadya again for more tests. Shouldn't be long," he said, misinterpreting the reason she was having a meltdown. Holding her head in his hands, he kissed her lips. "She will be alright."

"You don't know that," Leslie managed to say through gritted teeth. She watched her husband's mouth pop open at the venom in her tone. "I don't want or need a dose of your optimism. So unless you've earned a degree as a medical doctor overnight, keep your thoughts to yourself." As the words spewed from her, she acknowledged that she was in attack mode. Typical mama-bear behavior. But Aaron hadn't deserved her tongue-lashing, not when he was trying to be supportive and was just as worried about their daughter as she was.

His eyes went glacial but his words were kind. "I know you like to be in control and Nadya's illness is messing with your equilibrium, but you didn't need to come at me like that. We're on the same side and we might have a long road ahead of us, so now is not the time for us to be at odds."

"You're right. I'm sorry." She massaged her temples. Toni, Celeste and her father stepped out of the empty room. Her father appeared shaken but…together. The opposite of how she was feeling. Just seeing him sparked an angry flame and she bit her tongue to keep from hurling insults.

He looked like he wanted to say something, and deep down, she wanted him to take back his words, tell her she had had an out-of-body experience and he hadn't spun her life further off-axis. But his haggard expression declared the truth. There was no going back. The truth, once spoken, was like a prickly vine, winding its way around her very soul.

For a beat, no one said anything.

Keen, her husband must have picked up the vibe between them because he asked, "Is everything okay?"

Flailing her hands, she said, "I don't want to talk about it," before heading into Nadya's room. Plopping onto a chair, she felt a huge headache climbing from her temples to her forehead.

Moments later, Aaron trailed in, shutting the door behind him. With his lanky build, brown hair, light beard, Aaron would be forgettable if it weren't for his large baby blue eyes. He took the seat next to her and held her hand. "Your friends just brought me up to speed before going to get their physicals done. I don't get why I'm always the last to know, but I'm sorry. I'm really sorry your father dumped this on you now."

Leslie removed her hand out of his and faced him. "Are you making this about you?"

"No. No. I'm just saying I wish you had told your husband before you told your friends."

"My friends were here before you, in every sense of the word."

His brows rose. "Wow. Wow. That was uncalled-for. We're one in ways you and your friends will never be."

She glared. "Are you sure about that?"

His eyes narrowed while he considered her words before he smirked. Jabbing a thumb at his chest, he shot back, "At least I've never lied to you the way your father did."

"Don't you go there."

They were saved from a heated argument when the door opened and Nadya returned. Her eyes lit up. "Daddy, did you get my ice cream bar?"

Aaron wiped his hands on his pants and jumped to his feet. "Y-yes. The nurses promised they'd let you have it after you've had your soup."

Nadya's face twisted. "Soup? I don't like soup."

Leslie got to her feet, pushing herself to act the way she normally would. Scooping up all her emotions, she swept them to the back of her mind and ambled to her daughter's bed. "The vegetables are good for you."

Edwin chose that moment to enter and he was carrying a pink rabbit. Nadya squealed when she saw him and Edwin offered to tell her a story. Like he had done for Leslie as a child.

"I'm not a child, Grandpa."

Grandpa. Leslie wanted to yell that he wasn't. Not really. Not by blood. But her daughter had a look of awe on her face. Kind of like what Leslie would bestow upon Edwin before today.

Leslie was content to stand back and let him do his thing, but then Edwin gestured for her to join in on the fun. A bitter bile of resentment formed in her throat. He shouldn't be in here like all was hunky-dory between them, fully expecting her to play along. It was too much. She closed her eyes. She couldn't do this. Pretend. Play nice. Not when she wanted to lunge at him and snatch that stuffed rabbit out of his hand.

"Take a moment. Get some air. I'll text you if anything changes."

Opening her eyes, she welcomed the understanding reflected in Aaron's eyes. She gave a jerky nod and departed to the sound of laughter in the room. She couldn't help but wonder if she would ever have a reason to laugh again.

She walked the hallway, the sound of her shoes on the tiles as hollow as she felt. Zombie-like. Instead of going outside, she slipped inside the nearest bathroom to wash her face. To give herself a pep talk. Get her mind right and tap into the inner strength she knew she possessed.

Staring into the mirror, she reminded herself that she was Leslie Bronwyn—Edwin's daugh— No. No. Time for a paradigm shift. Take two. She was her own woman. And she would get through this like she had everything else in her life. Simply because she had no choice.

And she still had her friends.

Her father's words came back to her. *She might have other family too…* Leslie gripped the sides of the basin. Creasing her brow, she leaned forward into the mirror. Were there others who shared her face? Her genetics. Hope sprung like a tiny sprig after a huge outpouring of rain. She was adopted. What if she had family? Flesh-and-blood relatives who might be a potential match for Nadya? Goose bumps prickled her skin.

She covered her mouth and allowed that possibility to sink in. Yes. Yes.

She could redirect all these feelings into finding her parents. This is what she was good at. Turning her pain into purpose. Grabbing paper towels to dry her hands, she tossed the refuse in the wastebasket, and brimming with energy, she rushed into the waiting room to tell Celeste and Toni her plan.

12

Yasmeen

JANUARY 3

Yasmeen stomped out of the court that evening, battling feelings of helplessness and rage. Darryl had been arrested for a crime he didn't commit. Once she learned about Nadya, Yasmeen had called her coworker to cover her shift. She dreaded seeing what her paycheck would look like, but she couldn't dwell on that now. After her donor check, Yasmeen had then headed straight to sit in on Pookie's arraignment so she could hear his charges and how much it would cost to bail him out. She dabbed at her eyes, frustrated her boyfriend had become a walking cliché.

There was no way he was involved in that armed robbery. But his gun had been. It had been stolen by a "friend." A friend who was a known gang member. A friend who Pookie had allowed to spend the night in his house. A friend who refused to clear his name. That's what Pookie had told her, and she believed him. Pookie was many things, but a criminal wasn't one of them.

She stood with a hand wrapped around the door handle of Leslie's SUV and sniffled. She didn't want to leave him there. But unless she could come up with twenty thousand dollars, he was stuck behind bars until his trial, with an overworked defense attorney who was already pushing him to take a plea bargain. Serve time. "Take the five years" had been the attorney's advice. Pookie had pled not guilty. As he should.

Yasmeen didn't have that kind of cash and there was no way her friends would help with bail money. Not for someone they viewed as a lowlife bringing her down. She could do way better than him, was their advice.

She could.

But she didn't want to.

For some reason, Pookie had gotten under her skin and crept his way up to her heart. Pity it had taken all this for her to acknowledge she might have some genuine feelings for the man. Feelings that transcended their weekly hookups. Their... arrangement. All because Yasmeen saw his potential. His ambition.

Jumping into the vehicle, she scoffed. *Potential* didn't pay debts. For that she needed cold, hard cash. She saw she had a voicemail. It was the casino calling to say they had hired someone else but would keep her in mind. Blah. Blah. Blah. This was the story of her life and one she wouldn't ever want to read about.

A sob escaped her and she covered her mouth. She had to get back to the hospital.

By the time she arrived, Yasmeen's tears had tapered down to a mere sniffle. She whispered silent prayers for Pookie's protection behind bars. Though she dreaded telling her friends and hearing their disdain, Yasmeen knew she wouldn't be able to keep this to herself. Not if she wanted to maintain her sanity; her anxiety was at peak levels. First Nadya and now Darryl.

Hunger clawed her insides like crabs in a basket. Speaking of crabs, there was a great seafood place nearby. She imagined everyone at the hospital would be hungry. But then she checked her bank account. She had just enough left over from the money Celeste gave her to top up Leslie's tank and get everyone some food. If she went to the nearby Chinese restaurant instead, she could order a variety of choices. It was the most economical choice, and the average wait time was never more than twenty minutes.

Decision made, Yasmeen called and rattled off a few things from the menu. She held in her gasp when she heard the amount due and then made her way to the gas station. Burrowing into her coat, Yasmeen rushed inside and bought a couple bottles of iced tea. Then she stopped at the dollar store near the Chinese place to get napkins, utensils, plates and forks.

Just as she grabbed the food, Toni texted. Girl, where are you?

On my way. Picked up food for everyone.

That's what's up.

Be there in 10.

When she pulled into the hospital, Toni and Celeste were waiting for her by the entrance. Luckily, she found a parking spot close by. See, that's why she loved her girls. They had come out to help her carry everything. She snorted. Or they were just plain hungry. Either way, she was grateful for their assistance.

Opening the passenger door, Toni snatched a couple bags. "Girl, some things popped off while you were gone and we want to bring you up to speed before we go back inside."

Getting out of the vehicle, Yasmeen grabbed the jugs of tea. "What's going on?"

"Edwin just told Leslie he's not sure he'll be a match for Nadya," Celeste said, giving Toni the side-eye. She picked up the remaining bags and closed the door.

"Why not?" Yasmeen activated the alarm before circling to join her friends. Her ears were already burning from the cold. She wouldn't be surprised if it snowed that night.

Toni shook her head. "We had our own live version of *The Maury Show*," she said.

"I don't get it." Yasmeen pressed the button to open the automatic doors.

Celeste exhaled. "You know Toni has to be dramatic. Edwin confessed to Leslie she was adopted."

Yasmeen froze. "Adopted?"

"Yes," Toni whispered. "Leslie is heartbroken."

"She's not the only one," Celeste mumbled. Something in her tone made Yasmeen curious about Celeste's situation.

When they entered the waiting area, everyone but Leslie was present, since she was with Nadya. In a matter of hours, Leslie's life had changed. Her friend liked balance and order, and all this was pure chaos and...a hot, sorry mess.

A somber procession queued up to eat their first and possibly only meal of the day. Yasmeen made herself a plate, although her stomach was now unsettled, especially with Edwin behind her in the line. She avoided looking at him because, really, what could she say? He had lied to his only child.

This entire day needed a do-over.

Picking at her food, she sat with Toni and Celeste, who were in the farthest corner from the entrance. "What's going on with you?" she asked Celeste.

"Wade is leaving me for real," Celeste said.

"Say what?" Yasmeen gasped, touching her chest. Celeste and Wade had been together since college. She couldn't imagine the carjacking would break them apart like this. "When did all this happen?"

Toni took in a huge breath. "But I thought you said you guys were working things out," she said instead of answering Yasmeen's question.

"He's giving up." Celeste's voice cracked. "I can't believe after all these years he would walk out on me like that." She bit into her eggroll and started to chew, but it looked like it was because she needed something to do rather than because she was enjoying it. "Like Leslie, I'm heartbroken but I'll deal with my stuff later. Right now, it's all about Nadya."

Anger boiled like hot, burning lava. Yasmeen spewed out in a furious whisper, "I'm sorry to hear about your marriage, but you can't put yourself on the same level as Leslie right now. She's facing something of epic proportions she didn't choose."

"Ladies," Toni warned, "let's not lose focus."

"What's that's supposed to mean?" Celeste asked, her eyes blinking rapidly.

"For one thing, your situation can be fixed." She emphasized the word *fixed* so it sounded like *fixedt*. "Leslie can't do nothing 'bout the fact that the man she looked up to for most of her life betrayed her. And, I'm pretty sure that if she could trade places with Nadya she would. All you have to do is get help and you refused. He's been asking you to do this for months. You had you a good man and you couldn't meet him halfway," she huffed. "So don't get me started." Resting her plate on the empty seat next to her, Yasmeen fanned her face.

"Easy now," Toni said, her voice firm. "Tensions are high, so I suggest you two stuff your mouths with food to keep yourselves from saying something you both might regret."

Yasmeen rolled her eyes. "I'm saying my piece. I have no regrets."

"Listen, you don't have a right to dip your mouth in my

marriage. Not when you've only dated bottom-of-the-barrel men," Celeste snapped.

"Pookie, uh, Darryl, isn't a lowlife. He just picked the wrong friends."

"You're defending a grown man who calls himself *Pookie?*" Celeste's voice dripped with disdain. "Point made."

That blow pierced. Especially since he was incarcerated. "At least he hoses me down on the regular."

As soon as she said that, Yasmeen wished she could take the words right back into her mouth. Celeste inhaled a shaky breath, her eyes filling.

Springing to her feet, Toni huffed, "You two need to quit it. Right now you're behaving like a couple of entitled school girls. Don't let Leslie come in and witness you all at each other's throats. Her plate is toppling over. She needs us to hold her up, not the other way around." She stormed over to turn up the television, mumbling, "I need to listen to something else to calm my nerves."

Chastised, Yasmeen pressed her lips together.

After a beat, Celeste went back to eating, but her face was flushed red. Yasmeen knew their argument wasn't over. She tapped one foot with fury. Too bad. She thought about Darryl spending a night locked up and wished he had an ounce of Wade's accomplishments and ambition. He wouldn't be where he was now. And, oh, how she would treasure him. But Celeste was too bougie and prideful to bend.

Still, yet, she should have heeded Toni's advice and left well enough alone. Now both women were mad at her. She pulled her phone and earbuds out of her purse and accessed her Libby app, intending to finish rereading *The Hookup Plan* and not engage with anybody else.

Clicking through the channels, Toni settled on the news. Yasmeen listened with half an ear. The news reporters were talking about the prior night's lottery numbers, which had a single winner. A winner who hadn't stepped forward. That got Yasmeen's attention.

She addressed Toni, "Turn that up, please."

"We may not have a winner, but we have identified the store that sold the prized ticket." The camera zoomed in on the gas station. Yasmeen frowned. That looked just like the one she went to yesterday, where she purchased her own lottery ticket. The numbers flashed across the screen. What if…?

Her heart raced. Even as she dug into her purse for the ticket, doubt swarmed. According to the newscast, her odds of winning were one in two hundred and seventy-three thousand. She scoffed. There was no way she had that kind of luck.

Her father hadn't raised her to believe in luck, anyway. Anything good came from God. That was his mantra. The numbers flashed again.

Still…wouldn't it be something? Squaring her shoulders, she kept searching until she located the ticket. Her hands shook and she berated herself for daring to hope, but she just had to see. Wiping her sweaty palms, Yasmeen held the ticket high and waited for the numbers to appear once more.

By this time, the reporters had moved on to another story involving a dog or something. Yasmeen kept her eyes peeled on the screen.

18…24…57…38…33…6

She wiped her eyes, her head darting between the paper in her hands and the screen. Her mouth popped open, but no sound came out. She stood and walked closer to the television.

"Your head isn't made of glass," Toni shot out.

Yasmeen nodded and dropped to the floor, folding her legs in an X.

"Girl, have you lost your mind? Have you heard of MRSA? Get up off that dirty floor."

Her heart pounded and her chest heaved. She would wait again. She gripped the paper between her fingers.

18...24...57...38...33...6

She looked at her ticket and spoke each number aloud. "*18...24...57...38...33...6.*" By the time she got to the *six*, she was shouting. Then she flopped back on the floor, spreading her arms up and down, like when she was a kid making angels in the snow.

"What? What is it?" she heard Celeste ask.

Edwin came over and hauled her to a stand. He was looking at her with curiosity and concern.

Excitement began to build. She jumped and hopped around like she was in grade school.

"Why are you acting like you stepped in an ant's nest?" Toni bellowed.

Finally. Finally. Her voice box released the words, making it real. "I won. I won. I won."

"Won what?"

"I won the lottery!" she squealed, waving the ticket. "The solitary winner, it's me. It's me. I just won 10.5 million dollars." Crumbling to the floor again, she dissolved into tears.

13

Celeste

JANUARY 18

The past fifteen days had been some of the toughest of her life, but Celeste was still standing, even if she had to use the wall to prop herself up. She leaned against the doorjamb of her bedroom and stared out the window at the white flakes falling gently, quietly. Everything looked so peaceful on the outside. She inhaled, praying for an internal calm to counteract the havoc in her personal life.

She wore a figure-hugging sweaterdress and knee-length boots the color of camel in preparation for her meeting with the girls later on that day. But her garb was also a means to boost her confidence. Contrary to what she'd expected, Wade hadn't returned home to her. Instead, after all those days of silence, he had called the night before to say he had signed a lease to an apartment and would be coming for the rest of his things.

He stood a few feet away from her, packing with precision, refusing to look at her tear-streaked face or acknowledge the sounds of her sniffles. The click of the lock, the zip of a suitcase, the screech of the packing tape made everything...final.

Dressed in a pair of jeans, a sweater and a bomber jacket, he traipsed back and forth with the boxes to pack the small U-Haul. And still he didn't look her way. Not when she asked if he wanted any of their photo albums, and he'd said no. Not even when he walked through the door of this house they had bought together ten years ago, where they'd once smiled and posed for the camera, holding the keys to their forever home.

Her heart felt like it had been raked with a gardening tool. As she watched him, the moment was surreal. He really was leaving her.

From the look of it, he had made up his mind.

When he was done, Wade stood by the entrance, the key to the house in hand. Unlike Celeste, who had bags under her eyes and who had lost weight, her soon-to-be ex-husband looked good. So good it made her heart hurt. "Where should I put this?" he asked, dangling the key.

She shrugged and wiped her face with the back of her hand. "Keep it. In case of emergency." Accepting it would mean she accepted the fate of their marriage. "Where are you going?" she asked.

"If that's what you want." He slipped the key into his pocket. Hope lingered. "I moved in the apartments five minutes away from my office. You know the ones they were renovating..."

"You mean the very building that Tula lives in?" She curled her fists, her nails digging deep enough into her palms to hurt. *Don't snap off. Keep cool.*

Now he shrugged. "That doesn't matter to me."

She believed him. Celeste sighed. "Are you eating?" Anything to prolong having him there. She would stretch this moment like string cheese.

He rocked back on his heels. "Yes. Very well." He gave her the once-over. "Are you?"

She shook her head. "I try." She hated this stilted conversation, as if they were strangers. As if the past fourteen years were a dandelion blown in the wind. And all she had left was the stem, the wonderment of its past beauty. She eyed him. She loved this beautiful man.

"How's the job going?" he asked, seeming to waver, perhaps feeling nostalgic for what had been. Perhaps delaying the last step through the door and what it signified.

That question became a defibrillator for her broken heart. "It's going fine, meeting deadlines, getting it done. But I took the rest of this week off. For obvious reasons." She waited for her words to sink in.

He released a whoosh of air. "You took time off? You didn't do that after the carjacking. You went right back to work like nothing had happened." His long legs closed the distance between them. Wrapping his hand around her arm, he frowned. "You lost weight." He knew her body well. She had lost about seven pounds.

"Turns out losing your husband is the secret to weight loss and a much-needed minivacation," she scoffed. Then she slipped out of his arms and walked to the kitchen. "I haven't been able to sleep, eat or concentrate. When I found myself performing simple calculations over and over, I knew it was time to use all those vacation and sick days I barely touch. We both know it was the best thing to do." She tossed her hair to convey a lack of concern. "Once the bookstore becomes profitable, I'll probably go into that full-time."

He placed his hands on his hips. "Let me see if I get this straight. You would leave a six-figure job to work at a bookstore? Something you have no experience or knowledge about.

I could see you doing it part-time, like a hobby, but this is a big risk." The incredulity in his tone made her decision sound rash.

"Money isn't everything," she shot back. "And I love books. Books are my only bed partner right now." Her heart pumped in her chest and regret twisted her insides. She occupied her suddenly shaky hands by putting a K-Cup in one side of the double coffee maker.

"Money is something when you don't have it."

"Good thing I married well, then, isn't it?" She swallowed, regretting her cheap comeback.

He stalked into the kitchen to reach into the cupboard for two mugs. She suspected Wade was acting on reflex. Not that she would remind him he didn't live there anymore. She welcomed any normalcy between them and simply placed another K-Cup into the other compartment.

"I think this is a stunt, a ploy to have me worry about you," he ground out, grabbing a couple of sugar packets, shaking them, tearing them open before pouring them into her cup. She added creamer.

"Not a stunt." She gave him a knowing glance, then got a small teaspoon. "Like you, I need a change." She stirred her coffee hard enough that her spoon clinked against the mug.

"You think I'm enjoying this?" He plopped a fist on the counter before approaching until he was near enough for her to feel his breath on her face, to feel his suppressed desire mingled with fury. "You think it's easy leaving you? These nights without you have been torture." His chest rose and fell, and his eyes darkened as he stared at her like a tiger watching its prey.

"A torture of your own doing." Hope was alive now, resuscitated. She put down her cup, placed a hand on his chest, looked up at him from under her lashes and whispered, "It doesn't have to be."

"Stop," he muttered, dipping his head toward her.

Yes. She tilted her head back and their lips met. Savage hunger rose between them, and within seconds, they were out of their clothes. Wade snatched her in his arms and carried her over to the couch. Opening her like a flower, he loved on her innermost parts and she returned the favor. He entered her with one smooth stroke, rhythmic, building the madness, the agony until their release came, hot and fast.

Far too soon for her liking, they were getting dressed.

"We shouldn't have done this," he murmured, ramming his feet into his boots. "I'm sorry for giving off mixed signals."

"Mixed signals? We're married. In the eyes of God and the world, we did nothing wrong." She grinned, her body humming from their recent lovemaking. "I have no regrets."

Wade sat across from her and clasped his hands. She figured this was his attempt at resetting the boundaries between them. Plopping onto the couch across from him, where they had just made love, she folded her arms.

"I'm still leaving."

"I'm not stopping you," she said, anger flaring in her chest.

"Good. Then, I guess that's settled." He wiped his brow and cleared his throat. "So what will you do with your time?" His demeanor came across as slightly condescending. "Hibernate in the house all day?"

"I'll be devoting my energy to making the bookstore a success." She crossed her legs.

He cocked his head. "Are your friends doing the same?"

"They will. In time." *She hoped*. Leslie was understandably preoccupied with everything going on in her life, but at least Nadya was going home tomorrow. Toni was acting a little dodgy and secretive, though Celeste didn't have the mental capacity to push her for details. And all Yasmeen could talk about was her plans for her winnings, which included purchasing a house. But Celeste was willing to put in the work needed in the meantime.

"Ha. Watch and see. You're going to be the only one who goes all-in. Just don't go dipping into our savings."

"About that…" She coughed. "I made a withdrawal to tide the business over until our launch." She wouldn't add that she had also invested some of their money with the hopes of recouping all she had taken out.

Wade jumped to his feet. "You should have consulted me. That's our retirement fund."

"I know what I'm doing. I deal with money for a living," she snapped back, resentment building.

His lips curled. The very same lips that had whispered nasty things as they trailed her body moments before. "Your reckless actions prove I did the right thing by leaving you."

Standing, she pointed a finger at him. "You didn't build that nest egg by yourself. I contributed as well."

"Yes, I know, and that's why we'll split our assets down the middle. You probably should think about putting this house up for sale."

She sucked in a breath. "I was happy in our apartment. You were the one who said you wanted to be closer to your job and have a place suitable for entertaining the bigwigs. Your words, not mine."

He rubbed his head. "Let's not start the blame game."

"Oh no. You started this and I'm going to finish it." She jumped up and got in his face, sputtering angrily. "You think you're better than me because you got therapy. You're rising above this tragedy. Well, the blame for that night is all on you. If you hadn't been speeding, we wouldn't have gotten held up by those racist punks. How you like that, if you want to talk about blame?"

Instantly, she knew she had gone too far. He gaped. His eyes went wide, filled with pain and hurt. Her harsh words hung between them while her breath wavered. Without another word, he reached for his jacket.

"Wade, honey, I—I… I didn't mean that." He slipped his arms through and zipped it closed, then stormed toward the door. "I'm sorry. I—I don't know wh-what made me say that. I don't blame you," she rattled on, racing after him. She grabbed his jacket. "P-please don't leave like this. I was angry. I didn't mean it."

He turned to face her. "The thing about anger is it's a revealer of truths. I always felt like you blamed me, though you denied it," he choked out. "Now I know how you truly feel."

"B-but I don't." She clutched his arm, peering into the depths of his eyes, praying he would accept her apology. On the inside, she wondered why she had railed at him like that. That kind of venom was not her.

"Words once spoken, cannot be taken back. We are only left with the consequences."

And with that, he was gone. Celeste went to sit on the couch, too shocked by her own behavior to cry. She sent out a text to her friends, postponing their meeting until the next day. Leslie chimed in that they should meet at her house in the afternoon, since Nadya would be discharged. Both Toni and Yasmeen responded with the thumbs-up emojis.

Great. I'll bring the food.

Mustering all her energy, she called the catering company and was relieved they were willing to change the date and location without cost.

With that handled, she replayed her words to Wade. She cupped her mouth to keep from screaming, knowing she had lost him, knowing she deserved it. Her corresponding tears felt hollow, but they were all she had and she welcomed them.

14

Toni

JANUARY 18

Toni sat on the edge of the couch in her living room and flicked her wrist to glance at her smartwatch. The stylist was due to arrive at ten and she needed to get her mind ready.

She yawned, having spent most of the night before with Leslie and Nadya at the hospital. They had started Nadya on an immunosuppressive therapy and the doctor had performed the biopsy, which confirmed his diagnosis. They needed to find her a donor. Soon.

Seeing the constant worry on Leslie's face, her lack of sleep, her sitting by Nadya's side all night, made Toni ache for her friend and goddaughter. But in an odd way, it also made her yearn for a child even more. Someone to love, to fret about, to care for… Which was why Toni had forced herself to get back to her wedding plans. It was either that or obsess on her *old ovaries*.

Her second opinion appointment was the following month and all she could pray for was different results.

When she wasn't dwelling on her inability to conceive, she was agonizing over her digital stalker. Her anxiety skyrocketed every time she had a notification chime. That's why she had started putting her phone on silent.

Today was when she would post wedding dress options for her fans. She then called Joe, one of her best go-to photographer/videographers, and he was now whistling while setting up the lighting on the other end of her living space.

Joe wore a biker jacket, earrings lining both ears and green army pants along with a pair of black, chunky, buckled boots. His eyes were heavily lined with mascara and his nails were painted black.

"I'll be right back. I need to get my other camera," Joe said, then headed out the door. That was code for he needed to smoke. Just two drags since he'd promised his wife and four gorgeous daughters he'd quit.

Restless, she jumped up off the couch and walked over to the wall where she had installed three large decorative mirrors. She scrutinized her face and checked her teeth for lipstick stains, then turned to study her wide-leg tan pants, her matching turtleneck, black blazer and silver-tipped brown cowboy boots, and nodded. Her social media glam was on point. As usual.

She closed her eyes for a second and wondered how her followers would react if she posted a pic of herself au naturel. She'd been tempted a few times, but wearing her cloak of perfection was easier than facing any potential backlash or criticism. Her parents had done enough of that to last her the rest of her life.

Not wanting to sit idle, Toni decided to do a quick stream. She retrieved her copy of *Just the Nicest Couple* and placed it on her lap, then went live. "Heyyy, everybody, jumping on real quick to share some news with you. So, you already know that I've begun wedding plans. But what you don't know yet is that I plan to open a bookstore with my friends, because you know, I love my man and my books." She giggled, eyeing lots of hearts and well-wishing emojis. "And what better way to combine my love for the two than by having our wedding at the bookstore launch." She waved her hands in the air, loving the positive responses. "Yep, you'd better keep your eyes and ears on this page to stay in the know about that."

She already had thousands watching live. Toni picked up her book and held it to the screen. "Now, it's time for Toni Talks Books. So, this was my book club's twisty read for January and I hope you're reading along with me. Be sure to post your thoughts and comments and one lucky person will receive a special gift from yours truly." She blew a kiss. "Until next time…"

The doorbell rang just as she ended the stream. She hurried over, thinking the stylist had arrived with her wedding gowns, but that wasn't the person on the other side of the door.

"Leslie? What are you doing here? Is it…Nadya?" she asked, heart thumping. Toni could see the snow was still falling. Kent had shoveled her driveway, but it was already covered with a thin white layer dotted by her visitors' footprints. She stepped back so the other woman could enter.

"Nadya woke up with a fever, and now they are talking about not releasing her, so I—I needed a minute. I had to get some air," she said, her voice quivering, like she was fighting to keep from crying. Judging from her reddened eyes, Toni would say Leslie had already been doing that.

After exchanging hugs, Leslie shucked off her coat and stomped her boots on the welcome mat. Her hair appeared oily, hanging lifeless on her shoulders. Toni was pretty sure Leslie had worn the same sweat suit the last couple days. Toni hadn't even known Leslie owned casual clothes.

Toni hung the coat in her hallway closet. "Is Nadya okay?" she asked, heading back to sit on the couch.

Leslie unzipped the jacket to reveal a T-shirt with the words *Nadya's a Survivor* emblazoned on the front. She had gotten tees for all of them.

"Honestly? I don't know. They are running more tests." Leslie sank into the armchair and ran her fingers through her straggly strands. "Aaron is with her... You're the closest to the hospital."

Actually, Leslie's father was closer, but Toni knew better than to mention that. Since his big revelation, Leslie refused to talk to Edwin. "Can I get you something to drink?"

"No. I had some tea." Toni doubted it but she didn't push. Leslie took in the setup in Toni's living room. She waved a hand and whispered, "What's going on here?"

Toni couldn't meet Leslie's eyes. "I'm trying on wedding dresses... I'm sorry. I planned on coming over when I was done." She busied herself by reaching in her purse for her powdered makeup to blot her face.

Leslie touched Toni's shoulder. "Why are you sorry? You have been a good friend, sitting with me 'round the clock at the hospital when I know you have plenty to do. Your wedding is mere months away. You do need to pick out your dress. In fact, Celeste and Yasmeen are going to be mad you didn't tell them."

"I don't think so. Yasmeen's been too busy house hunting, and I did reach out to Celeste but she didn't answer her phone."

"Isn't Yasmeen's check clearing today?" Leslie asked. "I think that's what she said when she came by the hospital yesterday, but I don't have the bandwidth to keep track of everything."

She slapped her forehead. "Oh snap, I think you're right. That *is* today. No wonder she's gone incognito. She borrowed a pair of my sunglasses, this humongous scarf and a long wig last week when she went to claim it. She's probably trying to hide from Pookie 'n 'em. She's about to have cousins hitting her up from all over. That's some serious dough." The women giggled.

"She's an only child and so were her parents," Leslie added, and they cracked up even more.

"I'm glad you're here with me," Toni said, once their laughter died down. "How is your search for your birth parents going?"

"It's going." Leslie sighed. She scooted deeper into the couch. "I hired a private investigator because I haven't had a hit as of yet on any of those genealogy searches, but it has only been a couple weeks. I've read his reviews, and though his main office is out of Philly, he's meeting me here today at a diner. I figured since I was born in Philly that I should get someone with contacts up there." She shrugged. "I need to find them. The wait is torture and Nadya isn't getting better." Tears brimmed and she wiped her eyes. "I promised myself I'd stop crying, but here I go."

"Cry all you want," Toni said, dabbing at her own eyes. "I'm not her mother and I'm crying nonstop. You don't know how much I wished one of us was a match." Her voice caught. Receiving the negative results had crushed her heart. "I think you're so strong."

"Not that strong. I don't know what I would do without you all." Leslie hiccupped. "You have been my rocks." Her chin wobbled. "I need answers."

Toni went over to hug her. "Something will give. It has to." She felt Leslie nod her head. The doorbell rang. Releasing her, Toni patted her back. "I'd better get that."

Leslie sniffled and rubbed her hands, her smile appearing forced. "I knew I chose the right stop. You're good for a much-needed distraction."

As in, anything going on with her was fluff? Ugh. She wished her friends would ease off with the jabs, as if what she did lacked impact.

Toni bit the inside of her cheek to keep from asking Leslie to clarify because she knew she would be asking with an attitude. She didn't want to hear an answer that had the potential to upset her. Because her infertility wasn't fluff and she needed to talk to her friends, then Kent about it. She was lying to him, feeding him a hope that would never come true, and she needed to stop, come clean, even if it meant losing the man of her heart.

"Are you okay?" Leslie asked when she stood unmoving with her fists curled. This time Leslie's tone held concern. Which was almost Toni's undoing.

Tell her. Her chest tightened. That would require...vulnerability, admission of hurt. She released a breath and waved a hand. "Yes, of course. This is going to be fun," she said, with forced enthusiasm before letting in the stylist. Yet resentment built.

Good old Toni. Good for a laugh. Good for a comeback.

Her heels clicked, the marble floor sounding as hollow as she felt for even being upset, for taking Leslie's words so seriously.

"Wait until you see what I have for you." Sable, her stylist, flounced inside, holding the gowns high, her assistant straining to keep the trains off the floor. "I managed to score three designer gowns and one of them is vintage. They are absolutely delish."

The women exchanged air kisses. "I can't wait to see them."

Her fake British accent was even more pronounced today. Probably because Leslie was here. Toni held in a snort. She would be writing the check to Jane Lamb from Alabama, but as Sable said, no one trusted a plain Jane.

"Alright, let's get you undressed." Sable stood six feet in flat shoes and her blond hair looked like it had been hacked with a jagged knife. She had striking grayish eyes and wore a circular barbell in her nose.

"Will I be in your way?" Leslie asked. She patted her hair as if she just realized she hadn't washed it in days.

"Nope. You're fine."

The cameraman returned and Toni gave introductions. She glanced out her window. The way that snow was coming down, they might end up with twelve inches.

"Are we ready?" Joe asked.

"Ready as ever," Toni said, then paused. "Wait. Can you take a few pictures of my friend, first?"

"Sure." He went over to the white backdrop.

"What? No." Leslie touched her chest. "I look like I've been run over with a snowblower."

Toni held out her hand. "It's for our eyes only. You needed a distraction, remember? And...you're an overcomer."

"We'll wait over here," Sable said, moving to the other side of the room. Her assistant pressed against the wall, as if trying to be invisible. Considering Toni struggled to remember her name, she would say the young woman was doing a great job.

After a brief hesitation, Leslie stood. "Headshots only." She placed her hand in Toni's. A silent indication of trust. Toni blinked back her tears and gave a little nod.

"Hang on, I might have something she could wear," Sable said, rattling off instructions to her assistant. The other woman rushed out the door, leaving it open. A blast of cold air chilled the room.

"I—I don't want to cause too much trouble," Leslie said.

"Nonsense," Sable said. "Every woman needs to evoke her inner queen every now and again."

"I agree," Toni said, before dragging Leslie into her bathroom to get her a much-needed shower.

Leslie protested, "I don't have underwear."

"Go without them."

She scoffed. "Tell me you're kidding."

Toni waved her into the shower. While Leslie got cleaned up, Toni went to get the outfit Sable had in mind. It was a black sweaterdress that Toni knew cost a few weeks' pay. Plus, there were a pair of tights. "This is perfect. How?"

Sable smiled. "A girl is always prepared."

"Add it to my tab."

"On it," Sable said, patting Toni's arm and losing her accent. "This is sweet for you to do."

"She needs it. She's going through some things."

"I'll make sure she shines," Joe added.

Toni rushed to get Leslie a toothbrush and a great face scrub. Then, once Leslie was dressed, Toni applied her foundation, having been gifted several shades ill-suited for her skin tone, plus eyeliner and apple-red lipstick. Toni completed Leslie's mini makeover with a waist-length wig.

Leslie placed a hand to her mouth. "I don't even look like me."

"You're you. Just bringing out your inner diva." Toni washed her hands. "Okay, let's go take some photos."

With Joe's prodding, she watched Leslie go from shy and self-conscious to a confident woman striking a pose.

See, that's why she hired Joe. She dabbed her eyes and joined her friend so they could get a few shots together before Leslie helped Toni into her first dress. With a big thank-you and a kiss to Toni's cheek, Leslie eventually returned the wig and left, her spirits a little cheered.

Toni's heart lifted.

Joe put on the live stream. "Let's do this."

Ninety minutes, three dresses and at least a hundred photos later, Toni closed her front door and collapsed onto her couch. Once Joe emailed her his top choices, Toni would create a video to post to her social media accounts.

She dug into her bag to look for her cell phone. Her followers had posted memes and fire emojis during her stream, and lots of hearts. Reading their comments, Toni smiled. It felt good knowing her thoughts and actions mattered and influenced others. A lot of women were asking what color shade she wore on her lips and where she bought her shoes. Toni took the time to answer some questions, but she couldn't respond to thousands.

Maybe it was time to hire a full-time virtual assistant. Kent had been pressing her to do so. She usually contracted out, but it would be great to have someone devoted to her needs.

Thinking of the stop she would have to make at her postbox to collect the samples various companies sent her way, Toni decided to post a graphic on her Instagram page along with the caption "I'm looking for an assistant."

Within seconds, she had people sharing and commenting that they were interested and asking for her contact information. Okay, that wasn't a wise move. She updated her post with "Follow my page for more details." Now she had thumbs-up emojis displaying under her post.

Her eyes landed on a comment in all caps and her stomach muscles clenched.

@BLSTFRDAPST2: I SEE YOU.

Her stomach dropped. He was back. Panic prickled her spine and her forehead beaded with sweat.

@BLSTFRDAPST2: DOES HE KNOW WHAT YOU DID?

Despite her surreptitious digging, she hadn't been able to tell if Skins had been released from prison, and he hadn't responded to her direct messages via social media. Maybe it was time to do what Leslie had done and hire a private investigator. She couldn't ask Leslie for her contact, because then Leslie would want to know why and would tell the others. Toni had never told her friends the real reason she had moved to Delaware.

She tapped her leg. Something told her Skins was in Delaware and was about to mess with more than her equilibrium. But Toni wasn't a teenager anymore. He was trying to come for a grown woman. She looked back at her phone before snapping to attention.

@BLSTFRDAPST2 had DM'd again. Finally.

Hello. It's been a long time.

At least he had stopped writing in all caps.

She wasn't about to waste time with this fool.

Skins??? What do you want? she responded, praying he would ask her for money. Then she could go after whoever this was for extortion.

I go by Lamont now.

Her heart pounded. It was him. It was really him. She wiped her slippery palms on her jeans.

Thought you got life?

Ha Ha. Flying like a bird now.

She tensed. So he was out.

We should catch up...

Smart buzzard. He wanted money, but he wasn't going to say it in writing.

Name the time and place.

Skins mentioned a car dealership twenty miles away, asking her to come by that evening, but she pushed it off until the following week. She and Kent had a cake tasting and she needed time to mentally prepare to see him again. Luckily, he agreed.

She tossed her phone into her bag and swung her legs while her mind prepped. If he asked her for money, she would tell him to go back to jail and rot. Of course he was asking for money. She was only going to meet with him so she could tell him he wasn't getting anything. Not even an old, twisted copper penny.

Lie.

Truth was, she wanted to talk with someone who shared her loss, since she couldn't tell her friends or fiancé. Even if that someone was a despicable, conniving backstabber. He had been the father of what would be her only child. He'd been there for her when she had curled up with pain after the surgery. Right before his terror, he had been gentle. Her eyes became moist. That's who she needed to see.

Unless she called her parents...

Nope. Not a good idea.

She stood and traipsed into her bedroom, going into her closet and turning on the light. Reaching for the hidden spare key from out of her favorite red bottoms, she opened the small safe and pulled out a crumpled, rectangular piece of paper. She hadn't looked at this in years.

Slowly, reverently, she smoothed the lines of the ultrasound picture of her unborn child. The only image she kept. Her heart constricted and a sob broke loose but she tightened her lips to regain control. "I'm sorry, little one," she whispered, clutching her stomach. "I'm so sorry." She hugged the small piece of paper close to her chest and closed her eyes, allowing herself the luxury to mourn.

Her parents had not tolerated any tears. The milk was already spilled, cleaned up and dried. She needed to get over it and move on. Forget she'd had life inside her. That had been their advice. She emitted a low, guttural groan. She should have been allowed to cry.

"Toni?"

She shrieked and jumped to her feet at that bass voice. The paper fell out of her hands to the floor, fluttering by her feet. "K–Kent, what are you doing here? I thought we were meeting up later for cake testing." She inched forward, her heart thumping, while she prayed he'd keep his eyes on her and off the floor. The seconds ticked by, feeling as long as the day.

"I—I came to see you in between appointments. I feel like

it's been a while since we connected, with everything going on, and I had a rough day. But then…" He cocked his head. "Were you crying?"

She shook her head. "No. No. I was just…cleaning my shoe." Carefully, she covered the paper with her shoe and flicked it backward. She swore he could hear her heart beating as fast as her chest was moving. Inhale. Exhale. Sweat formed on her forehead.

Kent's eyes narrowed. He looked like he didn't believe her.

"I missed you," she said to distract him. Toni pushed against him, causing him to back out of the closet. She shut the door behind them.

Whew.

Then she pressed their lips together and closed her eyes. A picture of her baby flashed into her mind. With a gasp, she broke the kiss.

Kent furrowed his brows. "What's wrong?" he asked.

She lifted a hand and ducked around him. "I—I gotta go. I have to meet up with Yasmeen, check on Celeste."

"Toni?" he called out. "Do you have to do that now?"

"Yes, catch up with you later."

She scampered out of the room and snatched her coat. Shoving her arms into the sleeves, she bolted through the door. But no matter how fast she ran, she couldn't outrun the image of the baby she could have had.

15
Leslie

JANUARY 18

In a little over two weeks, Leslie's life had undergone drastic changes. Changes she had no idea how she would ever bounce back from. She had learned her father wasn't her father and her daughter, who had never been seriously sick a day in her life, was suddenly very ill. But then there was Aaron who, for the most part, had changed for the better.

He had been a strong support for Nadya. A father. To Leslie's surprise, Aaron had even managed to persuade his superiors to allow him to change his hours. He devoted a huge portion of his days to Nadya and worked even more in the evenings, which sometimes meant more overnight visits. He said most physicians were glad to meet when they were done with their patients for the day. She didn't know how he managed those erratic hours, but he was there every morning and Nadya's beaming face was all Leslie needed to see.

But they did disagree on one thing: her desire to find her family. After Leslie left her impromptu photo session, she had received a message from Aaron asking about the withdrawal from their checking account. He'd been adamant they have a conversation before she met with the private investigator. Ugh. If he made her late…

She swung into her driveway and pulled up next to Aaron's car before running inside. Scurrying into their bedroom to don clean underwear and another pair of tights, she could hear the shower going and Aaron attempting to sing the latest dance song. She caught her reflection in the mirror and padded closer, smoothing her new dress. It made her appear curvy, desirable, and the material was like butter. Leaning into the mirror, she turned her face this way and that. The concealer Toni had applied made her skin look flawless. She sighed and stepped back.

Her heart felt ravaged, shredded, bitter as lemon zest.

On autopilot, Leslie took out a pair of underwear, socks and an undershirt from Aaron's chest of drawers and rested them on the bed she hadn't slept in for days. Then she sat, careful not to ruffle the spread too much, and tapped her feet. When she wasn't thinking about Nadya, Leslie was thinking about her unknown relatives—Nadya's potential lifesavers. She glanced at her watch and groaned. The shower was still running. She had a limited amount of time before she had to be back at the hospital. "Aaron, could you hurry up?" she called out, curling a fist around the edge of the duvet. Ugh.

"Alright," he shouted, and she heard the tap squeal. Seconds later, he came into the room with a towel hanging low around his waist, his hair standing up in wet spikes. She saw he had shaved and given his hair a trim so it rested on his nape. Water dripped off his body, a sign he hadn't wiped his feet before getting out of the shower. She pursed her lips. Nadya's health and well-being superseded her personal gripes.

"How's Nadya?" she asked. She went to the corner of the room to dig through the pile of clean clothes in the laundry basket before choosing a pair of black wrinkle-free slacks and a black sweater. Leslie shuddered to think of the laundry room and the two other baskets waiting for her. The doctors had allowed her to bring Nadya regular wear, so the laundry had accumulated. But she would return home and take care of it tonight once Nadya had gone to sleep.

Aaron's eyes roved her face and body. He dropped the towel and gave her *the look*. She rolled her eyes and stuffed the clothing into his hands. Sex was the last thing she wanted. If he knew her, he would know that what she wanted was for him not to hassle her over the funds she needed to get their daughter help.

She folded her arms and watched him with dispassion. "What did you want to talk about?"

With a heavy sigh, he started getting dressed. "You took out a hefty sum for a PI when you could have spoken to your father to get information about the adoption." There was a twinge of worry in his tone.

"I didn't ask my father anything because I don't trust him to tell me the truth. The PI has excellent reviews," she huffed. "It's not like we can't afford it. You've blown a ton on less. Just last month, you said we lost thousands because of some investment opportunity that flopped, and you're still at it. This money is about our daughter's care. Is there a price too high for that?"

Aaron wiped his brow. "N-no. I just… Forget it."

With everything going on the past couple weeks, Leslie hadn't paid much attention to their finances. Most of their utilities and credit cards were on autopay. Still, his demeanor put her on alert. "Are we having financial difficulty?" Even as she uttered the question, she was already telling herself that wasn't possible. They had investments and shares and 401(k)s and a significant amount in their savings.

"I... We're good." He slipped his feet into his trousers and fidgeted with his waist. His pants hung loose. He'd lost weight. Leslie, on the other hand, had gained three pounds, though she barely ate. Stress showed itself in different ways in different people.

He shoved the sweater over his head, yanked it down and changed topics. "This isn't about Nadya. This is about you. You're searching for something you already have."

She paused. His words nicked her heart. "I'm trying to find more donors for Nadya." She stalked into their closet to get him a belt, doubting Aaron noticed his pants hung low on his rear.

"No. No. I know you. It's more than that. Yes, this is about Nadya, but it is also very much about you. Edwin destroyed your orderly life and you want to make him pay. Spite him. Possibly even find a replacement family. He's at the hospital every day—even now as we speak—and you refuse to acknowledge him, tuning him out, and I can't believe I'm the one who has to say this, but it's wrong."

The truth slashed her gut. She pressed the belt into his hand, tempted to use it as a binder for Aaron's mouth. "You never liked my da—Edwin. So what's it to you what I do? He did a horrible thing."

"Thanks," Aaron muttered, pulling the leather through the loops. "I agree, he was wrong for keeping that from you, but he did it out of love."

"Love isn't about deception." She paced the room.

He came over and held her arms to still her movements. Their eyes met. "Maybe he didn't tell you his deepest, darkest secret because he was afraid you would do what you're doing now. Reject him." He swallowed. "Leave." His eyes pleaded with her to be understanding.

She pierced him with her gaze and engaged in a staredown.

It felt like she was having a dual conversation. Like he was talking about more than her messed-up situation with Edwin. Since she wasn't certain, Leslie made sure her husband knew her position. "I don't tolerate being lied to," she whispered. "Lying is a sign of weakness."

"It's a sign of humanity," Aaron urged, drawing her close. "You need to forgive your dad. He kept this from you to protect you. Nadya needs him. You see how she lights up when her grandpa enters the room. And you're too stubborn to admit that you need him too."

She lifted her chin. "I can't pretend he didn't crush me. I can't unhear what he said. My heart isn't a squeegee. I can't clean this off, not when he's ripped away my trust."

"I'm not asking you to do that. I'm asking you to understand. To empathize." He wrapped his arms around her and kissed her head.

She stood, frozen. "I can't do that."

Aaron released her, giving her a look of disbelief, his arms hanging loosely by his sides. "This doesn't sound like you. I thought this was a manifestation of your stress, a defense mechanism to not deal with your hurt, but you're serious. Unforgiving, even."

"This *is* me and I'm very serious. I'm done talking about second chances with that man. He wasn't who he said he was. I thought he was my hero but he…he lied to me," she said, flailing her arms. "My stress management is action. Finding my blood relatives gives me hope for Nadya," she emphasized. "Are you coming with me to meet with the investigator? It won't take long and I can see if Toni is available to sit with her. Or, are you going to stay with Nadya until I return?"

He shook his head and stuffed his hands in his pockets. "I've got to get to…work. Edwin promised to watch her as long as we need, so she's good." Though relieved Nadya wouldn't be alone, she wouldn't admit her gratitude to Edwin. Aaron looked like he was waiting for her to say something, relent, before he shrugged. "Suit yourself."

He left without a backward glance or giving her the usual peck on her cheek. Whatever. She rushed out the door and tore out of the driveway. While she drove, she replayed her conversation with Aaron, haunted by those pleading eyes.

Nadya's illness had given her something she had always wanted—Edwin and Aaron working together. But it appeared their truce involved ganging up on her. She stopped at a queue in a three-way intersection. Imagine Aaron accusing her of being unforgiving. It was like he didn't get that Nadya could die. As in, not be here anymore. His parents were both deceased, and both Leslie and Aaron were only children. Edwin's deception was costly. Sorry, she couldn't get over that so easily.

She gripped the wheel. What she could do was find people to add to their numbers so her daughter had a chance at life. Nadya was on the donor list, but she wasn't in the top ten. She turned right and headed into the parking lot of the diner.

There was only one other vehicle present. She grabbed her purse and went inside, choosing a seat that gave a view of the rear of the property, where the snow was like a white, untouched blanket, a visual depiction of serenity.

A large man wearing sunglasses and a cap approached. This must be him. Her stomach knotted.

Taking a seat, he shook off his cap, revealing a head full of ginger curls. Up close, he reminded her of a supersize elf. He stuck a hand out and introduced himself, "Rick Brown."

She relaxed, shook his hand, then laced her fingers together in her lap. "H-hello." She sounded breathy, nervous. "I'm so glad you could meet me."

"No worries. As my website says, I'm flexible." His voice was warm and soothing. She suspected Rick was quite adept at putting people at ease, despite his imposing size. "Did you bring your birth papers?"

She nodded and picked up her purse. Snapping it open, Leslie took out a copy of her birth certificate.

He placed everything inside his jacket pocket. "I have access to many databases and acquaintances, so I'll do some digging."

"Finding my birth parents is a matter of life and death," she said, telling him about Nadya's condition.

"I'll track them down," he said, his conviction firm.

She nodded. "Good." Leslie took out an envelope and handed it to Rick. "I have the deposit you requested."

"Thanks." Rick slipped it in his pocket without counting it—an indication of his trust, which in turn made her trust him. "I'll be in touch," he said with a wave before departing.

All that anxiety for a five-minute conversation. She gave a little laugh and sipped her coffee. How anticlimactic. But the main thing was she had taken a step and soon she would have answers. Her cell buzzed. It was Edwin. Nadya's fever had broken.

Thank goodness. Though she didn't respond, she rejoiced at this good news. She gulped her coffee, settled the tab and went over to the hospital. As soon as she stepped through the door to Nadya's room, Edwin grabbed her and hugged her, lifting her off the ground.

For a second, she closed her eyes and inhaled his woodsy scent. She welcomed his strength and her eyes misted. But then she stiffened and shoved at his chest. She refused to look at him, to see the pain etched on his face, to relent.

He released her and she scooted around him, eyes on her child. Nadya had color in her cheeks and her smile was bright. Leslie kissed her face and forehead, ignoring Nadya's frown. "Mom, stop." She wiped the spots Leslie had kissed. "The doctor said I can go home tomorrow if I don't have any more fevers," she said, dipping her spoon into her Jell-O. "Pop Pop said I might be able to go to school soon."

Edwin had no right to tell Nadya that. "I talked to your

principal about putting you in homeschooling. A teacher will come to the house and help you with your studies."

Nadya's face fell. "But I want to see my friends."

Leslie touched Nadya's hair. "I can't risk you getting sick. You're immunocompromised."

"I want to go to school like normal kids my age."

And just like that, she was the bad guy. "You can video chat with them," she offered.

"It's not the same." Nadya's mouth downturned. She dropped her Jell-O onto the tray and looked away. "I hate my life right now."

Edwin came to stand next to Leslie. "Listen to your mother," he said. "She's only doing what's best for you."

"Can I still go to gymnastics at least?" Nadya asked.

"I'm sorry, honey, but no," Leslie said, her heart wrenching when Nadya cut her eyes away.

"You just enjoy controlling my life," her daughter snapped.

Leslie didn't bother to continue the argument. She walked over to peer out the window while Edwin tried to cheer up her child. It was tough always being the one to say no. If Aaron was here, she doubted Nadya would respond this way. She felt a hand tap her shoulder and her father pointed at the door.

Edwin then kissed Nadya on the cheek. "I'll be back, pumpkin. I just have to talk to your mom for a second."

She trudged behind him as he led her to the waiting area. Mercifully, it was empty. Once they were inside, Edwin rounded on her, his hands on his hips. "This cold war between us has got to stop. Nadya's been asking questions."

"What kind of questions?" she asked.

"Like why you seem so mad all the time. That little girl is perceptive and she knows something is wrong. It's time you cease with this temper tantrum."

It was his dad tone that set her off. "You don't have any right to talk to me that way. You lost that right when you made me live a lie for all my life."

"Listen, I get that I hurt you and I am sorry for that. Believe me when I say I regret the pain I caused you. I can't sleep at night," he choked out. "But if I'm being honest, you're being spoiled. You're not twelve years old. You're a grown woman with a child of her own and old enough to understand that no parent is perfect. Your mother and I made mistakes, but we loved you like our own."

"*Like* your own," she shot back, her anger venomous. "As in, I am not your child."

"You are my daughter." His chest heaved. "No matter what you say or how you act, nothing is going to change that."

Leslie had to puncture him. "I'm looking for my real parents."

He gasped. "You were always nasty when you were hurt, and this time it's no different. Well, missy, I told you about them because of Nadya. If they are able to help my granddaughter, no one is going to be happier than me. But not everything is black-and-white. You might not like all the answers you find."

His words sounded ominous. Like he knew something she didn't. "Edwin, I'm not—"

"It's *Daddy* to you," he commanded, his voice stern. He lifted his brows and folded his arms.

Her insides shook like when she was sixteen and had been caught smoking. She knew that tone and bit back a snappy protest. "Fine. Daddy, Daddy, Daddy." She waved her hands as if it were no big deal. But she willed her heart to calm. She was grown and had no reason to be scared. Or so she told herself.

"Yes, I'm glad you know who I am because despite what you say, you're going to need me, and when you do, don't hesitate to knock on my door."

16

Yasmeen

Yasmeen stomped across the bed of snow in her new designer boots, trudging a diagonal path toward her brand-new SUV parked outside the county jail. The insides of her boots were like clouds and she felt like she was walking on a puff of air. The quiet crunch accompanying each step left a new rhythm, a satisfying sense of hope.

She had paid for these as soon as she saw her total cash winnings totaling $4,867,800 available in her checking account. Yup. Yasmeen had opted for the lump sum amount and had paid the hefty lottery tax so she wouldn't have to worry about it anymore. The bank had cleared a portion when she deposited it last week, and waiting for the rest had been the longest and most exhilarating time of her life. She kept logging into her account from her new cell phone to check her balance, to assure herself she wasn't in a dream.

She knocked the snow off her boots, hiked herself up into the vehicle, and snatched off the borrowed wig and sunglasses, relieved to be done with her disguise. Now that she had posted Darryl's bail—wealthy women with class wouldn't say *Pookie*—it would take a few hours for him to be processed and released.

Darryl would find his way home. She started up the truck and her audiobook began to play. The stereo system was doing that smooth narrator voice justice. *I Am Debra Lee: A Memoir* was one of the books she was considering putting on display in the bookstore. Maybe she could reach out to Debra's publicist to see if the former BET CEO would come to Delaware.

That would be a huge draw. She bit her lip. Or Sunny Hostin. That was a big leap, but hey, as Daddy liked to quote, "You have not, 'cause you ask not."

Right as Yasmeen left the station, Toni called, saying she was coming with Yasmeen on her house-hunting quest. They agreed to meet up by Celeste's house so they could carpool to the four places under consideration.

Yasmeen hadn't been able to sleep the night before, knowing that today she was going to choose her first home. Something neither Yasmeen nor her parents had ever owned. She'd spent most of the night searching real estate sites, looking at houses for sale in the area of Dover where President Biden used to reside, and she had packed her Pinterest account with decorating ideas. The luxury of not having to choose properties by price but by location was one Yasmeen never imagined possible. But her new account balance showed it was not only possible, it was actually going to happen.

Today. Her insides fluttered. She shrieked and danced in her seat. This all felt surreal, but when she gripped the steering wheel, this vehicle was very much real. *Rich* was her new normal and she had the paper to prove it. *Holla!*

Now that the check had cleared, she would tell her parents. She wouldn't relish that conversation because she knew how her Daddy viewed gambling. "Casting lots," he called it, using the phrase from the Bible. She could almost hear him saying, "I don't cast lots or depend on luck. I get what I have from honest hard labor. Consider the ants..." She snorted. Bet the church won't say no to that 10 percent tithe though.

She arrived at Celeste's house, noting the oil stain on the driveway from her previous car. It had been satisfying to junk that car and watch the yard workers crush it, signifying a literal end of her former life and the beginning of a new one. She pulled right over that stain and honked her horn, pausing the audiobook. She would offer to repair Celeste's driveway, although it was very much unlike her friend not to have done so already.

Minutes later, Toni came out, her arm cupped around Celeste's shoulder. Yasmeen frowned. Celeste was hunched over, her head lolling with each step. Yasmeen pressed the unlock button, and Toni opened the rear passenger door to assist Celeste inside. Now, Yasmeen knew Celeste had anxiety about driving, but this was more than that.

"What's going on?" she asked, turning to face her friend.

Celeste leaned back into the seat and closed her eyes, shaking her head. Toni got inside the front seat. "Nice wheels, Yasmeen. When did you buy this?"

Yasmeen gave a little nod. "Thanks, I got it this morning."

"What did your parents say?" Celeste asked, sounding weary. She took a few tries to get the seatbelt fastened.

"I didn't tell them yet."

"I'm not surprised," Toni said. "I can see Pastor Adams preaching fire and brimstone because you played the lottery."

Yasmeen resisted the urge to slap that smirk off her face. Never mind that she herself had been thinking that, which is why she'd stalled until that money was deposited in her account. She didn't want her daddy guilt-tripping her over her winnings.

"I'll be happy to take it off your hands if he makes you return it," Toni said. "When you tell them, at least show up with gifts for your parents, like the Wise Men did for baby Jesus."

"I'm grown grown. My daddy can't tell me what to do," Yasmeen said. "And quit your teasing. You're making me sorry I invited you." Still, that was a good idea. Presents, especially things they needed, would be a good icebreaker. More things to buy. The Jamaican phrase her daddy often sang—*Money is a funny thing. A very quick to done thing*—was so true.

"You don't mean that," Celeste said from the back seat, her voice a whisper.

"You're right, I don't. I need my girls with me." Yasmeen twisted around to see Celeste shifting in the back seat like she was trying to get comfortable. "What's up?" she asked.

Toni replied, "Wade came by for the rest of his stuff this morning. She was laid out on the couch when I got here. That's all I could get out of her."

"I didn't feel like talking," Celeste said, her voice sounding hoarse. "Still don't."

"Fourteen years…" Yasmeen's heart squeezed. "I'm so sorry, Celeste. We don't have to do this if you're not up to it. We can veg out and trash talk if you'd like." She still believed Wade was a good person, but so was Celeste. Despite her feelings on the matter, she hated seeing the devastation on her friend's face.

Celeste shook her head, her eyes popping open. Yasmeen could see they had been reddened from crying. "No, I need to snap out of it, and what kind of friend would I be if I couldn't be happy for you?" She visibly pulled herself together and snapped her fingers. "Let's get going. I can't wait to see what you plan to get now that you're a high roller."

"Are you sure?" she asked.

"Yep. I want to celebrate your fortune with you. I'm a big girl. I'll be alright." Her determined tone put Yasmeen at ease. Somewhat. A part of her was shocked Wade had actually moved out for good. If she didn't know anything else, she knew that man loved Celeste. Goes to show you could never say never. Because she would never have imagined anything breaking up these two. She tapped the screen to bring up the maps and typed her destination in the search bar.

"Where is your first showing?" Toni asked, slapping her oversize sunglasses on her face. Yasmeen slid Toni a glance and gave her the once-over. Toni was all glammed up and looked a perfect ten, even in the midst of a snowstorm. Yasmeen patted her hair, done in neat cornrows. Soon she'd be just as fashionable as Toni.

"All four houses are within minutes of each other," Yasmeen said. "You know I'm not trying to move far away from my girls. Or the bookstore." She backed out of the space and made her way out of the development, then stopped at a light. A peek in the rearview mirror showed Celeste had her eyes closed and lips cinched tight. So far, so good.

"I know we're supposed to be meeting tomorrow but let's talk about the bookstore for a minute," Toni said, offering the perfect distraction. "I'm meeting with a website developer to set up our page. I'm thinking that we would each need to get headshots, I'll take care of that, and then under each of our names, I'd put our titles and a brief bio outlining what we do and anything else you think we might add."

"That sounds great," Yasmeen said.

"Yes, I like that idea," Celeste added.

"Good. Since we have a majority in agreement, I'll bring Leslie up to speed."

"I'll have my book list together by tomorrow," Yasmeen said. They would need to order the books in advance to make sure the stock of new and trending releases arrived before the opening. Yasmeen planned to set up meetings with the head librarians for the two libraries in town to get suggestions as well. She couldn't let her newfound fortune distract her from her commitment when her friends were depending on her to do her part. Although, with everything going on in their lives, she wondered if they should even continue their quest of launching the business.

Yasmeen posed the question, "Do you notice all this upheaval started the minute we partnered together to open this bookstore?"

"Whoa." Toni held up a hand. "Don't tell me you're thinking this is some sort of sign."

"Signs, actually. Celeste and Wade broke up—"

"Separated," Celeste clarified.

"Nadya fell sick, my boyfriend got arrested, and Toni—" she flailed a hand "—well, all is fabulous in Toni's world." From the corner of her eye, she saw Toni tense and rushed to add, "You do have your wedding to plan, which is a major transition."

"This is all coincidence. If anything jinxed it, I would say it was Celeste saying we're going to have the best year of our lives." Toni shook her head. "What a way to usher in the new year. It's only mid-January and I'm already ready for a new one or a do-over."

"Listen, we can't back down," Celeste said. "I'll pick up the slack. This has to work because I'm not trying to have Wade be right." Her voice took on an edge.

"But the bookstore isn't guaranteed," Yasmeen felt the need to add. "Do you know how many places I've worked for that closed within six months of opening?"

"She's got a point." Toni snickered. "And you know before she settled at the nursing home, Yasmeen done worked for almost all the stores in town."

"Whatever." Yasmeen rolled her eyes, though a chuckle escaped. "All that's behind me now. I emailed my resignation letter the night I won the lottery. Well, it wasn't a letter, it was a simple *buh-bye*."

"Yassss. Goodbye to the simple life. You messing with the big boys now, girl," Toni said.

Yasmeen remembered her idea. "Speaking of big boys, or in this case, big girls, what do you think of us reaching out to see if Sunny Hostin would have a signing at our store?"

"That's a genius plan. I read *Summer on Sag Harbor* last year and loved it. I'm pretty sure she will come if her schedule allows," Toni said, pulling out her phone.

"Wait... You've got Sunny on speed dial?" Yasmeen squeaked.

"Yep." Toni's eyes were glued to her phone.

Yasmeen turned off the main highway into a private lane. The snow had been cleared from the streets, and all the driveways as well. Dang. According to the smooth female voice on GPS, she had a mile to go. From one block to the next, the homes changed from modest to massive. These houses filled a block with plenty of bedrooms and had yard space to spare. Her stomach knotted and she swallowed. Yasmeen wiped her brow. A severe case of imposter syndrome struck her confidence. Her heart raced in her chest. Maybe she needed to make a U-turn.

"Sunny said she'll check her schedule." Toni must have seen something on Yasmeen's face because her next words were, "Breathe, girl, you have a right to be here as much as anybody else."

"Yes, friend. The only color they care about is green," Celeste encouraged, though her voice sounded tight, like she had *squeezed* out those words.

Yasmeen released a breath and spoke in a hushed tone. "We're almost there." She kept right below the speed limit. She wasn't trying to get pulled over in this neighborhood.

A quick glance behind her showed Celeste gripping a stress ball. Seeing a red light ahead, Yasmeen reduced her speed until the light changed. Two hundred feet away, the navigator declared she had arrived at her destination. All three women bent their heads to peer out the vehicle and take in the sprawling mansion to their right.

"From now on, we partying at your house," Toni said with a cackle.

"That's if I let you in," Yasmeen said. That released their tension. They cracked up.

Toni jumped out of the vehicle and Yasmeen followed suit, stepping into the frigid air. The temps were below freezing and her old coat wasn't helping. Both Toni and Celeste were well bundled and snuggled deep into their winter garb. She made a note to stop at the mall. Wait. No, she was going to use Toni's stylist to give her the hookup. Yasmeen dug into her jacket for a cap and placed it on her head.

"You made it, Celeste," Toni said, emitting a cheer and doing a little jig.

Celeste opened the door, releasing a blast of cold wind. "I guess anger is the cure for anxiety and depression. It made me get out the house." They headed up the driveway. The Realtor was already waiting inside.

"No, therapy is the key," Yasmeen added.

"You just had to go there, didn't you?" Celeste snapped.

Toni looked around before hunching close. "Listen, this is not the time or place for you all to act out and show your butt. Do you see where we are?" The Realtor chose that moment to open the door and beckon them inside.

Celeste inhaled loudly and then nodded. "You're right."

"I only spoke the truth," Yasmeen mumbled. "Wasn't trying to start nothing though."

Toni looped her arms through both of theirs and chided, "Well, truth spoken at the wrong time does more harm than good."

"True dat." Celeste gave Yasmeen the stink eye.

As they made their way inside, Yasmeen apologized. "I love you and I mean well."

"I know," Celeste said. "But sometimes a friend just needs you to be there and no comments are needed."

"Noted," Yasmeen said, before they hugged it out. Then they went inside what might be her future first home.

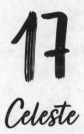

17

Celeste

JANUARY 19

Celeste watched her friends watching her as they sat around her living room table and ate the finger foods and charcuterie board she'd had delivered for their meeting that afternoon. If she hadn't postponed already, Celeste would have canceled today. When she awakened, she'd felt Wade's absence in every part of her body.

Reality had set in like rigor mortis and seeped through to her very bones. His final departure made the space empty, hollow, and all she heard was the echo of her solitary footsteps as she padded to the bathroom. Besides the gush of water and the squeak of the faucet while she washed her hands, it was so silent she could hear herself breathe. So still.

Thank goodness for friends.

And their mess.

Somehow Toni and Yasmeen knew she needed them. They had shown up within minutes of each other early that morning to sit with her, turn on the television, leave water rings on her coffee table and crumbs on the countertops, and she could take a breath and enjoy the normalcy, the durability of friendship. Of them being there.

And they planned to stay the night. *Sweet.*

She went to sit with them and placed a couple pieces of pineapple, chunks of cheese and a handful of grapes on her plate so Toni and Yasmeen would relax and not worry about her so much. She stuffed a yellow cube of sharp cheddar into her mouth and forced herself to chew, then swallow.

It was close to 3:00 p.m. and Leslie had texted to say Nadya's fever had returned so she would remain in the hospital under observation. There were manila folders and stationery placed before four chairs. Both Celeste and Toni had brought their laptops.

"Let's start the meeting. I'll bring Leslie up to speed."

"Great. I have been waiting to do this." Yasmeen dug into her oversize designer purse—also new, along with the diamond rings on both her index fingers glistening under the lights—and pulled out two checks. She handed one to Celeste and the other to Toni. "That's to cover my portion in the business. I was beyond grateful for the handout, but I'm so relieved I can pay my own way."

"Thanks," Celeste said. "Though you know you didn't have to pay it back."

"I feel as if I can hold my head up with the rest of you," Yasmeen said.

"Whether you have a dollar, or in this case, a million, you're our girl. We got you." Toni reached for a pen and endorsed her check before sliding it toward Celeste. "Put this toward our expenditures."

"We right here," Celeste said and pointed between herself and Toni.

Yasmeen's eyes sheened. "Thanks for having my back, guys, all these years. This morning I stopped at the gas station to fill my tank and I stuck my ATM card in that machine without a worry in the world. You don't know what it felt like not having my heart race because I'm not sure if it's going to go through." She dabbed at her eyes.

Since she was closer, Toni reached over to squeeze Yasmeen's hand. "Don't squander your blessing, girl."

"Save some and multiply the rest. It's all about residual income," Celeste advised and then cleared her throat. "Okay, we're not about to engage in a cry fest when we have work to do."

Toni took charge. "Alright, so we're going to take a few minutes to work on our bios. We'll each have individualized photoshoots at our residences."

"I close on my property soon. My Realtor was able to get the sellers to agree on a quick close since I waived the inspection and other contingencies," Yasmeen said, giddy, bouncing in her seat.

"So you made up your mind?" Toni asked. "You were driving me up a wall yesterday when you couldn't decide."

"I just needed to sleep on it," she said, moving her hair out of her face.

"Which one did you choose?"

"The first one."

The biggest and most expensive. It also needed some maintenance. "Are you sure?" Celeste asked. "I don't want to burst your joy bubble, but you want to make sure it's a good buy." Yasmeen was acting like someone who hadn't eaten for days. She was gorging herself when what she needed was to take small bites.

"I can afford it," Yasmeen said, a little haughty and defensive.

"I ain't mad at ya," Toni said, giving her a high-five.

Celeste needed to utter words of caution. "Just because you can, doesn't mean you should."

"Doesn't mean you shouldn't either," Toni said, ever quick with the comebacks.

"Will you stop encouraging her?" Celeste said.

"I get that you mean well for me," Yasmeen said in a much meeker tone, "but I won't go overboard. I just want to treat myself. If you think about it, I'm just getting what you guys have, except you accumulated your stuff over time. I'm catching up."

"Alright. I get it." Celeste decided to drop it before Yasmeen got the impression she wasn't happy for her. Many companies had gone bankrupt because of frivolous spending and not minding the money right, so she knew the pitfalls of having too much at your disposal. At least Yasmeen was buying things she needed.

Like diamond rings?

Toni tapped the table to get her attention. "That bio isn't going to write itself."

For the next half hour, the women crafted what they wanted to highlight about themselves. Toni was clicking away at her keys, in a groove. Yasmeen was hunched over, chewing on the pen cap, her brow furrowed. Celeste pulled up her résumé on her laptop and cut-and-pasted some of that language onto her bio. She started to add that she was happily married for fourteen years when she remembered… With a heavy heart, she highlighted those words and hit the delete button.

Her heart constricted. That was how fast Wade had deleted her from his life. Not even a text or a phone call. She sniffled as the tears flowed unbidden down her cheeks. Two heads bobbed up and looked her way.

"You good?" Toni asked.

She nodded and wiped her face. After reassurances that she was fine, the women reviewed what they had written and made suggestions. Toni sent their documents off to the website developer and slammed her laptop closed. "That's one thing down, a thousand to go. It feels good working on our goal."

Yasmeen pulled a few sheets of paper out of her bag. "I made a copy of my book lists for each of you, and I added blurbs." Toni placed a copy for Leslie in the spare folder.

Celeste scanned the lists. "I like the cookbooks and the historicals... I tore through Piper Huguley's book on Ann Lowe..."

"Yes," Yasmeen said. "She's got another coming later this year, I think. *American Daughters*. I'll have to look up her pub date."

"I believe it's out already but you can double check." Celeste tilted her head. "I don't think I read *Queen of Exiles* by Vanessa Riley. I'll have to check that out. Wait... ReShonda Tate wrote a historical? How did I not know this?"

"Yes, *The Queen of Sugar Hill*. I've already ordered the audiobook," Yasmeen said. "It's about the life of Hattie McDaniel."

"I'm loving all these titles with *queens*," Toni said. "Give us our just due." She glanced at the list. "These travel books and memoirs sound fun."

"Thanks. I stalk all my favorite authors' social media pages." Yasmeen preened. "But I did have help from actual librarians."

"Smart," Toni said, then snapped her fingers. "We have got to have *Spare* in stock. And, Michelle Stimpson is a hoot. If I remember right her newest book, *Sisters with a Side of Greens*, is due out in March and I've already one-clicked."

"Trust me. They are all on the list." Yasmeen beamed, then looking at Celeste she added, "Right along with Vanessa Riley's *A Gamble at Sunset*."

Celeste rubbed her temples. "Whew. So many books..."

"...so little time," they said in unison, then cracked up.

"I'll check our funds and contact the warehouses to make sure we will have enough in stock." Celeste studied the pages again. "Oh, I see you have suggestions for how many I should order. You've thought of everything."

"I try," Yasmeen said, lowering her lashes.

"Although I do think we should double the amount for Kennedy Ryan's *Before I Let Go* and Sadeqa Johnson's *The House of Eve*."

"Good idea." Yasmeen nodded. "But you do see I did myself a favor and added a lengthy romance list. I've got Farrah Rochon, Robyn Carr, Alyssa Cole, Jayci Lee, Julia Quinn, Brenda Novak—"

"Ooh, I love me some Brenda Novak. Her and Donna Hill's books are automatic one-clicks for me," Celeste said. "You'd better add thrillers and YA for Leslie."

"I did. I've got Sandra Brown's *Out of Nowhere* and Heather Graham's *Shadow of Death*, and I'm waiting on more recs from my library friends." Yasmeen made a note. "By the way, did you know *Confessions in B-Flat* is about to be a movie?"

Celeste did a high-wave. "*Holla!* I sure did. Donna's doing her thang. I'll support, but you know the movie is never as good as the book."

"You ain't speaking nothing but the truth," Yasmeen said.

"We can plan a girls' night when it comes out." Toni exhaled and splayed her hands. "We did good, y'all. We just need Leslie to find our location and choose our furnishings, etcetera. I'll reach out to see if she's done any digging yet but I imagine Nadya is her priority right now."

"I can assist with that, if Leslie doesn't feel up to it," Celeste offered.

"I'll let you know. I don't want Leslie to think we're pushing her out."

They sampled more of the fruit and cheese. Toni boxed some to take to the hospital and Celeste put a small portion in her refrigerator. Then the doorbell rang. "I'll get it. It's probably Leslie." She pushed back and scurried to answer the door, opening it with a flourish. The gust of wind made it swing wider than she'd intended.

There was a stone-faced-looking man at the door. "Can I help you?"

"Are you Celeste Coleman?" he inquired, his coat flapping in the wind.

"Yes."

He handed her a brown manila envelope. "You've been served." Then he was off and speeding down her driveway.

She lost her breath and closed the door, then hunched over and clutched her stomach. This couldn't be happening.

"Who was it?" Yasmeen asked, her chair scraping back as she stood.

Toni jumped to her feet. "What's wrong?"

"We literally had sex yesterday, and now he's..." She held up the letter-sized envelope in her shaky hand. "I think these are d–divorce papers." Her knees buckled under that knowledge. Fortunately, she had her friends to hold on to. Imagine what it would be like to receive this news alone.

Toni and Yasmeen ushered her over to the couch. She plopped on the soft cushions, the envelope falling out of her hands and to the floor. Her friends flanked her sides, after Yasmeen bent to retrieve the document.

"Stay calm," Toni soothed and rubbed her back.

"Deep breaths." Yasmeen used the envelope as a fan and directed her to inhale and exhale.

"You think he would've texted me to prepare me, so I'd know they were coming," she said, touching her chest and leaning into Toni. The light scent of roses and vanilla soothed her.

"Um, he probably figured you would avoid it," Toni said.

Yup. She sure would have.

"Whatever. I think that's grimy." Yasmeen was fanning so hard, the paper made a clacking sound.

Celeste lifted her head and patted Toni's hand. "What I

wouldn't do to trade places with you. I wish I had your carefree attitude about life. Maybe now I wouldn't be so heartbroken."

"I thought I was the only one who felt that way," Yasmeen chimed in. "Your life is so fab and you're marrying the man of every woman's fantasy."

Toni froze, then stood. "What is up with you all thinking I have it easy?" She smoothed her hands over flat abs and appeared to wrestle with herself before saying, "I won't try to one-up you guys, but just because I'm not as effusive with my emotions, it doesn't mean I can always shrug things off so easy. Sometimes that blasé attitude is a facade, covering deeper issues." Her voice caught, alerting Celeste that this wasn't just talk. Something wasn't right. Celeste placed a hand on Yasmeen's arm to still her movements.

"What's wrong?" Celeste asked.

With a heavy sigh, Toni came to sit beside her. "I don't want to pile my stuff on top of your laundry, but I can't keep this to myself any longer." Her bleak tone made Celeste's stomach knot.

"Tell me," Celeste said.

"You're scaring me," Yasmeen said, the envelope now resting in her lap.

Toni hunched her shoulders. "A few weeks ago, I found out I can't have children, and both Kent and I want to be parents." Her tone sounded bitter. "How's that for being perfect?"

"As in *ever*?" Yasmeen asked, at the same time Celeste asked, "Are you sure?"

Toni gave a nod. "I'm getting a second opinion," she said, sounding defeated. "But I've been told I have old ovaries."

"Say what, now?" Yasmeen's brows creased. "That sounds like something for women in menopause. You're way too young for that. I wouldn't worry your pretty head about that diagnosis. A second opinion will clear all that up."

Toni didn't look confident. Celeste rubbed her back while Yasmeen continued speculating. "For all we know, this doctor could be looking to make some money off you. You're a celebrity in these parts. D-list, but still. He's probably hoping you'll put him on your show."

"Okay, I have no idea what you're even saying right now," Toni said, "but I appreciate your support."

Yasmeen chuckled. "I guess I did go off on a tangent, but you get my drift."

"What did Kent say when you told him?" Celeste asked, redirecting the conversation.

Before Toni could respond, Yasmeen was on it. "I just know Superman said all the right things."

"Yasmeen, would you quit your chattering and give Toni a chance to talk?"

"Sorry, you know I just…" Yasmeen trailed off before she gestured to Toni to speak.

Toni slumped onto the couch. "I didn't tell him."

This time Yasmeen remained silent, her brows hitting her hairline.

"Please tell me you plan on telling Kent," Celeste said, her voice clipped.

"I can't tell you that," Toni said.

"Bad idea," Yasmeen chimed in. "Honesty is important in a relationship."

"I agree." Celeste nodded. "You're marrying this man, and you can't keep something like this from him. You're asking for your marriage to end before it's even begun."

"He might not see me the same," Toni whispered.

"Or he might support you," Celeste countered.

"You should listen to Celeste," Yasmeen said. "She was married for a long time before, well, you know, she got served her walking papers. She knows what she's talking about."

Celeste lost patience. She wasn't sure if Yasmeen was being genuine or throwing darts at her relationship. "Why don't you stop talking? At least Toni is in a committed relationship.

You're busy messing around with bottom-of-the-barrel men like Snookie once a week for your—" she made air quotes with her hands ""—tune-up.'"

Yasmeen gasped. And even Toni was looking at Celeste sideways. She wished she could retract her words, but she was tired of Yasmeen judging her. She had no idea what it was like breathing, walking, sleeping with nonstop anxiety.

"Wow, that was low." Yasmeen shoved off the couch. "Darryl isn't that bad, and it's *Pookie*." She sounded hurt, but Celeste wasn't in the frame of mind to apologize.

"Guys, let's take a breather before this gets out of hand," Toni interjected, but Yasmeen wasn't having it. She paced and continued with her verbal diarrhea.

"Yeah, I know I had to bail him out of jail yesterday morning, but it's because he insists on fooling with the wrong crowd. I'm pretty sure he's learned his lesson though," she huffed.

"And there you have it," Celeste said. "Point made."

Yasmeen stormed off into the bathroom and slammed the door behind her. They paused for a beat.

"Dang," Toni exhaled, breaking the silence. "Maybe instead of opening a business, we need to book a vacation or buy several gallons of ice cream."

"We're not quitting this bookstore." Celeste wagged a finger. "And you're telling Kent the truth as soon as you leave here."

"Let me see what this other doctor says first. For all I know, she might say everything is good to go. I don't want to alarm him unless I have to."

"You're hedging."

"I…I don't want to lose him."

"If you lose him, then he didn't deserve you."

"We'll see."

"Do you need me to come to your appointment with you?" Celeste asked.

"No, I know what it's like for you venturing out. You were

going hard on that stress ball yesterday. But you were a trooper. If I need you, I can always video call."

"I had fun and I would do anything for my girls," Celeste said.

Yasmeen came out of the restroom and returned to her seat. "Sorry I stormed off," she said. "I—I think I might have feelings for P—Darryl or I wouldn't be insulted when you all are just speaking the truth."

"Of course you have feelings," Toni said. "You're not the kind who can do hook-ups or flings."

Celeste's heart warmed. "Aw. I didn't know you had feelings for him. I'll be mindful of what I say in the future. You could be a good influence on him," she added to be supportive, though she wasn't sure Darryl wasn't just using her friend. "And I'm sorry if I came off catty."

"And just like that, we're peas and carrots again," Toni joked.

"Yes, that's why I am going to open this when you both are here." Celeste inhaled and picked up the envelope. She slipped her finger under the flap and tore it open. Surrounded by her friends, she read the petition of dissolution for the end of her marriage. Wade had been generous, a sign he was ready to move on and close this era of his life. He had also returned the house key.

When she was done reading, Toni said, "You have thirty days to respond. What do you plan to do?"

Celeste didn't hesitate. "Fight."

"Messing around with you is going to make us miss the opera," Wade said, giving her a wink. "Not that I have regrets. But this is the last night Blue *is playing." They were on their way to the Kennedy Center in Washington, DC, and were on Highway 50, about 27 miles from the Chesapeake Bay Bridge.*

A yellow light loomed ahead. Wade pressed on the gas.

Celeste placed a hand on his chest. Her diamond ring, a gift for their tenth wedding anniversary, flashed in the glimmer of moonlight. "Slow down, honey. We'll make it." Still, he kept going. Her stomach muscles clenched and her body raised up off the seat as they approached a yellow traffic light. "Wade, stop. Please."

A second before the light turned red, a car swerved over into their lane. With a grunt, Wade slammed on the brakes, his tires skidding on the sleek, wet road at the intersection.

"It's okay. It's okay." Wade gripped the wheel and moved into the slide with the car. Celeste's chest heaved and she hunched her shoulders, preparing for impact.

Screech. Swerve.

She gritted her teeth, her right foot pressing the imaginary brake.

The car came to a stop, inches away from the back bumper of the vehicle in front. Whew. Impact avoided. She released short staccato breaths of relief. From the corner of her eye, she saw Wade relax his shoulders. "Wow. That was close." She fanned her face. "Slow down. I don't want to see the show that bad."

He grinned. "I got skills, babe," he said, then waggled his eyebrows, "and not just in the bedroom."

Celeste touched her hair, which had been up in a neat bun. "Testify."

They shared smiles and joined hands.

That's when they heard a loud rap on her window. Celeste turned, her mouth popping open when she saw the barrel of a gun.

It was her scream that jolted her into consciousness. Awake, Celeste bounced to a sitting position, hand on her heaving chest, hair damp on her face. She struggled to catch her breath, her legs twisted in the sheets. *It isn't real. It isn't real.*

Inhale. Exhale. Inhale. Exhale.

The clock beside her said 3:28 a.m. Celeste sighed as her eyes adjusted to the dark room, with shimmers of light from the moon, and the empty bed next to her. Normally, when she had her nightmares, she would snuggle against Wade, his presence soothing her to sleep. Now on her own, she knew there was no way she would go back to sleep.

Untangling from the sheets, Celeste made her way downstairs to put the kettle on, the kitchen floor cool under her feet. She needed to soothe her insides with a cup of the chamomile-and-lavender tea Yasmeen had gifted her a few months back. She plopped the tea bag into a cup with a couple sugars. While she waited for the water to boil, Celeste went to adjust the thermostat.

The sing of the kettle amplified the night sounds of crickets outside her kitchen window. She padded back into the kitchen to finish preparing her cup of tea. Her stomach rumbled, reminding her that she hadn't been able to eat after receiving the divorce papers. She cut a small slice of cinnamon bun fetched from her bread box.

Settled at her kitchen table, she'd picked up the bun to take a bite when her eyes fell on the divorce papers propped on top of their book of the month, and she dropped the treat back on her plate. Talk about an appetite suppresser. Never had she imagined this would be her life. And it wouldn't be if she had her way.

Ugh. That brown manila envelope was an eyesore. She was so tempted to toss it in the fireplace. Then a thought occurred. Grabbing the envelope, she snatched out the contents and ripped them in half. What a satisfying sound. Her heart lightened. She would put those in the mail for Wade later that morning.

Dropping them on the table, she crossed her legs, sipped her tea and read until the sun rose on a beautiful new day.

Toni

JANUARY 26

"Is everything alright with you?" Kent asked, using his knife to cut a slice of avocado to eat with his omelet.

"Yes, why do you keep asking me that, babe?" Toni bent her head and sliced into her Belgian waffle to keep him from seeing the irritation she knew had to be etched on her face.

They were seated at a local diner, in an alcove that provided her some measure of privacy. Kent had invited her to breakfast in a public place. He had interpreted her running off the week before to mean that Toni was dedicated to keep their vow to abstain before marriage. Toni wasn't about to correct that notion. But she had been on edge thinking about seeing Skins again after all these years. She had trailed off during conversations with Kent and he had had to repeat himself several times. And at their cake testing, she had excused herself several times because of the text messages. As a result, Kent was what he called *concerned*, and what she characterized as…clingy.

"You're not acting like yourself." He moved to touch her shoulder and she jumped. "That's what I mean. It's like you don't want me to touch you."

It was the pain in his voice that made her eyes connect with his. They both stopped eating. Toni pushed her plate to the side.

"That's not true," she said. "You know you're the man for me. The only man. I show you in so many different ways how I feel about you." Just that morning, she had given him a mustard sweater—which he was currently wearing. "I love giving you gifts."

He nodded. "I'm not questioning your loyalty or your generosity, but I do believe you're hiding something."

Dang. Her man was perceptive. Yasmeen's and Celeste's advice came back to her. Maybe she did need to tell him about the infertility. Naw. She would wait until she had her second opinion. Her appointment was a little over a week away. She could hold out until then. If the results came back the same, she would have to tell him.

Toni flailed her hands. "Of course I'm hiding something. I'm planning a wedding of epic proportions. I think I have found the dress and decided on the color scheme. Lilac-and-cream will be all the rage once I'm done."

"Don't… Just don't. I'm not buying any of that." Kent leaned deeper into the booth and observed her.

"Don't what?" Her heart beat faster in her chest.

"Don't patronize me or treat me like one of your viewers. Tell me what's on your mind. I know you. Something is eating you up on the inside. I've tried to give you space to sort it out but… Now I need to know."

She raised her brows. Seeing Kent's stern face, Toni knew she had to give him something. She slumped her shoulders and decided to voice a different truth in the hopes that would satisfy him. "I know I chose this life and I make money being in the spotlight, but it comes with serious baggage. Sometimes it can be a heavy lift. I have to look perfect, be perfect all the time, and frankly, it's exhausting." Her body went limp at her words. "I can't just enjoy my wedding. I have to think about my followers and my sponsors."

"We can do a private ceremony," he said.

She paused for a beat. "No. I can't have that. I have to live stream. I need my haters to see me winning at life."

"Be serious." Kent reached across to take her hand. "I don't need you to be perfect," he said. "I just need you to be your authentic self, and I don't want you treating me like your audience. You don't have to put on a show for me or keep your true feelings to yourself. I am in love with you. I want to spend my life with you. Not a plastic doll."

His earnest words made her eyes moisten. "Ditto. But I only want you to see the best of me." And she had made sure he had. Her hair, nails, makeup were always done, even during her workouts.

"I get that, and I'm not saying you shouldn't look good on the outside, but I'm concerned about the woman underneath. I want you to know the love I have for you isn't based on anything superficial. When your hair is thinned and your teeth are falling out and you have to get a full set of mouth dentures, I'm still going to love you."

"See now? That's why they have hair extensions—" she tapped her teeth "—and caps. You won't see none of that."

He chuckled. "Whatever. You get the point." He returned to his meal and she did the same. "There's no fighting the aging process, so I plan to embrace us growing older together." Kent gave a look filled with desire. "And I'm always going to find you the most beautiful woman in Delaware."

"Just Delaware?"

"Well, I can't say the world because I haven't seen all the women in the world and I don't want to tell a lie."

Toni cracked up, tossing her napkin at him. "I can't win with you."

"I'm glad we spoke. I feel better."

"Good. So does that mean you're going to stop watching me like a hawk and get back to work?"

He nodded. "Yes, I rescheduled my day to make sure you were okay."

Her heart squeezed. "See, it's stuff like that which makes me fall for you more each day. By the way, did you decide on the cake flavor? We tried the lemon, the strawberry and the vanilla, but I couldn't tell your preference."

"I'm good with whatever you decide." Kent stood and kissed her flush on the lips before making her scoot over so he could sit next to her. "I can't wait to show you how much I love you."

His words fanned her heat. Their arms touched, electricity pulsing through them. It was a good thing they were in public because, baby, she was ready. "Yes, me too. Let the countdown begin."

He put the last of his omelet into that fine mouth of his before leaning over to whisper in her ear. "You know what else I can't wait for?" His deep voice drummed through her body.

"What?" she asked, breathy, and not a little turned-on. Toni took a sip of water to cool down.

"Seeing your stomach swell with our child."

She spewed the contents out of her mouth.

Later that afternoon, with Kent leaving for work, Toni jumped on the highway, heading to her appointment with Skins, or what she called a high-class shakedown.

The dealership—a ratty joint, as ratty as Skins—was one town over, which suited her fine. She didn't need someone from Kent's job spotting her and getting word back to him. Toni couldn't wait to confront the man who had sprung from her past to mess with this mighty good life she had going on. Kent thought she was going to visit Leslie, and she was, just not right away.

Once again, guilt at her dishonesty engulfed her, but after this evening, she could go back to her life as it now was.

Toni sped past a huge building with a For Rent sign and stomped on the brakes, ignoring the screech and the honk of the drivers behind her. She pulled off to the side and jumped out of her Mustang, forgetting her coat on the passenger side. Shivering, she released short, puffy breaths and wrapped her arms about her. Dang, it was ridiculously cold out here. Holding her hand across her forehead to shield her eyes from the setting sun, Toni tilted her head and scanned the two-story brick structure with wide-open windows. If she remembered right, this used to be a pharmacy and then a flower shop. Toni bounced back and forth and blew into her palms. Angling her phone, she snapped a pic, then sent it to the group chat.

Isn't this perfect?

While she waited for the others to chime in, Toni called the phone number on the sign and asked about the cost and when she could see the space.

Celeste was the first to respond.

Whoa. Yes it is.

Me likey, Yasmeen added.

Leslie asked, When can we get a tour? Is it available?

Toni answered the most important question. I made an appointment for early next month since the owner is out of town

and they are working on renovating the building. We can carpool in Yasmeen's truck.

She squealed and popped back into her car, turning up the
heat. This was going to be their spot. She knew it.

Just before she drove off, Toni realized that was the same date
she had her appointment. She sent another text to her friends.

My appointment with the OB-GYN is that morning. How about
we make a day of it?

Might as well have our book club meeting then too, Celeste
suggested.

Toni remained on a high about that location and the space
until she arrived at the dealership. It was on a corner lot and
the streetlights flickered like they could go out at any second.
She noticed the sign was tilted and on the verge of collapse.
There were a few cars in the lot, and the sign boasted that everyone would drive, even those with no credit. Getting out
of her car, she peered at the listing of one of the vehicles and
shook her head.

Everyone would drive, but the interest rate was double the
norm and worse, there was no warranty. The interior of the car
was littered with beer bottles and there was a huge crack in the
windshield. Legal robbery, in her opinion. Her car had a zero
balance and an amazing warranty package, thanks to the engagement gift from her honey. Even though she told him she
could afford to buy her own, he had insisted.

She picked her way across the gravel lot. She had made a dire
mistake, choosing to wear six-inch stilettos, but she wanted to
tower over Skins, who was her height without heels. But one
smart thing she had done was to put away her engagement ring.
Toni wasn't taking anything for granted.

The door was slightly ajar and the interior dark. She gave
it a light push, the accompanying creak loud in the otherwise

quiet evening. She stepped inside and called out, wrinkling her nose at the smell of herbs, and taking in the chipped off-white paint, the dingy furnishings and the rug black with dirt. There was a water fountain and a cup dispenser, but she knew her lips wouldn't touch anything in this place. She saw a shadow approach, and seconds later, Toni found herself facing her nemesis, her blast from the past.

"Well, look who it is," Skins said, coming over with his arms opened wide. He was thinner than she remembered and dressed in a T-shirt and jeans, despite the weather. His arms were covered with tattoos and there was one of a snake roped around his neck.

She looked around him, hoping to see another person. The owner. A witness.

She averted the embrace and folded her arms. "Hello, Skins. I see our justice system is failing since you're not behind bars."

He tilted his head to lock eyes with her. He had tensed at her words, and for a second, Toni wondered if he was going to get physical, but he relaxed and tapped her arm. "As I said, I go by Lamont now. And to answer your question, I got released early because the real perpetrator confessed."

"You'll always be Skins to me. And more like, some poor man you threatened took the fall," she scoffed.

His eyes narrowed to slits. "The justice system failed me and I'm seeking litigation so I can be compensated for my wrongful conviction."

"*Litigation. Compensated.*" Her eyebrows rose. "Nice five-dollar words. Too bad you're as guilty as sin." Toni knew it was risky taunting such a dangerous man, but she had to make him think she wasn't afraid. Though her insides quaked.

Skins chuckled. "I'm not falling for your bluff. You're trying to goad my temper and possibly get me arrested." He stepped into her face, his breath smelling of marijuana. "I'm not falling for it." He averted his eyes. "I'm a changed man."

"You're still the same snake," she said. "Blackmailing me."

"Blackmail?" He lifted a hand. "Read my messages. Money was never mentioned."

"No, but it was implied. I know you."

"If you choose to help me get back on my feet since my release, I'd be most grateful, but I am not threatening you in any way."

He was so oily. So grimy. She suppressed a shudder. "Fine, have it your way. I can see coming here was a mistake." Toni spun around and headed for the exit, but Skins was faster than she was. A wiry hand slammed the door shut, sandwiching her against it. The hair on her arms rose. Her heart rate escalated and her chest heaved. "Move your hand," she commanded.

"Don't go ruining our peaceful reunion," he said, leaning close and whispering in her ear.

"Get away from me," she said through gritted teeth. He gripped her shoulders and turned her to face him.

Skins's eyes were filled with fury. "You killed our child. You're constantly talking about wanting to experience motherhood. I watched the video where you opened packages from sponsors with gifts for your little one when it comes. Rambling on about how excited you are to start trying for your first. How touching. Imagine the scorn you'll face if they learn the truth."

Toni's mouth dropped. "You made me get an abortion. You took me to a shady doctor and I almost died. I was a child myself and I refuse to feel guilty for a choice I made years ago. I'm free from all that. That's my private business, but if you decide you want to tell the world, go right ahead." She would need to tell Kent and her friends first, though, because they would be hurt that she hadn't confided in them.

"Oh, confident, are we?" He changed tactics. "I wonder what would happen if your fan base learned you are nothing but a thief, pretending to be something you're not. You were the driver for the getaway car, driving without a license. I wonder what that would do for your squeaky image if that got out?"

His words slashed her gut. She curled her fists, itching to slap his face. Her eyes were wet. "You claimed you were teaching me to drive. I didn't know what you planned when you went into the laundromat."

"No one will believe that. You knew who I was, yet you dated me." He gave her a cunning look. "Did you know the owner died of a heart attack after that robbery? I learned about that after I got arrested and they tried to pin her death on me."

"N-No, I didn't..."

"I did eighteen months for that and I didn't rat you out."

She swallowed the bitter taste of that truth. "You would have gotten more time if they knew you had brought a minor to help with your crimes. This is all about you wanting to control me, like you did when I didn't know better."

"No, this is about your hypocrisy, Antoinette," he snarled. Her shoulders slumped. Skins was right. She was a hypocrite. She could see the swirl of her image, her wealth, her relationship flushing down the drain. After all her hard work. One post could bring her down. The very source of her wealth could be her demise.

She blinked to keep from breaking apart. She wouldn't give Skins the satisfaction. "What do you want?" Her voice trembled.

"A small portion of what you have. You won't even miss it."

"And what if I say no?"

"Then, prepare to see your reputation tarnished and all you have worked for blown to smithereens. Like they say, the truth shall set you free." He tapped his chin. "I wonder what your fiancé would say if he learned who you really are? You think he's going to stay with you after what you've done? Does he even know your real name?"

"K-Kent loves me," she said, hating how her voice was tinged with doubt.

Skins cackled. "That's because he's in love with your image. He doesn't know the real you and what you're capable of."

His words punctured her confidence, deflating her complete certainty in Kent's devotion. She took several seconds to study the man who could have been the father of her child, feeling a mixture of regret and relief. Regret that she hadn't listened to her parents' warnings and relief that she didn't have a permanent tie to him.

Toni shook her head. "You're the sorriest excuse of a human being I have ever met. I've got to get out of here." She spun on her heels, and this time, Skins didn't stop her. She opened the door, welcoming the cool air, the freedom.

"I'll be waiting to hear from you," he yelled out from behind, sounding cocky and sure.

Toni rushed to her car, not caring about the laughter trailing behind her. She slammed her door and sped out of the lot, her tires squealing in the otherwise quiet night. She wasn't going to give him any money. He would be a parasite for life. But if she didn't...he could destroy her relationship and end her career.

It's best that she paid him, but she had left without finding out how much the sleazebag wanted. Just as she pulled into the main entrance of the hospital, she had her answer. Skins had sent a number to her inbox, carefully phrased.

Have you ever heard of the show *A Million Little Things*?

She gasped.

One million dollars.

A price she had no idea how she would ever pay.

19

Leslie

JANUARY 26

"Oh, Toni, I'm so sorry to hear about your infertility," Leslie whispered, squeezing Toni's hand. They were seated together in Nadya's room and Toni had filled her in while her daughter slept. "I completely understand that kind of pain, but you'll get through it. Kent is a good man. He'll understand."

"He's dreaming of me carrying his child." Toni leaned against the wall and closed her eyes, her tone so sorrowful that Leslie's heart squeezed. "That's why I can't tell him."

"That's why you must. Level with him now," she said, the memory of Edwin's deceit making her voice harsher than she intended. She twirled her pearl bracelet. "Don't wait too long because the truth is a bitter pill and time won't make it any easier to swallow."

Toni's eyes popped open. "How's things with your dad?"

"I'm that obvious, huh?"

"Yep."

Leslie gestured to the door, and the women walked out of the room. She didn't want to chance Nadya waking up and over-hearing their conversation. Once they were in the hallway, they gravitated to the nearest wall, so they weren't in the way of the nurses, doctors and patients. She sighed. "I don't have much to say to him. But I met with the detective, Rick Brown, and he sounds confident he'll be able to find my family."

Toni rocked back on her heels. "Are you ready for that?"

"If by *ready*, you mean do I hope that my biological parents will be a match for my daughter, then yes, I am ready."

A brow arched. "Snarky, much?"

"Sorry. I don't mean to be testy." Leslie played with the fringes on her sweater.

"What I meant was, are you ready for the emotional load that comes with finding your bio fam? Do you think you can handle all that?"

What was up with everyone asking about how she was going to feel? Her dad, Aaron and now Toni. This was about Nadya. This wasn't about her. Yes, there was a small part of her who wanted the-man-she-called-Daddy-but-who-technically-wasn't to suffer, but as each day passed with her daughter being un-well, she just needed Nadya better. "I will have to be," she said.

"What if your birth parents want nothing to do with you?"

She hadn't considered that. For a second, doubt filled her chest, but then she thought of Nadya. "I can't let that stop me," she whispered. "This is my child's life we're talking about." Her voice held an edge. "If they refuse to help an innocent child, their grandchild, then that would be it for me. I'd be done with them for life." She exhaled. "But hopefully, it won't come to that."

"And do you plan to tell Nadya any of this?"

"Oof." She rubbed her cheek before shaking her head. "Yeah, probably not a good idea. Too much for her to process."

Toni lifted a brow. "Humph. Imagine that. Not telling your child something because you're not sure of how they might react."

Leslie pursed her lips. She knew exactly what Toni was saying. "Whatever. This is different. This isn't a pot-kettle-black thing. Daddy had ample opportunities to tell me when I was no longer a child. And the fact is he hadn't planned to if this hadn't come up."

"Maybe he had his reasons…" Hmm… Sounded like Toni was talking about herself.

"No. No. No." She would stomp her foot if it wouldn't make it seem like she was having a temper tantrum. "You need to 'fess up to Kent before you walk down that aisle. I'm not going to let that man get married under false pretenses."

Toni rolled her neck back and forth. "You wouldn't. I wish you would tell him. You need to mind the business you get paid for and stay out of mine."

"Well, if you can't handle my opinion, then keep your trap closed." Had she just snapped off at her friend? A friend whose eyes had gone glacial. Leslie backed up and drew in deep breaths. The tension between them was as tight as a guitar string.

"I'm going to pretend I didn't hear you say that because I know we are both stressed right now," Toni said, "but you'd better stop writing checks with that smart mouth of yours if your butt ain't ready to cash 'em. I know I'm grown, but I'm not beyond taking out my earrings and going old-school on your behind."

"Duly noted," Leslie said, before she cracked up. "Girl, I know I'm tripping, but you sounded like you were straight outta Philly just now and not from downtown Delaware." She snickered. "Can you imagine us fighting like a bunch of reality housewives?"

Toni relaxed her shoulders and tapped her head. "Nope. I

paid too much for this weave. Besides, you're my sister from another mister."

The two friends hugged it out.

"Where's Aaron?" Toni asked.

Leslie's comeback was quick. "I don't even know and I don't really care."

Toni frowned. "Everything alright with you two? You can't be fighting with the two most important men in your life."

All Leslie could do was shrug. "He's been here with Nadya most days. And when he's not here, he's working late at night. We're like two ships sailing in opposite directions and I've got too much on my mind to care."

"Whoa. Is that what marriage is going to be like for me a few years from now?"

She lifted her shoulders. "I can't say what happened. But it's like you're going and going, floating in this sea called complacency—and I'm not sure why I'm giving these water analogies—but then you wake up one morning to an empty bed, and you realize, meh, you don't care too much. As long as the bills are paid, you're fine with the status quo. Just don't rock the boat and we're good."

"Oh, Leslie, that's sad."

"Pshaw. Don't feel sorry for me. I have enough on my mind." Her voice caught. She hated the tears misting her eyes. When she wasn't thinking about Nadya, Aaron was on her mind. She had called his office the night before, where he'd said he would be, and he hadn't answered. But when she texted, he said he was out with a client. She didn't have the mental bandwidth to process what that could mean. She had refused to entertain scenarios and what-ifs. Her marriage was some sad song that she didn't want to listen to anymore.

Toni placed a hand on her arm. "Just know I am here if you need me." Her sympathetic tone was almost Leslie's undoing.

She cleared her throat. "Same." Right as they turned to head back into Nadya's room, her cell phone rang and she eyed the screen with amazement. "It's the detective."

"Already?" Toni shot out. "Pick it up."

"Rick?" she said, after pressing the answer button.

"Hello, Leslie. I've got an update for you. Turns out both your parents are alive and right here in Delaware."

She exhaled. Her parents had lived in this state the whole time while she had been living her life, clueless. That didn't sit well with her. Did her father know that?

"Oh snap," Toni said. "That was fast." She signaled to Leslie that she was going to check on Nadya, and all Leslie could do was nod.

"H-How did you…?" She trailed off. Her heart was beating as fast as a woodpecker on a pine tree.

"Where should we meet up?"

"Ugh. I'll meet you in the parking lot here at the hospital," she stammered out.

"I'm working another case here, so I can be there in about fifteen minutes."

In fifteen minutes, she would have the names and addresses of her biological parents. The people who had given her up. She pictured two teens, young and in love, who had been too immature to have a child, been forced to give her up and carried that guilt for all their lives.

Her hands shook and she darted into the nearby bathroom and into a clean, empty stall. Closing the door, Leslie released short, staccato breaths. She felt sweaty. Sitting on the lid of the toilet seat, she texted the friends group.

I need you all here with me. Got news about my folks.

Then she thought about her husband. She probably should call him, let him know. But when she did, she got his voicemail once more.

Celeste was the first to answer. Wow. Can someone pick me up?
I got you. That was from Yasmeen.

Using toilet paper, she wiped her neck and under her arms.
At the same time, the small space tightened around her. She
needed air. She exited the stall and washed her hands. Daring
to look in the mirror, Leslie gave herself a pep talk. "Don't
chicken out now. Think of what this means for Nadya." She
scuttled into the room to get her coat and made her way toward the entrance. She hovered by the door until she saw Rick
pull up. Then she huddled under her coat and raced outside.

He rolled down the windows and they completed the exchange. She gave him the certified check for the balance and
he gave her the documents.

"Good doing business with you," she said, her breath releasing in short puffs. She had forgotten her cap inside, and her
ears were burning.

"Likewise." Then, with a rev of the engine, he was gone. She
stood there, clutching the brown manila envelope, she wasn't
sure how long, until she saw Yasmeen's truck turn into the lot.
Gosh, that truck was ritzy, with the fancy wheels and all that.
She thought it was way too pricey and ostentatious, but if she
said anything, she was pretty sure Yasmeen would think she
was being jealous or catty.

Her lips quivered. The wind chill made it feel like it was
minus-six degrees but she waited for her girls to make their
way to her side.

Celeste's cheeks looked apple red and Yasmeen was blowing on her hands.

"It's freezing out here," Yasmeen said. "Thankfully, the roads
aren't icy."

"Only for you," Celeste said, opening her arms. Celeste's face
appeared gaunt and she had dark circles around her eyes. Leslie
couldn't imagine what it must have felt like getting served like
that. She thought of her own marriage. Shoot, she might end

up in the same yacht as Celeste. No way were they going out in a simple boat.

They huddled together, the envelope folding between them. Surrounded by her friends, she knew no matter what the news was, she would be alright. Her cell buzzed and Leslie broke the embrace. "Let's go," she huffed out. "I bet that's Toni wondering where we are."

"Yup."

They went into the building and made their way to the same waiting area where Yasmeen had heard about her lottery win. Toni was already inside. The room felt toasty, and the dim lighting made it a soothing backdrop to calm her nerves.

"Hey, did you move into your house yet?" Leslie asked Yasmeen, taking off her long coat.

"Soon," she said. "I had to get some repairs done. I'm staying in a hotel in the meantime."

Yasmeen shrugged out of her coat.

"How did your folks react when they heard you won the lottery?" she asked.

Toni smirked. "She hasn't told them yet."

Yasmeen rolled her eyes. "I plan to. Tonight."

"So, your parents aren't wondering where you've been staying?" Leslie had to know though she could see Yasmeen wasn't feeling this conversation.

"I told them I was hanging with one of you guys," Yasmeen muttered.

"Yep. She's fibbing to the pastor," Toni joked.

"Leave her alone," Celeste chided, giving Toni a light jab. She also had taken off her coat and held it in her hand. "Yeah, what Celeste said," Yasmeen mumbled. "Besides, we're not here about me. We're here for Leslie."

They sat close together, knees touching. "You don't know what it means to me to have my girls with me." Squaring her shoulders, she slid her finger under the flap to open it. She pulled out a photo, placed the envelope on the chair next to her and gasped. A diminutive woman, the image of Leslie in the future, stared back at her. Only her eyes were brown and her hair a shade darker. "Wow. She looks like me."

Despite the heat, she felt chilled. Dropping the picture in her lap, she rubbed her arms. The woman was leaning into a tall, burly man. Leslie bent her head. Wait. Was that man her father? He had green eyes and thick blond locks, both the exact hue as Leslie's. "I have his eyes and hair," she whispered. "This is my father. My parents are together." Waves of sadness, happiness, outrage washed over her, engulfing her under their crescendo.

She leaned into Celeste's shoulder, the first tear rolling down her face, with many more to follow. She sucked in her cheeks, but there was no holding her sobs at bay. "I...I didn't know... it would feel like...this." She hiccupped.

Toni snatched the photo up to examine it before passing it around. She could make out their head nods through her blurry gaze. Celeste reached for the manila envelope and withdrew the other papers.

"There's a birth certificate and an address." Celeste dangled it before Leslie's face.

Curiosity won. Leslie raised her head.

Toni dug around in her bag and pulled out tissues and hand sanitizer.

"Thanks." Leslie cleaned herself up and then took the paper. "Their names are Henry and Julie Johansen. They are still very much together." She scoffed to cover the tornado of hurt in her heart. "Johansen. Could you picture me as Leslie Johansen? It sounds weird, right?" Leslie squinted. "Wait, it says here they named me Louisa. Louisa Johansen. Nope, it doesn't gel with me."

"Louisa?" Yasmeen chuckled. "It's a good thing you were adopted."

"Bad taste," Celeste said, running her hands through her strands.

Leslie rubbed her eyes. "And look at the address. That's about forty-five minutes away from me." She shot to her feet and her friends did the same. "I've got to go see them." She grabbed her cell phone and texted Aaron to see if he would be able to leave work early to sit with Nadya, telling him she had found her birth parents. His response was immediate.

I will be there.

Her stomach muscles relaxed. She hadn't realized she'd been unsure of his availability—or that he'd even respond—until then.

"You want to go now?" Toni asked, jutting into Leslie's thoughts. When Leslie nodded, she countered with, "Not a good idea."

"Yes, let's make it a road trip," Yasmeen said.

"Why not now?" Leslie shot back. "I have an ill child. Their grandchild. Henry and Julie Johansen need to know that."

"You can go tomorrow," Celeste offered. "Or see if Aaron might want to go with you. Slow down a little."

"Slow down?" Leslie held up the birth certificate. "I have so many questions. I—I need to know. I..." She picked up the photograph. Judging by their outfits, the Johansens appeared to be upper middle class. Maybe they hadn't been the struggling youngsters she pictured. Resentment built in her chest. "I need to ask them why they gave me away." Yes, she deserved to know that.

"Do you really want to go there?" Yasmeen asked. "I wouldn't dig up past history. Just keep it about Nadya for now."

"We can feed two birds with the same seed," Leslie said.

"What?" Toni scrunched her nose.

"I'm not trying to kill birds with a stone," she said, flailing her hands. "It's cruel. But meeting them could serve a dual purpose."

"I actually agree with Yasmeen," Celeste said. "You can get all the answers after they're tested as potential donors."

"Agreed." Leslie dipped her head.

Toni sucked in a breath.

"What is it?" Yasmeen asked.

"Do you realize the current upheaval in each of our lives could be summed up in four little words?" She looked at Celeste, "You're getting a divorce," then Yasmeen, "You won the lottery," and Leslie, "Edwin's not your father," before pointing to herself, "and I can't have children."

The four women went silent for a beat.

Then Yasmeen busted out laughing. "That's wack. Go back to the drawing board with that one. Because this money is nothing but blessings for me." She retrieved her wallet from her purse and took out a wad of hundred dollar bills. "Blessings, blessings and more blessings. So speak for yourself."

"You ever heard of mo' money, mo' problems?" Toni shot back.

Toni and Yasmeen volleyed insults, cracking up as they did. Leslie tuned them out and picked up the photo. She wandered to the corner of the room. Henry and Julie Johansen. Were they together all these years? Or, did they get back together later in life?

She had all these questions, and these two people smiling in the photo were the ones with the answers. If they had gone on with their lives without her, happy, successful, then her truth was she hadn't been given away for adoption for her own good. She sniffled. She had been given away because they didn't want her.

20

Yasmeen

JANUARY 26

Since her friends were busy discussing Leslie's feelings of abandonment during their excursion out to the Johansens' home, Yasmeen concentrated on driving, and thinking. For most of the way, they would be on US 1, Delaware's main highway. She let the conversations carry on around her, because every time she opened her mouth of late, she came off trite and insensitive.

"Why are you so quiet?" Toni asked, interrupting her thoughts. She was sitting in the front passenger seat, with Leslie behind Yasmeen and Celeste behind Toni, as she had been before.

"Just contemplating my next move," Yasmeen said, keeping it vague.

"If you're thinking about telling your parents about your

lottery win, I think they are going to be grateful you're able to help them now."

"I hope so," she said. "I doubt they will leave that apartment building, but I plan to ask them to move in with me. They've been there twenty years. If they won't come with me, I can pay up their rent for two years and see if the landlord will move them into a first-floor apartment. That's one way I'll be putting this money to good use."

"I think that's a good call," Celeste said.

"I'm glad you approve." Yasmeen chuckled. "Because I felt the heat of your glare when I paid close to a million for my house."

"That house is a good investment," Toni chimed in. "A house usually appreciates in value over time. At least you can see where your money went."

"I'm not mad at you," Celeste said, "but I do think you would have been just as fine going with the smaller home that was half that price. I just don't want you spending and spending without consulting a financial advisor to help you manage your funds. Plus, don't forget you'll have property taxes to pay. You should think about investing some of that money so you can live off residual income."

Yasmeen nodded. "I will. To tell you the truth, I've had close to nothing for so long, it's great not to juggle and skimp and count pennies. Literal pennies. Now look at me. I'm giving rides instead of begging for them. Won't He do it?" She shook her head, her hair swaying. She had taken out the cornrows and now her natural curls popped. She should be able to rock this look for at least a week— Well, if the cold held out and it didn't rain.

"So what kind of repairs are you having done to your place?" Leslie asked.

"I had to get a new HVAC and pipes put in. The new flooring should be finished in a couple days. Then once my furniture is delivered, I'll finally have a place of my own. Bought and paid for in cash. So you know I'll be throwing a housewarming. It will be the four of us and my parents, if they want to come."

"I'm curious how you've kept your other purchases like this car, your coat, your clothes from your parents though," Leslie said.

"I told them I caught some great finds at Goodwill as far as clothes. And they think I borrowed this truck from a friend." She hunched her shoulders, hating how sheepish she sounded. "I don't want them thinking I'm dating a drug lord or something."

"Are you serious?" Toni said. "Girl, you're acting like you're some freshman in high school."

"That's it. Make sure you tell them today like you said," Leslie demanded, her tone sharp. "All this lying and subterfuge from everyone around me is giving me hives."

Toni cleared her throat. "Since we're all together, can we change the subject for a minute? I want to talk about the bookstore. I consulted with my photographer, and Joe can fit us in on the weekend. I'm waiting on the bios to get posted, but if you type in our store name, you should see our website pop up."

"Cool," Leslie said. "I'll get my bio done now and text it to you. I'm sorry I haven't been as active but—"

"Stop apologizing," Yasmeen said. "We got you."

"This looks so professional," Celeste said. "I'm impressed. I need to start on the book orders. I cleared out my garage so we can use that space until we get a place." Yasmeen stole a glance in her rearview mirror. Celeste was swiping away at her phone placed on her lap, her other hand squeezing the stress ball. She didn't seem to notice it was getting dark and they had stopped at a couple red lights. Yasmeen's heart moved. Celeste's love for her friends was bigger than her fear.

"I'll send you the book order, Celeste." Just then, her cell phone rang through the car's speaker system. It was Darryl. Great. She really didn't want to talk to him with all these ears in the truck. Though she knew she would regret it, she accepted the call.

"Hey, thanks for bailing me out," he drawled. "Although it would've been nice if you had been there to give me a ride home."

From her peripheral, she saw Toni cover her mouth with her hand and she heard Leslie's shocked gasps. Yup. Should not have answered.

"He was in jail?" Leslie asked, evidently not caring if Darryl heard and sounding slightly distracted. Yasmeen figured she was working on her bio for Toni. "You need to leave that loser."

"I can hear you," Darryl said, his tone dry.

"Yes, I've my girls with me." Yasmeen hoped he would see that as a hint that they would talk later. But this was Darryl.

"Hello, ladies." He dragged the word out, his voice sounding melodic. Her traitorous body quivered on the inside. It had been a minute since they had gotten together.

"I'll call you back later," Yasmeen said, her thumb over the end-call icon.

"No, no, wait. I need a loan," he said. It was like he could sniff when she had a few extra dollars, because there he was, asking for a handout.

Toni snickered and Celeste uttered an, "Oh my."

Since she hadn't told him about her fortune, she asked, "What makes you think I have any money to give you?"

"Someone told me they saw you driving some fancy truck, so between that and you bailing me out, I figured you came into some extra cash and thought it wouldn't hurt to ask. 'You have not 'cause you ask not,' is my motto."

"Actually, it's my daddy's favorite saying and James from the Bible said it first."

"Whatever, you get my drift." He chuckled. Again, that voice. Her insides. But his next words dried up that loving feeling. "I have to pay back this dude I owe or it's my head."

Fear knotted her gut. Yasmeen knew she had to let this man go, no matter how she felt, no matter how good he was at curling her toes and making her squeal. She had to stop thinking with her nether regions and believe he was the user he had consistently shown her he was.

And he wasn't done. "Wait, you didn't go ahead and replace me, did you? That would be messed up to do while I was incarcerated."

"While I was incarcerated," Toni echoed. "This brother is a trip."

"A hot, greasy mess," Celeste added.

"Can I talk to my woman without the Upper Crust Crew chiming in?" he asked.

All Yasmeen could do was shake her head. Her friends were telling nothing but the truth, but her heart refused to accept it. She kept hoping and hoping...

"There, I'm finished," Leslie announced from the back seat. "I just sent my bio to you, Toni."

Toni nodded. "Great. I'll check it out."

"I don't have any money to give you, Darryl," she said loudly, above her friends' chatter. Being with her girls bolstered her to do what she needed to do, what she should have done long ago, despite her disagreeable heart. "You know what, don't call me again. I'm done with you. All you do is ask for a handout, and I'm through. You got locked up, and instead of staying far from these so-called friends, you're right back in the thick of it."

Her friends did a happy dance and Toni thumped her on the shoulder. "You go, girl."

"No, no, you don't understand," he said. "I'm trying to get into culinary school. I do want to change. I just need help."

She felt herself caving and bit on her lower lip. Maybe she could help him one last time.

"Don't back down," Toni said.

"Don't listen to them," Darryl said. "Don't let anyone stop you from being the generous person you are."

"Please, that's in-your-face manipulation," Celeste said. "Yasmeen, it's time to stop buying what he's selling, because it's rotten to the core."

She straightened and gripped the wheel, making up her mind. "I'm done with you. For good. Lose my number." Then she pressed the end button. The navigation system told her to make a right turn. The Johansens were eight minutes away. Eight minutes until Leslie would meet the people responsible for her being in this world.

The women quieted.

"We're so close now," Leslie said, her voice sounding tight. "Guys, I'm nervous. Maybe this wasn't the best move."

Seeing a chain pharmacy, Yasmeen pulled over into the parking lot. She put the car in Park and turned to face Leslie. "It's okay to change your mind. Just say the word and we can go back home."

Leslie nodded, her hands tented in her lap as she fidgeted in her seat.

"This isn't just about Leslie though," Toni said. "It's about Nadya's health."

"Unlock the door," Leslie said. "I need a second to breathe."

Yasmeen complied and Leslie jumped outside. She started to pace and it looked like she was talking to herself.

"Man, it's freezing out there. One of us had better go join her," Toni mumbled.

"I'll go," Celeste said. "I need to stretch my legs."

Toni's cell phone pinged with a message that captured her attention. Yasmeen figured it must be Kent checking on her. See, she needed a man like that. One who reached out to her just because, and not because he needed to mooch off her.

Leslie and Celeste scurried back to the car.

"The cold got to you, huh?" she asked, driving out of the lot and back to their route.

"Ugh. I feel nauseous," Leslie said instead of answering her question. "What if they turn me away?"

"Don't throw up in here, please," Yasmeen screeched. "Give me notice so I can pull over again."

"Do you need us to come in with you?" Toni asked. Yasmeen gave Toni *the* look. Toni creased her brows, giving Yasmeen the stink eye. "Why are you looking at me like that?"

Yasmeen jutted her chin. "You see the neighborhood we're in, right? You think these people are going to open the door to three Black women rolling up on them?"

"Not everything is about race, Yasmeen," Toni said. "I want to be there for my friend. This is huge and she might need us."

"Some things are very much about race. Tell that to some of our people locked up behind bars," Yasmeen shot back, the visual image of Darryl getting tackled on her mind.

"Like you pointed out, we're not in the hood," Toni said.

"I can go with her," Celeste said.

"Why, because you'll blend in?" Yasmeen asked, a little snooty.

"I'm not even going there with you right now. I'm taking the high road," Celeste said, making Yasmeen feel bad about her snide remark. "Darryl was arrested because of his involvement in petty crimes. To reiterate Toni's point. That wasn't all about race. That was about him being straight-up guilty."

"He's not guilty," Yasmeen defended.

"Guys, you're not helping," Leslie said in a small voice, clutching her stomach. The three of them instantly apologized. Leslie waved a hand and sighed. "It's better if I go alone. Bad enough I'm showing up uninvited. I'd better not bring an entourage. I'll be okay." Except, she didn't sound okay at all. Yasmeen's heart squeezed. She uttered a silent prayer that meeting the Johansens would bring nothing but good for Leslie's family, but especially for her goddaughter.

21

Celeste

JANUARY 26

Celeste knew there was no way she could walk twenty feet in Leslie's boots. She couldn't even begin to imagine what Leslie must be feeling right now.

If it was her, Celeste doubted she would seek her bio parents out. That wasn't her MO. She would spend her time trying to get Nadya moved up on the donor list and leave this truth bone alone. That joker would fossilize before she ruined her status quo. Celeste would rather carry on with her life, pretend as if she didn't even know, before she messed with her equilibrium.

Hmm… Maybe that was why Wade had left her? Celeste shoved that thought aside.

He hadn't acknowledged receipt of the torn divorce papers,

which made her feel small. But she hadn't despaired for long. Instead, she had texted him to tell him about Leslie's adoption surprise and her subsequent quest to find her birth parents, but again, he hadn't responded. Celeste knew it wasn't due to a lack of caring. Wade knew her—if he engaged in any normal conversation with her, she would take it to mean everything would be alright between them again. And he would be correct.

Answer me, please, she begged on the inside, eyes on the screen. This was one way of her fighting: subtly, slowly creeping back into his life inch by inch until they were back to the way things were before. Yet he wasn't playing along. Which meant he was serious about the divorce.

Which meant she was going to have to fight another way.

Yasmeen pulled to a stop in front of a large two-story home with charcoal veneer stones and gray siding. The lights were on inside. There were two sedans parked in the driveway, as well as an RV camper.

"Looks like your normal middle-class family," Toni commented.

"Yeah," Leslie said, sliding closer to Celeste so she could peer out of the window. "I don't know what I was expecting, but from outward appearances, the Johansens look stable and relatively well-off. Google didn't do this house justice. It looked smaller in the picture."

Celeste patted Leslie's hand. "You know you can't trust what you see all the time. Look at me and Wade."

"Aw, how are things?"

She shrugged. "Oh, it's the same old, same old." She gave a jerky laugh. "We'll catch up on my stuff another time. You have a lot to deal with right now." She tilted her head. "Are you ready?"

"No. Not even close." Leslie released a plume of air and wiped her hands on her pants.

"Do you want us to just head back home?" Yasmeen asked, turning to face her.

Leslie fretted with her bottom lip before she sighed. "No, this is something I have to do."

Toni cocked her head. "Get on out there. We'll be here waiting, looking out for any sign of trouble."

"There's a strip mall nearby," Celeste added, tapping on her phone to search for restaurants. "Maybe we can wait there while you visit." She didn't want to stir the embers of the earlier race argument and get Yasmeen going again, but she didn't need the Johansens concerned about three Black women in a dark SUV parked outside their house.

"That sounds like a great idea," Leslie said, voice shaky. Then she squared her shoulders. "Here goes everything." She dabbed her eyes and gave a nervous chuckle, most likely at her paraphrasing of the cliché. "I'm going in." She opened the door and got out, slamming the door behind her.

"You good to go to a diner?" Yasmeen asked Celeste, while they watched Leslie's slow trek up the driveway.

"I could eat," she said, diverting from Yasmeen's real question. She reached into her coat pocket and squeezed her stress ball. "If we get a booth and I can sit so I can see who's coming and going, I should be alright." She hoped. Without another word, Yasmeen headed back onto the main road. Her anxiety seemed to be worsening with time instead of getting better. Ever since her breakdown, she noticed the least little thing got her heart racing. She had read online that many therapists recommended yoga and the use of stress balls or lollipops, and she had chosen the former. It helped center her and redirect her energy. But at nights, she still had those horrible nightmares, even more now that her bed was empty.

Maybe she should go see Wade at his apartment. Surprise him.

She suggested as much to her girls once they had been seated, she with her back comfortably against the wall.

"Negative. Negative," Yasmeen said, moving her finger back

and forth. "Don't creep up on that man when he's not expecting you."

"Um, 'that man,'" Toni said, using air quotes, "is her husband. She earned that right lying on her back for over a decade."

"I wasn't always on my back," Celeste had to point out.

"I ain't mad at you," Toni hollered, gyrating her hips. "Ride that pony."

Yasmeen gave Toni a light shove. "What's up with you acting so hood all of a sudden?"

"Can't I just be me for a minute?" Toni asked. "I just want to kick it with my girls since there's no camera around. Can I do that?"

Yasmeen rolled her eyes and picked up her menu.

"Ease up, you two," Celeste chided before looking at Toni. "And, girl, I sure would ride it if I could."

They high-fived. "That's right. That's right. Go see your *husband* and get it for the both of us, because you know Kent and I sure aren't."

"You two just plain nasty," Yasmeen said.

They busted out laughing. The server brought their waters and then hovered. They turned their attention to the menus.

"What do you think you're going to get?" Yasmeen asked. "This will be my treat."

"Girl, we can pay our own way," Toni said, shaking her head. "Acting like you a Rockefeller. You took the lump sum, so you didn't even get all the ten million dollars. Be smart with what you've got left. At least invest some of it."

"You really need to ease up," Celeste said to Yasmeen. Realizing the server was listening in to their conversation, she asked, "Can you give us a minute?" Once the server had left, she continued. "Dang, he was counting our teeth just now."

"Not to brag, but I thought he was caught up because I was here," Toni said, tossing her hair. "You know, possibly a little starstruck."

Yasmeen's and Celeste's eyes locked before they cracked up.

"You are so vain," Yasmeen said, holding up a strip of paper. "Nice thought. But he snuck me his number."

"That fast?" Celeste laughed. "I love this. I'm glad I came out. You two got me here giggling when I would be home moping or texting Wade."

Yasmeen and Toni each took one of her hands. "That's what we do, sis," Toni said. The server returned to take their orders, giving Yasmeen a playful wink. They each picked salads so they would get fed quickly, with Celeste choosing the vegan, though she added a basket of cheese fries for them to share. Comfort food. Celeste ordered one to-go for Leslie as well.

"He must have overheard us talking about your money," Toni pointed out once he left.

She rolled her eyes. "Great, why did you have to say that?" She ripped up the number and tossed the scraps on the table. Then she sighed. "It's probably for the best, since I'm not about to allow another man to slide into my goody box anytime soon."

"You weren't going to call him anyhow," Celeste said. "You still into Darryl. The man has you whipped like butter."

Her joke fell flat for a beat before Toni held up a hand.

"Okay, I am going to need you to pocket that joke and never bring it out again."

Yasmeen picked up her bag. "Guess what I bought?" she said. She held up a copy of *The Davenports*. "It's autographed. Plus, I bought the audiobook."

"I want to read that," Toni said. "I love the fact that it shows successful Black families in the 1910s."

"Meh. I don't read YA unless it's for book club," Celeste said.

"I bought us all autographed copies," Yasmeen declared. "Remind me to get them out the trunk. They got dropped off at the front desk of the hotel today." She gave Celeste the side-eye. "See, I did something good with my money."

"You wrong for that." Toni put a hand to her mouth. "You trying to bogart your way into Leslie's month."

"No, silly. We can read and talk about this now. It's an in-between read." Yasmeen didn't appear to feel the slightest bit of guilt.

"Leslie's going to have your head if you mess with her book of the month," Celeste warned.

"Yes, but we know YA is also Leslie's jam," Yasmeen said.

"Let me see the back of this book." Celeste admired the yellow cover with the African-American women looking regal. She took a minute to read while a different waiter returned with their meals. "This actually sounds good," she said. "Maybe I'll start it tonight."

"Yeah, girl," Yasmeen said, patting Celeste's hand. "Books are the best, most reliable company, especially if they have a fulfilling conclusion."

She could say the same about her husband...

Toni's cell chimed. When she saw who it was, she sucked her teeth before excusing herself and stalking out of the restaurant. She was agitated enough to have forgotten her coat. Sure enough, seconds later, she whipped back inside to get the garment.

"Are you alright?" Celeste asked.

"Yeah. Yeah. Just..." Toni gave a jerky nod. "Got to take care of something real quick. I'll be back."

Once they were alone, Celeste and Yasmeen dug into their meals. Celeste's salad had nuts, quinoa, edamame, olives, along with the usual greens, and paired with the vinaigrette, it was delicious. Maybe she would give this vegan lifestyle a try. Something new.

"What do you think is going on with her?" Yasmeen asked, nodding outside toward Toni.

"Who knows? With Toni, it could be something minor like a missed appointment or something huge like her hair is on fire. Either way she's going to be just as dramatic. We have to wait until she's ready to talk though. No point in pushing her. Either way, we'll have her back."

"True dat." Yasmeen nodded before changing the subject. "So, please tell me you've dropped this idea of surprising Wade at his place."

"I can't."

"I know it's tough, but you need to reflect on why he left." Celeste hunched her shoulders; she didn't want to hear this. Yasmeen jabbed a finger on the table. "Has anything changed? Showing up to seduce him will only give you both fleeting satisfaction. But when he's done and drops his head on the pillow, he's going to realize that the sex didn't resolve the issue. And the gulf between you might widen instead of narrowing." She shrugged her shoulders. "But hey, don't listen to me. What do I know?"

Yasmeen was right.

"When did you get so smart?" Celeste leaned back in her chair. "Maybe I do need therapy to help me figure out how to save my marriage."

"Your marriage was never the problem." Yasmeen gave her a pointed look. Meaning she was. "But hey, you can start with finding professional help. Make the call."

The door swung open and Toni stormed inside.

While they ate, a thought popped in Celeste's head. Maybe she could invite Wade to go to therapy with her. At least she would have a legitimate excuse to see him. And he wouldn't say no. In fact, she could use Wade's therapist.

Even better.

She picked up her phone and texted her husband. **What's the name of your therapist again?**

This time he answered and her heart whooped. He gave her name and contact information.

Thanks, she texted, then ate a mouthful of her salad.

Toni and Yasmeen were still talking about that Davenport book, so she let their conversation flow, knowing they wouldn't be paying her any mind at the moment.

He responded by placing a heart on her text. A heart, not a like. She pushed her food aside. Her own heart galloped. *That has to mean something.* You know what, she would keep this conversation string going.

I'll give her a call tomorrow.

That's good to hear.

This time it was followed by two hearts.

That had to be code for he missed her. She sent two hearts back and he hearted that. What the heck, she would go for it.

How about I stop by for a minute? Just need to talk about this.

Even as she pressed Send, she was looking at how dark it was outside.

It's getting dark. I'll come there. Wade texted.

Her fingers couldn't type fast enough.

Out with the girls. I'll text when I'm home.

Three hearts. Three flipping hearts. Oh, it was on. The bra would be swinging from the fan when she was done.

She slipped her phone in her bag, her spirits high. She couldn't wait to get home. Yasmeen's warning came back to her, and for a second, she reconsidered. Naw. Bump that. She was getting her man any way she could.

And she had just the right outfit to wear.

22

Leslie

JANUARY 26

Leslie pulled her hat lower to cover her burning ears, and she put on her gloves, tucking the manila envelope under her arm. She shouldn't have shooed off her friends. As soon as they turned the bend, her courage deflated and she started walking the block in circles.

What was weird, though, was she wasn't the only one out walking in the cold night. Leslie had passed one dude jogging wearing shorts—yes, shorts—and a coat, and an older lady twice her age speed walked past her. Ridiculous. But here she was, waving at them as she circled the block for the fourth time. They were going to be friends her next time around. Leslie rubbed her hands. She paused in front of the Johansens' home once more and slapped her hands to her sides.

Forget this. She hadn't come all this way to lose her nerve. Squaring her shoulders, Leslie trudged up the driveway and pressed the doorbell. Her heart hammered faster than a moonshine runner dodging the cops, as her daddy would say. Yes, sigh, she was back to calling him Daddy for now.

She tucked her shaky hands in her coat and watched the door. As it began to swing open, slowly, slowly, she released shallow breaths. Her chest heaved and her throat tightened. Keep calm. Keep calm. An older woman wearing a blue-jeaned dress pushed open the screen door. Leslie lifted her hand to her mouth and gaped.

Her real-life mother stood before her. Julie Johansen. Leslie's eyes blurred.

"Yes?" Julie smiled wide, clueless, eyes sparkling. "How can I help you?" Her voice was refreshing, reminiscent of an effervescent drink. The scent of cinnamon wafted from the house, teasing her nose.

"Ahh, I, um," Leslie croaked out, wiping her tears. She hadn't expected to feel...overwhelmed. Her mother hadn't recognized her, peering at her with kind but unknowing eyes. Her heart punctured and Leslie realized she had expected Julie to be able to tell, to feel an instant connection and maybe open her arms. But the other woman stood waiting.

The smile dropped and the eyebrows furrowed. "Are you alright, dear?" She wrapped her arms around herself. "It's freezing out here."

Leslie clutched her throat and forced the words. "I'm sorry to intrude on you, ma'am, but I need to talk to you about something really important." Goodness, she should have rehearsed what she was going to say. She shivered and her teeth chattered.

"Do you want to come inside to warm up? My husband will be here any minute." Julie was already turning to give Leslie entrance. Looks like Yasmeen was right. She couldn't believe the woman was so trusting, welcoming a virtual stranger into her home without asking any more questions. That probably wouldn't be the case if all her friends were with her. But then again, this was small-town life in Delaware.

"Yes, thank you," Leslie said. She stepped inside the warmth and drew in a deep breath. Besides cinnamon, she smelled peppermint and the distinct scent of baking. Julie took her coat and hung it in the small linen closet. The wooden floors glistened, the mirrors shone and everything had its place. The decor was charming with soothing grays and whites, and she could hear the wood crackling from the fireplace. The Johansens' home felt inviting, lived-in…happy. Without her. She didn't quite know how to articulate her feelings about that.

"Now, how about I get you some coffee?" Julie asked.

"Thanks." *Get it together, Leslie. You have a lot more to say than thank you.* "You have a lovely home."

"How sweet of you to say." She walked down the short hallway and Leslie followed. "Henry and I moved here after we had our children." She gestured into the living room. "I'll be right back. Have a seat and get comfortable." Julie wandered off, presumably toward the kitchen, without realizing how this bombshell news had gutted Leslie, who fell onto the couch and processed, clutching the envelope.

Children. As in more than one. As in, others besides her. Siblings. Leslie swallowed. That's when she noticed the pictures hanging over the fireplace. She took in the smiling faces of Julie and Henry with two boys and a girl and blinked back tears. From the look of things, Henry and Julie had pawned her off and then settled into a nice life. Picture-perfect. Without her. Sudden resentment ballooned in her heart and she jumped to her feet. But then she remembered Nadya. And she sank farther down, enveloped by the thick, soft couch.

Children.

She heard the tinkling of cups and Julie returned, unaware that Leslie's secure world of seconds ago had been upended.

Julie poured coffee in each of their mugs. Just like Leslie, she had two packs of cream and one sugar packet. That similarity gave Leslie goose bumps and fueled her anger. How had Julie missed that? How could she not see that Leslie was her replica? Leslie left her coffee untouched. If she drank any, she knew she would hurl.

"There now," Julie said, settling a few feet from her. "What can I do for you?" She smoothed her dress and gave Leslie an expectant smile.

"Does this date have any significance for you?" Leslie told Julie her birthday. The older woman's eyes went wide. Her cup clattered when she rested it on the coffee table.

"Oh." Julie zoned in on her and Leslie saw when realization dawned of exactly who she was. Julie cupped her own cheek with her hands. "Louisa?" Her voice held wonder, mingled with curiosity and joy.

"Actually, it's Leslie. Leslie Bronwyn."

"Oh, I see." Julie dipped her chin to her chest and fidgeted with her collar. "I always knew this day would come. I dreamt about this moment for years." Tears pooled in her eyes and she reached out a hand like she was going to touch Leslie's cheek, then second-guessed herself. She clasped her hands together and cleared her throat.

"I'm sorry to barge in on you, but I just found out I was adopted a few weeks ago," Leslie said. The question of why her parents gave her away pressed against her chest, her mind, her heart. But this was about Nadya. "I'm married and I have a little girl."

"Oh wow."

Leslie shifted to face her. "Yes, her name's—"

The front door opened and a draft of air flooded the room. "That's Henry. Your—um, my husband."

Her stomach knotted. She was about to meet the other individual responsible for giving her life.

Both women turned to await the newest arrival. From where she sat, she could see a tall figure by the doorway with his back turned.

"The lines were so long at the checkout," he said, "and I had trouble using my debit card. I have to put on this brisket in the cooker now or it won't be ready by the time the kids get here."

So she had interrupted a family reunion of sorts. Keenly aware of her exclusion, Leslie stood. Hurt expanded like metallic claws piercing in her chest. She had to get out of here so she could breathe. "I'd better get going." The stomping of feet drew close... He was a heavy walker.

"No, no. Please don't rush off," Julie said, also standing, her lower lip quivering. "I'm sure you—"

Henry stomped his boots, while she took in his shoulder-length locks. He gave his head a light shake before he noticed her.

"Well, who's this?" Henry said, motioning in Leslie's direction and giving his wife a kiss. He had two brown bags in his hands.

"Henry, this is Leslie," Julie said, carefully. "She's our..." She shook her head, choked up. "We know her as Louisa."

Leslie lifted her chin to look up at him. Henry made eye contact with his wife and frowned. Then, as the silence yawned, his eyes darted between them, and his mouth popped open.

"Leslie," he breathed out, understanding the significance of what Julie had said. He dropped the bags by his feet. A couple of oranges rolled under the couch, but he stood transfixed, scanning her from head to toe. "I can't believe this. You're here." Henry went over to take his wife's hand. Julie leaned into him, and Leslie had her first look at her parents together, aged from the picture she had seen earlier that day.

Her heart pounded and she touched her chest. "Hello," she said, an underwhelming greeting for this moment, before settling back onto the couch.

"How did you find us?" he asked, the first to recover, the first to take charge. He tugged Julie to sit on the loveseat across from her, then looked at Leslie with eyes she knew so well. Surreal. She needed a couple hours to gawk and process.

"I...I hired a private investigator." Words jumbled in her mind as she struggled to think coherently. The people who sat before her were her strongest genetic link and also complete strangers. Perhaps she should have brought her friends or Aaron with her to keep her grounded. Then she had to add, "You were ridiculously easy to find."

Her pointed jab met its mark. Henry's face reddened.

"She just found out about us," Julie whispered.

Finally, Leslie's lips loosened some more. "I don't think I would have ever known if my daughter hadn't gotten sick. She has been diagnosed with severe aplastic anemia and needs a bone marrow transplant." Leslie curled her fingers. "Neither myself nor my husband are a match. That's when my dad told me the truth of your existence. So here I am."

"This is a lot to take in," Julie said, dabbing at her eyes. "I have another grandchild."

"What's her name? How old is she?" Henry asked.

"Her name's Nadya and she's twelve years old." Leslie took out her phone and pulled up a recent photo.

They gushed over Nadya, which, prideful mother that she was, made Leslie's heart warm. "Of course we'll get tested. And we'll ask our children." As if realizing his faux pas, Henry fumbled his words. "Our other children." He cleared his throat. "I'd better put away the butter and sour cream." He retrieved the fallen oranges and the groceries, then excused himself, probably to gather his composure, leaving the two women alone.

Julie ran her fingers through her hair, focused on a point above Leslie's head and started talking. "I was eighteen, barely out of high school. I had been dating Henry since tenth grade and my parents wanted me to go to Connecticut for school, most likely to break us up." She gave a little laugh. "But then I found out I was pregnant. Henry was only nineteen and neither of us had ever even had a job. There was no way we could take care of a child." She looked at Leslie with pleading eyes. "We wanted to keep you, but our parents refused to support us, to help. They wanted me to... But I wanted you." She touched her abdomen. "No one would hire me, but Henry worked at a fast-food joint and for a while, we thought we could do this."

Leslie wiped her eyes. "I understand. I get it."

Henry came in and continued, "For a few months, the three of us were a team. It wasn't until winter came in and we were holed up in a rinky-dink apartment on the other side of town, freezing our butts off in single-digit temps, with a landlord who refused to replace the boiler, that we decided to consider adoption. Our parents didn't stop us."

"It was a closed adoption, but we chose the Samuels for you," Julie said, "because they were financially stable and such loving people."

"Were you happy?" Henry asked.

Leslie nodded. It felt unreal talking about her parents with her biological parents. But this was her life now. "I had a blessed childhood and the most amazing mom and dad a girl could ask for... My mom died when I was eight, and it's been me and my dad ever since."

Julie put a hand to her mouth, leaning forward. "I'm sorry to hear about your mom."

"It was just me and my dad until I met my girls in college. My friends are the best... They are my sisterhood, the siblings I never had...or didn't know I had..."

Leslie broke eye contact. Of course her eyes landed on that huge family photo again. The one that mocked her with her absence, that showed her how the people who claimed they loved her had moved on better than fine without her. She hated the internal pity party, but she was an attendee, nonetheless.

"Yes, it's good to have friends you can count on…" Julie looked down on her hands.

"After we gave you up, we were tortured and burdened with guilt. That broke us up," Henry said.

She straightened then. "Oh, you weren't together all this time?"

"No, we didn't see each other for a good ten years, and we both lived in different states. But we came back to town for a mutual friend's funeral, and as soon as we saw each other, it was like we never left," Julie replied. "We both had been married and divorced before, so there was nothing keeping us from being together. We were married within a month and started making more babies." She chuckled before averting her eyes, maybe because Leslie wasn't laughing.

"Why didn't you search for me?" Leslie asked, voice raw.

"We started to," Henry said, "but by then, you would have been about eleven or so and we didn't want to upend your life."

Or theirs.

So, instead of coming to find her, they got busy with her replacements. When Julie rushed to get the family album to share pictures of the past, it compounded the resentment. Leslie sniffled. "I've taken up enough of your time. I need to go." She texted her friends to let them know she was ready.

We outside, girl. Waiting. You good?

Her shoulders slumped. Thank goodness for her sisters not by blood. She sent an emoji with a downturned lip. Be there soon.

Henry looked at his watch. "Are you sure you don't want to stay for a few minutes? Your bro— I mean, you could meet Scott, Simon and Skylar."

Wow. They all had *S* names. Except for her. The odd one out.

Hurt wrapped around her heart. Despite the eagerness in

their voices, this rejection was too much. She was about to crumble under all these emotions swirling around her core, her soul. If she didn't get out of here, Leslie knew she would fall apart, and she couldn't do that. She couldn't let these people see how tenuous her control was right now. She stood and slipped her purse onto her shoulder before picking up the manila envelope. "No, I have to get back to the hospital. Perhaps another time."

Julie huddled close. "May I hug you?"

Leslie shook her head. "If it's alright with you, I'd rather not. I…" Her voice cracked. She looked at the brown envelope in her hand and placed it on the coffee table. "It was nice—" No, this didn't feel nice. "Thank you for allowing me to meet you." She dug into her bag and pulled out two swab kits with stamped return envelopes, then placed them on the coffee table. "I—I didn't know there were more, um… I can mail you more for the—uh, rest. If you could swab your cheeks and send these off, that would be helpful."

"We will do that tonight." Henry handed her a business card. "I wrote both cell phones and the house number on the back. Call us anytime."

Leslie stuffed the card in her pocket and scuttled to the door. With each step, a teardrop rolled down her face. Julie called out to her, holding her coat in her hand.

"Oh, thank you," she said, blinded by her tears. She ducked her head, but Julie must have spotted her wet face.

"We've upset you," she cried.

"I'll be alright," she said, and rushed out the door. Yas's truck roared to life and an old-school jam blasted through the speakers, making some noise in the neighborhood. The wide-eyed look on Henry's and Julie's faces made Leslie chuckle despite her heartache. "Those are my friends. No, they are my sisters," she said, squaring her shoulders. "They're here for me, my ride or dies." Celeste opened the door and stepped out, and then Toni and Yasmeen followed.

"Ride or die? I'm sorry, I don't know what that means," Julie said.

"It's okay. You don't have to know. I do, though, and that's what matters." With that, Leslie made her way down to where her friends stood huddled, waiting with open arms.

23

Yasmeen

FEBRUARY 3

Yasmeen gestured for her parents to enter her house. She had decided the best way to tell them about her fortune was to show them, so she had waited until the house was ready and had driven them over the very evening the contractor had informed her that all her renovations were finally completed. She didn't know how she'd managed to keep this from them, and the beans she hadn't spilled pinged inside her tummy.

The entire ride over, her parents had begged her to tell them her news and they had shared so much laughter while they guessed at her surprise.

Her parents took a tentative step past the entryway, looking around with furtive glances.

"Are you sure it's okay that we're here?" Willie said, his voice hushed.

"Yes, the owner is quite alright with you being here. I promise." She smiled, her heart expanding. The house smelled of fresh paint and the huge bouquet of chrysanthemums resting on the table by the entrance.

Yasmeen closed the door behind them and led them into the living room area. She had the lights off and couldn't wait for them to see their enlarged family photos.

Dixie stopped by the huge two-sided staircase and gaped. "I don't want someone to call the cops on us." Her mother twisted the button on her worn brown coat, looking behind her like she expected to get caught for trespassing.

"That's not going to happen, Mom. I promise all this will make sense in a few minutes."

Their feet squished down the long hallway. They passed the library she had filled with thousands of books. Books of all kinds.

"If you owned this, I could see you living in there with all those books," her mother said, with a laugh. "I would camp out with you too."

She planned to. Yasmeen had a chaise lounge and a fireplace along with armchairs. She couldn't wait to host the next book club and had posted pictures in her friends' group chat earlier that day.

"Is this your new job? Are you cleaning houses now?" her father asked just as they arrived in the living room area.

"No, this isn't a job." She turned on the lights and grinned, enjoying the myriad expressions across her parents' faces, ranging from quizzical to uncertain, and then to astonishment.

"That's us." Her mother pointed at the supersize picture of them holding her as a baby on a rare trip to the island of Jamaica West Indies. Her parents had taken her to meet both sets of her grandparents. She had her hair in two Afro puffs and a piece of corn husk in one hand—her unofficial teething ring. Yasmeen adored that picture, especially since her parents looked hopeful with their bright smiles.

Her father whispered, "I need to clean my glasses because my eyes must be deceiving me." Then he rested his gaze on hers and splayed his hands. "Yasmeen, what is the meaning of all this?"

She squared her shoulders. "Mommy and Daddy, all our problems are over. I found out a few weeks ago that I won the lottery!"

Willie reared his head back and repeated the words *the lottery*, like he had never heard them before, like they were some ancient, repugnant infestations new to the earth.

"What do you mean you won the lottery?" Dixie asked, her voice echoing in the huge space. "I'm confused."

"Remember the day our electricity went out? That's when I bought the ticket."

"You gambled your hard-earned money on a chance?" her father asked, tone judgmental.

"Yes," she breezily replied, belying the fact that her heart was beating fast at his evident disapproval. "And the chance paid off. Big-time. To the tune of 10.5 million dollars. I took a lump sum, and close to seventy percent went to taxes and all that, but what does it matter?"

While she rambled, Yasmeen led them to sit on the couch. Her parents leaned into each other, holding hands, and perched at the edge, like they were afraid to relax on it. Yasmeen plopped onto the chaise lounge across from them and propped her legs up, boots and all, ignoring the fact that it was white, plush and had cost a fortune to import.

Her mother gasped. "Take your foot off the couch. Why did you buy white? You really should cover it with plastic."

A vivid memory of the backs of her legs burning from her parents' hot plastic couch of past summers made her cringe.

"This isn't like back in the day," she said. "A living room is meant to be lived in. So get comfortable."

Neither moved. In fact, they seemed to curl even more into themselves. She offered to take their coats and to order them something to eat, but they refused. And her father didn't look pleased.

"How is it going to look to the church that my own daughter engaged in something I preach against?" he asked, shaking his head. "They cast lots for Jesus's robe at his crucifixion."

And there it was. She'd known it was coming, but his words pierced her chest just the same.

"From where I'm sitting, I think it will look just fine," Yasmeen replied, a slight edge in her voice. "I'm sure the deacons won't complain when they see the tithing envelope."

Her mother gasped. "Wow. I'm surprised at your cavalier attitude, Yasmeen. We didn't raise you to have such a bad attitude and a blatant disregard for our beliefs. Your father is voicing his feelings, and you shouldn't blow off his concerns."

"I'm sorry, Mommy." Yasmeen slumped. "I'm being defensive because I knew you wouldn't like it. I knew you would make me feel guilty, but I'm grateful. For once, I have money and I can buy whatever I want. I see that as a blessing. Maybe God gave me those numbers."

Her father's mouth popped open. "I can't believe you would say that to excuse your actions."

"I can't pretend I'm not happy though." She jumped up and twirled, spreading her arms wide. "For the first time in my life, I have a house. I have never been so happy. I'm free and I'm rich." She stopped in front of them and pleaded, "I want you to live with me."

Her father's eyes held hurt. "We might not have been able to give you a downtown parade when you were a little girl, but you were loved. We might not have had a table overladen with food, but we shared what we had and we were satisfied." He choked out the words, though his back was straight with pride. "I didn't know I would lose my job, but whatever I gave you, I earned by the sweat of my brow and the work of my hands."

Yasmeen's heart constricted. "Daddy, I didn't mean it the way you're taking it. I know you love me. I know how hard you worked to give me everything I need. You and Mommy have gone without so I could have. This is my chance to give you back tenfold."

"There's more to life than money," her mother said, standing.

"It's something, though, when they turn off the electricity in winter," she couldn't help but say.

Her mother shook her head. "The amount of dollars in the bank isn't true wealth. Good friends and family in your corner cannot be quantified. They are what makes your house a home." Yasmeen couldn't believe her mother was lecturing her like this, joining her father's side.

Both her parents stood, their bodies bent with disappointment. "Take us home, please," her daddy said.

"Why can't you be happy for me?" she asked, guiding them to the door. Tears pricked her eyes. Why couldn't everyone be thrilled? Instead her friends were cautioning her about how she spent and her parents were acting like someone had passed. Could she just have a moment to celebrate her fortune the way she pleased?

It was a tense, silent ride home.

After she pulled up to the building and her mother left the vehicle, her father patted her arm. "Be wise in all you do, my dear. Remember, a fool and his money are soon parted."

"Well, that's good to know because I'm no fool," she joked.

He pointed upward. "His words. Not mine." And with that, he was gone.

24

Toni

FEBRUARY 5

Since their meeting over a week ago, Skins had reached out at least half a dozen times with subtle messages, the gist of which was asking when she would have his money, at the most inopportune moments. Like now, when she was dripping wet and fresh out of the shower. Toni knew this was a part of his tactics to keep her off-kilter. She dashed into her bedroom and placed her phone on top of her copy of Vanessa Miller's *The American Queen* and the hardcover of Bonnie Garmus's *Lessons in Chemistry* on her nightstand. She dried off, then rubbed lotion onto her body while she contemplated.

No matter how much she told him she didn't have it, he would answer with Tick Tock.

The man was both a menace and a nuisance. And it seemed the only way to get rid of him was to give him the money. But he was a leech. Paying him now meant she would be paying him for life. That was his nature, and she didn't believe Lamont for even a millisecond when he said he was a changed man. But what else was she to do?

Toni slipped into her underwear, the only sounds the swishing of the hangers in her closet while she decided what to wear. The temperature outside today was close to sixty degrees and the sun was already out. Tomorrow, they predicted temps in the high thirties and rain. When you lived in Delaware, you learned to roll and adjust with the unreliable weather. She continued her internal debate.

Or she could tell Kent, her sister friends and her viewers the truth. Out herself before he did. But that could mean possible jail time. Never mind that she hadn't known Skins had committed a crime when he asked her to drive. Toni was still an accessory by default. She didn't know what the statute of limitations was on that, but she did know the damage to her social persona would be irreparable.

Gnawing her lower lip, she settled on a pair of designer sweats with a white tank and four-inch red bottoms due to hit stores in the spring. Toni would never get tired of the perks of her life as a social influencer. She quickly applied her makeup before taking a picture holding up *The American Queen* and posting to her media pages.

Skins liked her photo, then hit up her inbox with a question mark. She shuddered. She might as well answer his message or he'd keep this up all day. With her doctor's appointment and the book club meeting today, she didn't need any distractions or to arouse her friends' misgivings.

I need time to get that kind of cash without raising suspicion. She hit Send.

No response. Ugh. He knew how to get to her. Her doorbell

rang and she opened the door to greet Yasmeen and Celeste. She tucked her phone in the rear pocket of her sweats. "Where's Leslie?"

Celeste answered first. "We waited for twenty minutes, but she never came out, didn't even answer the door. When she called, she said she couldn't leave Nadya alone as Aaron hadn't shown up yet. He went out of town on business and hasn't returned. I think that's an excuse though. Meeting her bio parents messed her up big-time." Nadya had finally been released, and since then, Leslie had lived in her house like a bear on hibernation. "We reminded her about our book club meeting at her house and she said she wasn't up to visitors, plus she hadn't read the book."

Leslie not reading Alyssa Cole's book was a glaring sign of her mental state. Sister friend wasn't doing good.

"It doesn't matter if she hasn't read it. We can't allow her to miss book club. It's been our glue for over a decade. It's kept us together through some tough stuff," Yasmeen said, holding up an index finger. "If it weren't for book club, I don't know how I would've made it when I flunked out of school. Now, Leslie might be able to push her father away, but she's not going to do the same to us. We are going to bang on that door until she answers."

Toni nodded. "I'm down with that plan. And after we talk books, I want to hear all about the fact that you're sleeping with Wade again."

"What?" Yasmeen's eyes were wide. She clucked her tongue. "You know that's a bad idea."

Celeste's mouth popped open. "How did you know—"

Toni rolled her eyes. "Don't forget I know you. But in the eyes of the law, that's still your husband, so you do you, boo boo. You don't have to hide." She needed to take her own advice.

"You got a point there," Celeste said. "I haven't said anything because it's been fun sneaking around." She gave Yasmeen the side-eye. "And I didn't feel like hearing anybody's mouth about it. Especially those who aren't in a proper, committed relationship."

Yasmeen pursed her lips. "I mean nothing but good for you, Celeste. We go way back. That's why I tell you the truth. Sleeping with Wade isn't going to magically solve what's wrong. I just want you to get help. Real help."

"I am," Celeste muttered, lowering her lashes. "Just not in the way you think."

Yasmeen swirled her finger. "You can string that man along like he's Polly-O String Cheese, but he's not going to stop the divorce proceedings. You need to go to actual therapy and deal with your trauma."

"And you need to mind your business," Celeste fumed. "I'm doing fine at my job, fine with my friendships, and my marriage is going to be fine as well, no thanks to you."

Alright, Toni could see their argument was a pendulum that would keep swinging back and forth. She didn't have time for that. And she didn't like to see her friends arguing. Reminded her too much of her parents. Toni moved toward the door to get her coat. "Let's get out of here. Messing with you two is going to make me miss my appointment."

Neither said a word as they piled into Toni's Mustang. Yasmeen had her earbuds in, listening to her audiobook, and Celeste was texting on her phone. The air in the vehicle remained tense for most of the car ride. Toni knew how to fix that. She pressed the button to open the sunroof. When both Yasmeen and Celeste called out, she hid a grin and asked what was wrong.

"Naw, girl. It's too cold for that," Yasmeen protested. "I don't have my hair in braids like yours."

"My blowout won't survive the wind," Celeste agreed.

"I was trying to let out all the bad air out," Toni said, pressing the button again to close it. "This car is too tiny for all these negative vibes."

"You are so dramatic," Yasmeen said, though she did cackle. She returned her attention to her book.

"I can't with you." Celeste laughed. "You are ridiculous."

Toni's chest loosened. "What I am is scared. Scared about these results," she whispered.

That made her friends pay attention.

"Whatever happens, you'll get through this. You're Toni Marshall. Nothing can keep you down," Yasmeen said, using one of Toni's slogans.

A slogan as fake as her name. Right now, she was feeling very much like Antoinette Masters, the scared girl from Queens, visiting the backdoor clinic with her boyfriend. A boyfriend who instead of taking her home immediately after to recuperate, told her to sit behind the wheel of his Buick Century while he ran inside the laundromat and held up the owner, an elderly woman. She sniffled.

A hand moved to rub her arm. "Kent loves you."

"Yeah, even if you have old ovaries." Yasmeen snickered.

No one else laughed.

Toni glanced her way. "Too soon." If it was anybody else, she would be furious. But this was Yasmeen, who had a big heart but sometimes didn't think.

"Okay, I'm sorry about my poor sense of timing." Yasmeen cleared her throat. "I just don't want you worrying about Kent's loyalty. He's the real deal. Trust me. I've waded in enough crap to know Kent is a diamond in the rough."

Toni paused a beat, then busted out in laughter. "Diamond in the rough? Did you really just quote a line from *Aladdin* to me?" she asked, referencing the Disney movie.

Yasmeen gave her a light shove. "Whatever. See, this is why I don't try to be sentimental because you all can't handle it."

"I'm just messing with you," Toni said. "I appreciate your kind words." Sooner than she was prepared for, she was pulling into a parking spot. Her girls flanked her sides. She donned her sunglasses and pulled her cap over her hair. Today, she was dressed in sneakers, jeans and a sweater, with the intention of blending in.

She signed in, admiring the reeded front reception desk lined with a gold metal kick plate, then went to sit with Yasmeen and Celeste in one of the pink velvet chairs in the far corner of the waiting area. In the center of the room was a concrete coffee table with various health magazines and a white ceramic vase with gold vines. The space was picture-perfect. Too bad she couldn't record this visit.

By now her heart was moving at rattlesnake speed, right along with her leg. Yasmeen placed a hand on her thigh. "You'll be alright."

"I don't think so," she said. Soon, her name was called and she was nodding at her friends' encouraging gestures and trudging behind another chatty physician's assistant. This one rambled on about the weather and how the more it rained, the more babies they saw, and Toni had to clench her jaw to keep from snapping at the woman to be quiet.

The examination room boasted an orange examination chair that matched the cupboards. A nice change from the drab blue color present in most rooms. In fact, the room was bright and airy, and devoid of the stock photos of smiling mothers and babies. Instead, there were words of affirmation along with the usual pelvic posters citing various feminine conditions.

Thankfully, after directing her to undress to just her bottoms and adjusting the chair, the woman left the room stating the doctor would arrive shortly. Minutes later, Toni found herself on her back, feet in the stirrups, staring at the ceiling, hand across her abdomen, willing herself to stop shaking, to stop worrying and to pray for better results. The room was cool, so she was glad she had been allowed to keep on her sweater. She lifted her head and pulled out the small blanket to cover her lower half.

The door creaked open and the receptionist peeked inside. "Excuse me, Ms. Marshall. I have a Kent Hughes here to see you. Should I let him in?"

Kent was here?

She gave a jerky nod and the receptionist departed. Toni lifted herself up on her elbows and closed her legs. A few seconds later, he came inside and shut the door behind him. "What are you doing here?"

"Leslie called me. She said you might need me." He walked to her side. "I saw Celeste and Yasmeen in the waiting room."

"Leslie?" Toni repeated with a shake of her head. There was no way her friend had done her like this. She heard the faint sound of her cell phone vibrating and figured that was her friends warning her of Kent's approach. "What did she tell you?"

"Nothing much. She texted me yesterday and strongly advised me to show up here today. So I cleared my schedule for my favorite lady." He kissed her cheek before going to sit on one of the two stools in the room. Scooting close, he held her hand.

"Thank you so much for coming, but you don't have to wait here with me. I don't want you getting squeamish." Toni gave him a smile, though her left eye ticked. She was going to give Leslie a good telling-off when she saw her later.

"I'll be fine. You know I was premed before I switched majors, right?" He gave her a reassuring pat. "Besides, we're going to be husband and wife…"

"Going to be," she emphasized, "as is in, not yet. If I'm being honest, I'm not comfortable. I don't need you seeing my hoohah until our honeymoon or when I'm fresh off a Brazilian wax." Never mind that she had indeed gotten that taken care of because she was visiting the gynecologist today. *Hello.*

He chuckled. "It will be fine. I have no intentions of looking down that end. I promise." The chair squeaked under his frame as he moved closer to kiss her forehead.

On the inside, she sighed. There was no getting rid of her

beloved. She pouted. Leslie had no right to interfere, to meddle...to help? Whatever. She sniffled. Kent was here now and she couldn't order him to leave. She adjusted the blanket on her lower regions and turned her head toward the door, a tear sliding down her cheek.

Maybe it was good that he was here now and learned the devastating news so she could cut the umbilical cord on this relationship. Her phone buzzed yet again but she ignored it.

Kent tilted his head. "Unless...you don't want me here?" His question had a touch of vulnerability, like the thought hadn't occurred to him until that very moment.

Until he spoke those words, Toni hadn't realized how much his presence meant. "Of course I want you with me. Always." Or at least until he learned she couldn't give him children and was part of a robbery, and he left on his own will.

The doctor came inside with the PA and her pulse escalated. After making sure Toni was comfortably situated and verifying she wanted Kent there, the doctor turned and began the ultrasound.

At first, Toni kept calm. But then the doctor kept clicking. And clicking. And clicking. Her body began to shake.

"Whoa," Kent said, holding her hand. "What's going on? It's just a routine exam."

"No, there's nothing routine about this." She hiccupped. Her face was wet from the constant flow of tears. "I should have told you, but I needed to get a second opinion."

"Sec—" Kent must have thought better about talking in front of strangers. He placed a hand over his lips and went to get her a tissue, then kissed her forehead. "We'll talk after," he whispered, being his sweet wonderful self, which made her cry and shake even more.

"We're almost done," Dr. Ako said, her voice full of compassion. "Hold still." Her eyes were still on the screen. "Just a few more angles and then we can talk."

Thankfully, the PA remained silent. Once she was finished, the doctor told her to get dressed and meet her in her office. Feeling grim, Toni nodded and sat up, waiting until they had departed. Kent moved to leave.

Toni clutched Kent's hand. "Don't go," she croaked out. "Just turn around."

He stood with his back to her, straight and proud. "Should I be scared right now? You said you needed a second opinion and I don't know what in the world to think right now."

"It's not cancer, if that's what you're afraid of..." Her phone buzzed.

"Humph." That was his only response.

The only sounds were the crinkling of the paper when she slid off the chair and the swish of her putting on her clothes. When she was finished, he held his hand out, and together, they stepped down the hallway to the doctor's office. Toni's heart was filled with wonder. Was this what marriage would be like? What having a true partner was like? Not that she couldn't walk this alone, but right now, why should she, when she had this man willing to walk the path with her?

Dr. Ako greeted them and then confirmed the diagnosis. Primary ovarian insufficiency.

She swallowed. Her second time hearing those three words. Confirmation. Her shoulders slumped. She couldn't look at Kent, but he gave her hand a squeeze as Dr. Ako explained what that meant. Toni tuned her out, having heard it before.

"What does that mean in terms of having children?" Kent asked.

"It means it's highly unlikely," the doctor said.

"Unlikely is not impossible," Kent said.

"I've learned to never say never," the doctor replied. Diplomatic and noncommittal.

Kent's optimism annoyed her. She swung to face him. "Unlikely, as in not going to happen, so give it up." Toni jumped to her feet and ran her hands through her braids, her tears a heavy curtain. "Thank you for your time." Then she was through the door, her arms folded about her. She sniffled. She'd had no trouble getting pregnant for a man she despised, yet getting pregnant for the man she loved would be nothing but trouble.

Kent caught up with her at the end of the hall. He placed a hand on her shoulder. "Hey, wait up. We need to talk."

She tucked her chin to her chest. "I'm sorry I snapped off at you. I—I just want to be alone for a while. I can't look at myself or you right now." She sped toward the waiting area, where Celeste and Yasmeen were waiting, wishing Kent would leave her be, but he was right behind her and then beside her. He was everywhere. Ugh, when she left here, she would have a few choice words for Leslie.

Kent pulled her into an empty room.

"I don't want to abandon you when you need me," he said, rocking back on his heels. "I don't want to leave and then have you say that if I cared I wouldn't have left no matter what you said."

She heaved a sigh and touched his cheek. "I know you grew up with a single mom and that makes you more sensitive to the female psyche, but I'm fine. I have my friends and we're going to talk books. I'd rather talk books than dwell on my inadequacy, my failure. Plus, I have to prep for my interviews in a couple days, to snag a virtual assistant."

"Alright, I'm going to go because I know Celeste and Yasmeen will take good care of you, but I need you to know that I love you." She averted her eyes and nodded. *Please, Kent. Just go.* He cupped her cheeks and said, "Look at me. Don't ever describe the woman I love as inadequate or a failure." She peered into his earnest brown eyes and felt her heart shift. "I love you and I'm not going anywhere. You are more than enough for me. You're all I want and need. You are in a class by yourself."

Those words squeezed the doubt, the fears out of her being.

"I love you," she breathed out. "You're the best friend I never knew I needed."

He gave her a sweet kiss before pulling away. "Now, I shouldn't have heard about this appointment from Leslie. That's not what we're about. If I ask you what's going on with you, I need you to be honest. Is there anything else I need to know?"

She was about to shake her head when her conscience struck. "Yes, there is." She twisted out of his arms and squared her shoulders. "I… When I was fifteen, I messed with the wrong guy and ended up pregnant." She swallowed. "I terminated that pregnancy, and now look at me." Her heart thundered like wild stallions in her ear.

He stepped back. "What does that have to do with your ovaries? Did you hear what the doctor said?" Then his brows rose. "Whoa. Please don't tell me you really think that's why this is happening to you now." She did think that, but all she could do was lift her shoulders. "Sweetheart, you were a child and that was years ago. I don't think the two are related or she would say so."

"Oh." In a couple seconds, Kent had slashed the guilt she carried like a weight on her back with good old-fashioned common sense. Leaning into his chest, all she could do was sob as she found her release. When she left here, she was going to thank Leslie for butting into her business. "You're the absolute best."

"I hope you think so after my confession," he said, "since we're being honest."

She tensed. She was still keeping secrets. Toni could barely keep her gaze on his while she waited.

"I really don't like the lemon cake," he said.

Toni laughed. "Vanilla, it is."

25

Celeste

FEBRUARY 5

As soon as Toni pulled in front of the building, Celeste felt a tug of anticipation in her tummy. This was it. She was looking at the spot for Besties, Books and Bevs. Or, Triple B for short.

"Talk about a prime location," Yasmeen said, opening the front door. "You did good, girl."

Celeste clasped her hands. "I don't know what brought you to this side of town, but it feels like more than fate."

"I guess you could call it that," Toni said, uncharacteristically low-key about her discovery. The Toni she knew would be chatty, giving all the details of how she chanced upon the space. But she did raise her hands and rock from side to side. "Ooh, I love it better in the daylight."

"It has ample parking," Celeste added, looking around the large lot. There was a food truck on the other end of the pavement, with a small line. It looked like it was a barbecue joint, judging by the smoke coming from the back of the truck. Maybe they could skip their lunch reservations and stop over there. Yasmeen had joined the golf club—though she had never picked up a club once in her life, and no, miniature golf didn't count—and she wanted them to have fresh seafood from the five-star chef on the property.

That girl sure knew how to spend, but Celeste hadn't chided. She didn't want Yasmeen to think she wasn't happy for her, and their friendship wasn't about her constantly lecturing her.

"Now, we've got to play it cool," Yasmeen said. "We don't want the landlord upping the rent because we acting too thirsty."

"I ain't go'n lie," Toni said, "I'm ready to drink the water, girl."

"Keep calm," Yasmeen said.

The three friends huddled arm in arm in front of the building and silent squealed. The brick building with white shutters took up a large portion of the end of the block. Next to it was a bakery and a barber shop. From the look of it, the place appeared to be well maintained. There were round metal table-and-chair sets along the sidewalk and Celeste could already picture patrons reading while enjoying one of Yasmeen's teas. Speaking of which, she needed to ask Yasmeen about that.

A gentleman who appeared to be in his late forties, early fifties opened the door. He had salt-and-pepper hair closely shaven to his scalp and was dressed in brown trousers and a brown-checkered sweater along with some dress shoes. "I'm Nelson, and you must be my prospective renters." His head touched the doorjamb, making him about a good five inches taller than Wade. He scanned the group before his eyes rested on her, and his mouth widened into a smile. *Oh my.* She returned his smile with a shy one of her own.

It wasn't until she placed a hand to her chest that she realized that she wasn't wearing her wedding ring. Nelson stepped aside so they could enter. Celeste caught Toni looking at her, her eyes wide.

Yasmeen passed to enter first, one of her poofs grazing Celeste's cheek.

"Someone's got an admirer," Toni whispered, holding Celeste's hand to give it a squeeze.

She raised her brows. "Girl, I am taken."

"It's still nice, though, isn't it?" Toni asked, jabbing her in the ribs.

"Can't fault him for having good taste." They high-fived. Toni scurried after Yasmeen, who was plying Nelson with questions. They disappeared around the wall.

As soon as Celeste stepped into the wide expanse, her heart warmed. There was a fireplace and an area that looked like it could house the café. The rest of the store had space, lots of big, open windows, which made the atmosphere bright and cheerful. They could probably squeeze about thirty people in here, along with the books. She looked up and gasped. Was that a loft?

In her mind's eye, she could picture the books, the long wooden ladder to get up there. A couple of comfy sofas.

"Celeste, you've got to come see this," Toni yelled, her voice echoing in the empty space.

"Where you at, girl?" Yasmeen shouted, several octaves above her usual pitch.

Celeste chuckled and hurried to have a look. So much for playing coy. The wooden floors creaked with each step of her boots, but some area rugs would help with that. When she turned the bend, Celeste stopped. Then smiled. She got it. She understood their excitement.

"Is that a nook?" She pointed. The space by the window took up the entire wall. She couldn't believe it. This place was designed to win the hearts of book lovers.

"Yes, yes." Toni broke off into a full-fledged, old-school dance move.

Nelson dusted the wood. "It needs reinforcement and a fresh coat of paint."

"You heard that? All we have to do is repair the wood, give it a little TLC," Toni shrieked. "It's perfect. We can even store books on the shelves underneath. I mean, pinch me, somebody." Then she lifted a hand. "Okay, don't."

Celeste snapped her fingers. "We can put in a nice mahogany or deep cherry flooring up there." She nodded, her excitement heating. "And we can get some sage cushioning. Man, I can see it now. This place is going to be fire when we're done."

Toni held out a hand to Nelson. "We'll take it." Her enthusiasm was contagious. Yasmeen gave a thumbs-up.

"We didn't hear the cost yet," Celeste said. "We have to make sure it's in our budget."

"Don't matter. I want it," Toni said with a wave of her hand. Nelson chuckled.

Yasmeen held up her phone, snapping pictures, and then made a video call to Leslie to give her a virtual tour.

"We need to look at the restrooms," Celeste said. "Check out the plumbing."

"I just had the bathroom renovated and the plumbing lines replaced," Nelson said. "And, I'm willing to negotiate. I'm a book lover myself and it would be nice to have a bookstore. I love reading Harlan Coben." There he was giving her warm looks again.

"I'm sure Celeste would hook you up," Toni said. She pushed Celeste closer into Nelson's space, like she was a part of the bargain. She took a few steps back and gave Toni a look of warning to ease up.

Call her Suspicious Sally, but this place seemed unreal. She met Nelson's eyes. "How is this spot still available? Why hasn't anyone grabbed it?"

"Is it for sale?" Toni asked.

"Well, uh, I don't know if you heard, but the flower shop folded when the owner died trying to climb up that loft. Well, she fell and then died en route to the hospital, but no one finds that tale as salacious as saying she died here." Nelson wiped his brow. "A lot of people knew her and they are a bit hesitant to rent the space." He lifted his hands. "Thus, the overhaul. I had a café in mind, but a bookstore would be the perfect addition to this mall."

"My followers would eat that up," Toni said, obviously not deterred by the fact that someone had passed. "Let me research this real quick."

"Please show a little tact," Celeste said to her friend. But Toni was tapping away on her phone, her face the picture of fascination while she read about the previous renter's demise.

"I would consider doing a lease-to-own kind of thing," Nelson said. "My wife died a couple years ago, and I've been thinking about moving out of state to be closer to my children. I own this entire strip and I've been fortunate to have wonderful tenants." He looked at Celeste. "I feel as if I could trust you to take care of my property if you wanted it."

She lowered her eyes. The finance major in her admired the fact that Nelson had residual income. "Would you be opposed to us building a staircase to the loft and putting in an enclosure?" she asked.

"That's a good idea." He placed his hands on his hips and walked up to the spot. "I know just the builder for you too." He tapped his chin and paced back and forth, mumbling to himself. Every now and then, he looked up at the ceiling before continuing his think-thru. He reached in his pocket and made a phone call.

By this time, Yasmeen had ended hers, and both she and Toni had joined Celeste while she waited for Nelson.

"Leslie is in," Yasmeen said, her eyes shining.

"I love the mystique, and imagine what we can do during Halloween season," Toni added.

Celeste gave her a cutting glare. "We cannot capitalize on someone's death, Toni."

"I'm trying to make it into a positive experience," Toni explained with a little more decorum. "And a haunted-house adventure in Halloween season would make us a fortune."

"Say what, now?" Yasmeen said, her eyes darting between them. Toni rushed to explain what they had learned. Yasmeen twirled her index finger. "I don't want this woman's ghost haunting me because we took over her place," she said.

Celeste bopped her on the shoulder. "You are so superstitious."

"I'm serious," Yasmeen whispered. "I'll be doing what I need to do to invite calmness into this space." She shuddered. "I'm ordering my sage and candles tonight and I'm going to add this location to my father's prayer list."

Celeste rolled her eyes and bit the inside of her cheeks. "You are straight-up ridiculous."

Toni busted out laughing.

Yasmeen scowled and folded her arms. "Whatever. Laugh if you want. But I'm doing it."

"How about we go check out the bathroom, the storage area and the office?" Toni looped her arms through theirs.

Celeste put a hand to her mouth. "I was so caught up that I forgot there was more to see." They finished the tour, loving the large area in the back, which had an entrance for deliveries. She could picture the rows of shelves housing their excess books.

"As soon as I go home, I'm prepping a vision board," she said. "I'll get with Leslie to see about ordering the necessary supplies."

"Whoa, so you've made up your mind?" Toni whooped. "We're doing this?"

"Yes. We are."

The women cheered, then dabbed at their eyes.

"I had to handwrite my book lists," Yasmeen rushed out. "My new computer hasn't arrived yet and I didn't have time to go to the library." She reached into her bag and took out some sheets of paper with neatly written words and handed them to Celeste. "I will have more for you soon."

Celeste dropped them in her bag and gave it a pat. "I'll take care of it."

"I'll get my interior designer to come and take a look to give us a quote," Toni said.

"Aahhh!" Celeste jumped. "This is exciting."

"I know, right? Let's go see what Nelson has to say," Toni offered. They returned to the main area.

"We definitely want this space."

"So, I can get this place ready by mid-April," he said. "I know when you called, you were looking for late June, early July, but how do you feel about moving up your launch to May? My son just called and they are planning a cruise and want me to come, so I would want this all settled before then." Nelson then quoted them a sum well below their anticipated rate. "After a few months, we can revisit the idea of your purchasing this unit outright. What do you think?"

She looked to Yasmeen and Toni to get their reactions.

"We have everything in order, so I think moving up the date would work," Yasmeen said. "Maybe the first week in May could work."

"And I can talk to Kent about moving up our wedding date to match," Toni said. "We don't have a huge guest list. Most of our attendees will be virtual and the rest are all local, so I think moving it up will add to the hype. It could work."

Wow. It really was all coming together.

"I think you have a deal," Celeste said, shaking his hand. He lingered a little too long for her liking, so she added, "I can't wait to show my husband this spot. He's going to be over the moon."

She took in the slight tightening of the lips before Nelson gathered himself. "He's a lucky man."

"You should tell him that," she joked, but her words fell flat, and her tone came across as pleading.

But Nelson was too much of a gentleman to comment, and thankfully, her friends didn't either. With a dip of the head, Nelson excused himself, leaving to prepare the lease documents.

Mentioning Wade did dampen her delight somewhat, but Toni and Yasmeen had more than enough eagerness to cover whatever she lacked. She took a moment to snap a picture of the exterior to send to Wade, who gave her a thumbs-up sign.

That was it. Unless they were hooking up, he didn't have much to say. It was paltry but she would take it.

Are we meeting up later? she texted, tapping her feet while she hoped he responded in the affirmative.

Raincheck?

She pictured the salmon she had defrosting in the sink and sighed. She had to keep things light and easy until she had reeled him back home full-time. Sure. Catch you later.

This time she got another thumbs-up. Celeste felt a sudden urge to tell him she was more than a booty call. She was his wife. But if she did that, chances were Wade would agree and cut things off permanently. And, she was oh-so not ready for that.

She swallowed her impatience, her pride, and sent him the only response she could.

A heart.

26

Leslie

FEBRUARY 5

From her bedroom, Leslie pulled up the Ring app on her phone to see who was at her door. The call with Yasmeen, giving her the tour for their bookstore, had depleted her energy. Spotting her three friends waving at the camera, she groaned. "I told you I wasn't up to visitors tonight." She noticed they had balloons and paper bags that she would bet held Italian food.

"If you don't come answer this door," Toni shot back, "I am coming through the window."

"You know this neighborhood isn't ready for that," Yasmeen hollered.

"We're not leaving until you answer the door," Celeste stated.

"We're just going to talk about this book from right here," Yasmeen said.

"Yep, even if we're freezing," Toni shouted. "And disturbing the peace."

"Just open the door," Celeste commanded.

"You turkeys are stubborn enough to stay out there all night if I let you," Leslie mumbled with a shake of the head. She might as well let them in. "Whatever, I'm only letting y'all in because I see you have food. I'll be right there."

She passed her reflection in the hallway mirror and screeched, touching her drooping strands. She hadn't yet showered, and she was still in her jammies and a robe. Her kitchen was littered with dishes and her living room area filled with takeout boxes. She sniffed under her arms. Oh no, this wouldn't do. She rushed back to her room to brush her teeth and freshen up. Raking a comb through her hair, she tugged it into a bun. Then she searched for a clean sweater and a pair of jeans.

The doorbell rang.

"Mom," Nadya yelled, ringing the tiny bell Leslie had thought was a good idea to purchase. "Can you get the door?" There was a home healthcare nurse on duty until 11:00 p.m., so Leslie knew she didn't have to worry about Nadya. Unlike the rest of the house, Nadya's room was immaculate. That's where Leslie devoted her time and energy.

"It's your godmothers," she yelled back. "They're here for book club. I'll get it in a second."

Goodness, they were leaning on that doorbell. When she was suitable, Leslie raced down the stairs to let them inside.

"Took you long enough," Toni said, giving Leslie a hug before giving her the once-over and scrunching her nose. Leslie ignored her, eyes on the large paper bag in her hands. Her stomach rumbled.

Celeste and Yasmeen followed, carrying more bags.

"Ms. Moneybags insisted on getting seafood," Celeste said.

"Whatever." Yasmeen kissed Leslie's cheeks.

Their faces registered their shock when they saw the condi-

tion of her house—the sun's glare highlighted the dust bun-
nies, the cobwebs high in the ceilings, the layer of grime on
the coffee table. She shrugged. Bless their hearts, they didn't
utter a word about it and she closed the door.

Instead of asking the real question: *Why is your place looking
like a scene from* Hoarders? Yasmeen asked, "Where's Nadya?"

Toying with the frayed edges of her sweater, Leslie said,
"She's upstairs. The nurse is with her. The social worker on
our case arranged that service to give me respite." Not that she
ever took a break. Leslie didn't allow the nurse to do much. She
had to do it all, show Nadya how much she loved her, wanted
her. She needed Nadya to know Leslie would be there for her
for life, that she wasn't about to abandon her or shirk on her
duties, even if she was too exhausted to do anything, not even
sleep at night.

"Okay, we'll go visit with her after book club," Toni said.

Her friends picked their way over the clutter and gravitated
to the family room, where they usually congregated when it
was her turn to host. Leslie felt her face go hot when her friends
got bug-eyed at the papers tossed on the couch and the floor,
right along with a litter of empty cookie boxes, ice cream car-
tons and candy wrappers.

Toni and Yasmeen placed the food on the corner of the coffee
table, the only free spot, then perched on the edge of the couch.

Shame washed over her entire being.

"I've been meaning to clean up, but…" She trailed off, tears
brimming in her eyes. She sniffled and wiped her face. "I told
you I would skip book club this month." Her shoulders shook.
"I didn't even read the book. I just… I don't know," she choked
out, sobbing now. "And it was my turn to choose the book, but
I…" Her voice cracked. "I'm just so…overwhelmed."

Her friends surrounded her, their faces filled with compassion and tears. "I can't think straight. I have all these books
around, and I can't get past one chapter. I don't know what's

wrong, but I'm not me." She lifted her hands, her vision blurry. "I don't know who I am." She swallowed, fighting the tears as the words flowed. "Every morning when I wake up, all I can think about besides Nadya is that…I wasn't…wanted. And I learn if any of the Johansens are a match…next week."

Her birth mother, Julie, had called to let her know all the family had swabbed and sent off the packages, but Leslie had avoided any other contact. Her newfound siblings had reached out, wanting to meet, but Leslie hadn't returned their calls. Plus, according to Julie, there was a whole slew of relatives. And a yearly family reunion.

She couldn't face them, face her jealousy.

"I don't know how I'm going to tell Nadya all of this." She splayed her hands. "How do I even start?" She felt a hand on her back. "It's too much."

Leslie's knees buckled, but her friends were there to support her, to steady her, banding their arms about her, rocking her, hushing her, allowing her to break down but not fall apart, their love a *strength*ship, a bond.

A sisterhood.

"We don't miss book club," Yasmeen said, her voice wobbly as she recited the mantra that had united them through all their experiences over the years, both good and bad.

"We don't miss book club," Leslie repeated.

"This is what we do, girl," Toni said, patting her shoulder. "Now, go sit down somewhere. We got this." She left the room and returned with a trash bag and some of the latex gloves Leslie used when cooking. Both her and Yasmeen slipped on a pair and began tossing the garbage. Celeste ushered Leslie to sit on the couch and went to help Toni and Yasmeen, ordering Leslie to eat.

The bag crinkled as she dug around to pull out one of the Styrofoam containers. This one had seasoned corn. Her mouth watered and she took a bite. It was delicious. Corn juice flowed down the sides of her mouth.

"You guys need to eat all this food before it gets too cold," she called out, reaching for a salmon-and-cucumber appetizer.

While she ate, her friends cleaned the family room.

Though she knew they were being helpful, Leslie was mortified. "This place is messy to the point of condemnation."

"That's a gross exaggeration," Celeste said, clucking her tongue, wiping her hands.

"Naw, girl. She's telling the truth," Toni said, stuffing more refuse in the almost-full bag.

Yasmeen pulled out her cell phone. "I'm calling a cleaning service."

"Humph, there you go, spending money again," Celeste said. "We can get this done in a few hours for the bargain price known as friendship."

"Did you see the rest of this house?" Yasmeen flailed her hands before making the call. "Hello?" She headed out of the room as she talked. "Yes, I wanted to find out about your emergency cleaning..."

Emergency cleaning. Wow. She looked around her space with fresh eyes. Her house was really that bad. A reflection of how she felt on the inside. Her minor in psychology was coming in handy. She rubbed her temples. She didn't have a trash bag in which to dump all her emotional distress.

The women washed their hands, then came to sit by her and helped themselves to the meal. Celeste went to the kitchen and returned carrying a tray with iced tea for all of them. While they ate, Toni put on some country music.

Leslie bobbed her head to the beat, but then she heard the faint sounds of Nadya's bell and stood. "I'll be right back."

Celeste must have been watching her because she came over and pushed on Leslie's shoulder, commanding her to let the nurse do her job, promising to go check on Nadya after turning up the music to drown out any other sounds.

Now her friends teased her about how she danced like a

chicken, but Leslie didn't care. She lifted her hands and hopped around, doing her signature steps.

Celeste, Yasmeen and Toni came over to dance with her.

"Bawk, bawk," Yasmeen teased, mimicking Leslie's steps.

"You just sorry you can't copy these moves." Jumping around, Leslie said, "Everything I learned, I learned from my dad." A dad she missed but couldn't call to tell him so. Thinking about Edwin made Leslie recall something he had said.

You're going to need me, and when you do, don't hesitate to knock on my door.

She paused mid-dance before she gasped. While her friends frolicked, she marched to get her cell phone and punched in Edwin's number.

The minute he answered, she railed, "You knew all along, didn't you?"

"Knew what?" he asked, sounding like he had awakened from a nap.

"You knew that my real parents were nearby and had other children. That's why you were so certain, warning me almost, that I was going to need you," she raged. She heard the music come to an abrupt stop and her girls hovered close.

"Yes."

That one word sliced her gut. For some reason, she had expected him to deny it. She released staccato breaths to cool her temper. And her hurt.

He continued. "I ran into them at a natural food store down by the beach a few years ago. I don't know if they saw me, but I definitely saw them."

"I thought it was a closed adoption."

"I searched them out. Your mother's death shook me, and all I could think was if anything happened to me… But I never reached out."

"You are unbelievably selfish," she shouted, "and I want nothing more to do with you." Then she ended the call. Ball-ing her fists, she swung around to face her friends. "Ugh, I hate being lied to. I hate it with a passion." Fury boiled, stirred by hurt, adding venom to her words.

Yasmeen's eyes went wide. "What's going on?"

"Ooh, my father made me so mad just now, I could scream." She pumped her fists in the air.

Toni gestured for her to be quiet. "News flash. You are screaming, girl. Bring it down."

"Why does he say he loves me if he keeps lying to me?" Leslie scowled, her voice still raised several decibels above normal.

"Easy now. You don't want Nadya overhearing you," Celeste advised, going to sit on the couch. Leslie nodded and took several deep, long breaths. "Speaking of Nadya, maybe just tell her that you found some long-lost relatives who are testing to see if they can be her donor. You don't have to get into the weeds of the details, just tiny pieces of truth that add up until you have served her the whole truth pie."

Leslie cocked her head. "Dang, that's some good advice." She gave a small chuckle. "I might need you to come with me when I talk with her."

Celeste gave her a thumbs-up, then Toni chimed in. "I think that's something you and Aaron should do."

"Or maybe you and your father," Yasmeen added. She must have seen Leslie's fury at that suggestion, because she lifted a hand. "Never mind. Classic case of foot in mouth, again."

Leslie waved her off. "Don't worry about all that. I know your intentions. It's all good."

Yasmeen gave a little smile, her diamond rings flashing under the lights. "I'd better go wash my hands and then we can talk about this book."

Concern for Yasmeen's spending brought Leslie out of her own funk to pay attention to someone else's. "Please tell me she's wearing costume jewelry. That's a lot of bling on those fingers."

Celeste sighed. "They are the real deal. Yasmeen isn't making the best choices with her money right now."

"We're worried about how much she's spending so fast," Toni said in a low tone. "But I don't want her thinking we're not happy for her."

Leslie shook her head. "I'll refer her to our accountant. He'll help get her on a good track."

"Hopefully, she'll call him up," Toni said, before clearing her throat. "There's something I need to tell you—all of you—but I'll wait until after our book club meeting." Toni reached over to help herself to some of the food after dangling that announcement.

Uh-oh. Leslie sat in the armchair. She looked to Celeste but Celeste appeared to be clueless. "Alright," she said. "We'll talk afterward. I'm dying to know what you need to tell me, to tell us. So let's talk about this book so Toni can spill the beans."

"I'm sure I'm not the only one with things to talk about." She gave Celeste a pointed look.

Yasmeen shuffled into the room and took a seat at the far end of the couch. "What's this about spilling beans?" she asked.

Celeste patted Yasmeen's leg. "Later."

"I'm so glad you all came," Leslie said, slapping her thighs. "This was just what I needed to distract me from this crazy new normal known as my life. I want to hear it all. I've been in a bubble and we need to have our girl talk."

"The night isn't long enough," Celeste said wryly. "But we have to talk shop when you have the mental space, now that we're moving up the launch date. We got to get everything in order."

Leslie gave her a thumbs-up. "We'll set a date before you leave. Thanks for picking up my slack." She extended her gaze to her friends.

"No worries. Your cup is full and overflowing. We understand," Yasmeen said.

Settling into the plush cushions, Leslie released a long breath. For just this moment, she was going to allow herself to relax, enjoy the night with her girls. Tomorrow, she would go back to worrying and imagining all kinds of subterfuge. Reaching for a plate to get more food, she said, "Let the shenanigans begin."

27

Toni

FEBRUARY 5

She ignored the laser-like focus of Celeste's questioning eyes on her. Toni was determined not to let anything interfere with their book club meeting.

She reached into her bag for her copy of the book and rested it on the table. Next, she took out a folder and her laptop, placing those on her thighs.

"Since I knew Leslie wasn't prepared to host tonight, I planned our games and discussion questions."

"You're a lifesaver," Leslie said. "So thoughtful."

Toni's heart warmed.

Yasmeen snapped her fingers. "I just had an idea for when we expand the book club at our bookstore. We can post our monthly reads online and then plan games around the characters like bingo and charades. It could be a great chance to even connect with other book clubs across the nation."

"I like the way you think," Leslie said, mouth full of food.

Toni handed her a napkin. "We can start in the fall. I'll add that to our website once we decide on the book." Yasmeen opened her mouth and Toni held up a hand. "Don't say you know just the book. We're not venturing down that rabbit hole."

The women cracked up. Toni led them through all the fun activities, while they ate and laughed like they had many times before, like their lives hadn't been upended over the past thirty or so days. It felt good. And it was very much needed.

When they had cleared their trash, she met six expectant eyes and Toni knew it was time for her share. Her friends scooted close. Her heart pounded and she found herself hesitant.

Squaring her shoulders, Toni began, "There's no easy way to say this, and though this is my second time around today, it doesn't make it any better."

Yasmeen placed a hand on her shoulder. "Just spit it out. Kind of like what you do when—"

"Yasmeen!" Celeste yelled, then slapped a hand over her mouth.

Toni couldn't hold the chuckle. Just her girls being themselves was putting her at ease.

"What?" Yasmeen said, patting her poofs. "I was going to say 'spit out sunflower seeds.' What did you think I was going to say?"

Celeste rolled her eyes. "You are just too much."

Leslie toyed with the bracelet on her wrist and asked Toni, "So, what did you want to tell us?"

Toni read the trepidation in her eyes and sought to put her at ease. "Before I moved here, I was going through a rebellious phase and I started seeing someone who was into some bad stuff."

"What kind of stuff?" Yasmeen asked.

"At first, drugs, petty crimes. But then he started robbing and hurting people. Scary stuff."

Yasmeen raised a brow.

"Yeah, well, I was a kid, and no more interruptions. I've got to get this out." Toni ran her hands through her braids. "To get to the point, I ended up pregnant. I wasn't ready to be a mother, so I terminated my pregnancy." She inhaled. "I was walking around with a massive amount of guilt and thought it could be the reason behind my infertility, but of course, I know now that isn't the case."

"Okay...and?" Leslie gestured for her to continue.

Toni shook her head. "That's it." Her conscience squeezed. She should just tell the rest—the crime, the blackmail—and be done with it. But a tiny part of her was afraid of their possible rejection. It was ridiculous, didn't make any sense, but that was the crux of it.

Leslie shook her head. "But you said you had big news to share?"

Celeste pursed her lips. "I think she just did."

"So you pumped us up to tell us about your teen pregnancy?" Yasmeen said. "Dude, I hate to burst your bubble, but that has already been done." They all laughed. Her words reduced the tension in the room. She continued, "What kind of petty women do you take us for? We're not going to hold anything you did in your past against you. Besides, you know, I'm in no place to judge."

Toni marveled. Her friends really were the best. She hadn't known how Leslie would feel, but all she saw on her friends' faces was understanding. "That was pretty much how Kent was feeling when I told him. I was worried how he would react."

"Hold up. You told Kent?" Celeste asked. "That's major."

Really? That's what impressed them?

"I'm proud you put yourself out there," Leslie said, her tone filled with approval. They shared a hug, with Celeste and Yasmeen joining in.

"Honesty is the best foundation for a strong relationship," Celeste added, puncturing Toni's contentment.

She was still lying. She had only told half of the story. But to reveal everything was to risk everything. It wasn't that she didn't trust her friends. It was that she didn't trust the truth. The more people you tell about something, the more chance of it spreading like a red spill on a white gown. But if she kept it to herself, the truth would be buried with her. Contained.

Or would it?

Skins knew.

Her good feeling deflated. She pulled out of the embrace and lowered her chin to her chest. The truth bludgeoned her resolve, cracking her facade, brutally forcing huge, racking sobs out of her body.

"Oh my goodness, Toni, what's going on?" Celeste asked.

"There's more, isn't there," Leslie stated, matter-of-fact.

With a nod, Toni wiped her face. "I've buried it for so long that I had forgotten about it, until Skins came along and…"

"Wait, who's Skins?" Yasmeen asked, shoving a napkin in Toni's hand. "Girl, you're going to have to slow down because I can't keep up."

Leslie got her a glass of water. She took a few gulps to calm her insides. "He's the guy I told you about. The one I used to date. He's dangerous, he's scary and he's here."

"Here?" Yasmeen asked. "As in *here* here?"

"Yes." Toni's tongue loosened. "I was actually on my way to meet him when I saw the building." She gave a little chuckle. "Well, it's our building now."

"That explains what you were doing on that side of town," Celeste chimed in.

She gave a jerky nod, wadding the crumpled tissue in her hand.

"Why on earth would you be going to see this man when

you're engaged?" Leslie's tone suggested she had a problem with it.

Toni's head popped up. "He's—he's…blackmailing me." She fanned her face and apologized.

"Wh-Why?" Celeste asked, scooting closer to push Toni's braids out of her face and dabbing at Toni's tears as she repeated how sorry she was. Celeste tucked her finger under Toni's chin. "Why are you sorry?"

"Because I'm not who you think I am and I did something bad. Something really bad." She straightened and wiped her nose. "And unless I pay Skins a million dollars, he's going to tell the whole world what I've done."

28

Yasmeen

FEBRUARY 5

After she had uttered those words, Toni clammed up. No matter how much they prodded, Toni refused to provide any explanation for her cryptic comments. Yasmeen quit asking and backed off, but made it known she was there when Toni was ready to talk.

By then Yasmeen's phone had pinged at least four times. Darryl kept sending her raunchy messages and they were hard to ignore.

She excused herself to go to the bathroom again to give him a call. Her friends were going to think she had a stomach bug if she kept this up. She wished this man would leave her alone, but her traitorous heart skipped when his name appeared on her screen. Yasmeen rushed into the bathroom and pulled up his number.

"You've got to stop sending me pics," she said. "I told you we were done." Still, her heart raced, just knowing she was talking to him. She shouldn't be feeding this fascination.

"C'mon, baby. This is what we do. You get mad and then you take me back." He groaned long and deep. "I got to have a taste of your oatmeal cream pie."

She snickered. "You need to stop with the nonsense." She heard the lilt in her voice and could have slapped herself. Great. Now he would see that as encouragement.

"Where you at, baby?" he asked. His deepened voice made her insides feel like jelly. "I've been low-key stalking your parents' crib, trying to get a glimpse of you, but you holed up in there. Your books can't give you what I can." Darryl's voice held a sensual promise she knew he could deliver. "You don't need to read about romance when I can give it to you. Check your phone." He'd sent her another pic.

Whoa. He had missed her. Though Leslie kept her house cool, sweat formed on Yasmeen's forehead and under her arms. Dang, she had forgotten how sexy he was. Okay, she had tried to forget, but this was a very huge reminder.

"Darryl, I can't mess with you. You're no good for me."

"I agree. I don't deserve you, but I still got to have some whip cream with my pie. I baked some just for you."

Shoot, he knew she loved it when he talked food and sex. Her mouth watered. "Did you layer the top with cinnamon?" She licked her lips.

"Mmm–hmm, just the way you like it."

Whew. "That's it, I have got to get off this phone. I don't need to be your booty call."

"Listen," he huffed. "You're more than that delicious booty to me and you know it. I have genuine feelings for you, girl, so don't come at me like you're one of many. You're the only one I'm dealing with. That's the kind of bro I am. And you too stubborn to say so, but I know you must feel something or you wouldn't have bailed me out of jail. Thank your crew for putting up the cash." Yasmeen could correct him but she wasn't ready to deal with his leeching just yet. He continued. "I'm trying to get into culinary school, but they saying I have to pay for the classes this time since I jacked up the financial aid when I didn't finish the mechanic class."

Funnily enough, his words fueled her passion more. Her body responded to the ambition in his voice. Plus, for real, he could cook like nobody's business.

"Alright, alright, I've got to go because I'm at Leslie's house. She got a lot going on and so we all here trying to cheer her up—"

"See, that's what I love about you. How you care for others. Call me later, then. The time don't matter. I'll keep it hot for you," he said.

"I'm not at my parents' anymore," she blurted out. "I—I moved into my own place."

"Say what?"

Her video tone went off. She accepted, and soon his face filled her screen. "Why you just now telling me you moved?" he asked. His voice and face held hurt.

"I— It's a long story." She squared her shoulders, calling herself all kinds of foolish, and told him. "I won the lottery."

He laughed before he must have realized she was serious. His mouth hung open. "The *L-O-T-T-O*?" Then he covered his mouth. "Baby, this is good for us. Text me your address to your new place. I'll hit you up later. We can celebrate in proper style. Order us some Alize and caviar."

"I'm sorry I told you," she said, her shoulders deflating. Now she felt unsure, exposed. "All I see in your eyes are dollar signs."

He stopped laughing. "That's not even right. You obviously don't know me." He lifted his chin. "You know what? I'm out."

With that, her screen went blank.

Yasmeen hesitated, her hand wrapped around the doorknob. Maybe she should call him back. But then she heard Toni hollering for her. Knowing Darryl was vexed with her dampened her enthusiasm a little, but the mantra We Don't Miss Book Club, which she had recited that very evening, propelled her out the door and back to her friends.

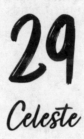

29

Celeste

FEBRUARY 5

Celeste undressed and, leaving her clothes on the carpet in her bedroom, traipsed into her shower. She turned on the tap and yawned, the sound echoing. This day felt like it'd had forty-eight hours, and she was ready to relax. The good thing about being exhausted was that when she fell asleep, she probably wouldn't have any nightmares.

Once she'd dried off and dressed in her comfy nightdress, she wrapped up her work on a financial planning presentation for the facilities executive board she had the next morning. Since Wade wasn't coming over, Celeste rewarded herself with a good book. Her perfect companion.

She scanned the books in her e-book library. She had purchased hundreds she had yet to read. One of her secret passions was reading Harlequin Amish romances. They were like a midnight snack before bed.

Quick, delicious, and of course, you couldn't read just one.

A few years back, Celeste had been wandering the book aisle at Walmart when she spotted an Amish woman checking out the romances. Dover was home to a thriving Amish community, so she was used to seeing them ride past in their buggies and enjoyed shopping at their bakeries. But for some reason, she thought they only read the Bible. Celeste had no idea that they enjoyed English pastimes.

The young woman's face had shone, enthralled by the contents on the back of the book. To see an Amish person reading a book about the Amish fascinated her. Celeste wanted to take a picture but refrained because the Amish didn't like photographs. But as soon as the young woman scuttled past her with the book in hand, Celeste had been curious to see what had captured her interest, and a new thirst was born.

Besides her faves, like Jacquelin Thomas, she now added authors of Amish romances to her never-ending to-be-read (TBR) pile. There was definitely going to be a small section of the bookstore dedicated to Amish books.

She typed the name Patricia Johns into the search bar and selected *Her Amish Country Valentine*. Celeste leaned against her headboard, crossed her legs and sighed. *Perfect*. She had been eager to read this one.

Her eyes burned, but Celeste couldn't stop until she was done. She heard a ping in her phone. It was a text from Yasmeen. Celeste was surprised to see it was well after midnight.

What you doing? I can't sleep.

Yasmeen had never texted her at this hour when Wade was there.

You alright?

Yes.

You lonely in that big house of yours?

Yassss!!!!!!!

Celeste chuckled. No one told you to get that monstrosity
of a house.

Yasmeen didn't disagree. Come over. Let's have a sleepover.
Her poofs must be snatched too tight.

Girl, you know I don't drive after hours. And even if I did, I'm in
my bed reading. Why don't you do the same?

Got tired.

Whatever. Celeste dropped her phone next to her and continued her novel. It was finally getting to the good part. Another ping. Another two words.

Coming over.

Her response was fast. Noooo!!!! I am almost done with this
book and I got work in the morning.

😮

Celeste looked upward and groaned. That meant she was
going to have to get up to go answer the door. She loved her
friends, but sometimes a girl just wanted to be by herself with
her books. Plus, for once, her feet were just right, under the

blanket, and if she moved, she might not achieve this level of comfort again. She gripped the sheets. *Why? Ugh.*

Tossing back the covers, Celeste got out of bed and trudged down the stairs to put on the kettle so Yasmeen could get some tea. Then she put a couple K-cups in her Keurig along with two mugs. It wasn't until it started brewing that she realized her error. She had been on autopilot, used to making coffee for herself and Wade.

Her heart pinched.

He should be there with her. By her side.

All she needed to do was go to therapy and he would probably come back home. That wasn't a big ask. But when she'd been going, her nightmares were worse, her emotions seesawed and her fears magnified. Therapy jarred her status quo. How was that a help?

Hard pass.

Plus, she had to function. She had to work. Celeste went to the window to look out for Yasmeen's truck. She hadn't taken any time off after the carjacking. Sitting at home would leave her more room to think about what had happened, and she couldn't have that. But she had told Wade she would go and she knew there was a limitation on how long he would accept her excuses for why she hadn't yet had an actual appointment.

But she was enjoying their hookups in the meantime. His hands, his lips. *Whew. Think of something else, Celeste. Think about the Amish. The weather. Anything but sex.*

Yasmeen's car turned into her driveway and Celeste scuttled over to open the door, wrapping her arms about her to shield herself from the draft of cool air.

"Hey, bestie," Yasmeen said with a wave. She opened the passenger door and took out an overnight bag with a Coco Chanel label.

And just like that, she was alright with her friend dropping by. A smile pulled at her lips. "Get in here."

As soon as Yasmeen crossed the threshold, she shut the door behind her and they hugged like they hadn't seen each other in weeks. The kettle whistled so they made their way to the kitchen. A very clean kitchen.

Remembering the condition of Leslie's home made her shudder. That house needed a top-to-bottom cleaning. Celeste planned to give Yasmeen money to aid that cause. The two friends worked on preparing their hot beverages. Yasmeen flipped through the different tea bags before making a selection.

"Darryl called, begging to see me, and I had to get away from that temptation or I was jumping back down that rabbit hole," Yasmeen said, rocking her hips. "Because, baby, it's been a while."

"Really?" Celeste chuckled. "It's only been about a week or two."

"Whew. Too many days. A sister has needs."

Celeste waved a hand. "Well, you came to the wrong place because I got nothing for you."

"Don't knock it till you try it," Yasmeen cackled, wagging her brows and pouring sugar in her cup.

"Say what?" Oh, she was very much awake now, her eyes wide.

Yasmeen changed the subject. "Anywho, I've been working on the signature tea for Besties, Books and Bevs—I can't believe we have a business—" she squealed "—and I have about three concoctions that might work. I didn't think to bring my herbs with me."

"Your herbs...?" Celeste shook her head. "Maybe it's the lateness of the hour, but for a second, I thought you were talking about a joint."

"Went to that party, danced to that jam," Yasmeen shot back, swaying her hips. "Meh. Didn't like that tune."

"Who are you and what did you do to my friend?" Celeste put a hand on her hip. "How am I just hearing all this?"

"I was curious." She didn't even sound repentant.

"It's always the preacher's kids," Celeste said, with a chuckle. "Pastor Adams had you on lockdown when we were in high school."

"Yes, as soon as I hit eighteen, I was going to experiment." She gave Celeste a sly glance. "The joint was Leslie's idea."

"Shut up." Celeste chuckled. "I don't believe that Leslie was the one to suggest that. Not even for a second." Celeste wagged a finger. "If she were here, she would have your head."

"One thing about me, I keep receipts." Yasmeen pulled out her phone and after a few swipes and taps, showed Celeste a picture of Yasmeen and Leslie, faces scrunched together, laughing. "We ate two bags of chocolate chip cookies that night."

Celeste's chest heaved with laughter. "Why wasn't I invited?" Not that she would have gone... Would she?

"If I remember right, you were on your honeymoon and Toni was on some trip with her job, but Leslie was free." Yasmeen flailed a hand. "You acting like you didn't try nothing. Don't forget I was there at your bachelorette party to see your Magic Mike moment at the strip club. You and Leslie were a hot mess, screaming and kicking your feet like you never seen a penis before."

"I don't know why I let Toni talk me into going." Celeste knew her face was brick red. "Girl, that man was doing some things... We made it rain that day." She fanned herself. "But that was it for me. It was hot and sweaty in there."

They cracked up, laughing until tears rolled down their faces.

"Yup. Me and Toni stood back watching you two acting like a couple of thirsty heifers. I think I recorded it too, but Toni made me delete the videos." Yasmeen sipped her tea.

"I'm glad you're here," Celeste said, dabbing at her eyes.

"Same."

Celeste grew serious. "I miss Wade."

Yasmeen's brows furrowed. "I know you do, honey. You two are the real deal. There's no impersonating what you two have."

"He gave me the name of his therapist, but I've been stalling." She recounted some of her earlier thoughts, then said, "I just don't want to keep rehashing that tragedy."

"But you are reliving it. Every night when you close your eyes. In fact, what could have been a tiny crack sealed with professional help, is now a chasm, destroying your marriage."

Yasmeen had a good point. "I'll think about it."

Her cell phone chimed and Yasmeen looked at her screen. "There he goes, sending me a pic of his junk to get me worked up." She turned the phone but Celeste lifted a hand.

"Naw. Keep that to yourself. I don't want to see all that."

"Suit yourself." She placed her phone face down on the counter. "It's not just physical for me, you know," Yasmeen whispered, placing a hand to her chest. "I think he has potential. He wants to take some culinary lessons at the tech center. That man can cook his butt off." She brought her fingers to her lips and smacked them. "You name it, he can make it. He even makes oxtails better than me, and he's not even Jamaican. And when he's not with his boys, he's kind and thoughtful…" She waved a hand and dipped her chin to her chest. "Let me shut up, because I know you don't want to hear about Darryl."

Hearing the yearning in Yasmeen's tone touched Celeste's heart. The man Yasmeen was describing made Celeste realize she might be judging him too harshly. Just a wee bit. "You should help him," she said.

Her brows rose. "I'm surprised to hear that coming from you."

Celeste shrugged. "Maybe I'm being too hard on *Pookie*. You're good people and if you see something in him and want to help, you should. Doesn't mean you have to be *with him* with him though. Let him earn the right to be with you."

Yasmeen gave a nod, the relief in her eyes evident. "Thanks

for listening. You're my oldest friend and what you think matters to me."

"Aw, come here." They hugged it out.

Celeste gulped the rest of her coffee, glad she had used the decaffeinated cups, and then reached for the other since Wade surely wasn't there to drink it. She knew she wasn't going to sleep that night. Eventually, the two women found themselves snuggled on her couch watching reruns of *Virgin River* on Netflix.

Minutes into the fourth episode of the first season, Yasmeen's head began to tilt. It kept its descent until she was slobbering all over Celeste's shoulder. Celeste gave Yasmeen a gentle tap to wake her before helping her into the guest room. Curling under the covers, Yasmeen turned on her side, a small smile on her face.

Celeste remembered when she would go to bed smiling, but sadly, those days were behind her, and now when she closed her eyes, mostly all she felt was fear.

30

Yasmeen

FEBRUARY 7

Yasmeen thanked the driver of the deluxe car service and tipped him well before stepping out into the overcrowded streets of New York City. She took a moment to breathe in the air, take in the sounds of the horns, the whoosh of the city bikers, and smiled. "I'll meet you back here in a few hours," she breezed out, then said, "Ta-ta," instead of a simple *goodbye*, before adjusting her oversize sunglasses.

She had decided to take a day trip to New York City. A solo trip, because she didn't feel like hearing her friends' mouths about how much she was spending.

This was her money. She should be able to spend it how she pleased without fear of being reprimanded like she was a child.

She was grown and about to do some grown-woman spending. Enjoy her *Pretty Woman* shopping spree. But first, she was going to have breakfast at Tiffany on Fifth Avenue. Yep, just like the movie starring Audrey Hepburn. The Blue Box Café had gone through major renovations and she planned to drop some dollars after snagging a reservation. It would have been for four, but her girls were straight-up tripping, pecking at her like hens in a coop, as if there wasn't enough corn to go around.

After having her tea, avocado toast and truffle eggs, she was going to make sure she left with a trinket or two in that special Tiffany Blue box. She had already studied the website and decided to purchase Darryl an Atlas watch in stainless steel. After her talk with Celeste, Yasmeen had paid Darryl's tuition and let him back into her bed.

Over the past thirty-six hours, they had blessed a good number of rooms in her house. All but the kitchen.

And he had arrived with a closet worth of clothes, his knives, pots and pans into her kitchen to cook her the most delectable meal. If she were being honest, he had moved in, but she wasn't about to admit that to herself or her friends.

With her head held high and a sashay of her hips, Yasmeen strutted behind the hostess to her designated table. Then she placed her order, loving the deferential treatment she received, especially when they saw her American Express Centurion Black card. *Mm-kay.* She was a part of that 1 percent now, and she was loving it.

While she waited, she people-watched the throng of shoppers dressed in everything from jeans to designer garb. It always amazed her how this city could cram so many people in a single store. But New Yorkers didn't seem to mind the jostle, the dance, the constant movement, all while minding their own affairs. In fact, they thrived on it. Even now, the buzz of chatter, the flash of the eyes, gave the city a beat that not many could dance to.

Not so Yasmeen.

She knew how to blend.

Her food arrived, and while she ate, she thought about the other items she planned to get—matching jewelry to gift her friends at the launch. Following that, she would let her eye decide and her hand do the swiping, and she wasn't going to deny herself anything she wanted.

A lithe young woman, dressed in a cream turtleneck and suede jacket along with matching four-inch-heel boots, slipped into the seat next to her. Yasmeen admired her bronzed skin and wondered what the woman used for her skin care routine. The woman tucked her bags in the corner and gave Yasmeen a smile.

Yasmeen couldn't keep her eyes off her. She had a quiet confidence, the look of old money, giving Yasmeen a case of imposter syndrome, as if she were the kid on the playground watching the other girls in their clique, all wearing the newest pair of sneakers and the coolest clothes.

Then she pulled up her account and looked at her balance.

Nope. She was good. Her money was just as good as everyone else's in this store. She placed her phone back into her purse and finished up her meal. After settling her tab, Yasmeen wandered over to look at the trinkets.

She eyed several pieces before she gasped and touched her chest. A sterling-silver bracelet offset with pearls glistened under the light.

The saleslady must have seen her gawking, for she sidled near. "Those are freshwater pearls."

"Ooh."

"Yes, we have our own special source. That piece was inspired by the New York City skyline," the lady said, adjusting her glasses. "It's part utilitarian with a bit of glamour."

It would be nice to have a piece of New York with her in Delaware. Yasmeen asked to try it on, loving the care with which she was treated. And the trust. As soon as the piece circled her wrist, Yasmeen fell in love. She had never owned anything so beautiful.

"I'll take it," she breathed out. The saleslady gave a nod and moved to undo the clasp, but Yasmeen placed a hand over it. "Leave it. I'll take the box though."

"That's gorgeous," she heard a wispy voice say. It was the woman Yasmeen had been admiring at the café.

"Isn't it?" She preened, holding out her wrist for the young lady to get a look-see, before addressing the saleslady. "I'll take three more of these for my friends."

"Whoa, how generous." Her new companion's voice was smooth, carefully modulated, like she was a singer. As she drew closer, a scent of jasmine teased Yasmeen's nostrils. The woman smelled wonderful as well.

"Yes, well, I have great friends." Yasmeen put distance between them and pulled out her credit card to hand over to the lady. Thinking about how she didn't have to worry about her card declining made her want to weep.

"I'm Cashmere," the sister said, holding out a hand.

Yasmeen shook the other woman's hand and introduced herself.

Cashmere flipped her hair. "I know this is an odd request, but I was about to hit up some stores and my coworker bailed on me. Do you want to shop together?"

That invitation was a little off-putting. Yasmeen shook her head. "No, I'm good. I don't plan on being here too long. I'm heading back to Delaware soon. I made this daytrip on impulse."

"Delaware?" Cashmere's brows rose. "You won't believe it, but I'm from Middletown. Delaware born and raised."

"Really?" Yasmeen moved closer. Somehow, hearing the woman came from the small state made her feel more like an ally than a stranger.

"Yes. I'm in finance and just finished a deal with a Fortune

500 company when I decided to stay an extra day and get some serious retail therapy done." She lifted her hand to touch Yasmeen's shoulder, her huge solitaire on display. That further put Yasmeen at ease, and she was flattered Cashmere thought she was good enough to hang out with. Didn't mean she was going to though. Still, she didn't want to be rude.

Yasmeen gave a little laugh. "I hear you. I had the same idea in mind, so I hired a car service and came up here." Riding in the luxury vehicle had made the trip seamless and enjoyable.

The saleslady came over with her package. Yasmeen's chest puffed as she held the trademark Tiffany bag in her hands. She slipped her card in her wallet.

Cashmere looped her arm through Yasmeen's. Though Yasmeen wasn't sure how she felt about that, she was so impressed by the attention, she didn't want to offend the woman. "It feels so good to run into another sister in here."

"Um, we're not the only Black people in this store."

"Yes, but I can tell we're both on another level." Cashmere waved a hand. "When I leave here, I'm heading to Dubai for business. What about you?"

"No set plans…" A feeling of inadequacy yawned. Cashmere had a tight grip. Yasmeen extricated her arm, feeling claustrophobic and with a sudden urge to lose her newfound company. She was a stranger and a bit too much. "Well, it was nice meeting you, but I have to pick up a watch for my boyfriend." She huddled her packages close to her chest.

Cashmere backed up and twisted her ring. "Okay, sorry if I came on too strong. My dad always said I was too friendly. When I was a child, he said, I would tell complete strangers my name and phone number." Cashmere snickered. "Actually, before you go… I came in here to pick up a gift for my dad, and I had my eye on a couple things. Would it be too much to ask for your opinion?"

Yasmeen was a daddy's girl. She didn't hesitate. "S-Sure."

She shuffled after the other woman, battling a sudden case of suspicion. Something about this young woman didn't settle right with her. But maybe this was how the younger generation operated—and she was out of touch. Old-school.

Cashmere whispered to the saleslady before gesturing Yasmeen over. The women opened the display case and took out a key ring with a Swiss Army knife.

"This could work." Yasmeen turned the sterling-silver jewelry in her hand. She debated whether to get one for her dad but decided against it. She didn't want Cashmere to view her as a copycat.

"It's either that or…" Cashmere took her hand and led her over to look at a beautiful fountain pen. "What do you think?"

Yasmeen rolled back on her heels. "Definitely the pen."

"I agree." She clapped her hands. "Thank you. My father is going to be ecstatic because of you." She settled up with the saleslady, then took out her phone and snapped a couple pictures of her purchase. "Let's exchange numbers so I can reach out to tell you what he thinks."

Yasmeen supposed there wasn't any harm in that, so they traded contact information.

"Now we are officially friends." Cashmere swung the small signature-blue bag.

Her beatific smile made Yasmeen relax and shove her doubts aside. "If your offer still stands, I'd like to take you up on it. I could use the company."

"Awesome. Let's explore Fifth Avenue. The world's our big apple today, or something like that."

"Lead the way."

A few hours later, when she was on her journey home, Yasmeen reflected on her new companion. Cashmere was both savvy and smart. Yasmeen had told her about the bookstore and had been delighted to hear that the other woman was also an avid reader. In fact, she'd read many of the books Yasmeen had.

That she was another book partner warmed Yasmeen toward the other woman more than anything else. In fact, she had invited Cashmere to their next book club meeting. She couldn't wait for her new friend to meet her besties.

31

Leslie

FEBRUARY 13

Ugh. If she heard that tinkle one more time… Leslie buried her head under the pillow and pinched her lips close together to keep from screaming. Once her friends had left, she hadn't been able to sleep so she ended up staying up most of the night reading *The Cuban Heiress*. The girls had raved about it, which reignited her interest. It felt good to lose herself in the story, eyes burning, and not think about the chaos that was now her life. But that bell pulled her back to reality.

Tinkle. Tinkle.

She slid a glance toward Aaron, snoring next to her, a strong urge rising within her to bop him with a pillow. He hadn't arrived home until close to 3:00 a.m. and had gone right to sleep, so it was up to her to cater to Nadya's needs. She didn't know how he was able to tune out that sound. But he had also done a remarkable job of ignoring the mess in the house. Although that could be because he wasn't around long enough to be bothered.

Tinkle. Tinkle.

She rued ever giving Nadya that bell.

It was only 5:07 a.m. What could Nadya want at this hour? Her daughter was doing this on purpose because Leslie had taken her cell phone. Since her hospitalization, Nadya had gotten used to playing Roblox on her devices for hours. Now that she was home, Leslie had reinstated the policy of no electronics use after 8:00 p.m. Nadya had jutted her lip, but Leslie was immune to that face. Well, okay, she had made sure not to look her daughter in the eyes. It was hard to deny a sick child. But, she reasoned, a spoiled, sick child would be intolerable.

Tinkle. Tinkle.

Maybe the walkie-talkie app would have been a wiser choice but it would have meant Nadya using her phone.

Rolling from under the covers, Leslie plodded through the plush carpeting to Nadya's room and opened the door. It was really a suite because her daughter had her own bathroom. Her walls, painted light purple, featured other gymnasts, and there was a mat on one side of her room. A flash of Nadya doing her floor routines made Leslie hold in a sob. All the irritation she felt oozed out of her being.

She wiped her face. "What's going on, darling?" She went to sit next to Nadya on her bed.

"I'm really nervous about today, Mom," Nadya said, her voice trembling. Her hair was matted on her face because of sweat, and her eyes looked darkened, hollow, like she hadn't slept at all. Leslie's heart squeezed. She'd taken Celeste's advice and told Nadya that newly discovered relatives had tested to see if they were a match and that they would learn the results today. She hadn't divulged the true nature of their relationship—yet. She would though, if—no, when—Nadya got better.

"I know." She kissed the top of Nadya's head. "But if everything goes right, you'll be better soon and you'll be able to go back to school and your friends."

Nadya wiggled. "That will be awesome. What time are they supposed to call?" She finished her question with a big yawn.

"The doctor's office should be phoning sometime close to noon, so you need to go back to sleep."

"I—" yawn "—don't want—" yawn "—to sleep." Nadya rubbed her eyes. "Can I play—" long yawn, slow blink "—on my cell phone?"

"No, what you can do, is close your eyes and rest." Leslie kissed the top of Nadya's head and turned off the main light. Nadya was too busy yawning to argue. She took a moment to look up at the galaxy projecting from the small oval in the corner of her room. Aaron had placed it there when Nadya complained about sleeping in the dark.

Leslie returned to her room and decided to get a shower. Knowing she wouldn't be able to fall back asleep, she figured she might as well straighten up before the cleaning service workers showed up, then work on the inventory for the bookstore. She would reward herself by finishing her book. She gave her body and hair a good scrub and then donned Rihanna's Savage X Fenty underwear that Toni had gifted her. Leslie had been worried about being accused of appropriation, but Toni had waved her off, saying nobody was worrying about what she was wearing under her clothes, and that Rihanna's clothes were for everyone.

Leslie ran her hands down the sheer mint-colored bra and matching panties and turned to study her luscious figure. Her lips widened into a smile. She looked and felt desirable. She went into her room and put on a plain housedress, hating to cover up all that goodness.

Eyeing the book on her nightstand, the impulse to read won over the chores. She trekked down the stairs, brewed a cup of coffee, and under the quiet of the morning, turned the pages until she got to the end. Closing her eyes, Leslie placed her book to her chest and sighed, grateful for this time of true respite.

Now she could get on with her day. Looking at the clock, she sucked in a breath. It was close to seven thirty and she hadn't picked up a single article of clothing off the floor. The door-bell rang and she rushed to get it, knowing her face would be flaming red. She could see crimson spread across her chest and decided she would avoid eye contact with the cleaners, sparing herself from seeing the silent judgment in their eyes.

But when she opened the door, Edwin stood there. Without a word, she moved aside to let him in.

"This has gone on long enough," her father said, his wool cap in hand, his chest heaving. "After that phone call last night, I have had it with your little stunts. It's time for you to act like the grown woman you are."

They headed toward the kitchen where she braced herself for the showdown. Her father stopped to pick up some of the laundry, his nose upturned. Leslie bit her cheek to keep from explaining, or breaking down again. She took the clothes from him and rested them on the chair.

"I have cleaners coming today," she said, but her father still picked up what he could. Like he had done when she was a child.

His anger was a building block adding to the tension in the room.

She found his fury off-putting. It wasn't often that Edwin got mad at her. "This isn't a stunt," she said, her voice steely. "You hid my true parentage from me. Something I should have been told when I was old enough to understand. Something I shouldn't have had to learn when my child was in a hospital, fighting for her life."

"When? When your mother died?" he shot back, tossing some of her containers in the trash before hauling it out of the bin.

"No, but maybe when I first got my period or went on my first date or had my first kiss." She ran her fingers through her hair. "It would have been nice to have a woman to talk to."

"I didn't think I was too poor of a stand-in, but I get it." He held the trash bag in a beefy fist. "I did the best I could." Edwin went to take out the garbage and then returned. He washed his hands. "Look, you didn't grow up the classic poor little rich girl. You had plenty of love, and your mother and I were devoted to you. You were well taken care of, and I dare to say, you turned out alright."

"I know. But you deceived me." Leslie shook her head. "It's the fact that you were never going to tell me that rankles the most."

Edwin drew in a deep breath, visibly trying to calm himself. "Regardless, it doesn't excuse your abhorrent attitude toward me. Nadya is perceptive. I don't need her picking up on bad vibes between us. I love her too much to add to her stress."

His barb couldn't be ignored. "Don't use Nadya as a shield for your wrongdoing. I'm not adding to my child's stress. I'm all about getting her better."

"Glad to hear that. Now, quit behaving entitled and spoiled."

"How do you expect me to act when you had me living a lie for *thirty-four* years?"

"Act like a parent who understands that sometimes you keep things from your children if you don't want to hurt them."

"Keeping this from me did hurt me."

"We are going round in circles. When all I want is peace."

"And all I want is my child to get better, which is why I'm waiting to hear if one of my relatives is a donor."

He rubbed his head. She scrutinized him. Edwin looked tired, haggard, like he hadn't been sleeping. Guilt squeezed her heart. She knew it was because of her.

He sighed and rubbed his eyes. "When will you know?"

"I'm supposed to get a call today. The doctor said right before the lunch hour. If all goes well, Nadya will be heading back to the hospital to begin prepping for the bone marrow transplant."

Just then, Aaron entered the kitchen. He wore a plain T-shirt and pajama bottoms and his hair was standing up in all directions. He grunted a greeting and went to get the Keurig machine going. He asked Edwin if he wanted a cup, and her father nodded before slipping out of his jacket, placing it on the back of a chair and taking a seat.

Leslie wanted to lash out at him for practically inviting her father to stay, but Nadya would be up soon, and she didn't want to distress her daughter by arguing with Aaron. Besides, that would give credence to her father calling her spoiled.

"I checked on Nadya, and she's still asleep," Aaron said, almost as if he had read her mind. He leaned against the counter while the coffee percolated.

Edwin stretched his legs. "How's the bookstore going?"

"We found a location for a reasonable rate. If all goes according to plan, we should be ready to set up shop soon. Actually, we moved up the launch date."

"Oh, that's wonderful," Aaron said, pouring two cups. He came over to give her a kiss on her cheek. His eyes dipped under the top of her housedress and he obviously spotted the sexy lingerie underneath.

The eyes that met hers had darkened, and she did her best to pretend she was unmoved by the desire reflected in their depths. She couldn't handle one more thing in this Jenga game called her life. Instead, she broke eye contact and went to turn on the morning news for her father.

"This is delicious," Edwin said, unaware of the friction between Leslie and Aaron, or maybe he was very much aware and trying to ease the tension. Who knew?

She wasn't too happy with either of them at the moment to care about it too much though.

The faint ring of Nadya's bell made Aaron jump up, stating he would go check on her. Edwin volunteered as well. She supposed neither of them wanted to be in her company and she was fine with that.

The doorbell rang, and the cleaning crew, consisting of four people, trooped inside, holding supplies and other paraphernalia. She admired the women's pink-and-white uniforms and the men's navy blue ensembles.

After quick introductions, they got to work, and the house began to smell like bleach, lemon and wood cleaner. Aaron retreated to his office to take a few work calls and her father turned up the television to watch his home improvement shows. Leslie spent time with Nadya and then ordered bookshelves for the store and furnishings for their café.

When the cleaning service crew was finished, they opened the blinds and she welcomed the rays of the sun glistening against the freshly cleaned window.

And she thanked her friends.

Then the phone call came. Together, Leslie, Aaron and her father huddled with Nadya as Leslie placed the phone on speaker and heard that there was a match. Two actually, but one had an autoimmune disease. The doctor marveled at the impossibility, the unlikelihood of finding two potential matches, then droned on about the months of prepping, but no one cared. Amid all the whooping and joy around her, Leslie fell to her knees and lifted her hands. The fear around her heart eased and all she could do was cry, her body racked with relief.

Her baby was going to be alright.

Her baby was going to be alright.

Her baby was going to be alright.

32

Toni

FEBRUARY 14

The website was ready. Their professional photos were up.

The only thing left was her official announcement to her followers about the bookstore launch and her wedding date. A double whammy. And there was no better day to do this than Valentine's Day—a suggestion from her new assistant. When Aliyah proposed that during her interview, Toni had hired her to start that very hour.

Aliyah had been posting all week that her viewers needed to tune in at 2:30 p.m. today for Toni to make a special announcement. Then she had hired Joe, who was setting up in his usual spot for her shoot.

Kent had been ecstatic when she suggested moving up their

wedding date, since his father and stepmother were planning to relocate to Florida after the ceremony and they could move in time to have their annual Fourth of July celebration. He was also more than ready to consummate their union.

In fact, his exact words had been, "I'm ready to be your husband and to call you my wife and once we've recited those wedding vows, be prepared." His voice had dropped, causing tingles to run up her spine. "I'm going to need days," he had said, "days to make love to you. And a few more days to do it again."

Whew. Standing in front of her mirror in her living room, Toni wiggled. Talk about a promise. She plumped her lips and ran her hands down her sleeveless black St. John jumpsuit, similar to the one Michelle Obama had worn on the Jimmy Kimmel show a few years back. She admired her sculpted arms, the thick red leather belt that had taken a couple extra inches off her waist and the red kitten heels. Talk about fierce.

Aliyah had chosen a winning ensemble. She was efficient and like the little sister Toni had wished for but never had.

Overall, the vibes were positive in her world.

Except for Skins. He was like a splinter in her finger, a pesky food particle stuck in her teeth. She couldn't wait to be rid of him. Toni had decided to pay him the money and had already begun to make withdrawals in increments so as not to trigger her bank into an investigation. Her friends had told her to call the cops, to report him, stating he would use her like a sieve, a never-ending cash flow. She agreed.

There was no way Skins would be satisfied with one million dollars. If she was able to give him one, then she would be able to give him two. That was his mindset.

She knew this, but she had to meet his demands.

Her reputation was worth that and more.

It was either pay him or end up behind bars. Possibly.

Every time she spoke with her friends, they would gently

nudge her to explain what she was afraid of that was so bad she would pay her extortionist.

Each time, Toni changed the subject or said, "I'll take the *L* on this." She just couldn't risk seeing the shock on their faces and dealing with questions she couldn't answer, like why she had kept this from them so long. At first, it had been to protect herself, then it was because the relationships were new, but soon, the lie became a shield, a way of blocking her view to her past. It had just been easier to say nothing.

Aliyah came over to let her know it was time to go live. Since she had done a few takes to work out the kinks of her message, Toni felt comfortable using live stream over recording. Besides, she wanted to see the comments as they were coming in and address her fans. She checked her teeth to make sure there were no traces of the salad she had consumed earlier. Next, she refreshed her lip gloss before throwing herself a kiss.

Once she was settled on the couch, Toni began with a practiced calm.

"Hello, Toni's Troopers! I'm so glad you have tuned in. As promised, I am coming to you live today to share some exciting news." Her feed already showed that she had over ten thousand viewers, and that number kept climbing. She took the time to give a shout-out to some of the people, waving or sending out a hello, and then cleared her throat.

"First, many of you know I use my time as an influencer to talk about things I am passionate about, like food, books and my boo." She clasped her hands and zoned in on the camera. "Well, in just over two months, I am pleased to announce that my friends and I will be opening Besties, Books and Bevs, a bookshop and café dedicated to giving a space for marginalized voices to be heard, to be seen and to be valued."

Countless hearts, thumbs-ups, and celebratory emojis and GIFs popped up on her screen. Her stream's numbers had increased to forty-five thousand viewers.

"In addition, on the day of our launch, Kent and I have decided to live stream our vows as man and wife at the bookshop. So keep an eye on my social media pages for the exact date, time and location. The first twenty people to comment will receive complimentary tickets to attend our ceremony in person."

Rapid-fire messages now filled the timeline.

Toni smiled. "Until then, stay sweet and be on the lookout."

"That was some good stuff," Joe said with a wide grin. "Your viewers are going wild. This event will catapult you to another level."

"I hope so," she said. "Now, remember to respond to the RSVP. I have a small VIP list and you're on it."

Joe swallowed. "That means so much to me. I can't wait to be there to film your special day."

She waved a hand. "Oh no, you're not on duty. You're a special guest. Give my assistant a few names and we'll secure a couple of them."

"Yes, but it would be an honor to work this for you. It's good PR."

"Understood. Okay, consider the job yours. In the meantime—" she placed a finger over her lips "—mum's the word on that date and time."

"You got it," he said, before beginning to pack up his equipment. "You really need to get you a real office space."

"I will," she said, tilting her head toward Aliyah. "She's on it."

Her phone buzzed, and even before she glanced at the screen, she knew who it was. Skins.

New due date. See you at the bookstore launch.

And just like that, her good spirits plummeted to the sole of her shoe. She placed her head in her hands. She was never going to be rid of him. And that last text proved he wouldn't be able to keep his word and his demands would spread like bacteria.

Unless…she took away his power.

33

Celeste

MARCH 15

"Dang, you upended my whole world just now. In a good way."
Celeste clutched the sheets and stared up at the ceiling in her
bedroom while she regained control of her breathing.

"That was...wow. Epic." Wade plopped his chiseled naked
body next to her and folded his arms behind his head.

"Do you need water?" she asked, wiping her brow. She had
a glass of water on her end table.

"I'm good." His tone sounded clipped. She could tell he was
disappointed in himself again. His weakness. Each time they
made love, Wade would say that was the last time, that he didn't
want to confuse the situation, and she had agreed, knowing his
hormones would win the war against his will, his good inten-

tions. For her, it was simple. They were still married. As far as she was concerned, she wasn't doing anything wrong.

The silence yawned between them.

"Did you call the therapist?" he asked.

"Y-yes." Celeste flipped to her side so her back was to him. She couldn't look him in the face while she lied. "They were booked solid but promised to call if there was a cancelation."

Wade sat up and swung his legs off the bed. She turned around and placed a hand on his arm. "You don't have to leave, you know."

"I do." He ran a hand down his five-o'clock shadow. "Ugh. You need to stop sending me pics with skimpy underwear. You need to stop sending me pics, period. I need to stop looking."

She had been reading a romance where the heroine had sent her man photos, and Celeste had decided to try it out as a lark. She hadn't expected to see Wade at her door twenty minutes later. Stifling a grin at his tortured expression, she tried to sound penitent. "Okay, but would you prefer I send them to someone else?"

He whipped around. "Be serious."

"I am being serious. Aren't you the one who wants this divorce?" She ran a hand down her leg. "That leaves me free to pursue other...interests."

His eyes followed her hand before he balled his fists. "You're enjoying this." Grabbing his pants off the floor, Wade put them on. "This is the last time I allow you to manipulate me, to distract me from my decision." He pulled up his zipper on his taut waist and then looked at her. "You're not who I thought you were." Those words spoken with disappointment crushed her to her very core. She wanted to protest, to say she was very much still the woman he'd married and that he was the one who had changed. But the words wouldn't move past her voice box.

He spared her a quick glance. "I'll have my attorney resend another copy of the divorce papers in the mail." Those words were like cement lining the walls of her stomach. She watched him, stunned, as he stormed out of the room.

He was running out of her life for good. That knowledge punched her in the gut.

Celeste hurried out of the bed. Her hand knocked the glass over, spilling the water across the book lists she had placed there. But she would take care of that later. Drawing on the sheer robe she had worn to answer the door, Celeste followed him down the stairs.

"You can't mean that," she huffed, trailing behind. "We love each other."

He stopped at the foot of the steps and looked at her. "Yes, but love doesn't do this. Love doesn't take advantage. Love isn't about games." He lifted his hands. "I am done with the games." She read the hopelessness in his eyes. "Nothing has changed since I walked out of here weeks ago. You still haven't seen a therapist, acting like therapy is akin to the bubonic plague. I'm convinced you faked interest to make me get my hopes up, to get me into bed."

She couldn't hold back the sharp intake of breath. "It's not like that." Only it very much was, and hearing him utter those words made her feel shallow. Superficial. And childish.

Eyes that had looked at her moments ago with tenderness now held scorn, cutting at her heart. "Don't contact me anymore. If you need to reach me, you can contact my attorney."

She stiffened. "If that's the way you feel, I'll sign the papers."

With a jerky nod, Wade was out the door.

Celeste's legs folded and she dropped to the last step. Holding on to the banister, she fell apart. Hot tears rolled down her face as the fight left her body. She certainly wasn't going to beg someone to be with her if they no longer wanted to be. The disgust on Wade's face was a huge deterrent to any more schemes.

In time, she wiped her face and trekked back up the stairs to her bedroom, snagging her gown. She slipped it off her shoulders and tossed it in her bathroom trash before taking a long, cleansing shower. When she was done, she padded back into her room, the soft, fluffy towel wrapped around her body. Seeing the wet papers, Celeste retrieved a towel and spot dried the sheets before placing Yasmeen's book lists in the drawer of the nightstand. She didn't have the energy to do that now. Dropping the towel to the floor, she donned cotton pajamas and got under the covers.

Ugh. The strong scent of cedarwood teased her nostrils. Masculine. Wade.

In a fit of rage, she stripped the bed and dragged the covers and sheets and flung them down the staircase. Spent, Celeste dropped to the side of the bed, her chest rising and falling while she attempted to gain control of her frayed emotions.

She had an early morning meeting with a new facility her company was onboarding and had to finish working on their financial plan. Their past expenditures showed that their previous financial advisor had brought them to the brink of bankruptcy.

Celeste was proposing a drastic five-year budgetary plan to bring them into the black, and she couldn't do that if she were a bumbling mess. Working would relax her, redirect her and reinforce her confidence in her capabilities.

Gritting her teeth, Celeste staggered into her home office and logged into her workstation remotely. For hours, she plugged in numbers, working steadily through most of the night. Then she checked on her investments and pumped her fists when she saw that she had made a significant profit. Since she had used equal funds from her and Wade's personal accounts and the bookstore's account, she would split the rewards in half.

Celeste was about to withdraw the funds, when the thought came that maybe she could double their input and possibly quadruple their output. She chewed on her lower lip and contemplated. Normally, she wouldn't make such a move unless she had studied the market for weeks. She would call anybody else who did what she was about to do reckless.

But she remembered the disappointment on Wade's face when he had said she wasn't who he thought she was. She straightened. Well, she was very much the person he had married and more.

She couldn't wait to humble brag on her skills. And to prove him wrong.

Decision made, Celeste shifted the money into a higher-risk investment fund that promised a big payout. The higher the risk, the greater the reward, and whoever had penned the phrase "the best revenge was success" knew what they were talking about.

When Wade saw the zeroes behind the dollar signs on their next statement in a few weeks, he would never doubt her again.

And he would be sorry he'd ever uttered those words.

34

Yasmeen

MARCH 17

Standing outside the Bally's Casino entrance, Yasmeen considered her new life. A couple months ago, she had come here in search of a job. Now look at her.

If only her friends would truly celebrate with her the way she liked. Life was for living and she intended to try new things. Like a few hours of leisure at the casino and then dinner at the Royal Prime Steakhouse. When she texted the group chat, all she had gotten were lectures. She was spending too much. She needed to take it easy. But, Leslie? Leslie had been the harshest, writing in all caps.

STAY AWAY FROM THAT MONEY PIT.

She couldn't blame Leslie, since gambling almost ruined her marriage before it even started, but frankly, her ears were tired of hearing the warnings.

Thankfully, Cashmere was right there with her, encouraging her. Cupping her bag under her shoulder, she waited for the other woman to get off her call so they could get inside. Yasmeen was eager to try the slot machines. She had her rolls of quarters from the bank, and that was her limit.

Cashmere trotted over and they hugged it out.

"Thanks for hanging with me," Yasmeen said. "I brought enough quarters for the two of us."

"Yassss, let's do this," she said, waving her hands in the air. "We about to turn it up. Although blackjack is more my gig."

Blackjack made her think of Aaron. That and roulette were his kryptonite. Maybe it was because she was thinking about him that Yasmeen surveyed the area to see if she spotted him. When she didn't, she released a breath she hadn't realized she held.

"I've got to use the bathroom," Cashmere said, tugging her toward the ladies' room. "Let's go now so we won't have to get up if things get hot."

"Why wouldn't we just get up and go?" Yasmeen shook her head.

Cashmere stopped to look at her. "You're definitely a newbie. People wear adult diapers and some even pee on the seats because they feel they might hit the jackpot."

"Say what?" she gave the other woman the side-eye.

"Girl. You don't want to know what I have seen or smelled in this place."

"So that's why they have the air cool and the vanilla scent."

"Yup. The funk is real."

They arrived at the restrooms and Cashmere rushed inside. Just as she was about to follow, she gasped. Aaron was coming out of the men's restroom. She blinked. Then blinked again. It was definitely him. He wiped his hands on his pants, his dress shirt hanging out. He looked scruffy, unshaven. She stared straight at him but he didn't even look her way. Yasmeen trailed behind him.

Aaron meandered toward the roulette table. Yasmeen stomped across the space and bopped him with her bag.

Aaron jumped and held his head. "Ow. Why did you do that?"

"Because you're a moron." She placed a hand on her hip. "What are you doing here?"

"I—I had a rough day and came to play for a little. You know, a basic stress reliever."

"Losing money is not a stress reliever," she snarled, anger flaring in her chest. "You know better than to be up in this place. Gambling almost cost you your relationship with Leslie. Did you forget that?"

Aaron dashed toward the exit and she scuttled behind. "Don't you run away from me," she huffed. But he just kept moving. They sailed through the door. "I'm going to tell Leslie," she yelled. "I can't keep this from her." Even if Leslie's plate was overflowing and spilling over the sides, her friend would want to know. Had to know.

He came to an abrupt halt and faced her. "Please don't tell her. Leslie wouldn't understand. I'll stop, I promise. I'll get help. This was a one-time thing. A slipup. You've got to believe me."

She so wanted to. But he was doing the classic addict-in-denial speak. A man who would leave his sick daughter's side to go to the casino needed help.

"Did you win anything?" she asked.

He shook his head. "Not yet."

"How much?" she fumed. "How much did you lose that could contribute to the hospital expenses?" All he did was shake his head and lift his shoulders. "I know you have that good

good insurance, but you have copays, plus Leslie was thinking about getting a tutor. All of that takes money."

"Please…" Aaron begged.

Yasmeen's heart squeezed. Aaron would feel the edge of Leslie's heel when she kicked him out. She wasn't one who did well with tolerating weakness. Or lies. Leslie, along with Toni and Celeste, would have Yasmeen's head for not saying a word. Breaking the girlfriend code.

"Sorry. I can't keep this to myself." She dug in her bag for her phone.

Just then Cashmere opened the door and came over to where they stood. "What's going on?" she asked, looking between them.

Yasmeen kept her gaze pinned on Aaron, who looked ready to bolt again. "L-let me talk to her," he sputtered. "It's best coming from me."

"Girl, do you need me to step in and show out?" Cashmere asked, moving into Aaron's space.

Yasmeen held Cashmere's arm. "I've got it." The sparkle of the casino teased her peripheral vision, which swayed her decision. Slipping her phone in her bag, she told Aaron, "Alright, I'll let you handle your business with my girl. But you'd better do it tonight."

He nodded and started stepping back. "I w-will. I promise."

"My daddy often says 'Promise is comfort to a fool.'" She debated, guilt churning in her gut.

"Not this time. I know what I have. Not messing that up." Then he rushed off. Yasmeen waited until he exited the lot before going back into the casino.

"What was that all about?" Cashmere asked once he was out of earshot. Yasmeen was generally tightlipped about her friends' personal affairs, but Cashmere looked so concerned and she needed a sounding board. So she divulged about Aaron being addicted to gambling.

"You did the right thing backing off," the other woman said, leading Yasmeen back into the building. "You don't want to be the reason somebody's marriage ends. Any chasm needs to be organic. So I agree with Aaron. He needs to be the one to tell her. It shouldn't come from you."

"Hmm. I don't know about that. That's not how my friends and I roll. If it were the reverse, I would want to know. Would you?"

"Yas! But I'm not married and there is an innocent child involved." Cashmere paused. "Can you look your goddaughter in her eyes and see the pain of her face, knowing you helped put it there?" Something about Cashmere's tone made Yasmeen believe the other woman was talking about herself.

"How could I stay silent though? This is big…" She placed a hand on her chest. "The thing is, if Aaron tells Leslie about his gambling, the Leslie I know would help him get into rehab or something. But if he doesn't tell her and she finds out, she will chomp into his behind." A thought occurred. She reared her head back. "Wait… I wonder how much money he's lost?" She shook her head. "Oh no. This is too much. I'm calling my friend."

Cashmere placed a hand on her arm. "Girl, I know our friendship is brand new, but you need to step back. This isn't your business. Periodt." She slid a finger across her neck, the gesture signaling that should be the end of the discussion.

"Naw, girl, this is very much my business. The whole point of sisterhood is that sisters come first. I have to drop a dime on this. No, make that a whole dollar. This is 9.5 earthquake major. If Aaron is losing money, they could lose their home, their savings." She shook her head. "The more I hear myself talking, the more I know telling Leslie is what I need to do. Aaron can't be trusted."

"Alright, if that's what you feel to do, but can you do it later? A few hours won't make any difference in the situation…"

Cashmere tilted her head. "I say we get to playing and then I'll come with you when you tell her. How does that sound?"

There was no way Yasmeen was going to bring Cashmere along when she talked with Leslie. That was a direct violation of the girlfriend code. Besides, Leslie would be furious at Yasmeen blabbing her business. But Yasmeen appreciated the gesture. Cashmere had a good heart, so she gave her a gentle letdown. "That's sweet of you, but I'm good talking to my friend on my own," she said, scuttling toward the slot machine.

For the next couple hours, the women had fun at the machines. Yasmeen marveled at how quickly her coins disappeared. And Cashmere's. She had to spot the other woman some money, which gave her pause, but Cashmere said she had forgotten her wallet at home. When they headed to their dinner reservations, Yasmeen knew this adventure was a one-and-done for her. Cashmere tried to cajole her into getting them a room for the night, and massages, but Yasmeen declined, picking at her food. Her mind was full of Leslie.

She reached for her phone, intending to call her friend, when she saw an urgent text from her dad. Her mother had had an asthma attack. She called, frantic, and though her parents assured her that her mother was alright, Yasmeen had to go see for herself. She jumped to her feet.

"Do you want me to come with you?" Cashmere placed a hand on the table.

What's with this woman always wanting to come everywhere with her? Yasmeen drew a breath and banished the churlish thought. "No, finish that steak for the both of us."

"Alright... I, uh, I don't have my card with me."

"You're lucky I like you." Yasmeen gestured to the server to settle the tab. Then, with a "see you later," she was out the door.

35

Leslie

APRIL 2

There was no putting it off. Over two months had passed since she had met her biological parents, and she needed to step through that door and join the Johansens for dinner. Share a meal. And meet her siblings in person for the first time. She had spoken to them over the phone but hadn't sought any other contact.

Leslie stood outside the steakhouse, her hands in the pockets of her spring jacket, and watched her siblings and biological parents through the mosaic-tiled window, seated inside. Nadya was staying at the hospital for a few days while she began her first round of chemotherapy. The doctor had provided a long-winded explanation, but the overall gist of it was that they had to destroy the existing bone marrow cells so that Nadya had room for the transplanted tissue.

The Johansens had been solicitous, generous, welcoming.

She had been grateful but aloof, the question churning within: *How could they have made this glorious life without me, and be okay with it?* That plagued her through every interaction with them, and even now, it was a cloud looming over this beautiful spring day.

The hurt ballooned in her chest, the temptation to return home magnified. But then she thought of Nadya and her brother's sacrifice, and she took a tentative step.

Leslie opened the door and meandered through the restaurant to where they sat. She stopped by the end of the table. For a moment, their wide grins and tilted heads, mannerisms so similar to her own, jarred her. She'd had limited contact with Henry and Julie, so having her siblings present with their children proved overwhelming. Disconcerted, she held on to the chair and nodded and smiled as introductions were made, before folding her legs and taking a seat next to her brother, Simon. Scott and Skylar were seated across from her with their spouses and children on either side of them. She pressed her feet into the floor, fighting the urge to flee.

How could Aaron bail on her like this?

When she told her girls about today, they offered to tag along but she had declined, saying Aaron would be coming. She knew now she was wrong because Aaron had texted at the last minute to say he wasn't going to make it. She had no idea what to say to her brother, besides "thank you for helping Nadya," which she did, before falling silent.

"We requested a jug of sweet tea and another of lemonade," Skylar said after a beat. "We were waiting for you to arrive before we ordered."

She nodded, her thoughts scattered, her heart pounding. She

shifted, her shoulders bumping against her brother's burly ones, while the chatter flowed around her. Happy chatter.

The server appeared with water and the drinks, and she took a huge gulp of lemonade and ordered a steak when it was her turn. Then she pulled out her phone and texted her friends.

Aaron didn't show up.

Say what?? Toni said. I don't believe him. But we planned for this. Yasmeen is on her way.

Yasmeen? She frowned. It was like they knew Aaron wouldn't show up.

Yasmeen chimed in. I'm almost there.

Leslie chuckled. She should have known her girls would have her back. Thanks, girl. I'll look out for you. She waved over the server to add another steak order for Yasmeen.

Scott leaned over. "So, Mom tells me you're a homemaker?"

"Yes, but my three best friends and I are starting a bookstore near the end of town soon. I'll finally be able to put my degree to use." She knew from Julie that both Scott and Simon were attorneys while Skylar was a pediatrician. She wasn't about to come across as the weakest link of the bunch.

"Oh, that sounds impressive. Simon is an avid reader," he said, calling out to his brother and filling him in about the bookstore.

Simon, the one who was immunocompromised. "I used to spend a lot of time in hospitals when I was younger and I'd get lost in graphic novels and mysteries. I'd love to check it out. When is the opening?"

"We're aiming for May fourth," she said. She spotted Yasmeen and gave a wave. The knot in her stomach loosened a bit at having a familiar face around. Only Yasmeen hadn't come solo. She had someone with her. That must be the new friend and shopping partner Yasmeen had been raving about. She had taken quite a few trips down to the beach and the outlets with Cashmere. Yasmeen assured them that Cashmere had her own money, but if she knew Yasmeen, her friend was offering to pay. Leslie gave a polite smile and tried to capture Yasmeen's eyes. She really wanted to know why Yasmeen had brought that other woman, but Yasmeen was avoiding meeting her gaze. On purpose. Probably because she knew showing up with her was tacky to the umpteenth power.

Dressed over-the-top with large earrings, sunglasses and designer wear, they both looked more suited for a runway than a simple trip to the diner. Leslie and the others at the table were dressed in jeans and sweaters.

She stood to introduce Yasmeen, who hugged Leslie, then introduced her friend. Whatever perfume Yasmeen was wearing smelled amazing…and expensive. Cashmere jumped in and started talking it up with Skylar.

"Why didn't you tell me you were bringing her?" Leslie whispered, tugging her off to the side. She was going to invite Yasmeen to sit with her, but she didn't want to impose further with this other person.

"I didn't think it was a big deal," Yasmeen whispered back. "She just got back from Dubai yesterday. How's it going?"

"Alright. I just…" She didn't want to come off as ungrateful for Yasmeen's presence. "I just wish you hadn't brought an entourage."

"One person is not an entourage. We have a spa appointment near here, so it made sense to have her with me. Besides, we won't sit with you. I'll be close by."

"Okay, that's a good idea," Leslie said, mouthing a thank-you.

Yasmeen squeezed her hand. "Don't think too much. Just enjoy them." Her friend knew just the right words to say. Leslie was analyzing every action and word, which was adding to her stress. She took a deep breath and relaxed.

Yasmeen addressed everyone. "It was good meeting all of you. Our table is ready."

"I'll have the server deliver your meal to you," Leslie added.

With a nod, Yasmeen kissed Leslie on the cheek before heading to her table, within sight. Just knowing her friend was in close proximity put Leslie at ease. But she didn't appreciate the fact that Cashmere had pulled out her business cards and handed them out to everyone at the table, except Leslie, who had declined.

Their meals arrived. After she had taken a bite of her steak, she felt her phone buzz. It was her father.

Thinking of you.

Since he was watching Nadya, she had told him her plans to meet up with the Johansens. He had bunched his lips and she thought she'd seen fear in his eyes. Did he think he was going to be replaced? But, Leslie, stubborn woman that she was, refused to bend and assure him of his place in her life. She still hadn't forgiven him fully.

Another text came—a picture of her as a baby on Edwin's lap, laughing at something he must have done.

Then another of Edwin handing her flowers at her graduation from elementary school.

Her heart constricted. She felt more buzzes, which meant more pictures, but if Leslie kept looking, she knew she would burst into tears.

So, she placed her phone in her bag and focused on the people around her, joining in the conversation. A few times she caught Yasmeen giving her the thumbs-up or some other gesture, and she made it through the meal.

The dinner crowd thinned, and soon it was only Leslie and her family on that side of the restaurant. Yasmeen and Cashmere had departed by then with a wave. Leslie and the Johansens lingered, cracking jokes and making conversation. Her siblings even convinced her to entertain the idea of a sleepover at her house so Nadya could get to know her younger cousins. She had agreed. Both her belly and her heart were full.

Henry stood with his phone in his hand to capture several photos. Then her brothers and sisters left after giving her long, tight hugs. Right before she departed, her parents asked to talk to her.

Her father began first. "Leslie, as you see, we're a close-knit family. We told our children about you when they were really young, and they have been waiting for this day for what feels like forever. Waiting for the day when their sister would return to us. And it's happened."

She opened her mouth to ask why they hadn't sought her out if they felt that way. But Henry wasn't finished.

He dabbed at his eyes. "Julie and I wanted to add your name to our will. Claim you as our own."

Claim me as their own. As in erase my past?

Visions of Edwin's pictures were imprinted on her mind. There was no undoing Edwin's relevance in her life. And it felt like that's what the Johansens wanted to do. Maybe she was overreacting… Maybe they had good intentions… But she couldn't do that.

Leslie eased out of her chair, backed up and drew a deep breath. "That's a thoughtful gesture, Henry and Julie—"

"We hope you'll come to call us Mom and Dad," Julie said.

So she wasn't overthinking this. "I'm sorry, *Henry and Julie*," she emphasized, "but this is all too much, too soon." With that, she sped out of the restaurant and didn't slow down until she was in her truck.

None of the requests made sense, but they did put some things into perspective.

She exited the parking lot and accelerated, then kept going until she was at the hospital, her stomach tense during the entire drive. Darting to the elevator, she pressed the button several times, though she knew that wouldn't make it arrive any faster.

As soon as the doors whooshed open, she trounced inside, tapping her feet while the elevator ascended to Nadya's floor. The doors opened. She scurried out and down the hall, swerving around other parents and staff until she was at her daughter's room.

She swung the door open.

Nadya was asleep and her father was watching something on the television. He turned to focus on her, stood and opened his arms. Without any hesitation, she ran over to the man who had raised her, welcoming the familiar strength of her father's embrace. Leslie closed her eyes and remembered all the times in her life she had done this, and smiled. This was familiar. This was what she knew. This was…home.

36

Toni

APRIL 3

Toni scrunched her nose at Yasmeen's new "friend."

"Meh. I don't like her. She feels like she's trying too hard."

"You're just mad because Yasmeen invited her to book club," Celeste said, as they stood in Yasmeen's kitchen. For this month's meeting, Yasmeen had insisted they meet at her place. Toni had swung by Celeste's house for them to travel together. Now they were feasting on the spread on the granite countertop. Yasmeen had gone all out with three types of boneless wings, veggies, taquitos, two kinds of lemonades.

"She should have asked us first. Book club is our sanctuary," Toni said through gritted teeth before biting into a celery stick.

What she was actually mad about was Skins. He wouldn't

leave her be for this money and the pressure was twisting her up on the insides. Funneling a million dollars took...finesse, and she was short. Like four hundred thousand dollars short. She couldn't ask Kent for the rest of the money. Ugh. Maybe she would have to ask Yasmeen and then pay her back, but she didn't relish having to answer the natural prying questions. Whew. But that was a convo for another day.

Tonight, she had put her phone on silent and tossed it in her bag just so she could relax and talk books with her friends. Respite. Instead, she had to make room for this...imposter.

"You wanted to expand our book club when we open the store, so look at tonight as a soft start," Celeste said.

"Yes, but we also need to finalize the wedding plans and the launch and we don't need outsiders all up in the mix."

Toni decided to wait until Cashmere left before she brought out her for-real wedding gown as well as the bridesmaids' dresses. She didn't want to chance any pictures popping up on social media until the live stream.

Aliyah had vetted the twenty people who'd won VIP tickets with background checks, and she was now finalizing the guests list to send them the special e-vite. Another reason Toni knew she had chosen well with her assistant.

"Quit being a conspiracist. Besides, Yasmeen seems quite taken with her," Celeste whispered back, reaching for a couple of the buffalo wings.

"I don't see why," Toni muttered under her breath. "Look at her with her fake boobs, fake nails, fake everything." She jutted her chin. "I bet that fur coat is fake too." Yasmeen had introduced Cashmere to the friends, even calling the woman her new bestie.

Celeste smirked. "She reminds me of you, actually." She popped one of the wings in her mouth before taking a drink of her lemonade.

Toni looked at Cashmere with her bronzed skin and perfect

teeth, dressed in pink high-waisted pants, heels and a crisped white shirt and rolled her eyes. She had style, if not class.

"To say that is an insult of massive proportions. Everything on my body is the real deal. Authentic. I worked hard for it." She ran her hands down her jeans and black sweater. "I don't think she can say the same." Across the room, Yasmeen and Cashmere giggled like they were schoolgirls, while watching videos. Toni shook her head. "Something about her feels…off. Leechy."

Cashmere, with all her airs, was from the hood just as Toni was. Hood knew hood. She could see it in the way Cashmere walked, skulked around.

Toni had seen the young woman's speculative gaze taking in Yasmeen's home, like she was pricing everything. Yasmeen had given Cashmere a tour of her property once she had arrived from business in New York City in a car Yasmeen had paid for.

Toni made a mental note to urge Yasmeen not to share information about her winnings with this woman.

"Yasmeen said she's a big shot in the finance world but I've never heard of her," Celeste said. "According to Yasmeen, she has old-school money."

"Isn't that a red flag if you haven't heard of her?" Toni was going to google the mess out of this woman later tonight.

"Not really. Ever since the carjacking, I haven't been to conferences or kept abreast of what's new in the money biz. You need to ease up on your suspicions."

This time, Celeste ate a barbecue wing.

"And you need to ease up on those wings or you'll get a stomachache. I thought you were giving up meat? At least that's what you said last week."

Celeste wiped her mouth. "I know, I'm trying, but I need protein. I haven't been eating well, and have you had these?" She groaned and licked her lips. "Yasmeen said that Darryl made them. They are beyond delicious. I'll try to give it up tomorrow."

The food was tasty but Toni wasn't about to acknowledge that *Pookie* did anything well. Toni raised a brow. "Oh, it's Darryl now?"

"She likes him." Celeste shrugged. "I've decided to accept what I can't change." Her tone made Toni realize that Celeste was talking about the state of her own marriage as well. She placed a hand on her friend's shoulder.

"Did you sign the papers?"

She gave a small nod. "I mailed them off a couple days ago."

"What about your assets?"

"We are splitting everything down the middle. Fifty-fifty. It's a no-fuss kind of settlement." She slumped her shoulders. If they weren't in mixed company, Toni would have pushed for details and explored Celeste's feelings. Her friend seemed… resigned but determined at the same time.

Toni squeezed her hand. "I'm here if you need me."

"I'm good." She ran her hands through her hair. "In fact, I got a big return on some of our investments. I'll share that later when we talk bookshop." Celeste did a little jig.

"How much did we make?" Toni asked.

"A lot. A lot," Celeste said. "It's high-risk, but the rewards are…" She let out a loud whistle.

"Ooh, it was that good." Toni broke out into a dance move and they high-fived.

"Hey! Are you two coming over to join us?" Yasmeen asked, giving them a pointed glance. "We want to know what all that whooping is about."

"You'll find out soon enough." Celeste gathered a small plate of food, then tilted her head toward the other two women at the table. "Let's get over there before Yasmeen calls us out for being unfriendly."

"Aren't we waiting for Leslie to get here?" Toni asked just as the bell rang.

Since she was closest, Toni ran to open the door. She squealed

Leslie's name and hugged her tight, swaying back and forth. "I'm so glad you're here," she said, stepping back, "and that you cut your hair and showered."

Leslie ran her hands through her bob. It looked like she had added highlights and Toni admired how her curls framed her face.

She gave Toni a light slap. "Stop it, silly."

Yasmeen and Celeste called for Leslie to hurry up.

"I'm coming," she said.

"You looking good, overcomer." Toni helped Leslie out of her coat and asked, "How's Nadya?" Her goddaughter had begun treatments and had minimal side effects, but until the transplant, Toni wasn't easing up with the concern. "I'm sorry I couldn't make it over there."

"She's doing good. Daddy is with her," she said, walking toward the kitchen.

"Is Aaron working out of town tonight again?"

She rolled her eyes. "Please… I don't even want to think about him right now. He stood me up yesterday and didn't even have the decency to apologize." Her tone had a hard edge. "As soon as Nadya's good…" She shook her head. "Never mind. Not going there. I don't want to bring down my good mood tonight."

Toni's heart squeezed. As a woman who was about to get married, it didn't feel good knowing two of her friends had trouble in their marriages. Celeste was almost divorced, and judging by Leslie's tone, Toni would say Leslie and Aaron's relationship might be in trouble.

Celeste and Yasmeen called out to Leslie again, this time including Toni's name as well.

"We are being summoned," she said. Leslie reached for her coat but Toni waved her off.

"I got it." Toni retrieved one of the hangers and hung Leslie's coat in the closet. Her eyes fell on Cashmere's coat, and she glanced behind her before dipping her hands in the pockets. Her heart raced and she drew in small breaths. She felt like she was going to pass out. Goodness, she wasn't cut out for subterfuge.

The pockets were empty. She sighed. She didn't know what she'd expected to find. But then she saw there was another in the inner lining. Inside she felt the crinkle of paper and pulled out two receipts. One was from Tiffany's and the other appeared to be a bank receipt.

"Toni, we gonna start up without you," Yasmeen yelled.

Toni jumped, then jostled to hold on to the receipts. She shoved them in the back of her jeans. She would take a look at them later. Might be nothing. But it might be something.

She strutted around the corner and pushed the enthusiasm, to keep her guilt at bay. She had no right to invade the other woman's privacy and search through her possessions. Toni debated putting them back, but then she saw how Cashmere seemed to be agreeing with everything Yasmeen said.

If Yasmeen said she liked a character, Cashmere did the same.

If Yasmeen ate cauliflower, Cashmere did the same.

Naw. This woman was trying too hard.

The red flag was high in the sky and waving.

Oh, she was smart, poised and she obviously knew her books. But Toni dubbed her a cultured pearl. Manufactured.

In some ways, Toni and Cashmere were alike. This woman had reinvented herself, the same way Toni had. Except Toni had done so out of desperation, a fear for her life and her family. And Toni wasn't trying to scam anyone. She felt it deep in her bowels that Cashmere was all game and Yasmeen didn't know those rules to play. Her stomach knotted. She had to warn her friend.

And she did. As soon as Cashmere excused herself to use the restroom, Toni pulled Yasmeen aside and whispered, "You need to get that woman out of your house and out of your life."

Yasmeen's brows rose. "What do you mean?"

"She's no good," Toni said.

"She's cool people. We're shopping buddies and she's like a little sister to me."

"That's a Venus fly trap." Toni wagged a finger. "Keep her away from your money." She cleared her throat and whispered, "Speaking of money, I might have to borrow some." Toni blew out a little breath, hating how needy she sounded.

"Sure, you don't even have to ask," Yasmeen said. "And your warning about Cashmere is too little, too late. I hired her as my consultant since Celeste felt it would be a conflict of interest for her to manage my funds." Her voice didn't hold even a millimeter of concern.

"I don't believe you. Did you research this woman to make sure she's legit before you gave her access to your accounts?" Toni asked.

"I checked out her website and called the references she gave me. I just signed on with her last week."

Toni clenched her jaw. "Anybody can set up a fake account and use their friends for recommendations. Did you forget when I did that for you?"

"I sure do recall that's how I got the job at the floral shop." Yasmeen's eyes held fear. "You got my chest beating hard right now. You think I made a mistake?" She grabbed her phone and started tapping on the screen. "I'd better change my passwords."

"Good idea." Toni bit her lower lip to keep from voicing that Yasmeen might already be too late. She dipped her head to her chest. "For once, I hope I'm just being suspicious, because if I'm right..." She couldn't say any more. She couldn't even think it. All she could do was pray she was wrong.

37

Celeste

APRIL 4

Her calculations had been wrong. Very wrong. And she wasn't sure she knew how to fix them.

Celeste sat at the end of her dining table and blinked several times, hoping that the numbers she was seeing on the screen were incorrect. Maybe her contacts were out of focus. She leaned forward and scanned the spreadsheet again.

"No, no, no. This can't be right," she said, slamming a hand on the table. "I know I triple-checked the numbers before I prepared this presentation. I don't understand what I am missing."

She jumped up and paced the room, her heart hammering in her chest. She had no idea how she was going to explain this to her superiors. What's worse was that she didn't have time to find her error because her official presentation with the board was in thirty minutes and the ride to her office was twenty without traffic. She had to get going now.

Celeste had chosen her power suit with care—black, tailored, with a green silk blouse—but none of that mattered if she didn't have the proposal for the healthcare facility executive board. They wanted to take over another facility on the brink of bankruptcy and they were awaiting her recommendation, which would be a no based on her calculations.

If only her spreadsheet showed the same.

It was distinctly showing a profit.

She looked upward and flailed her hands. "How did this happen? How?" Of course, there was no response. Only the pounding of her heart and rising panic messing with the air in her lungs.

Looking at her watch, she saw she had twenty-eight minutes and counting.

Grabbing her coat and her laptop bag, Celeste dashed out to her vehicle. Before getting in, she bent over and took deep cleansing breaths to keep the panic at bay. She could fix this. All she had to do was explain her mistake and then share her recommendation. Maybe they would be alright with not seeing the numbers and she could fix it and send it back. Besides, she had the actual presentation to go through.

Yes, that's what she would do.

Celeste swerved out of her driveway and hit the gas. Her hands shook and her insides churned the entire way. When she got to her office, she prayed that the board members would be late, so she could do some recalculations. Again.

She was the chief financial officer and she couldn't get her numbers right. She shuddered, thinking of the impression this would leave on her bosses. When it came to money and numbers, Celeste Coleman didn't make mistakes. That had been her private triumph for years, which is why they had hired her when she was twenty-six. Even after the carjacking, despite her mental state, she had been able to manage the money.

Now, as she drove through the winding traffic on US 1, words like *error* and *mistake* plagued her. Words that had never been a part of her vocabulary. Before now. She was shaken, stirred and now unsure how to navigate her way through uncharted territory.

She sniffled. She had messed up. Messed up big-time.

Celeste remembered visiting the landfill with Wade back when they were about to move in together. She remembered how he had packed a U-Haul with furniture, clothes, stuff that they knew a local Goodwill wouldn't take. When they parked by the huge mound of earth, Wade couldn't get past the vultures and the stench. But for Celeste, what held in her mind was how, once they had emptied the rear of the truck, the man in the huge tractor came by, and within seconds, *seconds*, everything had been smashed to smithereens and buried.

That's how she would describe her confidence: smashed and buried.

To keep from breaking down, Celeste recited her talking points, which she practically had memorized. Once she arrived, she did her best to appear at ease, waving and exchanging pleasantries with the staff before scuttling toward the conference room.

All eight members of the board were seated, present and waiting for her.

Celeste squared her shoulders, greeted everyone, grabbed her stress ball in one hand and the clicker in the other, and began. She paced while she spoke, to keep them from seeing her legs shaking. And she kept her jacket on to keep them from seeing her sweat.

When she was finished, the people at the table praised her. Praised her efforts and accepted her recommendation, all without seeing the spreadsheet. All because they trusted her. And she didn't deserve it. She swallowed to keep the bile at bay and shook each of their hands, accepting their atta-girls, all while feeling like a fraud.

Celeste shuffled back to her office, locked the door behind her and sank to her knees before buckling over. Recalling the trust on their faces ripped at her heart. Wrapping her arms around her midriff, she rocked back and forth as the tears began to fall.

She had failed in her marriage.

And now she had failed at her job. Her job. She clenched her fists. The one thing she had always done right. That knowledge ripped her apart. Wracking sobs shook her body and she was powerless to stop the flow.

So she allowed herself to have a good, ugly cry, mainly because her soul didn't have a choice.

She heard a rap on the door. Then the rattle of the doorknob. She cleared her throat. "Yes?"

"Are you okay in there?" her administrative assistant asked.

"I'm good." Another rattle. "I just have a lot to do."

"Okay… Let me know if you need anything."

"I will."

Mustering her strength, Celeste got to her feet and shuffled over to her desk, where she grabbed tissues and wiped her face. She typed in her password and then pulled up the spreadsheet. Since she had two screens, she placed it on the left and opened up a blank one on the right. She was going to start over. She was going to sit here and rework everything until she got it right.

Hours later. Hours. She found it. A simple number reversal.

Once she fixed those two digits and had the system recalculate, everything fell into place. It was close to 3:00 p.m. and she hadn't eaten, hadn't left her desk except to use the restroom, but she had gotten it done. Thank goodness. Celeste drafted the email and sent off the document.

She sank back into her chair and released a huge plume of air.

Today had been nerve-wracking. But it made her acknowledge something she had been fighting for over a year. She needed help.

Professional help. Not to get Wade back. Not to please her friends. She needed help for her. And it was time she stopped resisting. If she hadn't had all those sleepless nights, she wouldn't have miscalculated. She couldn't work at her optimal performance if she was tired.

And frankly, she was tired of being scared.

Celeste reached into her bag, pulled out her laptop and typed the name of the therapist into the search bar. Then, before she could second-guess her actions, she called to schedule an appointment.

They had a cancellation for the next day, which she accepted.

For the first time in hours, Celeste smiled. She then opened her laptop and went to check the spreadsheets devoted to the bookstore.

She had already purchased the furnishings and supplies that Leslie provided. She scrolled through the inventory to see when the books would arrive. Then her eyes went wide. The books. Had she ordered the books? A mental picture of Yasmeen's list of suggestions flashed in her mind. She remembered water spilling on it and shoving it into her nightstand.

Her brows furrowed. But did she actually place the order?

She shook her head. She couldn't recall. She released short breaths. The opening was in thirty days and they couldn't launch a bookstore without books. She'd better get those orders in right away, dreading the cost for expedited shipping. When she reviewed their budget, Celeste's stomach knotted. She would need to allocate more funds because of her careless error.

Hold on. She drew in a deep breath.

"Don't panic, Celeste. You've got money from your investments." Celeste minimized the document and checked on her and Wade's investments, as well as the bookstore's.

There was a huge crack of thunder outside. She looked out her window and took in the darkened skies and the splatters of rain on the glass.

Turning back to the computer, her heart fell to the floor. Her eyes went wide and her mouth dropped open. They had lost everything. Celeste sent her friends a SOS text in the group chat for them to meet up at the bookstore, then sprang out of her chair. The morning's fiasco was nothing compared to this. If that was a fire, this was an inferno.

One that she had no power to douse.

38

Yasmeen

APRIL 4

The loud crash of thunder startled Yasmeen awake. Extending her hand, she felt nothing but cool sheets beside her. Darryl must be off to class already. She stretched and eyed the clock before she gasped.

It was close to three in the afternoon. She sat up and swayed, feeling sluggish. She had stayed up until sunrise, reading, but she couldn't say she regretted it.

Yasmeen yawned and padded across the plush carpeting to the master bath to take care of her morning, or in this case, afternoon routine. She loved the black-and-white decor and the checkered tile on the floors along with the light gray walls. Her favorite thing, though, was the floor-length mirror in the

MICHELLE LINDO-RICE

adjoining closet. Thirty minutes later, she was ready to face what was left of this day.

That's when she saw Celeste's SOS text.

She called out for Cashmere, who had spent the night, but there was no response. She shrugged. Such was the joy of youth. Cashmere was probably traveling to the airport to get to a business trip she had in Tennessee. The thunder clapped again, followed by a huge downpour.

Her doorbell rang.

Yasmeen rushed to the front door. When she opened it, she gasped at who stood there.

"Daddy?" she enquired, stepping back. "What are you doing here?"

"Hello, Yasmeen," Willie said. The rain pelted his face and back. He stood holding his cap in his hands, his shoulders hunched.

She looked around him, into the blinding rain, and ushered him inside, where he stood dripping on her mat. "How did you get here?" she asked, then muttered through gritted teeth, "I know you didn't drive because you refused to allow me to buy you a car."

"Sorry to mess up your rug," he said, tone subdued. "I took the bus and then walked from the main road."

Her mouth popped open. "Daddy, why didn't you call me? That's close to a mile." She waved a hand. "Come into the kitchen. Let me make you some tea."

"I don't want to mess up your place."

"I'm not worried about it," she said. "I bought some spice buns and Jamaican cheese from the Caribbean store."

"Yes, that would be good. I haven't eaten anything since this morning." His deferential tone sent off an alarm. Her dad wasn't acting himself. There was only one thing she could think of. Something was wrong with Mommy.

"Why didn't you eat?" she asked.

He simply shook his head before traipsing behind her like a recalcitrant child, all the way to the kitchen. He sat at the table. Yasmeen poured water into the electric kettle and went over to stand by him, her heart racing. "Is Mommy alright?"

He nodded. "Y-yes. She's at the church."

Yasmeen scrunched her nose. It rankled that her father had declined the charitable contribution, aka tithes, she'd tried to pay, because it was "the devil's money." She got a plate, opened the bread box to get one of the round buns and sliced him a good portion of cheese.

Then, while she waited for the kettle to sound, she sent the group chat a text.

My dad stopped by. Something's wrong. OMW soon. She took out a teacup and saucer and got some brown-sugar packets. Then she placed a tea bag inside the mug.

Ok. See you when you get here, Leslie replied.

He took a bite, closed his eyes and moaned. The food loosened his tongue. "I got a call from the senior pastor last week that the church had a water main leak. They have to dig up the entire foundation. We called the insurance company, but because we are in a flood zone and we bought the place with plumbing issues, they are fighting us to pay for the repairs."

She stilled, then met her father's eyes. "Daddy, are you asking me for money?"

"J-just until we get this settled."

"So…it's alright to take the money now?"

"This is an emergency."

"But isn't it still 'the devil's money'?" she asked. The kettle sang. She poured the hot water, mindful of the steam, so that it could steep the tea.

"Yes, but when the children of Israel were leaving the Promised Land, they took all kinds of gifts from the Egyptians."

"Wow." Her brows rose. "Are you calling me the Biblical Egyptian?"

"No, what I'm saying is we could really use your help. If you can."

Yasmeen relaxed and cracked up. "Of course, Daddy. I couldn't resist giving you a hard time for a bit. I am glad to help the church out, to help you out. Anything you and Mommy need, I got you. In fact, I bought her a brand-new set of Belle Calhoune's books, but I wasn't sure she would take them."

Willie laughed. "Thanks, my lovely daughter. You had me going there for a minute. And your mother is going to love those books. She'll tune me out, sit on that couch and read until she's done."

Yasmeen smiled. She was just like her mother with that. "It's not a problem." She poured his tea and took it to him. "Drink up." She went to her personal library for the box of books for her mother and rested them on the table, then she pulled up her phone and tapped on her bank app. "I'll send you some money."

"A check would be better," he said, wiping his mouth. "I don't trust those quick money-transfer gadgets."

Yasmeen giggled. "I am going to bring you into this century." She used her index fingerprint to log into her account. When she saw the balance, she froze. "No. No. No. This doesn't make sense."

"What's going on?"

"I don't know," she sputtered. Her heart began to race. This must be a mistake. She closed the app and then restarted it. Then logged in again. But the balance in her account was almost gone.

Willie got to his feet and came over to place a hand on her shoulder. "What's going on?"

"My money. My money is gone."

"What?" he said, taking her phone to look at the balance. "You only have $3,861?" he asked. "I thought you won a significant sum? Or did you spend it all on your house and car?"

"N-no." She hyperventilated. "Just yesterday, I had about

three million dollars in there." Yasmeen pressed the account summary, then gasped. "It says I did a wire transfer to some account." Struggling to breathe, she looked at her dad. "I don't have another account." She placed a hand over her mouth and sobbed. "I've been robbed."

Toni's words came back to her. She dashed toward the guest room. It was empty, cleared out. No sign that Cashmere had ever been there.

Her father was right behind her. "Do you know who could have done it?"

"I have a good idea. It must be my new accountant." She snarled on the last word. Yasmeen retrieved Cashmere's contact info and called her, but she was sent to voicemail. She tried again. And again. That meant one of two things: Cashmere's phone had died or she'd been blocked. Her gut said it was the latter.

Yasmeen released a guttural wail and gripped her phone to keep from tossing it in frustration. Her father held her against him and rocked her.

"What am I going to do?" she asked, her body convulsing.

"Call the cops."

"I gave her access to my personal information," Yasmeen screeched, panic permeating her being. Then her head popped up. "Celeste! Celeste can help me. She's a whiz with numbers. She might be able to trace who took my money." She grabbed her father's hand. "The girls are at the bookshop. I need to get over there ASAP."

"You need to call the authorities."

"I will. After I'm there. The last time we had an SOS, my goddaughter was deathly ill. I don't know how much more I can take."

While she drove, her father prayed, holding on to the box of books in his lap. She gripped the wheel and bit down on her lower lip to keep from screaming. Why hadn't she gone to a wealth management firm? Why had she allowed this woman to infiltrate her life and scam her? She was a fool. Plain and simple. A naive fool for trusting a complete stranger. The tears streamed down her face, wetting her sweater.

She screeched to a halt in front of the church.

"I thought I was coming with you?" her father asked, putting on his hat.

"No, you've got to deal with the church. I'll call you later."

He held her arm. "God's got this," he said. "Vengeance is His. He will repay." Then he kissed her cheek and tucked the box of books under his arm. "Keep me posted," he said, then got out of the car.

Yasmeen nodded but she didn't believe that. All she could think was, what if her dad hadn't come by? She might not have looked at her account until tomorrow morning or tonight. She watched him walk off, then sped over to the bookstore.

The last to arrive, she parked and darted inside. Her friends stood huddled in the center of the space. She could see Celeste was crying.

As soon as Celeste saw her, she ran over to Yasmeen and hugged her tight. Yasmeen's brow furrowed.

"Oh goodness, the money. The money is gone," Celeste wailed. Toni and Leslie came over to where they stood.

Yasmeen nodded, then cried, "I was scammed." But then Celeste's words registered. Wait...what? Yasmeen pulled away from her. "How did you know?"

"I took some major risks in hopes we would get a major payoff." She sobbed. "I withdrew the funds, but then I decided to go for it. I decided to throw it all in some stocks." Then she swallowed. "Only, I was...wrong. I was so wrong." She grasped Yasmeen's arms. "I don't have the money for the launch."

Toni held both their arms. "Wait a minute. I get that you two are in the midst of a breakdown, but you're not listening to each other." She focused on Yasmeen. "What do you mean you were scammed?"

"You were right, Toni. Cashmere took off with my money."

"Say what?" Leslie asked. "How on earth did you allow that to happen?" Outrage filled her voice and she was looking at Yasmeen like she was to blame.

Yasmeen swung around to snap off at Leslie. "I didn't allow anything. She tricked me. Made me trust her and then she wiped me out. Left me with barely four thousand dollars to my name."

"I told you," Toni said, pointing a finger. "I told you she was bad news."

All Yasmeen could do was nod.

Celeste wiped her face and shook her head. "Hang on. If you don't have cash in the bank, what are we going to do about the bookstore?" She then looked in Toni's direction and wrung her hands. "Can you loan me some until I earn it back? I'm pretty sure I will." Yasmeen hated to see the desperation on her face and hear her pleading tone. It wrenched her heart.

Toni lifted a hand. "Normally, I would pull out the checkbook, but I'm in sort of a bind."

"Oh yeah," Yasmeen blurted out. "I forgot you asked me for cash."

"Really? I asked you in confidence." Toni placed a hand on her hip. "You don't know how to keep a secret, do you?" She flailed her hands. "No wonder you got shafted, because you don't know when to keep your mouth closed. I mean who tells a complete stranger that they won the lottery?"

Yasmeen stepped back. "Listen, I don't appreciate how you all are coming at me, like I'm stupid or something. What happened to me was an honest mistake."

"Honest?" Leslie scoffed. "Even my twelve-year-old knows about the sanctity of keeping her business personal. She won't even let me know her password."

"Wow. Are you comparing me to a twelve-year-old?" Yasmeen tilted her head. "You are so judgmental. Acting like you better than me. No wonder your husband is barely home. He's probably sick of your lofty attitude." She slaked her eyes across her friends and snarled, "You all think that because you have college degrees that makes you superior to me, and you know what, I'm sick of it."

"If the shoe fits…" Leslie huffed, her eyes flashing.

Yasmeen kicked off her shoes and got into Leslie's face. "And what?"

Toni joined Leslie's side. "I wish you would."

"Guys, I know we're under stress, but let's not get ugly," Celeste said, coming to stand between them. Then she gave Yasmeen a pointed look. "And you need to get over yourself. Nobody here made you drop out of school. You did that on your own."

Yasmeen gasped. "Wow. Tell me how you really feel." Tears pricked her eyes.

"Yeah, wow," Toni said, turning to Celeste. "Don't you think that was kind of harsh? We all know she has a learning disability, even if she won't admit it."

"So, you all are talking about me behind my back now?" Yasmeen yelled. Her chest hurt. "You all think I'm stupid?"

"I would tell you to your face if I thought so," Toni hurled. "You're not the only one with a big mouth."

"Really?" Yasmeen asked. "This from the one who is the most secretive of us all. You hid your old ovaries from your fiancé. Why didn't you open your mouth then?"

"She does have a point," Celeste said.

Toni averted her eyes. "There's a lot going on." She looked away, fiddling with the collar of the A-line dress she had paired with black booties.

"Yes, I have a sick daughter I've been dealing with," Leslie chimed in before addressing Yasmeen. "So, please spare us the woe-is-me act. We all know how smart, talented and gifted you are. We believe you can get your degree but you don't believe it. Frankly, I don't think you wanted it bad enough," Leslie said. "And that's okay. There are many lucrative careers out there that don't need a BA. You just have to make up your mind. But you're all about taking it easy."

She worked hard and studied for hours to make those Cs, so Leslie's comments pierced her gut. Yasmeen released staccato breaths as her temper heated.

"Why does it feel like I'm being ganged up on?" Yasmeen asked, shoving her hands in her pockets.

"We're not ganging up on you." Celeste jabbed a finger in Yasmeen's chest. "I gave you a recommendation, but you didn't want to listen. You didn't take my advice to ease up on your spending when I meant good for you." Her lips curled. "But someone appears from out of nowhere and you hand over access."

Yasmeen exploded. "Well, isn't that the case of pot and kettle," she raged. "You think you're better than everybody. That's the real reason you refused to get counseling. You're a fine one to talk about getting advice when you only like hearing the sound of your voice. You lost a good man because you were pigheaded and stubborn. Now you all alone in that bed of yours while I am getting it good and plenty on the regular."

"That was low." Celeste swallowed, eyes filled with hurt.

Yasmeen's heart ached, but the apology remained stuck in her throat. She wasn't going to be the first one to say sorry.

Leslie shook her head. "The fact that we're fighting like this when we're about to go into business together is appalling."

"You know what else is appalling?" Yasmeen asked, chest heaving. "Your husband gambling away your money while his daughter is on her sick bed."

"Wh-what are you talking about?" Leslie asked. "That's

golden, bringing up his past. If my husband was gambling again, I would know it."

"Quit acting like you don't know what I'm talking about," Yasmeen piped up. "I ran into him at the casino a couple weeks back, and from the looks of it, he had been there awhile." She covered her mouth. "I made him promise to tell you. He didn't tell you?"

"No. No." Leslie stepped back.

Yasmeen's heart squeezed. She shouldn't have trusted Aaron to fess up. "I was going to call myself but then my mother got sick…" Regret twisted her insides. If she hadn't been caught up in shopping sprees with Cashmere, she would have called her friend.

Leslie barely seemed to be listening to Yasmeen's explanation. She rummaged in her bag for her phone and then tapped the screen. "Our checking account is fine." Yasmeen and everyone expelled long sighs. But then Leslie said, "Let me check something else." Seconds later, her eyes narrowed before going wide. "Oh my goodness. Nadya's college money is gone. All of it."

The friends gathered together to look at the small screen. It showed twenty-six cents. Their retirement account was also depleted. Leslie dropped the phone, her hands hanging loosely at her side.

"I'm so sorry." Toni led her by the shoulders to have a seat at one of the tables at the café.

Yasmeen rubbed her temples. How could she have forgotten to call? Leslie sat in the chair, shaking her head and mumbling under her breath.

"That can't be for real," Celeste said. "How are we all facing money problems?" Her tone held disbelief and dejection. "We might as well reach out to the landlord and tell him we can't take the property."

"I'm not surprised you'd suggest that," Toni scoffed. "We see how you behave when things get difficult."

"I was in a carjacking," Celeste said. "I could have died."

"You think you're the only one to experience trauma?" Toni asked. She opened her mouth to say something, but then stopped. "Whatever. Let's call this whole thing off."

Yasmeen froze. Toni's words sounded final. "The bookstore?"

She flailed her hands. "Yes, the bookstore…the book club… the friendship." She slipped into her coat. "I've got too much going on in my own life to dwell in this toxicity. If I don't come up with…" She cut herself off and shoved her arms in her coat before placing her bag over her shoulder.

A knot formed in Yasmeen's stomach. She couldn't lose her money and her friends in the same day. But she had no idea what to say after all the venom that had spewed tonight.

"I agree." Leslie popped up and pointed at Yasmeen. "You knew that Aaron was back to gambling, but you said nothing, knowing I have a child, a sick child. That's not friendship." She headed toward the door. Just before she left, Celeste spoke up.

"If after all these years, you all are willing to give up on us like this, I'm not stopping any of you. I've learned my lesson running after Wade. I'm not going to beg anybody to value me or my friendship." She straightened. "I'll talk with the landlord tomorrow." Her voice held ice. "The only time any of you will hear from me is when I have earned back your investment and then some. Until then…" She placed her bag on her shoulder and walked out the door.

Leslie was next.

"Toni," Yasmeen called out.

"It's over" was all she said. The door clicked behind her.

Yasmeen was left alone in the space. She walked through the building, taking in all the renovations. The dark green walls, the soft lighting, the shelves throughout. And the café.

The café with the built-in couches, just as she had envisioned, right along with more tables and chairs. This was supposed to be a space celebrating their sisterhood, their bond, but instead, it was the scene of their unraveling and the demise of years and years of friendship.

A sob broke through her chest and Yasmeen crumpled to the floor.

It was only at this moment she realized the true wealth she'd had—her sister friends, their love and their support—and the true wealth she had lost.

39

Leslie

APRIL 4

Leslie stormed out of the building and stomped over to her truck. Once she sat in the driver's seat, she gripped the wheel and screamed. Her heart had been pounded by a sledgehammer and it had some to do with Aaron but more to do with her so-called friend.

She couldn't fathom how Yasmeen could know something like this and not tell her. She couldn't fathom how she hadn't picked up on Aaron's behavior herself. How she hadn't seen the effects of his spending at all. Hadn't noticed.

But she did know one thing. No, make that two. She was done with her friends. And she was done with Aaron.

For good.

Bad enough he had messed with their retirement. But to touch Nadya's money? That made her chest burn. That was a floor below low-down and grimy.

She sniffled. But Yasmeen. Yasmeen had talked with her, ate with her, laughed with her, all the while knowing what he was doing. There were no accurate words to describe that betrayal.

The door opened and Toni came out of the building and traipsed over to her car. She drove off without a glance in Leslie's direction. Celeste had left before Leslie, so she knew Yasmeen was still inside, alone. Yasmeen. Her chest heaved. She ought to go back in there. Confront her. But Leslie feared she would do more crying than raging.

So she did the next best thing. She called her father and asked him to watch Nadya. When he asked what was going on, her words simply were, "I'm taking out the trash." She went home and packed. She packed and packed and packed for hours, refusing to stop until her trunk was piled high with all the possessions she could fit in. The rest she would sell or donate.

Then she went to the casino. Sure enough, Aaron's car was there. A secret hope dived to the pit of her stomach. Confirmation.

She unlocked his vehicle and systematically packed his car. When she was finished, she placed his golf clubs—a wedding gift he had never used—on the driver's seat.

A thought occurred. There had to be clues, but Aaron had made sure she wouldn't see them. She went to the glove box to check, then gasped. The hospital bills were inside. Opened. Unpaid. She sorted through them. They owed thousands.

Leslie shuddered. This debt could prevent her daughter from getting the surgery she needed. She clenched her jaw. Her temples throbbed. Leslie stuffed the envelopes in her pockets, slammed the door closed and pressed the lock button, welcoming the satisfying beep.

Her heart thudded with each step, but she made her way

through the deceptively sparkling lights, the excited jingle of the slot machines, until she spotted Aaron. She took in his face when he saw her—his rounded eyes, his slack jaw—and curled her fists to keep from slapping him into another state.

Aaron ran a hand through his hair. "I—I can explain."

Leslie lifted a hand. "Save it. I know everything. If I were you, I'd think about what you're going to tell your daughter." Then she uttered four parting words, "Don't bother coming home."

Celeste

APRIL 16

"I don't know if I can do this," Celeste said to the younger white woman sitting across from her. Even now, thinking about the task ahead, her insides fluttered.

"We can stop whenever you need," Therese said. "But if you don't face that day, it is going to continue to dictate how you live your life."

The therapist had a point. This was her fifth time meeting with Therese and she could see why Wade trusted her.

She thought about her marriage, her job, her friendships, her overall well-being, then drew deep, long breaths, took a sip of water, and began. "Wade and I were on our way to the Kennedy Center to see an opera show. It had been raining earlier, so the roads were slick. We were on highway fifty, the Chesapeake Bay Bridge ahead, and Wade was going a good number of miles above the speed limit when we saw a yellow light. Instead of slowing down, Wade decided to accelerate. I remember touching him and pleading with him to stop, but he was confident he could make it. Right before...right..." Her heart started racing. She took another sip of water.

"Take your time," Therese said. "I don't have another client until later this afternoon, so you can go at your own pace."

"Even though I begged him, Wade just didn't listen. Right before the light turned red, a car swung in front of us, so Wade had to slam on the brakes." Celeste touched her abdomen. "I remember my body tensing, lifting out of the seat because I was pretty sure we were going to collide with that car. But inches, mere inches from the point of contact, Wade came to a stop." She shook her head. "I don't know how—" She pointed upward. "Someone was looking out for us."

Therese nodded. "I will say amen to that."

Celeste wiped her forehead. "I remember the relief coursing through my body as I struggled to calm my breathing, and I looked over at Wade and said something like 'I don't want to see the show that bad,' so he needed to slow down. He grinned and cracked a joke about having skills and we held hands. That's when..."

She swallowed and gripped the sides of the armchair.

Her voice went high. "That's when I heard someone knocking on the glass, and I turned my head to see a gun pointed at me." Her body began to shake. "There were two of them. One was on Wade's side demanding we get out of the car."

"You're in a safe place," Therese reminded her, tone gentle. "You're okay."

Heeding that calm voice, Celeste squared her shoulders. "The men in front of us must have seen the car swerving, and though we didn't hit them, they had gotten out of their car to confront us. We held up our hands and Wade shouted that we didn't want any problems, we just wanted to be on our way.

But they started hurling profanities and calling us all kinds of names, saying if we didn't get out of the car, they were going to shoot me in the head."

She could hear her heartbeat thunder in her ears. "I could see Wade was livid, and he bunched his fists like he was going to attack them, but I grabbed his hand and I begged him not to do anything reckless. I begged him." Her eyes filled with tears. "Wade put the car in Reverse, backed up and took off. He made a U-turn, because after all that, you know we were going home. We thought that would be it. But I saw them running to their vehicle. They started to follow us."

Celeste shook her head. "I remember screaming to Wade that they were coming after us and he said he was going to outrun them. Well, I decided to call 9-1-1 and I told the operator what was going on. She told us to keep going and that an officer would be on his way."

"How were you feeling then?" Therese asked.

"Relieved, actually. I felt sure the cops would come quickly and take control. There was a handful of vehicles so we had an open road. And we kept going. But…then. There was another red light before us. Wade told me he was going to cut the light. But I insisted he stop because I was scared that we might hit another car if we did that." Her lips trembled. "So we stopped."

Celeste wrapped her arms about her and rocked. "If only we hadn't stopped."

"You did what anybody in that situation would do," Therese said.

Tears streaked down her face. "Because we stopped," she choked out, "those men caught up with us. They swerved in front of us, blocking us off and p-pulled their guns again." She sobbed. "They made us get out the car and lie face down on the ground. I remember praying for the cops to get there, but they started kicking Wade in the sides and his head, calling us highfalutin mongrels who needed to go back to Africa and give them back their country."

Therese gasped and placed a hand to her mouth, her brown eyes filled with compassion. "I'm so sorry that happened to you."

"I thought Wade told you…" she said.

"No…" She shifted, tossing back her chestnut curls. "But this isn't about him. It's about you."

"I remember thinking to myself 'we're going to die out here today.' And all because we stopped at a red light."

"It was then they directed their attention to me." Her body shook. "One of the men shone a light in my face. S-said I looked…white. Asked me wh-what I was doing w-with a t-tar baby, and he grabbed my hand and snatched me to my feet." Celeste covered her face with both hands. "I begged him not to hurt me. In the corner of my eye, I saw Wade lift his head. His eyes held shame, and I mouthed to him 'I love you, d-don't g-get up.'" She wiped her eyes. "I told him s-stay there. Over and over I told him, while that man wrapped his arms around my waist and licked my face." Her mouth twisted and she shuddered. "Thank God that's all he did, but it made me feel dirty. The other man called out to him to leave me alone."

She stood and walked over to the window. "We heard the sirens in the distance. They panicked and fled the scene in our car. Wade jumped to his feet and howled. I mean he howled at the top of his lungs, but I raced over to him and told him I was alright, I was alright." She cracked. "B-but I w-wasn't. I wasn't alright. We gave the police report, and though they found our car abandoned at an airport parking lot, they couldn't identify the men. Turns out the original car they had been driving had been stolen."

She met Therese's eyes and sniffled. "My marriage suffered after that… And eventually, my job…and now…" She quivered. "I've lost my friends and I don't know how to make any of that right."

Well, there was one little tiny thing, a possibility, but she couldn't dwell on that, couldn't dare hope.

"It's okay to not know what to do. To have yourself a good cry for no other reason than to just cry," Therese encouraged.

Those words were all Celeste needed to hear. She sobbed then. Cried until she was spent.

And Therese let her. Urged her to let herself cleanse, remove the toxins of that past experience from her body and brain.

Celeste cried until she had been wrung like clothes in the washing machine. She excused herself to use the restroom and wash her face. She took in her red eyes, her swollen lips and cheeks, and smiled. She hadn't felt this good in a long time.

"Take it one day at a time" were Therese's words when she returned to their session.

"It's too late," Celeste said, regret whipping at her heart. "I've lost everyone I loved and I have no one and very little of our investment left. And our bookstore… Our bookstore is now a pipe dream."

"Yes, you do have something." Therese leaned forward, her voice stern. "You have you. Start with you. Love you. Accept you." She jabbed her pen into her desk while she spoke. "Keep doing what you're doing now. Then, when you're ready, focus on restoration. Restoration in your circle of influence. That's the journey back to you."

Restoration. Restoration.

She snapped up. The bookstore. The bookstore was within her influence. She hadn't canceled the lease yet. She could start there. If she ordered the books now, they would still come in time for the opening. It had been twelve days since her fallout with her friends—the longest they had ever gone without talking—and nobody had responded to her So this is how it's going to be for real? text to the group chat. But you know what, she could do it by herself. She could run the bookstore. A spark of energy stirred, right along with excitement. "Thank you, Therese. I know exactly what to do."

41

Yasmeen

APRIL 30

The good news was the police had been able to trace Cashmere's whereabouts. They had located her in a one-bedroom, roach-infested apartment in Brooklyn and had confiscated all the things Yasmeen had unknowingly purchased. Turned out that heifer had racked up a good tab at several high-end stores and had them bill Yasmeen from the first day they met inside Tiffany. Most of the stores had accepted the returns, especially since Cashmere had kept the tags on most of the goods.

The bad news was most of her money was still missing. Cashmere used her smarts to manipulate and scam people out of their fortunes. Yasmeen had no idea how to read the intricate money trail.

The cops promised to have someone work on it, but they had warned it could be months, years even, before she saw a fraction of her money back.

But she knew if there was anyone who might be able to crack through this number web and find her money, it was Celeste. However, that would mean giving her former friend a call, something that required a huge swallow of her pride and taking a dollop of "I told you so."

"I can't believe your Upper Crust Crew exploded like an egg in the microwave." Darryl snickered. "Poof. Just like that."

He had just finished whipping her up an omelet garnished with tomato, avocado slices and a sprig of basil and placed it before her.

"I can't believe how they came at me. Ganged up on me. That's what I can't believe. That's why I didn't bother to answer Celeste in the group chat when she asked if this was how things were going to be from now on. They need to apologize to me first." She stabbed her fork into her meal and put a piece in her mouth, then stopped. She had to take a moment to welcome the savory sensations hitting her tongue. Dang, this man could cook.

"Hold on now, I'm mostly kidding," he continued. "From what you told me, you should have called your girl as soon as you saw Aaron at the casino. If one of my boys did that to me, I would be tighter than a sealed jar. That's not how we roll."

"I feel guilty enough without you reminding me of it." She slid Darryl a glance. "Maybe I was wrong about you. How about that?"

He kissed her cheek. "Naw, honey. From all that hollering this morning, you were right about that part." He tapped her nose. "I'm good for you."

"Whatever." She knew her face was hot after that remark. "Well, I don't know if I'll be able to hold on to this house much longer as I won't be able to afford the upkeep, so might as well enjoy all of it while we can."

"Don't worry, I got you," Darryl said. "I didn't spend all of what you gave me for school. You gave me three times what I needed. We can put this house up for sale and buy a condo or something. Then you can help me with my catering business."

"I can't handle all that studying."

"You can. I'll help you. We'll study together."

Yasmeen tilted her head. She could see he was serious. "You think so?" A fledgling hope pulsated in her chest. Before she waved it off. "Pshaw. I would probably end up flunking out, and I love to eat more than I love to cook."

He straightened. "Don't say that about the woman I love."

She gasped. "L-Love?"

"Of course I love you. You must know that." He tucked his finger under her chin. "I'm sorry for all the times I kept hitting you up for cash. That wasn't cool. Getting arrested put some things in perspective for me, showed me I couldn't keep lying with dogs and not expect to catch fleas. So I'm done with all that." He lifted his chin. "And though I appreciate all the money you gave me for school, I plan on paying you back with interest."

"You don't have to do that," she said, though her chest puffed. Her man was coming into his own. His next words proved that.

"Sometimes all a man needs is a chance and a woman who believes in him, and you're that woman for me. I won't let you down."

Yasmeen kissed him then, with all the passion she could muster. "I love you too. And I know you won't."

He hugged her. "We're in this together."

"We can't live off love though," she fretted. "I need my money back."

"You might not get everything but you will get something.

You probably should see if Celeste can help with that. She did reach out…" He sounded so sure, she believed him.

"Good idea… Maybe I'll get enough to keep the bookstore."

"If that's what floats your boat, go for it. I should have enough to get you going for a few months." Darryl gave her a light squeeze. "But give your friend a call. Naw. Bump that. You need to rap with her face-to-face. Pride don't feed the hungry."

"I will. Wow. How the tables have turned," Yasmeen said with a smile. Suddenly, her day felt brighter. She got on her tiptoes to give him a kiss.

He looked down at her. "I must say I love the view from here."

42

Toni

APRIL 30

She was supposed to be getting married in four days, and three
of the people she loved most wouldn't be there to celebrate with
her. Toni stood in her kitchen that morning, her untouched oatmeal growing cold in the microwave while she thought about
the two things she intended to do that day that could change
the course of her life. The past few days had been a flurry of activities around her wedding, including securing another venue.

Aliyah had called around and booked a nearby lodge, but
in her heart, Toni wanted to be married in the bookstore with
her friends. Truthfully, she wasn't sure if there was going to
be a wedding. Toni looked at the clock. She would know in
about an hour.

As the time drew close, Skins had become even more demanding, even more threatening. He had hinted at doubling the million dollars, and she was about three hundred thousand dollars short. But no matter how much she explained that to him, Skins didn't care.

His words were You'd better have my money. He wasn't even trying to be coy anymore. He was like a throbbing toothache and the only cure was to yank him out of her life.

Between her friends, her wedding and Skins, Toni was on the verge of a breakdown. Which is why she had to fix things by being honest with herself, with those she loved and then the world. It was the only way. Once she did that, she'd probably lose her influencer career, and she wouldn't have the bookstore or even her friends to rely on. But Toni Marshall would be free. Or she should say, Antoinette Masters.

She had already reached out to her parents as a courtesy to let them know what was going on, and their response had been that they didn't want to be involved. Not surprising. But they did shut down their social media pages as she had suggested, though the likelihood of anyone linking her name to theirs was small. She'd never posted about them or placed them in the spotlight with her.

She heard the lock jangle and knew Kent had arrived. She was supposed to be packed and ready to move into his place after their wedding, but Toni hadn't even taped a single box together.

Seconds later, she found herself wrapped in her fiancé's embrace and he was whispering the most wonderful things in her ear. Toni placed a hand on his chest. "We need to talk."

Kent stiffened. "How I dread those four little words."

All she could do was smile. Taking his hand, Toni led him into her living room and they settled together on the couch. She turned to face him, her legs touching his, and took his hand in hers. "I want nothing more than to become your wife, but I haven't been completely honest with you." Goodness, her heart was racing in her chest.

His brows furrowed. "What is it?"

Toni froze. Unsure. Once she started talking, there was no backtracking. Though it was unfounded, her fear that Kent would leave her returned. But Toni couldn't shoulder her past on her own. She hunched her shoulders. "My real name is Antoinette Masters."

"I don't get what you mean," he said, his voice even.

"I didn't tell you because I was scared and I grew up learning not to trust anyone. My friends don't even know most of what I'm about to tell you. When I was seventeen, I had to legally change my name." He gestured for her to continue, and it was hard to gauge how he felt about what she had just revealed. She dipped her chin to her chest. "I was dating a dangerous man who came after me and my family when I tried to break things off."

Kent touched her face. "Is this the same man for whom you had the abortion?"

She nodded. "But I didn't tell you everything." She drew in a deep breath. "This man has been extorting me for cash."

"Hold up. When did this happen?"

She drew a breath and let it all out. "A couple months back. His real name is Lamont, but back then, he was known as Skins. He was behind bars serving a life sentence for a home invasion gone bad, where three people got killed. But he recently got out because he had somebody take the fall for him. He found me through social media. If I had known he would get out, I would never have gone into influencing. Anyways, we met up at this used car dealership when—"

"Whoa." He interrupted her. "This man is here in Delaware?"

She nodded. "Yes."

"Where?"

Toni told him the location. With a snarl, Kent jumped to his feet. "Let me see if I am understanding everything you've told me so far," he said, his tone like steel. "Are you telling me you went to meet Skins, even though you knew he was dangerous? A killer?"

She rushed over to him and pleaded with him to understand. "My plan was to confront him, to get him to back off. Handle it on my own."

"This is the second time you've done this to me," Kent hurled. "First at the doctor's appointment and now this. What's the point in getting married if you're all about doing things on your own, like you don't need anyone? Like you don't need me?" He paced the room as if caged, anger evident in every long stride. "Something could have happened to you and I would have never known. How could you do that?"

Toni touched his arm, but he stiffened. She clasped her hands. "I wasn't thinking. I didn't want you or anyone to know about the real me, how messed up and confused I was back when I was a kid. I won't bore you with the details of my childhood, but I wanted to shield you, to protect you from my past. But Skins is threatening to go public if I don't pay him."

"Did you?" he asked. "Did you pay him?"

"N-not yet. He wanted a million dollars, and I'm short."

"A million—" He exhaled and lifted his hands. "Why would you...?" He stopped, then zoned in on her. "There's got to be more. I can't see you paying a million dollars because he knew you had an abortion and you were a messed-up kid. What does he have on you?"

Her chest heaved. "I was the getaway driver in a robbery. A laundromat. He lied to me, told me he was teaching me how to drive," she stammered out. "I didn't know what he had planned. But the owner died of a heart attack." Tears ran down her face. "That's it. That's everything." She lowered her head.

Kent folded his arms. "Have you got in touch with law enforcement or called an attorney for advice?"

She shook her head. "No. I was worried about my new life... my reputation...you."

"I'm so furious at you right now, I don't even know what to do with myself."

"I understand." She wiped her eyes. "I'll cancel the wedding. Tell everyone it's over." She moved to take the ring off her left hand.

"What are you doing?" he asked, stopping her.

Her head popped up. "Aren't you leaving me?" That's what she deserved and expected.

"No. I love you. Don't you see that?" he asked. "I'm not going anywhere. But we're going to secure an attorney, go to the cops and report this lowlife. Then you're going to tell everyone the truth. Starting with your friends." Toni had already filled Kent in on her argument with the girls and how they had decided to end their friendship. Something Kent had been vehement against.

Toni nodded. "I sure will. When Celeste texted in the group chat, I should have answered then, but my pride kicked in. I plan to rectify that today once we've spoken to the cops."

"And received an attorney's advisement," he reminded her. "This isn't my specialty, but I know who I can call."

"Yes. For sure. Thanks for looking out for me." Toni went over to the coffee table to show him the three handwritten notes she had penned that morning. "I've written Yasmeen, Leslie and Celeste letters asking them to meet with me in a couple days. Aliyah is coming by to get them and hand deliver them for me. I can't have them hearing this from anyone else or from social media." She massaged her temples.

Kent drew her close. "You're doing the right thing."

"You're right. I'm not trying to get arrested while live streaming. There will definitely be a fallout, and this scandal could be the end of my gig as a social influencer. And how will this all look for you? Your job at your firm?"

"Things might get hot for a minute, but you'll be okay. I'll be okay. If worse comes to worst, you can go into business for yourself."

She perked up. "That's right. I'll need time to lick my wounds, but eventually, I can open the bookstore. Run it by myself." She stood on her tiptoes and gave Kent a tender but searing kiss. "That's what I'll do. Thank you for loving me despite my stubbornness and my flaws."

"This love is for life. The sooner you know that, the better for both of our mental health."

She relaxed into him. "I'm learning it, babe. I'm learning it."

43

Leslie

MAY 1

Standing by the doorjamb on her front porch, Leslie looped her arm through her father's, its strength a warm blanket around her heart. The sun scorched her exposed skin, though she appreciated the gentle breeze that sent the leaves flapping.

The Johansen clan were due to arrive any second for breakfast. Julie had texted that they were five minutes away. Though the other woman had invited her to call her *Mom*, Leslie hadn't done so. She already had a mother, a wonderful one. Julie could be...a friend. By the look of things, she might need one. Leslie had been busy with Nadya when Celeste texted the group, but later, when she saw that neither Yasmeen nor Toni had said anything, she decided not to either. Besides, Yasmeen was dead wrong for not telling her, and every time Leslie thought about that, she got angry all over again. Still...she would rather argue over this silence.

Edwin patted her hand and gave it a squeeze, bringing her back to the present. "Now this. This is right."

"I agree," she said, her heart hammering in her chest. "This is how I should have done it the first time."

Edwin was the reason she had extended an invite to her new-found family to break bread with her. Vestiges of their conversation the day before played in her mind.

"I'm grateful I got to meet my birth family and siblings, and be-lieve me, nobody is more thankful than I am that they were able to help save Nadya's life. But having two families is too complicated for my peace of mind."

"You don't have two families," her father rebutted. "You have one family. Singular. A unit."

It took a moment before she grasped the implication of his words.

"There's always room for family, no matter how large or how many," he said. *"We make room. Always."*

That's when she had extended her version of an olive branch—waffles, eggs and home-fried potatoes. The scent wafted through the house.

Disengaging from her dad, Leslie made her way down her driveway to the mailbox, sidestepping the For Sale sign. She might as well check the mail while they waited. She opened the box, praying it would only contain junk. Anything but another hospital bill. She had to get her house sold so she could clear up the tab.

At least Aaron had paid the mortgage, and he hadn't touched any of the cards with Leslie's name on them. That meant when she downsized, she wouldn't have any problem securing the loan. He still came by every day to be with Nadya. Leslie didn't interfere with that.

She made sure to avoid eye contact so she wouldn't fall for the Puss in Boots eyes, or keep acting upon the urge to feed him. He wasn't her responsibility, she reminded herself, even as she fretted Aaron might be living in his car. He had asked to take showers at least twice, which she had allowed.

Leslie wasn't about to be spiteful or inhumane. She treated him the way she would anyone in need.

Surprisingly, when they broke the news to Nadya, her daughter had shrugged, saying she had friends whose parents had divorced and some who fought all day. Leslie deduced that with Aaron's prolonged absences, Nadya had gotten used to him not being around. Nadya had added that as long as her daddy didn't forget her, she was fine and that she would expect to get two birthdays and two sets of gifts.

That's when Leslie knew how much Nadya was going to be like her. She also knew she would need to get a job. She had been thinking about reaching out to the landlord about the bookstore. It wouldn't be the same without her girls, and it would be scary, but she found herself excited about that new venture. She smiled, thinking about that now as she returned to her father's side.

Hearing a sneeze behind her, Leslie turned to check on Nadya, who was sitting on the couch closest to the door. Her daughter had awakened with a stuffy nose and reddened eyes. Allergy season was on.

"You good?" she asked.

Nadya bobbed her head. "Yes. I'm excited to meet my uncle."

"Uncles," Leslie corrected.

"Yeah." She laughed. "I guess I'm focused on Mr. Scott since he is my match."

With a nod, Leslie turned in time to see a queue of cars come around the bend. Her stomach muscles tightened.

They pulled in front of the house and into her driveway, and when they came out of the vehicles, all she could see were their smiling faces, faces so similar to hers. Edwin left her side to greet them, his enthusiasm infectious. Her lips widened into a smile. Her heart eased. All would be well. All would be well.

Splaying her hands, she announced, "Welcome to my home."

44

Celeste

MAY 1

"Thank you so much, Nelson," Celeste said, shaking the property owner's hand. They stood outside the bookstore early the next morning and admired the store sign, which now simply said, Books and Bevs. It was a deep green with white lettering. She had already submitted the amended paperwork with the required change fees to rename their—um, her—business. Beginning a solo venture was going to take some getting used to.

She loved everything about the sign—the design, the colors, the font. Seeing the culmination of her nonstop effort these past few days made her chest puff. She had done it. She had restored something in her circle of influence. Celeste couldn't wait to talk to Therese about this when they met online tonight. The counselor was away at a conference but Celeste still asked to check in.

How she wished she could text a picture to the group chat or send one to Wade, but this was probably going to be her new normal...

Celeste parted ways with Nelson after accepting the four sets of keys she had ordered.

Those four keys were a physical reminder of what should have been.

She stepped inside the building, loving the smell of fresh paint. All the furniture had been delivered and set up and the loft was now a secure second floor. In short, it was a reader's dream. She looked over at the café, and her heart squeezed. That would remain closed until she hired someone. In the meantime, she would run the bookstore. Just the store. Celeste couldn't think of a book club without her girls. Maybe in time.

She walked into the back room to her office and opened the laptop. After hours of research and careful planning, Celeste had reinvested all the remaining funds, and yesterday, after a nail-biting wait, she had regained all she had lost and then some. Then she had called Nelson.

Celeste ventured to the bank and ordered cashier's checks for her friends and Wade. He had called her a couple times but Celeste hadn't answered. She figured he had signed the divorce papers, so for her, there was nothing more to talk about. She would wait for the finalized documents to arrive in the mail.

After updating her accounts, Celeste decided to tackle some of the boxes of books delivered earlier that day.

She headed back into the main room and stopped when she saw she had an unexpected guest.

"Yasmeen," she said, trying to keep the shock out of her voice. She edged close.

"This was my third stop," Yasmeen said. "I came here on a

whim, actually, after I stopped by your house and then your office. They told me you were on an extended leave…?"

"Yeah, I, uh, decided to still go through with the bookstore." Celeste ran a hand through her strands. "It's been a ton of work doing this on my own. But I'm excited."

Yasmeen rolled back on her heels. "It's impressive."

Celeste thought she heard a sliver of regret in Yasmeen's tone, so she asked, "Why were you looking for me?"

"I need your help."

"What's going on?"

Yasmeen told her about Cashmere getting caught.

"I'm glad they apprehended her. That must be a relief."

"Yes. Major relief," Yasmeen breathed out. "But I figured I'd ask if you could trace the funds?"

"Unfortunately, hacking into someone's accounts is a job for the cops to do, not that I could without a bank account anyway. But I can review your account records if you want. See if anything jumps out at me."

"Sure. Thanks." Yasmeen came over and tapped her arm. "If there are any discrepancies, you'll find them."

Her chest constricted. "See, that's why I've missed you. You're a real confidence booster."

"I missed you too." Yasmeen clung to her. "Now, you're going to need help in here…" She jutted her chin toward the café. "I'm still available if you're taking applications?"

"You don't need to apply, silly. I could use a partner to help me run things," Celeste said, tears flooding her eyes. "And I'm sorry for all that I said. It wasn't my intention to hurt you."

"I'm sorry too. I should have heeded you when you warned me about how I was spending my money. I got caught up. You know?"

"Yes, I understand."

Celeste remembered the check. She took out the envelope with Yasmeen's name written on it. "Oh, here, I almost forgot, I have something for you. I was going to put these in the mailbox today, but I got Toni's letter, so I'll give the others to them when we meet. Are you going?"

"Yes." Her friend tore open the letter and then gasped. "That's a lot of zeroes."

"Yes." Celeste nodded. "Not as much as you had, but it's something."

"It's a lot." Yasmeen jumped up and down before coming to snatch Celeste close. "Thank you. Thank you. Thank you."

"You're quite welcome."

Yasmeen spread her hands. "So that's how you were able to do this…" Then she twirled. "Are those books in those boxes?"

Celeste nodded, her eyes misty. "Yep. I got everything I could read off your list that wasn't blurred by water damage."

"I can't wait to get started." She placed the check in her purse, then rubbed her hands and squealed. "Let's open a bookstore."

45

Toni

MAY 2

She had sent handwritten invitations. They would come.

That's what Toni repeated to herself while she waited at the diner, facing the entrance, hoping her friends would show. She had rented a private room so they could talk without interruption, and so she wouldn't be recognized. It was about fifteen minutes before the allotted time, which meant Leslie should be walking in at any moment. If she was coming.

Kent had offered to come with her but she told him she didn't need him. She was more than capable of pouring out to the women she had known and had called best friends for almost two decades.

Leslie popped around the corner first and Toni gave a wave. The women exchanged awkward hugs.

"You look great," Toni said, admiring Leslie's flowy skirt paired with a jean jacket.

"And you look fabulous as usual," Leslie replied, scanning Toni's military-inspired jumpsuit.

They took their seats and Leslie clasped her hands. "How have you been?"

Toni opened her mouth to say the usual "I'm good," when it hit her that she wasn't. She was far from good, and she was going to need her friends. In a somber tone, she said, "I'll wait for the others to get here to answer that question." Almost as soon as she uttered those words, she regretted them. Now Leslie probably thought she was on her deathbed. She added, "I'm not dying, if that puts your mind at ease."

Leslie's shoulders slumped. "Yes, yes it does. You don't want to know all the thoughts that were racing through my mind."

"I'm glad to see things are going well with Nadya."

"Yes, she should be having the surgery soon. Nadya told me that her aunties have been reaching out." Leslie's eyes warmed. "I'm so glad for that. I wouldn't have known what to tell her."

Toni nodded. "I wasn't going to leave her hanging. No matter what." She had made sure to video call Nadya to ask how she was doing and she had gone in person a few times during the day. But she had thought she was the only one. So it was good to know Celeste and Yasmeen had also been in touch.

They entered the room and Toni caught how chummy they were, talking and laughing, relaxed. Her heart squeezed. Somehow, she didn't imagine anyone else had been in touch. That stung a little. She did notice that Yasmeen held a bouquet of flowers wrapped in cellophane and wondered if they were for her, but Yasmeen didn't mention anything, simply resting it on the cushioned seat.

The four women exchanged greetings and the server appeared to take their drink orders. Then they joined the buffet queue since Toni had prepaid for their meals. She noted how polite they were with each other, feigned, practiced, like each was making an effort not to offend. How she missed the natural pushing and shoving that used to occur when they came here for birthdays, parties...

They filled their plates and returned to the room. Once they were seated, Toni started talking before she lost her courage. She told them all about Skins, her name change and his threats. They listened in silence, but their eyes held kindness, sympathy, which was encouraging. Besides a clarifying question or two, they gave her the space she needed to tell all that was going on.

"I'm glad to hear you went to the cops," Leslie said, running her hand through her hair. Of course Toni noticed the absence of the other woman's wedding ring and her first thought was of Nadya. Her goddaughter hadn't mentioned anything, which could mean she didn't know. Toni had so many questions, but this wasn't the time.

"Yes, you did the right thing," Celeste added, her voice firm...confident. Toni gave her a second look. She sounded and looked like the Celeste that Toni knew before the carjacking. "Will the cops press charges?" she asked.

"No. They are going after Skins. To them, I was a minor being taken advantage of." She released a plume of air. "All this time, I was walking around with that guilt, that fear. But I faced my biggest fear only to see most of it was in my head. Kent has been a rock," Toni said. "I couldn't have done this without him." She squared her shoulders. "And before the wedding on Saturday, I'll tell the world who I am and what I did."

"You sure you want to do all that?" Yasmeen asked.

"Yes, I've got to take the power away from Skins."

Toni felt a pang at how well her friends seemed without her.

A spring of emotions welled, and Toni couldn't remain silent. "I miss you all so much," she choked out. "From the look of things, you all are fine, but I'm a mess without my girls. For the first time in I don't know how long, we didn't have book club, and that's tearing me apart. Plus, I've got this wedding and no best friends."

"I know that feeling," Yasmeen said. "You can't imagine how lonely I felt dealing with all this nonsense with Cashmere when we were on the outs."

"Oh, I forgot to ask how that went?" Toni asked.

"She's been caught but they still trying to find my money." Yasmeen squeezed Celeste's hand.

An image of the receipts Toni had slipped into her pockets flashed in her mind. "I might have something that can help your case. If I remember right, I had a bank receipt. It might be nothing..."

"But it might be everything," Yasmeen said, excitedly.

"It could crack the case," Celeste added.

"Don't get your hopes up, but I'll have my assistant get them to you. I put them in my jewelry box."

"What made you save them?" Leslie asked.

Toni shrugged. "I have no idea but I'm glad I did."

"You and me both. Time for more pleasant matters." Yasmeen picked up the bouquet and handed it to her. "I made this for you, like you asked. Kept my word. Just keep it in the refrigerator." It was a gorgeous arrangement of baby's breath and lilies, tied with the same color sash she had chosen for the bridal party. She was so choked up she could only nod to show her appreciation.

Toni started to sob then, unable to stem the flow of tears. She felt their arms surround her and they held her, as they had done many times before. The pain in her heart eased. When she was more composed, they continued their conversation, their meals sitting cold next to them.

"I missed you all something fierce," Yasmeen said, her eyes holding a sheen, "but I still read *The Messy Life of Jane Tanner*. I couldn't miss book club."

"I did too," Leslie said, with a small chuckle. "It's a habit now.

You don't know how many times I wanted to reach out to talk about this book because Brenda Novak did her thing, as usual."

"Well, since I'm opening the bookstore still, you know I had to read the book. It's going to be my first featured novel." Celeste touched her chest. "I'm scrapping the book club idea though."

"And I'll be helping with the café and working on developing my special blend," Yasmeen said.

Toni wiped her face and addressed Celeste. "You're going through with the bookstore? You and Yasmeen?"

Yasmeen didn't give her a chance to answer. "Yep. And she's got the sign up already too."

Toni's heart squeezed. "Good for you."

"This is really happening," Leslie said, with awe.

Celeste said, "Therese—my therapist—tells me that I need to take back what those men tried to rob me of."

"You went to therapy?" Yasmeen squealed. "You didn't tell me that."

"Yes, I've been going regularly." Celeste dabbed her eyes. "It's working."

"I'm so stinking proud of you," Leslie said, giving Celeste a hug. Of course, Yasmeen joined in and then Toni.

Toni's heart warmed. All was right with them again. She broke the embrace. "I've got to break this up before I fall apart and ruin my makeup," she said with an awkward laugh. Everyone dried their tears.

"That's some good advice—to take back what those men stole from you," Toni said. "Actually, that's kind of what I'm doing as well. I'm not going to allow Skins to keep this over my head. I'm going to tell my followers everything, right before Kent and I exchange our vows at the lodge."

Celeste reached over to take Toni's hand. "You know the bookstore is ready and available, if you still want to use it. Having you there would give us a great launch and turnout."

She slumped. "Yes. I would. Thank you. The invitations had that address anyway, so I will announce it live tonight." She squared her shoulders. "I hope you'll all reconsider standing with me when I marry the man of my dreams."

"My dress is dry-cleaned and pressed," Celeste said.

Yasmeen and Leslie promised to do the same. The friends hugged it out. "I'm getting married, guys. I can't believe even with my old ovaries and all my past drama that he wants to give me his last name. Still."

"I can. He knows the best when he sees it," Yasmeen said.

"If I have one piece of advice," Leslie said, "I would say, never stop communicating. Never be afraid of letting him know who you are, flaws and all." Her voice cracked. "He's showing you he's a man of good character now, and that's not going to change. When someone shows you who they are, believe them the first time."

Toni squeezed her hand. "I will." She pulled out her phone to reach out to the website developer and gave the okay for their website to go live. "Once I'm back from my honeymoon, my calendar is open if you still want a publicity manager...or desk clerk. Whatever. I just want to be around the books. And my friends."

"Of course, you did put in your money," Celeste joked. "I'll retain the lease for now, but when it's time to purchase, it will be in all our names."

"Sounds good," Toni said.

They all looked at Leslie.

"Of course I'm in. I need to start working pronto and this will be income I can count on as Aaron won't be able to give me alimony for a while." Her voice caught. "I'm glad we're back together."

"Glad to have you," Celeste whispered, squeezing Leslie's hand. "Hang on a minute. I've got something for the two of you." She took out two envelopes and handed one to Leslie and one to Toni.

"What's this?" Toni asked.

"Open it and see."

"Ladies, blink a few times to clear your eyes," Yasmeen said, with a chuckle.

Leslie went first. She tore open the envelope and pulled out a cashier's check. When she saw the amount, Leslie sucked in a huge breath. "Is this for real?" She held the check up to the light. "I spot watermarks. This is legit."

Toni opened hers and her eyes went wide. "What did you do?"

Celeste puffed her chest. "My investments paid off big-time."

"Thank you so much," Leslie said. "I'll put it in the bank today. I won't even try to pretend that I can't use this. It's a weight off my back to know I can pay off Nadya's hospital bills. Insurance goes but so far."

"Speaking of that…" Celeste's eyes shone. "I settled the bill."

Leslie gasped. "Stop it. You didn't." She held her head with her hands. "You did?"

Celeste grinned. "Yes, I used my share."

"But what will you do?" Leslie asked.

"Girl, you know Celeste wouldn't do that if she couldn't," Toni chimed in. "Just say thank you."

"I know that's right," Yasmeen said.

"I'm good." Celeste waved her off. "Wade said I can keep his profits, and I didn't argue. He mailed back the divorce papers unsigned, so I guess I'll hear what that means when I see him at the launch."

Toni raised a brow. "He didn't sign them?"

"He's showing you what he wants," Leslie whispered, then dabbed at her eyes.

Celeste blushed. "We'll see. Weddings do tend to make me raunchy, but I'm at a good place now, so…"

Toni waved a hand. "Girl, please. Who you think you fooling? You just want to make him sweat after all he put you through these past months."

"Maybe." She shrugged. The women giggled.

"I almost feel sorry for him," Yasmeen said. "Almost."

"I plan to make my man sweat too, but for a much better reason." Toni cackled. "Whew, chile, in forty-eight hours, this drought will be over and I plan on getting me a good long drink. You feel me?" She and Yasmeen high-fived.

"It's going to be a good night for all of us," Yasmeen said, waggling her brows. Then she drew in a breath and looked at Leslie. "I'm sorry. I didn't mean... Foot in mouth, again."

"It's all good," Leslie said, giving a small smile and waving her check. "Nadya has all my attention and I'm looking forward to my fresh start. I plan to put some of this money back into Nadya's college fund, and I'll give you a portion to invest so I can have a decent retirement fund." She tapped her cheek. "But next year, this girl is going to Italy to celebrate her freedom. You best believe I'll be saving those coins."

"You're not going to Italy without me," Toni jumped in.

"Me either," Yasmeen added.

"Let's just start planning," Celeste said. "I'm sure we'll have the most magical time."

Thinking about the last few months and all they had experienced made Toni laugh. "Famous last words."

46

Celeste

MAY 4

Celeste stood by the entrance of the bookstore, loving the sight of people milling through the aisles and eating cake and drinking punch. The sun was just about to set, the skyline a gorgeous mix of blues, whites and purples. It had been a beautiful day for a wedding. And a bookstore launch.

Which was why they had decided to set a tent up in the parking lot for Toni's nuptials. A smart move. The ceremony had been flawless. Toni's new assistant had been ecstatic at their viewership. When Toni went live with her confession before her vows, her fans had sent her nothing but love. Then one person posted a photo of Skins's location in Baltimore, which had led to his arrest. Celeste hoped Toni finally realized her worth.

Just as she had.

After the wedding, Toni and Kent had cut the cake, taken a few pictures, then ditched everyone to take off for their honeymoon. They would hold a splashy reception on their one-year anniversary. Celeste loved that idea.

Most of the crowd had thinned, but there were a few stragglers inside the bookstore, peeking at books and drinking Yasmeen's special tea from the café. They had hired food service workers to make the teas and serve.

Celeste and Yasmeen had arrived early that morning with boxes of books from each of their personal collections that would serve as keepsakes for the guests. She had had a hard time convincing her friends to part with their books. It was only the promise of new ones and the knowledge that others would enjoy them that had finally changed their minds.

Hearing laughter made Celeste smile. Leslie's niece was reading one of Nadya's books from when she was a toddler. She captured a picture for Leslie, who had left with Nadya right after the ceremony. Her bio family were lovely—and it was weird seeing so many people who resembled Leslie.

She waved at the pastor eating a huge slice of vanilla cake before she continued to scan the room.

One guest in particular captured her attention. He wasn't reading. He wasn't drinking the tea. He leaned against the wall, staring at her. As he had been for most of the past three hours. *Dang.* He didn't care who was watching him eating her with his eyes either.

Wade.

She bit the inside of her cheek to keep from grinning and smoothed her dress. He watched her movements as usual. As she knew he would.

Stepping inside, she clutched her purse and walked over to him, making sure her hips swung from side to side. Then she gestured for him to follow her. They entered her office and she closed the door. His woodsy scent assailed her senses. He reached over and turned the lock, cocooning them inside the small space.

"You haven't been answering my calls." His voice was deep, smooth, causing her insides to quake. Her body remembered that voice, those lips, those hands.

She lowered her lashes. "I've been busy."

"You signed the papers," he said, almost accusatory.

"You sent them," she shot back, then reminded herself to play it cool.

"I returned them to you," he said through gritted teeth, then mopped his brow.

She smirked. "Sweating much?"

He stepped into her space. "Woman, don't play with me. You know I didn't mean it."

"You left me," she snapped, mindful to keep her voice down.

"Physically. You had already done it mentally," he said, drawing closer.

Her eyes locked with his. She backed up until her butt met the desk. "I started therapy."

"Really? That's wonderful. I'm so proud of you for taking that step on your own."

"I thought you weren't coming back unless you knew I was in therapy," she challenged.

"Girl, I left to get your attention. I was always coming back." He leaned into her, placing his hands on the desk on either side of her. The feel of the length of his body against hers sent her heart rate into overdrive.

She released staccato breaths. "So, you just expected me to be waiting?"

"Listen, I need you as much as you need me, so quit stalling. I'm here to get my key so the movers can unload the truck. They are packing up my place as we speak."

Her heart somersaulted, but she gave him a light shove. "You just knew I would let you back in without a fight. You ain't all that," she scoffed.

"Oh baby, I am all that and I will gladly give you a reminder tonight."

She released a long plume of air. Then she opened her purse, took out his key and tossed it to him.

His eyes went wide. "How did you know?"

"Because, my love, I know you, just as well as you know me." She folded her arms. "And we have our first couple session with Therese next week."

His full lips quirked into a smile. "Girl, those are baby-making words."

She placed a hand on her hip and tossed her hair. "Let's get to it, then."

He shoved the key in his pocket and moved toward her with panther-like grace, with purpose. He curled his arms around her waist and snatched her close. And when he placed his lips on hers, Celeste knew what love tasted like, what home felt like. She had her friends, her man, her bookstore, and a girl couldn't ask for anything more.

Well…except for maybe one thing. She wrapped her arms around him and said four words, "The pastor's still here…"

"Mmm-hmm." Wade nuzzled her neck, planting kisses on her collarbone.

She stilled his movements and then uttered another four words to seal their new beginning. "Let's renew our vows."

★ ★ ★ ★ ★

ACKNOWLEDGMENTS

Thank You, Lord, for giving the talent and for opening the door so that after twenty years, I can see this goal realized.

A thousand and one thank-yous for my wonderful literary agent, Latoya Smith, and the team at LCS Literary, especially Sobi Burbano, who read my proposal and manuscript to give insightful thoughts and feedback.

To my amazingly wonderful editor, Dina Davis (flowers, flowers, hugs), who helped me bring stories to life at Harlequin Love Inspired and then took a chance on cultivating my foray into Women's Fiction writing here at MIRA, thank you, thank you, thank you. Dina has been a source of support and her patience and guidance helped to shape *The Bookshop Sisterhood* into the read it is today.

Thank you so much to the entire team at MIRA and Harper-Collins: Editorial Director, Nicole Brebner, and editorial assistants, Whitney Bruno (special thanks) and Evan Yeong. Thank you to the proofreading manager, Tamara Shifman, and the copyediting managers, Gina MacDonald and Bonnie Lo, as well as copyeditor, Jerri Gallagher. A special special thank-you for my publicist, Sophie James, for all the efforts made to help spread the word about this book.

I also have to give a shout-out to the individuals who work behind the scenes to get my book in front of readers. Marketing team: Ana Luxton, Ashley MacDonald and Puja Lad; channel marketing: Randy Chan and Pamela Osti; digital marketing: Lindsey Reeder, Brianna Wodabek, Riffat Ali, and Ciara Loader; subrights: Reka Rubin, Christine Tsai and Nora Rawn. A very special thanks to Loriana Sacilotto, Amy Jones, Margaret Marbury and Heather Connor; the production team: Katie-Lynn Golakovich for the manuscript and Denise Thomson for the cover and galleys; those in charge of sales: Heather Foy, Colleen Simpson, Kara Coughlin and Prerna Singh, among others; Carly Katz and Ariel Blake who served as the narrator and anyone else I might have missed. You are all appreciated.

Next, you can have an amazing product between the pages, but the cover is what attracts someone to pick up the book. So, I would like to thank the art team: Erin Craig and Alexandra Niit (special mention) for the amazingly wonderful book cover they gave this special story.

I'm beyond grateful for all your efforts and energy into making this book into the best it could be.

I've been blessed to have authors such as Brenda Novak, Kimberla Lawson Roby, Farrah Rochon, Rochelle Weinstein, Kristan Higgans, Annie Rains, Eliza Knight and Rhonda McKnight take the time to read early galleys to give blurbs and reviews. Thank you so much.

Thank you to my little Nova, whose smiling face helps

grandma remain motivated. Thank you to my parents who are a strong support and believer in my gift. And to my sons, Eric and Jordan, who are my sidekicks, my champions. Thank you to my daughter in love, Jasmyn, who is a sweetheart and so good for my son. I also must mention the children of my heart: Arielle, Erika, Erin, Dezirae, Destinee, Devyn and Siara.

Thank you to my sisters: Zara and Chrissy, who are some of my biggest cheerleaders. Thank you to my parents: Pauline and Clive, and my Agape church family: Velma, Marva, Olive, Marvelyn. My weekly prayer fam: Auntie Charmaine (Paula Ann), Andrea and Arlene. And special mention and gratitude to Theresa Bennett, my former boss, who has been a tremendous support and confidante at times.

Now, I can't write such a strong book about friendship and love without some incredible life-long friends of my own: Colette, Glenda, Lea, Michele, Teresa. Also, you have those you haven't spoken to in years but when you get together, it is like no time passed: Sarah, Sharon, Debra, Annemarie, Bridgette. (I am blessed with many, so if I forget you, don't hold this brain accountable because you know you're in my heart.) And, I am honored to know some remarkable husbands who inspired the men in this book—the real-life Kent and Wade—my brothers-in-law: Sean and Guillermo (DJ).

Finally, thank you to my husband, John (kisses, kisses), who came into my life while I was on this journey and who is now my biggest supporter, I thank you for being there and for being positive when I wasn't. I don't know how many times you heard, "Can I talk through this with you?" and how many hours we devoted to this, but it is really appreciated.

And thank you, dear devoted readers, for reading and sharing and talking about my books. You are priceless.

Love always,
Michelle